DANCE OF THE THUNDER DOGS

DANCE OF THE THUNDER DOGS

KIRK MITCHELL

BERKLEY PRIME CRIME, NEW YORK

THE BERKLEY PUBLISHING GROUP
Published by the Penguin Group
Penguin Group (USA) Inc.
375 Hudson Street, New York, New York 10014, USA
Penguin Group (Canada), 10 Alcorn Avenue, Toronto, Ontario M4V 3B2, Canada
(a division of Pearson Penguin Canada Inc.)
Penguin Books Ltd., 80 Strand, London WC2R 0RL, England
Penguin Group Ireland, 25 St. Stephen's Green, Dublin 2, Ireland
(a division of Penguin Books Ltd.)
Penguin Group (Australia), 250 Camberwell Road, Camberwell, Victoria 3124, Australia
(a division of Pearson Australia Group Pty. Ltd.)
Penguin Books India Pvt. Ltd., 11 Community Centre, Panchsheel Park,
New Delhi – 110 017, India
Penguin Books (NZ), Cnr. Airborne and Rosedale Roads, Albany, Auckland 1310, New Zealand
(a division of Pearson New Zealand, Ltd.)
Penguin Books (South Africa) (Pty.) Ltd., 24 Sturdee Avenue, Rosebank,
Johannesburg 2196, South Africa

Penguin Books Ltd., Registered Offices: 80 Strand, London WC2R 0RL, England

This book is an original publication of The Berkley Publishing Group.

This is a work of fiction. Names, characters, places, and incidents either are the product
of the author's imagination or are used fictitiously, and any resemblance to actual persons,
living or dead, business establishments, events, or locales is entirely coincidental.
The political and administrative settings of this novel are not meant to represent
the actual policies of any tribe or law enforcement agency.

PRINTING HISTORY
Berkley Prime Crime hardcover edition / November 2004

Library of Congress Cataloging-in-Publication Data

Mitchell, Kirk.
Dance of the thunder dogs / Kirk Mitchell.—Berkley Prime Crime hardcover ed.
p. cm.
ISBN 0-425-19836-7
1. Parker, Emmett (Fictitious character)—Fiction. 2. United States.
Bureau of Indian Affairs—Fiction. 3. Class Actions (Civil procedure)—Fiction. 4. Indians
of North America—Fiction. 5. Government
investigators—Fiction. 6. Comanche Indians—Fiction. I. Title.

PS3563.I7675D36 2004
813.'54—dc22
2004046880
PRINTED IN THE UNITED STATES OF AMERICA

10 9 8 7 6 5 4 3 2 1

1

T HIS IS A STORY *I heard from my father and he from his father. It happened long ago, but they told me it's true.*

*Half the year, Kingfisher made his home in a hole in the clay
bank above Lake Lawtonka. Like all kingfishers, he had a sharp bill, a
swept-back crest and a stubby tail that wouldn't weigh him down when he
swam. Kingfisher flew south in the winter, but came back to Lawtonka in
spring, when the creeks ran swift and clear out of the Wichita Mountains,
when the lake rose high behind its dam and fish dotted its surface. But one
year, the lake didn't rise. Instead of building behind the dam, the waters
gushed down Medicine Creek and went on their way to the ocean.*

*Muskrat, Salamander and Crawfish, who also depended on the lake to
fill each summer, went to Kingfisher. Muskrat said, "Something's wrong
with the dam. The waters won't rise, and how will we make our living if
they don't?"*

Kingfisher told them he was worried about the same thing.

*Salamander suggested, "Nobody knows more about dams than Beaver.
You should fly to him, Kingfisher, and ask him what's wrong."*

So Kingfisher flew over the mountains to where Beaver had built a dam of willow sticks along Sugar Creek, just below the springs there. He told Beaver about the problem.

Beaver scratched his long whiskers and said, "I know nothing about the dams Human Beings build, Kingfisher. Mine are made of sticks. Theirs are made of earth and stone. I'm sorry, but you are the better diver. You should go down and look for yourself to see what the trouble is."

Kingfisher flew home and told the other animals what Beaver had said.

Crawfish said, "Beaver is right. You should go."

Kingfisher thought about this for a while, but only a very short while, for he, too, was very worried about the lake. As low as it was, Lawtonka was too muddy to see the fish swimming, and if he couldn't hunt fish, he would starve. He agreed to dive to the bottom and have a look.

He waited until the May sun was high and bright, for the shrunken waters of the lake were heavy and dark with silt. Then he sprang from the tree branch and plunged into the depths. Soon, it was almost as dark as night, but Kingfisher kept darting down, holding his breath. Down and down he went, all the way to the bottom, still holding his breath. There he found a cave that wound back into the murky heart of the dam, and inside this cave was a kind of iron gate. It was jammed open, letting out the waters into Medicine Creek, keeping the lake from filling as it should.

Then Kingfisher could no longer hold his breath. He had to come back up.

He burst to the surface, gasping in his raucous, clattering voice.

"Are you all right, Brother?" Muskrat asked.

Kingfisher nodded. The other animals gathered around him on the shore and asked him what he had seen. As soon as he had breath, Kingfisher said, "I couldn't see much. The waters are like night. But something's stuck in the water gate. What, I don't know." He promised to go down again the next day, when the sun was at its highest again.

But the next day, Kingfisher had no need of the sun's light. Reaching the bottom, he saw that Human Beings had gotten to the cave. Two of them were swimming down there, with fires attached to their heads that lit up the water gate. The two could hold their breaths longer than any Human Beings Kingfisher had ever seen swimming in Lawtonka before, even though much of their air leaked up from them in long streams of bubbles.

It shocked Kingfisher to see what was lodged in the water gate, but then he himself was out of breath and had to rise.

On the shore, the other animals asked what he'd seen below.

Kingfisher said, "There's a Human Being stuck in the iron jaws of the water gate. That is what keeps it from closing."

Crawfish was not convinced. "Men are soft. They have no hard shell like I do. How can one keep the gate from shutting?"

"This Man is tied to a log," Kingfisher replied, "and it's this log that keeps the gates open."

"Why would a Man be tied to a timber?" Muskrat asked.

Kingfisher had no answer.

Salamander asked him to describe this Human Being.

"He is swollen with death. His eyes are wide open, and they're shaped like pecans. Like the eyes of the First People. But his skin is as white as a snowy egret, much whiter even than that of the Second People." Kingfisher could tell that the other animals found this all very strange. As he himself did. But then he had to explain nothing more, for the two Human Beings brought the body to the surface.

All saw that the dead Man had pecan-shaped eyes and skin as white as skin would be. He was lashed to a log, and his lower legs were missing where the iron plates had cut them off.

It was very strange, and the Human Beings who gathered around this sight seemed as puzzled as Kingfisher, Muskrat, Salamander and Crawfish. Yet, this was soon forgotten by the animals as the lake swiftly filled and life went on much as it had as long as anybody could remember. All horrors fade when life goes on as usual.

This is what my people told me.

2

PEOPLE. ALL THE PEOPLE.

Vehicles filled the parking lot of the Comanche Nation Complex along Interstate 44. Emmett Quanah Parker took the tribal "get-off" in his mother's thirty-year-old Dodge Aspen. Time to start thinking in Oklahoma idioms again. Get-off meant turn off. A glance in his side mirror reminded him that he was leading a convoy of three Parker family pickups, all with right-hand signals blinking through the twilight. They were driven by young relatives he'd scarcely recognized after his long absence. He was a stranger to much of his own family, and his hospital stay until six weeks ago had further distanced him from them. The doctors had feared infection to his damaged left lung—white doctors who didn't understand that you can't catch things from your own kin, only outsiders.

The outside world is infectious. Outsiders brought infection.

His mother rolled down her window on the evening heat of early June. It felt thick after all the years he'd lived in dry Phoenix. But there was also a vague comfort in its soft and familiar heaviness, the liquid warmth of the womb. *I'm home. I'm not dreaming about home. I'm actually here.* She held out her hand into the slipstream as if testing for a promise of coolness. Celia Ann Parker's fingers were curved and her knuckles swollen with arthritis. Her back was hunched. Age seemed to be making her tinier by the day. Still, she was full of life. Did her unbroken connection to home give her that?

Emmett led the convoy of family vehicles onto the small tribal holding, not a reservation but a few acres held in trust by the government. And of all the buffalo that had once roamed this vast quarter of the southern plains used by the Comanche, only a hundred or so remained. Some of these now placidly grazed in a fenced pasture across the road from the tribal head-quarters building, oblivious to the lost way of life they represented. Only human beings were given to nostalgia, and the Comanche less so than other people.

"Where we going to park?" his mother asked. The lot was full.

"Jerome left a message he'd save us a place." Emmett slowed for the river of people streaming down the road toward the arena, an expanse of trampled grass shining greenly under floodlights. Not just Comanches, but members of at least a dozen tribes Emmett recognized by dress. Not *dress*, he reminded himself. The right word was *regalia*: fabric, beads, and feathers distinctive to each people who'd been removed from their homelands to Oklahoma, a Choctaw term that meant *Place of the Red People*. He himself wore nothing elaborately Comanche, just black cowboy boots, Levi's, and a linen shirt with ribbons the tribal colors of red, yellow, and blue. He had every reason to dress to the nines, but hadn't felt up to it. He hadn't wanted an honor dance and would've declined if his mother hadn't been so pleased with the invitation. She'd had so little pleasure in her life. This morning at the Wal-Mart in Lawton, it'd been good to see her with her sisters, their daughters, and their granddaughters, filling plastic laundry baskets with foodstuffs and household items for the giveaway at tonight's dance. Every-thing was reciprocal in Comanche life, and even if offered something as in-tangible as honor, you were expected to return the kindness with cans of Spam, boxes of Ritz crackers, and rolls of paper towels.

I'm home. Why don't I feel like it?

More law enforcement than usual was on hand for a Thursday night dance, even if it was the kickoff for a weekend powwow. The tribal cops were reinforced by the Comanche County Sheriff's Department, and they by deputies from adjoining Caddo and Kiowa counties.

"There's Jerome," Celia said. "Oh my, he's gotten so heavy."

A jowly, grinning Jerome Crowe had stepped out into the Dodge's head-lights and was pointing at several parking slots he'd staked out for the ar-rival of Emmett's entourage. He was the same age as Emmett, forty-one, but three times his girth. He wore a fringed fawn-skin jacket that was too warm for the night; his neck and forehead glistened with sweat. Hard to believe he'd been a sprinter on the track team at the mission.

Emmett shut off the engine and stepped out of the car. Gingerly. Wait-ing for the sharp edges of his mending ribs to give him pain. They did, but less so than they had yesterday, or the day before.

Jerome looked him over. "Hell, *Pabi*—you're still skinny. What's your secret?"

His secret was a chest wound he'd gotten that winter while on assign-ment in upstate New York. He was thirty pounds lighter than he'd been at Christmas. *"Kima, Pabi."* Come, Brother. Emmett widened his arms to en-close him. "I haven't been able to stuff myself with mama's fry bread until lately."

He wanted the years to melt away. He wanted the feelings they'd shared at the Indian mission near Anadarko. Although they both eventually went to work for the Bureau of Indian Affairs, they'd seldom seen each other in the intervening years: Jerome had gone on to Yale Law School and served at the Washington, D.C., headquarters.

But the old feelings wouldn't come.

He barely knew this portly stranger, who said with emotion, "It's been too long, Emmett. We can't let this happen again." A minute passed before Emmett could disengage himself from the man's fleshy embrace and open his mother's door for her. But she looked delighted that, already, her son was being so warmly received.

Jerome, who, like Emmett, was a few inches taller than six feet, bent over to hug the little woman. "Good to see you, Mother Parker." He hugged her again. The Comanche were big on hugs.

She asked, "What brings you home from Washington?"

"Your son's dance. I wouldn't miss it for the world."

"You heard about this all the way in Washington?"

"You bet. The whole government keeps track of Emmett."

Celia took this in with a satisfied nod. Parker's face had been bolstered. The Comanche were as big on face as they were on hugs.

Emmett's sons and daughters were sifting forward from the pickups to await his instructions. Technically, they were his nephews and nieces, but these were white kinship terms. In the closely knit world of the traditional band, all persons were mothers and fathers, sons and daughters, or brothers or sisters. Even unrelated persons were often addressed as such. Emmett had seen these younger relatives so infrequently through the years that most of their names escaped him. Thankfully, his mother began organizing the transfer of goods from the beds of the pickups to the arena. The spaces Jerome had saved for them were next to the emcee's stand and the host club area—in this case, the Thunder Dogs, a warrior society that had taken its name from the original Comanche term for horse. Emerging from the mountains of Wyoming onto the northern plains four hundred years ago, the Shoshonean ancestors of the Comanche had been astonished to see these massive animals whose hooves shook the ground like thunder.

His mother asked Emmett to look after the blankets, and Jerome followed him to the rear of the old Dodge. "This your car, Em?"

"No, mine's in storage in Phoenix." Sometime soon, he'd have to fly back and pick it up. And perhaps close down his apartment. But that'd be the final admission his career was over. An admission he wasn't prepared to make. As much as he loved being home with his family, he couldn't imagine anything here that could fill his time. He'd begun to wonder if he'd adapted too well to the outside world. "How are things going for you in D.C.?" he asked Jerome.

"Not so good."

Emmett paused in the midst of opening the trunk to look at his boyhood friend. "How's that?"

"Let's save it for later. Here, let me help you with those. . . ."

Inside the trunk were blankets and a dance shawl purchased yesterday at the Eagle Trading Company in Anadarko. Most of the blankets had been modestly priced Mexican knockoffs with generic Indian designs. But four of them were the genuine trade articles, Pendleton blankets from Oregon, predominantly red, the color of protection. They had been three hundred dollars each. And the shawl had cost two hundred.

Comanche honor didn't come cheap.

They joined the file of Parkers who looked like porters on safari, bearing the laundry baskets of foodstuffs and boxes of oranges and apples. But before they could spread the gifts on a tarp near the drum group at the center of the arena, a law-enforcement type in a blazer delayed them to wave an electronic detector over their clothes and the blankets. "Who are you?" Emmett asked.

Jerome quickly intervened: "A couple VIPs might show later. You're not carrying your service weapon, are you?"

"No."

Jerome moved Emmett along as soon as they'd both been scanned.

The head drummer was setting up while trying to ignore the bomb-sniffing dog wandering among his group, twenty men with drums, and at least that many women singers, who were unfolding their chairs around their leader.

Emmett asked, "Mind telling me what's going on, Jerome?"

"You'll see," he said cryptically. But enjoying himself.

Emmett didn't like surprises, and last thing he wanted this evening was a big to-do.

But then the head man began beating his drum, and the hair stood on the back of Emmett's neck. He hadn't heard that sound in a long time. He squinted up into the artificial sun of one of the floodlights, listening with his belly to the beat. The sound seemed to penetrate his navel and travel along his bones.

I'm home . . . aren't I?

When he looked down again, Jerome and the arena director—a kind of event manager—were standing on his right, and two sons, twin nephews, had lined up on his left. He struggled to attach names to their faces, which had matured far beyond those fat baby faces in the photos his mother had mailed him. Home was filling his head with so many sensations he found it hard to concentrate on any one thing. Home was overwhelming him, but he wasn't sure he wanted to be here. That he belonged here. He visualized himself alone in his Phoenix apartment at this hour—if not content, at least sedated by the weariness of one more day on the job.

He glanced back at his mother, hunched in her white beaded dress, yet smiling. She waited at the middle of a second rank, this one composed of five elder Parker women. Behind them, more ranks of relatives, a phalanx of kin, lined up behind Emmett and his honor men.

Bobbie and Billie.

Emmett exhaled with relief. He'd just recalled the names of the twins, who were undertaking this obligation with somber expressions that both touched and amused him. Jerome was still grinning at Emmett as if he'd eaten the canary, brimming with the surprise he obviously itched to spring on Emmett. Strictly speaking, Crowe wasn't a relation. But brotherhood was too valued to be measured by blood alone, and their bond had been forged in the confines of an Indian mission run by the Order of St. Benedict, who invented the Christian monastic life. *Pray and work.* Jerome had submitted to the Benedictine way of life, finding solace and identity in it. Emmett had remained like many Comanche—insurgently acculturated.

"*Udah* for coming, folks," the emcee said over the loud-speakers. Emmett looked to the man up on the stand whose face was half-hidden by the shadow of his Stetson. Then, as was the custom at all powwows, the emcee translated for the sake of nonmembers of the tribe, "*Thanks* for coming. Welcome to the start of our powwow. This year, to get things rolling, we'd like to honor a son of the *Nuhmuhnuh,* as we Comanche call ourselves, *the People,* who's been gone too long from home. Do you have the song?" he asked the head drummer, who replied in the affirmative by striking his big drum once.

The males of the group began beating out a steady rhythm. Emmett had heard it likened to a mother's heartbeat her baby hears from the womb.

He started his family around the drums. It was a step dance, and the pace couldn't be too swift. This was a chance for people from the crowd to either approach Emmett and press crumpled currency into his hand or leave the money with the arena director, who'd doffed his hat for the offerings. The bills were wadded up so no one but the giver would know the denomination of the bill. He was confronted by person after person he hadn't seen for years. Young faces had turned old, and old faces had turned older. Each made an offering, then joined the rear of the shuffling column.

Thankfully, Emmett did not have to say anything at this point.

The head drummer fell into the honor song. There were songs for most occasions, and new ones were composed all the time in a continuation of the tradition, but the familiarity of this one sent a chill up Emmett's spine. He knew this song well. It was about his own family. How the warrior Peta Nocona, *He Who Travels Alone and Returns,* took Naudah, *She Who Carries Herself with Dignity and Grace,* as his wife. She'd been born Cynthia Ann Parker to Texas pioneers. In 1836, at age nine, she'd been captured by a Comanche raiding party. After a rigorous period of initiation endured by all captives, she was welcomed as a full member into the *Quahada* branch of the tribe.

So blood alone did not make you Comanche.

The drum women took up the story with shrill vibrato and made it soar through the sultry air: How, like all Comanche boys of that era, Quanah, the son of Peta Nocona and Naudah, had been pressed early into warrior service for his people. Quanah had barely been out of his teens when he led a war party against the U.S. Cavalry. His face painted black and riding a black horse, he charged the soldiers and shot one dead. Alone.

That is what the song emphasized. Alone he charged under the admiring gazes of his men. Alone he courted death.

Emmett looked over his shoulder at his mother.

Had she suggested this song to the head drummer? Her expression was blank as she planted each rhythmic step. But Emmett knew that she sensed his ambivalence about coming home—weakened by his wound and by a failed love as well. What was she trying to say with this song? That above all, courage and good cheer were required of a *Nuhmuhnuh?* That these were the things that made you Comanche? Had he lapsed, somehow?

I'm home in body, but has my spirit actually forgotten the way home?

The singers went on: How at the Battle of Adobe Walls, the last great fight against the buffalo hunters who were starving the People with their wanton slaughter of the herds, Quanah galloped through a withering fire from the big-bore guns of the hunters, leaned over, and grabbed a wounded comrade named Howea off the ground, carrying him to safety, although he himself was shot in the leg within minutes of the dramatic rescue.

The song ended on that high note. Of self-sacrifice.

The emcee descended from his stand and halted the column that was now fifty yards long. Hundreds of well-wishers had fallen in behind the Parkers in ranks of fours or fives, and Emmett's hands were filled with wads of cash. The arena director extended his hat to Emmett, who deposited the money in it. A thousand dollars, at least. It wasn't for the Parkers. All would be portioned out to the drum group and those who had helped put on the dance.

"Folks," the emcee broadcast, "Jerome Crowe will speak for Emmett Quanah Parker."

Jerome took the microphone. "Ladies and gentlemen," he said, draping his arm across Emmett's shoulders, "this is my brother. I'm going to speak for him. Afterward, he'll keep to the old ways and give to those who honor him. So bear with me while I take you back. . . ." Jerome paused, his round, sweat-damp face going still for a moment. "I'm of the *Kotsotekas* band, 'The Buffalo Eaters.' There are several bands of the *Nuhmuhnuh* and all of them are indebted to the *Quahada*, 'The Antelope Eaters.' From them came Quanah. . . ." Jerome smiled fondly as he repeated the name. "Mothers, you remember the smell of your new babies?" The women, especially the older ones, nodded. "Well, *Quanah* means *fragrance*, and it was with that fresh smell of the newborn in mind that Naudah named her son. He became a fine man, strong and tall like Emmett here. When the *Nuhmuhnuh* were forced to fight to protect the buffalo on which their survival depended, Quanah rose to war chief. He fought in the all the last great battles. When the war was done and the old nomadic life gone, he served us in another way. He took his mother's maiden name as a sign that we had to learn a new kind of living. We had to change. He taught us to adapt. He taught us to prosper, not just survive. And so the Parkers have always been counted among our protectors, all the way down to my dear brother and son here. . . ." Jerome gave Emmett's neck a tender squeeze.

Emmett tried to smile but couldn't. He felt sadly out of step with this heroic past. And the humid heat was pressing on his body, making him want to sit down. The full weight of the past was on him, like a boulder.

But Jerome was just hitting his stride, and it was an insult to make an honor speech too brief. "I call him my brother because we shared our youth together at the mission near Anadarko. I also call him my son now and again because I taught him everything he knows. . . ."

As the laughter swelled around him, Emmett gave a flicker of a smile for the first time. But then he was distracted by tribal workers setting up wooden barricades behind the emcee and Jerome.

"After getting his bachelor's degree in criminology and anthropology at Oklahoma State University," Jerome went on, "Emmett served five years with the Oklahoma City Police Department, first in patrol and then as a detective with the homicide bureau. . . ."

Two failed marriages during that tenure, Emmett recalled to himself. Long hours of work, punctuated by a haze of bars, parties, speeding drunk down the turnpikes late at night, driven by desire. Times the old people called 'roughing it out.' Nights that now shamed him for his lack of self-control. Quanah had been a master of self-control, finding balance and dignity in a world that had turned upside-down on him.

Am I Comanche only when I'm out in the white world?

"Three times, Emmett was decorated by the Oklahoma attorney general for valor in the line of duty. Incidentally, that A.G. went on to become governor and now occupies the highest office in the land. . . ." There was polite applause, a couple of boos for the current president. "Fourteen years ago, Emmett's talents and deeds as an investigator came to the attention of the Secretary of the Interior, who personally asked him to come on board the law enforcement division of the Bureau of Indian Affairs as a criminal investigator. Fortunately for Indian Country, Emmett agreed, serving initially at the Anadarko area office . . ."

His third and last marriage ended his first year with the BIA. Actually, he hadn't started in Anadarko. He'd started with an undercover assignment in Wounded Knee, South Dakota, although that stint didn't appear on his resume because it was still politically controversial.

"... and then with the Phoenix area office, where he continues to be posted, serving throughout the country as needed. Twice he has been named the Native American Law Enforcement Association's Officer of the Year...."

He'd missed the second presentation while in alcohol rehab. After that, he hadn't considered marriage again—until assigned on detail two years ago with Anna Turnipseed, an FBI agent of Modoc ancestry. That, too, was now finished. Of late, she wasn't even returning his calls. All in all, a smashing life capped by something he swore he'd never do—come home with his tail between his legs.

The crowd had gone quiet, and Emmett realized that Jerome had finished speaking and was offering the microphone to him. Taking it, he quietly thanked everyone for coming. Not much was expected of him after his spokesman had extolled his virtues. As was the custom, Emmett promptly returned the mike to Crowe and whispered to his old friend the name of the first recipient. Jerome nodded and announced, "Emmett Quanah Parker calls for our vice chairwoman." The tribal chairman was away on tribal business and had already sent his apologies. Emmett enfolded the vice chairwoman in the fringed shawl he had brought. Shawls for women and blankets for men.

Again, Emmett whispered to Jerome, who announced, "Emmett Quanah Parker calls for the Keeper of the Pipe of the Thunder Dogs."

A short but powerfully built man approached in the prescribed way, clockwise around the drum circle. Unsmiling, Michael Mangas extended his hand, and Emmett accepted it. They shook. In the formal silence that followed, Emmett presented him with one of Pendleton blankets. Mangas was now the FBI's head resident agent in Lawton, although Emmett and he had first met as boys while attending the BIA school just outside of town. Emmett had been expelled and went on to the Catholic Indian mission, but the two had met again as rookie patrolmen in Oklahoma City. He embraced Mangas. "Thank you for this honor. I thank all the Thunder Dogs for their consideration to me and my family. We won't forget this."

The agent kept a poker face, but it was apparent by a tiny frown that he'd picked up Emmett's intimation that the two of them weren't family. He and Emmett were related, although in a way most whites would find exotic. Quanah Parker had had seven wives. Emmett was a descendent of the first daughter of his first wife. Michael's line sprang from another of Quanah's wives—with an Apache twist. That branch had intermarried with Geronimo's band of Chiricahua, who had been detained at Ft. Sill after being run to ground by the U.S. Army. Despite his Comanche blood, Mangas had Geronimo's hard-bitten scrawl of a mouth, although Michael wasn't his direct descendant. Quanah and Geronimo had never cared for each other. Neither had Emmett and Mangas. But, given tonight's public occasion, the agent and pipe keeper thanked Emmett for the fine blanket and embraced him in turn, stiffly. Mangas had lost his son in the bombing of the Murrah Building. Emmett had not seen the man since that morning in 1995, but now was not the moment to offer his condolences. He'd do so at the first opportunity.

Emmett gave a Mexican blanket to some he had Jerome summon forward, a laundry basket of foodstuffs and household items to others. Making these choices was beyond him, but his mother stood slightly behind him, prompting in whispers even softer than his own, calmly telling him who should receive what.

They were down to the last few baskets when a bull buffalo lowed anxiously from the adjoining pasture.

Another sound swelled out of the northwest—the rotors of a large helicopter in approach. Everyone craned for a look as the aircraft swooped down into the glare of the floodlights. The white-over-olive-green U.S. Marine Corps helicopter dipped out of sight behind the grandstands.

Emmett found himself flanked by two Secret Service agents. They were marked by their lapel pins and the radio wires snaking up out of the blazers and into their ears. "Please step this way, Mr. Parker," one of them requested, indicating a gap in the barricades that led to a podium that had materialized there. It bore the presidential seal. News people were ushered before it. Camera crews were the first to notice the army staff car, borrowed from nearby Ft. Sill, pulling into the arena.

Emmett's mouth went dry as he realized that he now had a very big to-do on his hands.

3

"IT'S GREAT TO be home, Oklahoma!" the President of the United States declared to the cheering throng. Emmett noted that there were no boos. Everybody in attendance was now a supporter. "As I flew into Tinker Air Force this evening, I was informed by my staff that a celebrated *Nuhmuhnuh* lawman is being honored for his years of service to the people of our state and nation. . . ." His pronunciation of the tribe was right on the nose. "Once told the name of this lawman, I ordered a little detour for Marine One on my way home to the ranch. So I hope you don't mind if I drop by, say howdy, and add my voice to those lauding Emmett Quanah Parker!"

The people roared their approval. Many of the older women *lulued*, trilled their tongues. It was all a bit too much for Emmett: the camera lights, the frenetic energy whipped up by the Commander in Chief's sudden appearance. The only way he could bring himself back down to earth was to imagine the man as he'd first known him. A self-confident state A.G., already balding back then, profane when it suited his temper, petty in some ways, but possessed of a tireless ambition that set him apart from others.

Then he saw that the President was looking at him.

"Emmett, I've valued your friendship through the years, especially those years when we labored together in the attempt to rid our state of the scourge of drugs. Tonight, we're in debt to you for your courage and dedication. You have labored ceaselessly for the safety and welfare of the ordinary men and women of this country. . . ." Emmett acknowledged the applause with a wave, and after that spate of clapping, the president segued into the political message he'd been hammering home for the November election: "And it's for the ordinary men and women of this country that I will soon tour the Western states to spread the message of tax reform. . . ." The mostly Indian crowd quieted down, quick on the uptake that the President was now speaking to the cameras, not them. They were being moderately exploited, just as Emmett had been with the falsehood that he and the President were chums. As far as the president's mention of that distant task force, he'd been denounced recently by the other party's candidate for being soft on drug enforcement.

Emmett had now recovered enough to ask himself how this honor had come about. The President had been accused of being negligent toward the tribes, especially by the Indian press, and this evening served as a ready photo op to help put a dent in that criticism. But it had to be more than that. Presidents don't waste time on low-level federal cops.

Why is he here?

Emmett didn't have to look far for the answer—standing beside Jerome Crowe was a slim platinum blonde in her late thirties. Pretty, but a tad too high voltage to be pretty in a cuddly way. Her name was Dagen Kirsch. A perennial deputy. Presently, she was a deputy chief of staff to the President, but she'd first made her name in Washington as one of the deputies to the assistant secretary of the Interior, with oversight on BIA law enforcement operations. On a more personal level to Emmett, Dagen had been a fellow inmate at the Indian mission near Anadarko, the only white child to attend, an awkward girl with hair the color of straw and a history of pathetic crushes on boys older than herself.

She smiled over at Emmett with a self-assurance she'd lacked back then. He didn't smile back.

While with the Department of the Interior, Dagen had not been a friend to BIA law enforcement. She'd endeared herself to the party she now served by slashing jobs in the Bureau, particularly investigator positions, to the point the law enforcement division was only a shell of its former strength. In arranging this presidential visit, was she signaling that she wanted to kiss and make up with the BIA's cops?

Dagen Kirsch did nothing without an agenda.

"So thank you, everyone, for letting me be a part of this night. God bless you and God bless America!" The President was obviously looking for his escape when the vice chairwoman put her hand over the mike and asked him if he'd mind being smoked. Emmett noticed that he glanced to Dagen, who gave him a nod, as if it'd become a habit to rely on her counsel. "Be honored," he told the vice chairwoman.

Wendell Padduhpony stepped forward with dried sprigs of red-berry cedar smoldering in a stone bowl. The holy man was pushing eighty but his back was still ramrod straight. Long gray braids dangled out from under his black bowler, which he removed and handed to Michael Mangas. He wore a matching black kerchief as a tie. He prayed to the each of the sacred directions, then used the feather of a golden eagle to anoint the President with the cedar smoke, murmuring soft words of counsel all the while. Not every visiting dignitary got cedared, and Wendell probably rendered this honor as a decorated World War II veteran to his commander in chief, not as one of the president's partisans.

While Wendell went on ministering to the President, the vice chairwoman proved that she too had been caught unprepared for this visit, for she asked Emmett if he'd brought an extra Pendleton. He had, of course; you never held back at a giveaway. Minutes later, she enfolded the president in that blanket, at which point, the cameras flashed and clicked, catching the politically defining moment of the evening. The President motioned Emmett closer for a handshake that went on too long. "You were one hell of a cop." More photos while Emmett contemplated the significance of the President of the United States referring to his career in the past tense. The President promptly offloaded the blanket on an aide, and Emmett mused that he'd had no idea yesterday as he bought that Pendleton in Anadarko that it would wind up in the Washington warehouse where most presidential gifts gathered dust. A lesser blanket would've been fine for the warehouse.

Shit, what does it all matter?

Then the Secret Service trundled the President back into the army staff car for the short ride across the complex to Marine One. Unnoticed until that moment was an executive type with slicked back silver hair and a ruddy face, who got in and sat beside the President. Atypically, his name eluded Emmett for the moment, but the man ran an oil service conglomerate based in Tulsa. He was probably joining the first family for a few days at the ranch as reward for his generosity to the campaign. Or, more correctly, his foundation's generosity, whose critics claimed had been created with the sole purpose of skirting the new campaign finance reform laws the President was touting in public.

The vice chairwoman tugged apologetically at Emmett's sleeve. "Sorry about your blanket. I thought maybe the governor might show, not the *President*, and I didn't have a decent thing to give him."

"No problem, he looked cold," Emmett muttered. "He always looks cold to me."

Marine One lifted off and wheeled toward the western White House, the president's ancestral ranch eighty miles to the northwest in Dewey County. Then someone bushwhacked him with an embrace and emphatic kiss. Dagen Kirsch. She was still with Jerome Crowe, who asked Emmett, "How's that for a surprise?"

"Fine," Emmett said.

"Oh damn you," Dagen complained, "you can do better than that. You don't change a lick, do you, Emmett Parker!" She seemed prettier at close range, something he didn't recall from their days together at the mission. And there had been some close-range encounters back then, the most memorable on a swimming trip to Lake Lawtonka.

"You just miss your ride?" Emmett jerked his head toward the receding lights of the chopper.

"Nope. Secret Service from the Oklahoma City office is going to drop me off at the apartment I keep in Anadarko . . . unless one of you wants to drive me home?"

"Glad to, Dagen," Jerome volunteered.

"You're a dear. I'll catch up with the President on Monday morning. We all need a rest. The *campaign*," she added in a weary whine. "Don't tell any-body, but the party chairman is already among the walking wounded. Poor man, he just can't keep up with this kind of punishing schedule anymore—"

A loud clack startled her.

Emmett saw that the podium and barricades were gone, and the Thun-der Dogs had assembled in a line that stretched across the arena. They were dancing to honor him, loudly beating their round Comanche shields with their arrows. It embarrassed him to have been caught off-guard.

Swiftly, he faced the warriors with his full attention and didn't move a muscle until they were done.

Then the powwow began in earnest, and at last Emmett could get out of the spotlight and withdraw into the grandstands. He searched for his mother. Jerome and Dagen tagged along, chatting casually, so casually that Emmett suspected over the years in Washington they'd carried on their friendship from the mission. It was Jerome's strength and weakness: He was everybody's friend.

Standing on a bleacher, Emmett finally spotted his mother. She was sur-rounded by admiring women her age. This had probably been the high point of her life. Why wasn't it even close to being his? Tired, so tired. His legs felt like boiled okra. He was ragged from rubbing elbows with so many people out of his past, all hemming him in on one hot evening.

He sat, and within seconds, Michael Mangas was looming over him, his grim and naturally scowling mouth set in what the FBI agent probably imagined to be a smile. Behind him at a distance stood some other Thunder Dogs, still sweating in their finery.

Mangas eased down beside Emmett. He said nothing for the moment, just let the beat of the drums and the jingle of ankle bells fill the silence.

Emmett was first to break it: "I was sorry to hear about your son."

The FBI agent shrugged, and Emmett thought that closed the subject. But then, keeping his gaze on the arena, Mangas said, "High-functioning."

"Pardon?"

"Todd was what they call high-functioning," Mangas went on. "You know, for somebody with Down syndrome. So I was able him to get him a janitorial job there at the Murrah Building. He lived in this house in the city with other folks like him. He was doing great. . . ." The man paused, and when he continued there was a thin quaver to his voice, like someone retelling a nightmare that refused to go away. "I was driving there that morning from Lawton."

"To the Murrah?" Emmett asked.

"Yeah. A task force meeting scheduled for eight. Except there was an accident just north of Chickasha. I stopped to help 'til the troopers arrived. Back on road again, I saw the column of smoke rising from downtown. . . ." Mangas's voice trailed off, as if he'd finally come to grips with the fact that there was really nothing more to tell. Everything was explained by that ribbon of black smoke hanging in the bright April sky over Oklahoma City. When he spoke again, the quaver was gone, and he sounded determined to get something out of the way. "I know we've had our differences in the past, Emmett, but that shouldn't stand in the way of you joining the Thunder Dogs. The other guys have asked me to ask you. So that's what I'm doing. Asking."

Emmett pretended to watch the dancers while he thought up an answer. For generations, membership in the dancing societies had been reserved for warriors. In the modern era, that meant military veterans. Even law enforcement vets, like Emmett and Michael, weren't let in. Then, in the early 1980s, the Thunder Dogs Society was organized by Comanche men who wanted to perpetuate the old ways but hadn't served in the armed forces. Since that time, the Thunder Dogs had grown in prestige, and it was an honor to be asked, so much of an honor that Emmett felt the need to say, "I'm not ready right now, Michael."

Mangas exhaled, as if he'd expected no less. "On account of me?"

"No. Nothing to do with you. How's it said? *'The pipe finds its keeper.'* I'm sure you're a fine one." A sacred pipe was central to all the societies and the focus of their rites.

"Then what?"

"Me," Emmett replied. "It has to do with me. I just don't feel up to the honor. . . ." He tried to be as precise as he could in declining the offer. The old ways were inherently holy, and he didn't feel worthy of upholding them right now. Not after the past year, one marked by violence and so much anger and a crushing sense of failure. "I just don't feel right about taking this on right now."

Mangas said, "Suit yourself."

"But thanks." Emmett looked up at the other Thunder Dogs, who seemed more disappointed than the agent. "Thanks, everybody."

Then Mangas's beeper went off. He took it from his belt and read the message screen. "Got to go," he said, heaving himself to his feet.

"Trouble?" Emmett instinctively asked the fellow federal officer.

"Who knows? Summons is from Hawzeepa. Take care."

"You, too," Emmett said, as they shook.

Silas Hawzeepa, a Kiowa, was the Comanche County medical examiner, and one of Emmett's former brothers-in-law.

On the way out, Mangas stopped and greeted Dagen Kirsch. Without smiling. They exchanged a few words, then he hurried on. Mangas had not gone to the mission with Dagen and Emmett. His conduct had been satisfactory enough for him to remain at the now defunct BIA school on the outskirts of Lawton, unlike Emmett and his late brother, Malcolm. So the agent had met Dagen somewhere else along the line. An accomplished politico, she would know most everyone in area law enforcement, particularly federal officers who could do special favors outside the chain of command for the administration.

Mangas was soon gone into the crowd.

Dagen took the place on the bleacher the agent had vacated. She said nothing at first, simply gave Emmett a sisterly pat on the knee and watched the colorful action in the arena. "You miss this?" she eventually asked, obviously meaning the Indian world of Oklahoma.

"Much of it. How about you?"

"I get back quite a lot. But yes, I miss it when I'm in Washington. I miss the lack of intrigue."

Emmett had never found his home state particularly lacking in intrigue, but he didn't argue.

Then she abruptly said, "Malcolm killed himself."

Emmett wasn't sure if it had been a question, but he replied, "Years ago. While I was still with Oklahoma City P.D." He'd shot himself in their mother's kitchen.

Dagen took his left hand in both of hers. "Do you know why?"

Emmett shook his head, but found himself trying to explain. "He was under a lot of stress. Law school. And everything else a young person has to go through."

"I was crushed when I heard, Emmett. He was so sweet."

He nodded.

Then she asked, "I wouldn't be young again for the world, would you?"

"I'll have to think about that." His damaged forty-one-year-old body had been worn down by the evening, and he missed the vitality he'd felt twenty years ago. But what had he done with that precious gift? Not much, judging from his present straits.

Dagen was looking at him, hard. "I've missed you, Emmett Parker."

He wasn't quite up to saying that he'd missed her. But close. She was looking increasingly good to him. But then he noticed his mother being escorted toward him by Jerome Crowe, who said, "I'm taking Mother Parker home. She's tired."

"I'll drive you, Mama," Emmett offered.

"Just give me the keys," Jerome insisted. "You've got to stay for at least one more dance, or I'll be even more ashamed to call you my brother than I already am. Don't argue."

Emmett dug the keys out of his pocket and tossed them to Jerome. His mother gave him a happy peck on the cheek and walked off with Crowe, looking elfin in comparison to his waddling bulk.

As he sat again, Emmett realized that he'd failed to reintroduce Dagen to his mother. He apologized to her for the gaffe.

But Dagen said, "No matter. She knew who I was."

This was said with such hurt, he quickly added, "I've never heard my mother say anything but good about you."

"Celia never says a bad word about *anybody*." She clasped Emmett's hand again and grinned with damp eyes at him. "Don't worry. It was nothing." But her grin was brittle enough for Emmett to glimpse once more, after all these years, the hypersensitivity that had made her unpopular at the mission, even to the boys who'd found her attractive. Maybe she'd had cause for this annoying foible. Dagen was the orphan of a widower father, a medical missionary from Anadarko who left her in the care of the only parochial boarding school in the area, which happened to be Indian. He had died in a plane crash, and St. Benedict's had become her only home.

She let go of his hand as more well-wishers descended on Emmett. This time, he made sure to introduce her to everyone. But it was clear that the evening was wearing on her patience, for she checked her wristwatch more than once.

"Jerome should be back soon," Emmett promised.

Dagen held up a set of keys and jiggled them in his face.

He asked, "What's that?"

"Jerome's keys," she said mischievously as she sprang to her feet. "Come on, drive me home. It's been a long day, made longer by the time change."

"What about the Secret Service?" he asked, falling in behind her.

"To hell with the Secret Service." She shot a tentative look back at him with her blazing blue eyes. "You don't *mind* taking me home, do you, Emmett?"

The Keeper of the Pipe was back to being an FBI agent.

"*Icoño,*" Michael Mangas muttered in his fractured and largely scatological reservation Spanish. *Crap.*

He left the outer regalia he'd worn for the dance in his *bucar,* or bureau car, and strode inside Lawton Community Hospital. He flashed his credentials at the front receptionist and went past without breaking stride. He'd lived most of his life in Lawton, all of it in Oklahoma except for his time at the FBI academy in Quantico, and everybody knew him.

The medical examiner would be waiting for him in the autopsy suite in the basement, his intentions in summoning Michael unclear.

On May 21, almost two weeks ago, a discovery had been made by lovers along Medicine Creek where it wound through Medicine Park, a resort town in the Wichita Mountains with rock bungalows and a meandering river park lit by old fashioned streetlamps. One of those lamps figured prominently in the discovery, as it was by its mellow light that the lovers noticed something odd in a pile of branches heaped up along the shore by the spring runoff. A human foreleg, neatly severed just below the knee joint, shoeless and sockless.

Yawning, Michael punched the "down" button and waited for the elevator. It was slow in coming.

Concurrent with the ground search along the banks of Medicine Creek, the City of Lawton—which owned and operated Lake Lawtonka—had a seemingly unrelated problem of its own.

The elevator doors whisked open and Michael stepped inside.

The dam gate had been malfunctioning in such a way that it refused to hold back enough current for the lake to rise to its early summer level. Water, needed by area agriculture in the coming months, was spilling wastefully down into the Canadian, Arkansas, and Mississippi Rivers beyond. A commercial diving outfit from Galveston was hired to check the water gate.

The elevator doors opened to a dimly lit corridor, boxes of hospital supplies stacked on both sides all the way down to a locked door. Michael knocked, and after a minute, the long face of Dr. Silas Hawzeepa appeared in the opening. "Agent Mangas," the medical examiner said, stepping back for Michael to enter the bilious-smelling suite.

Agent Mangas.

Michael didn't care for the formality. Hawzeepa and he had known each other since they were boys. They'd gone to the BIA school in town together, along with Parker, before Emmett and his younger brother, Malcolm, ran off once too often to seek their father, an itinerant construction worker, and found themselves at the even stricter Indian mission. Amazing how little two brothers could resemble each other. Malcolm had been gentle and eager to please. Unlike Emmett. And Michael had never taken to Silas Hawzeepa, either. Stoic, aloof, and opinionated—a typical Kiowa, except that he was taller than most.

There it was, under strong lights. The reason the water gate had refused to close. At least, in part. "Where's the cross?"

"How did you know about that?" Dr. Hawzeepa asked. His precise diction and carefully modulated voice annoyed Michael.

"Word gets around."

"Stored in the property room at the police department."

As best Michael could figure, the vertical member of the rough-hewn cross had passed almost all the way through the submerged gate while it was open for the spring run-off, but the cross-beam had become lodged in it, preventing it from closing when the time came to hold back the waters. Otherwise, the entire crucifix would have been disgorged into Medicine Creek, and the spooning couple might have been privy to a religious experience instead of just a grisly one.

Frowning now, the examiner led him over to the autopsy table for a closer look.

"He was found nude like this?" Michael inquired. *He*, based on the undeniable fact there was a pecker.

"Yes."

Immersion did strange things to a human body. Bloated the face beyond recognition. Not just individual recognition, but racial as well. The lids and surrounding tissue swelled, giving the eyes an often misleading Asiatic cast. The bulbous lips had curled back to form a carp-like mouth, revealing a tongue so enlarged it distended past the gaping jaws. And the flesh of the entire body had a soft, soapy appearance. Michael ran a slow gaze over it. From head to knees. Only as far down as the knees, because both legs had been severed, presumably by the guillotinelike water gate, just below there. The left foreleg had yet to be found.

Here and there were nibble marks. The work of crawdads, the latest generation of the same crayfish he had hunted with bacon-baited hooks as a boy along Medicine Creek.

The corpse itself had not jammed the water gate. Despite its rigid skeleton, the human body was too soft a thing to have held open those massive iron plates. Again, it was the wooden cross to which the victim had been lashed that had kept Lake Lawtonka from rising. "You save the bindings?" Michael asked.

"Of course," Dr. Hawzeepa answered. "I realized you'd find the knots of interest, so I cut the nylon ropes some inches from them."

To Michael Mangas, interest and jurisdiction were synonymous. He saw no advantage in becoming fascinated with something that didn't involve him. Personal energy was finite, particularly these days. More than anything else, grief exhausted. "Why would I find any of this interesting?"

"Two reasons. First, Lawtonka lies on federal land—"

"Adjacent to the federal wildlife refuge," Michael corrected. "The actual lake is on city land." He paused. "Did the victim die of drowning?"

Dr. Hawzeepa declared, "No, his throat was slit."

Michael fell silent; he'd been hoping for a quick way out of this. A suicide by drowning would've done the trick, nicely. But it was unlikely that the unknown subject had lashed himself to a cross for the Easter holiday and then slashed his own throat. "Your second reason?"

"I believe the victim to be Amerind."

American Indian. Michael considered that possibility for a moment. The victim being Indian would squarely put the case in his ballpark, so he had to pin down Dr. Hawzeepa on this. "You have DNA to back up that conclusion?"

"Of course not. The body was just pulled to the surface yesterday afternoon. But the hair has Mongoloid characters—"

"Which can be either Amerind or Asian," Michael stopped him short again.

"There are the skull and jaw characteristics."

"How'd you see them, given this condition. . . ." Michael gestured at the misshapen face.

"X-ray. And given my long experience with this sort of thing, I'm telling you the victim is Indian, not Asian."

Michael wasn't sold, and in that he still had some hope this investigation would wind up back in the laps of Lawton P.D. But there was no reason to belabor this point at the moment; doing so would only make him look uncooperative. "What are the general time spans *with this sort of thing?*" He realized a second too late that his echoing of Dr. Hawzeepa's phrase had come across as sarcastic.

The examiner hid any possible displeasure by turning his attention to the victim's right hand, which he'd apparently just rested under an illuminating magnifier when interrupted by Michael's knock. "The hands become badly swollen three to five days into the immersion, depending on water temperature," he explained. "It's all dependent on water temp, and Lawtonka is cool but not cold this time of year."

"What are we talking?"

"Oh, about fifty degrees, Fahrenheit." Over Dr. Hawzeepa's shoulder, Michael could see the indentation left by the nylon rope around the right wrist, although it was nearly covered by the bloated flesh. The examiner lightly used a scalpel all the way around the base of the hand, while preserving the impression evidence of the binding. "In five to six days, the skin begins to slough off the body. Eight to ten days, the skin of the hands and around the fingernails separates . . ." With that, he removed the entire epidermis of the right hand. It came off like a glove, although with slight resistance and an unpleasant sucking sound. He spread it flat on a paper towel, then glanced up at Michael, his eyes owlish over the tops of his bifocals. "Your call, Agent Mangas—do you want this shipped off to our lab or yours?"

Michael paused, thinking. Fingerprint identification could prove the swiftest route to disputing federal jurisdiction in this, and nobody was better at that than the FBI's technicians, or *techies*, as they were called with mild affection. But some unwanted cases were acquired by concretion, one detail at a time, until there was no way you could get out of them. Michael was not opposed to taking on cases. Just ones that threatened to take gaping mouthfuls out of his private life for years to come. And Michael didn't care for the examiner's transparent desire that he, as head resident agent here, take over the case from the P.D. But after a long lull in the conversation, he found himself saying, "Let's ship both hands off to D.C."

"Fine." Dr. Hawzeepa was staring at Michael's neck.

Until then, the agent hadn't realized that he'd failed to take off the beaded choker he'd worn to the dance.

The examiner asked, "The powwow?"

"Yeah, an honor dance to kick it off." Then something made him tack on, maybe just to see Dr. Hawzeepa's reaction, "For Emmett Parker. Damned if even the president showed on his way to his ranch."

The examiner's face revealed nothing as he moved the magnifier to the other side of the table and began removing the epidermis of the left hand. His sister was tall, too, plus willowy—recalling from the last time he'd seen her on Emmett's arm, at an affair for the Fraternal Order of Police in Oklahoma City. "How is Emmett doing?" the examiner finally asked.

"On the mend," Michael said. "Some whacko damn near killed him with an ax while he was on assignment in upstate New York."

"How ghastly," Dr. Hawzeepa said with a faint but disagreeable smile.

4

EMMETT HAD JUST pulled out of the town of Apache and was headed toward Anadarko when Dagen Kirsch said in that odd tonal quality of hers that was neither a question nor a statement, "I heard you underwent the Sun Dance while up in South Dakota." In the soft glow of the instrument lights, she smiled over at him, waiting for his answer.

Jerome Crowe's new Cadillac glided almost noiselessly over the highway, past fields of sweet corn, the leaves glistening in the light of a moon that was just a slice off full. The ride would've been entirely pleasant but for the smell of the cigarette butts that overflowed the ashtray. Emmett felt a faint pang of guilt: He'd introduced Jerome to smoking while at the mission. Not tobacco. They couldn't afford the Lucky Strikes some older boys sold for a nickel a piece. Those who couldn't afford a nickel a smoke went out into the brambles and harvested the dry, pithy reeds of the wild grape vine and smoked them—at the risk of a flame shooting up the porous stem and scorching their mouths. "Who told you about the Sun Dance?"

"I have my sources." Dagen had kicked off her shoes and cocked up a leg with her bare foot resting on the seat. He kept his gaze on the center line, but her pale white thigh was firmly caught in the corner of his eye. "What was it like, hanging that way . . . ?"

Few knew about his undercover assignment fourteen years ago to infiltrate an offshoot of Indian militants, but he realized that Dagen could be counted among them. As a deputy to the assistant secretary of the Interior with law enforcement oversight, she would've had access to Emmett's file. There was little she wouldn't know about him, at least in terms of the record.

"Did you do it or not? Do you mind discussing this?"

"No," he said, turning right at Apache Wye.

"*No* . . . you don't mind, or *no* . . . you didn't undergo the ceremony?"

"Don't ask two questions at once."

"Are you telling me to shut up?"

"Ummm . . . no . . ."

"Fuck you, Emmett Parker." With that, she reached across the center console and undid the top two buttons to his ribbon shirt. There was something innocent and tomboyish in how she explored his right pectoral with her hand. She smoothly and quickly located the twin scars through which one of two wooden skewers had passed under the muscle, anchoring him by leather thongs to the sun pole. Then, she accidentally found his most recent scar, the indentation to his chest. "My God, what did *that* to you?"

"The fire ax from an airliner cockpit."

"I'm sorry."

"Me, too."

She withdrew her hand. "Please, Em—what was the Sun Dance like?"

Indescribable. Dangling on a shimmering liquid membrane of pain between Sun and Earth. All the clocks in the world grinding to a halt. At the time, he'd justified the experience as a means of gaining the trust of the militants, who were financing their activities by robbing banks throughout the northern plains. But soon after, he began to see that he had done this for himself. Like most people, he had always sensed that there was a part of himself he didn't have ordinary access to, and he wanted to glimpse it, if only temporarily.

The Sun Dance did that for you.

At last he said, "It's like being born and dying all in one moment."

"*Really?*"

"Really."

"But wasn't the pain intolerable?"

"No," he said quietly. Nothing like the pain of losing Anna Turnipseed. No word from her in weeks, and he now fully expected that she'd never contact him again. She'd said her last good-bye in her own bittersweet way. They'd meet again, months or even years down the pike, but only accidentally at some federal cop function. He'd get a swift peck on the cheek from her, feigned delight in seeing him. Then she'd peel off and keep company with her fellow FBI agents.

I will turn monk before I fall in love again.

"I can't stand the thought of you in pain," Dagen said. "Even if it's for something worthwhile. Like the ceremony." She set her foot back on the floor mat, and her skirt slid over her thigh, concealing it. "Am I making you uncomfortable?"

"Hell yes," he said, without lying, "you're even prettier than I remembered."

She undid her restraining belt to give him a quick kiss on the cheek, and for a second time this evening he saw the side of Dagen Kirsch that had not healed with time and success. She was still prone to flattery, something a number of boys at the mission had discovered and used rather callously. "Ask you something?"

"Sure," she eagerly responded.

"Are you seeing anybody right now?" Jerome had seemed quite taken with her, perhaps he'd always been, and Emmett didn't want to blunder into something his friend had going.

"What do you think, Em?"

Oh, boy, this one could be a minefield. "Whoever he is, he's a damned fool for not wrapping you up while he has the chance." Emmett thought she was going to kiss him again.

Instead, she cried, "Stop!" So sharply Emmett thought an animal was crossing in front of them. But she pointed at a modern Catholic church sitting back from the highway. "Turn in. Have you ever been back?"

"Never," he admitted, taking the lane that wound behind the church. A floodlight shone down onto the vacant parking lot, drawing a flurry of moths and bugs. It also illuminated a placard and small shrine to the Virgin. He pulled alongside and killed the engine. His two top shirt buttons were still undone and he felt no urge to fasten them again. He'd liked the coolness of her fingertips on his skin.

"Come on," she invited.

They both stepped out of the car, she in her bare feet. Her hair looked like spun glass in the strong light. Side by side, they stood before the bronze placard, and she took his hand as they read:

St. Benedict of Nursia Indian Mission

From 1888 until fire destroyed the main structure in 1979, the Order of St. Benedict maintained a school just north of here, which served the children of numerous tribes, including the Apache, Caddo, Choctaw, Comanche, Kiowa, and Wichita.

Erected by the Anadarko Knights of Columbus

Emmett could barely make out the gravel road in the overgrown grass that had once led up to the front entrance of the mission. There was no sign of that two-story brick main building, the convent, the chapel, nor the bungalowlike rectory where Father Jurgen had dwelled in a solitude Emmett could not have imagined for himself. A life without women. The once-pruned trees and shrubs now had the run of the grounds, sending up rebellious saplings wherever they pleased.

"Let's go have a look," Dagen said.

"Grab your shoes."

"I don't want to wear any. Too early for cockleburs."

As they walked up the abandoned driveway, the past enveloped him. In his senior year, Father charged him with teaching the younger nuns to drive. Unfortunately, the mission's car was an ancient Chevrolet with a three-on-the-tree stick shift and a clutch that was tricky to master. As they jolted and bounced along this very stretch of drive, Sister Angela stalled the Chevy for the dozenth time and exclaimed, "It's impossible—you need a trinity of feet to drive!" And beside a big stump Dagen and he now approached, in the summer shade once cast by the cottonwood that stood there, Sister Murtha, who was even more ancient than the Chevy, would conduct somber picnics for her native wards, sitting at the head of the long table and swatting flies with a vengeance. One killing spree was so wanton that Sister Angela reminded her that flies were God's creatures, too. "Vell," Sister Murtha said in the clipped accent of her native Austria, "if Gott vants them, He can keep them avay from me!"

Emmett and Dagen passed through a gap in the screen of boxwood and, still hand in hand, ascended the front steps that now led only to a low pile of brick rubble beyond. He tried not to think too much of Dagen's moist palm pressing against his. He told himself that the atmosphere of remembrance made this clasp natural. Almost familial. Together, they'd survived Sister Murtha, who had ventured from the heart of Europe with the flaming ambition to bring God, hygiene, and algebra to the Indians of North America. Emmett had always had the suspicion that the Indians of North America had disappointed her, being no more heroic and romantic than any other people, and their offspring proved just as resistant as any other group of juveniles to God, hygiene, and algebra.

Yet, Sister Murtha lived on inside him. In a set of anally retentive habits, she'd hard-wired in the soft putty of his formative psyche.

"What are you thinking?" Dagen asked.

"Do you still fold your towels and washcloth precisely on the rack as Sister Murtha taught us?"

"Oh God, yes!" She laughed.

Emmett kissed her. It seemed the right moment. But after only a few seconds, she pulled him back down the steps with both arms toward where the chapel had once stood.

Emmett halted, breaking her hold on him.

"What?" she asked impatiently.

He was staring at the tiled floor of the boys' shower room. It, of the whole structure, was most intact, and the porcelain gleamed, as if to spite him. In his last two years here, he'd served as a prefect, a monitor for twenty little boys, most of them chronically homesick for the close-knit families they'd been taken from. The mission was very different from that. Cold, like the tiled shower room. And right there, in the entryway, Father Jurgen, his narrow Germanic face red with anger, had scolded Emmett when his boys left the showers a mess. He ordered Emmett to clean the room for them. Emmett asked why he had to do it. "Because you are their supervisor." Brazenly, Emmett had then asked who his supervisor was. Father said, "I am," and stormed out without another word. Later that day, Emmett was strolling past the shower room when he saw that the door was ajar, as it was when the space was being cleaned. Father had tucked the skirt to his robe up around his belt and was down on his hands and knees, scrubbing the tiles with a brush. He stopped briefly, glared up at Emmett, then went back to work. Humiliated, Emmett withdrew to his dorm.

The old Benedictine knew enough about Comanches to make one lose face.

But Emmett still had for Father that curious mix of resentment and gratitude most children feel toward a parent. Whatever his faults, the priest had taught him how to get by in the working world, another loveless environment. And all the crucifixes here, hanging everywhere like grim sprites, had taught him early that the defining motif to existence was pain.

Yet, all of this marked the start of his journey away from being *Nuhmuhnuh*. And he knew that none of the signposts would be found among these ruins.

"Come on," Dagen urged, giving his arm a tug, "I've got a surprise for you."

The collapsed chapel had left a cruciform of tumble-downed bricks on the ground. Dagen and he filed through another slit in the rampant boxwood. Pushing through the foliage left its smell on their clothes. There, in the alcovelike space paved with flagstones, where Father liked to meditate, Sister Murtha's long picnic table survived. Except it wasn't quite as long as Emmett recalled.

"Remember this?" Dagen asked.

"Christ, yes—it took ten of us to move it out front under that old cottonwood." He followed Dagen to its far end, where she sat and faced him, her thighs exposed once more.

"You know what this place is?"

"Sure, the garden off the vestry."

"No, *stupid*—I mean this school, this parochial factory for good little Catholics."

He suddenly remembered that's what she'd called him in the sexually charged gamesmanship of their few moments alone together. And he'd liked her calling him that, understanding that the mild contempt only underscored her desire. He said nothing. Just waited for her answer.

"A hothouse for juvenile fantasies," she whispered.

"Did you have many here?"

"Oh, yes. You figure in a lot of them." Parting her legs, she pulled Emmett into her and took him by the neck so his mouth came down to hers. After a moment, she said, "And this was one of the hottest ones."

"Next time, I'll bring a flyswatter," Emmett said.

He awoke to the birdlike sounds of women speaking Comanche in a distant room. His chest ached, and as he continued to clench his eyelids against the sunlight, he imagined that he was back in the Indian hospital. But then a series of unhospitallike sounds interrupted the conversation: heels crossing an old hardwood floor and making it groan, a sink faucet being turned on and off. Then a resumption of chatter in Comanche. *"Unha nu naksupana inu?"* His mother's voice, asking the age-old question in all human exchanges, the longing as basic as the need for food and sex. Maybe it was the very first thing one person asked another. *Do you understand me?*

Emmett's eyes snapped open.

He was in his mother's house on the west side of Lawton. Not the house he'd grown up in. He'd not resided in Lawton after his parents divorced. His brother Malcolm and he had lived first at the Ft. Sill Indian School and then at St. Benedict's. *St. Benedict's.* Love among the ruins.

He sat up, gingerly, and tested his still-healing ribs with slight pressure from his hand.

He'd survived Dagen Kirsch. Barely.

Then he checked his wristwatch. Astoundingly, the hour was pushing noon. Jerome Crowe would be here any minute to pick him up. After Emmett had returned belatedly last night from Anadarko in Jerome's Cadillac to the Comanche complex, he and his old friend had made plans for the afternoon. It'd been all over Jerome's face as they parted: He'd surmised that something had happened between Dagen Kirsch and Emmett. Parker hadn't admitted anything of the sort. Or at least only to himself, sensing that—after the often mystifying and usually frustrating experience of Anna Turnipseed—he was lapsing into an old attitude that put no life-altering significance on sexual encounters, especially unexpected ones. He had known many women. It was only natural he'd know more. Still, he kept waiting for the heartache of Anna to fade, and making love to other women felt a bit like taking his medicine.

Throwing on his clothes, he continued to listen to the conversation. His mother and the other female speaker, yet unrecognizable, were one generation closer to fluency than he. One of his grandmothers had spoken nothing but Comanche. Not that she hadn't excelled at English studies at Carlisle Indian School in Pennsylvania. Carlisle had prohibited speaking any language but English, punishing her each time she uttered a word in her native tongue. Returning home, she vowed to her father, Quanah, that she'd never speak anything but Comanche again. And she didn't. If you didn't speak Comanche, you didn't exist. We create our cosmos with language, and his grandmother had understood this, perfectly.

Emmett ducked into the bathroom, the old floor creaking under his trod. He washed his face and combed his hair, avoided looking too carefully into his own eyes. He didn't count last night as a mistake. But neither did it feel like an achievement. He'd intended to drop off Dagen and return to the dance, but then he'd caved to her offer to go inside her apartment. There, in her political excuse of an Oklahoma address, they conspired once again—this time on the almost barren living room carpet—to make Sister Murtha roll over in her grave.

Emmett went out to the kitchen, where a woman as old and arthritic as his mother sat with her at the table. Her eyes shone up at him from deep folds of crinkled skin, and it was a moment before he recognized her. "Why, Mother Chocpoya, good to see you," he said, leaning over to kiss her cheek, which felt like an overripe peach.

"Sorry I missed your dance. I go to bed early these days."

"That's all right. I understand."

Mary Chocpoya had been a beloved friend of the family for years. She was so fiercely independent she insisted on walking from her small spread south of town instead of letting somebody pick her up in a car. And she never walked directly from point A to point B. Mary epitomized the *Nuh-muhnuh* love of roaming and exploring on whim. Yet, all was not joy and light within the old woman. Her left earlobe was missing. A traditional woman, she'd cut it off when she learned that her husband had frozen to death during the Korean War. She'd never remarried.

As Emmett rummaged through the refrigerator, his mother said, "There's some cold fry bread and boiled eggs—next shelf down. I already shelled the eggs for you." Emmett found them and was putting together an impromptu sandwich when Celia added, tartly, "Kitty Toppah called to congratulate you about the President coming and all."

"When?"

"Around nine this morning."

"You seeing one of the Toppah girls?" Mary Chocpoya asked in a slightly disapproving tone.

With his mother watching, Emmett took a moment to finish chewing before speaking. Kitty was a Kiowa nurse at the Indian hospital where Emmett had recovered. Some of the older Comanche didn't approve of liaisons with the Kiowa—on-again, off-again allies of *Nuhmuhnuh* through the centuries. But Emmett had wed one, and now that the heat of their marital battles had cooled with the years, he remembered Ladonna Hawzeepa as a warm and gracious woman. Kitty Toppah was also warm and gracious. Plus sexy. "Yes, Mother Chocpoyah," Emmett fessed up, "I'm seeing Kitty. Now and again."

Right away, he could tell that his mother found that *now and again* cavalier. She'd been very fond of Anna Turnipseed, so much so he found it impossible to reveal the darkness in the Modoc FBI agent's childhood that prevented her from ever settling down with a man. Even a man she loved. Emmett realized that his mother had known the ways of love: He and his brother Malcolm were proof of it. But each time he tried to tell her about his turbulent time with Anna, it felt like reciting the *Kama Sutra* to Mother Theresa.

A voice helloed from the front of the house, and Emmett raised his voice for Crowe to come back to the kitchen. *"Kima,* Jerome!" His mother *tsked* him for inviting somebody to enter in that manner, but the large man then proved he was Emmett's equal in rudeness by relieving him of the fry bread and egg sandwich before hugging Celia and Mary Chocpoya with his free arm. All of this made Emmett feel oddly juvenile.

Mary asked, "Jerome, you're still with BIA like Emmett, right?"

The question gave the attorney pause before he answered. "Right, Mother."

"You know all about MMS, maybe?" the old woman continued to press. The Mineral Management Service, a division of the Bureau of Indian Affairs charged with overseeing Indian mineral leases.

Jerome handed the sandwich back to Emmett. As if he'd lost his appetite. "I never worked for MMS, dear. I handled some cases involving the service, but that was years ago."

"But you still know about those things?" Mary asked hopefully.

"Sort of. You having a problem with them?"

"Yes." All at once, Mary's voice hardened. "That oil well they got on my land, it pumps all the time. Up and down, up and down. The trucks come and fill up. All the time. But you know what my check for last year was, Jerome . . . ?"

"No, I'm afraid I don't."

"Two dollars and twelve cents. How much does a barrel of oil go for?"

"Oh, around thirty dollars. But it's not always simple, how these royalties are computed."

"I know, but *two dollars and twelve cents*? Can you look into it for me?"

Secretly, Emmett was glad that Jerome and not he was bearing the brunt of this common complaint. Despite having more native employees than any other branch of government, except the military, the Bureau of Indian Affairs was not popular with the people it served. And no issue was more contentious than the royalties owed Indians for their resources and held in trust by the BIA. Emmett decided to rescue his friend from the ire of an eighty-year-old Comanche woman. "We're going to be late."

"Where you two headed?" Celia asked.

Jerome said, "Polo match, Mother Parker, and it starts at one."

Her eyes narrowed at Emmett. "You're not going to play, are you?"

Emmett chuckled, touching the injured side of his chest. "No way." Not after last night. Those two frenetic rides had been hard enough on him. Dagen wasn't a practitioner of gentle sex and had been direct in expressing that preference. "Be home before dark."

Jerome lit up a Marlboro on the front porch with a goldplated Zippo lighter. Tripping down the walkway to the man's Cadillac, Emmett had the past rush back on him—the headiness of adolescent flight away from either parental or parochial authority. It was so heady, he asked Jerome for a puff.

"Want a cigarette?"

"No, just a hit."

Emmett inhaled. It'd been years. He found the smoke raw and unpleasant, despite being mentholated.

They piled into the car, and Jerome cruised down the street. The west side of Lawton was the Indian and Hispanic part of town. A bit more rundown than he recalled. Smaller. All was smaller than he remembered, the houses and even the widths of the streets. There was a distant threat of rain, towering gray and white in the south, but all was sunny around them.

Jerome said, "Isn't it great to be home?"

Emmett impulsively reached over to clap his old friend around the shoulders. "Sorry about Mary Chocpoya's grilling. I had no idea it was coming."

Jerome's exhaled smoke through his nose, then frowned. "Oh, I get that all the time. She's right to be pissed off. That's the bitch about this mess. . . ." He pointed with his cigarette: "Hey, look—the Teepee Bar. It's still here. Remember the sign in the front window?"

"No Indians allowed," Emmett said, laughing along with Jerome at the irony. In Jim Crow Lawton, Indians had fallen into a crack between the supposed separate-but-equal status of whites and blacks. No drinking fountains, waiting rooms, or eating places were designated for Indians as they were for *colored*. So using most any facility was a roll of the dice for an Indian to see if whites took offense. Sometimes they did. Sometimes they didn't. But there was no consolation in that ambiguity.

Jerome drove him past the Southern-style colonnaded mansions along Gore Boulevard. Celia Parker had worked in one of them as a live-in housekeeper, then later for a general on the post at Ft. Sill. Emmett turned his thoughts away from those years of separation from her. He had no desire to revisit them. However, as the minutes passed and Jerome and he sped into the open range south of town, he wanted to get something equally unpleasant out of the way. It stood between him and what promised to be a good day. "What's going on with you and the bureau?" he finally asked.

Jerome kept his eyes on the road as he snubbed out his cigarette in the ashtray. "You honestly don't know?"

"Know what?"

"I've been suspended."

"You're kidding."

"I wish."

"On whose orders?"

"The director himself."

"Why?" Emmett asked.

"Long story. Don't want to bore you."

"Bore me. Are you suspended without pay?"

Jerome immediately lit up another Marlboro. "Oh, they're not that reckless. I'm on administrative leave pending the review."

"Review of what?"

"The mess poor old Mary was asking about. The trust funds. Do we have to go through this right now, Em? I just want to enjoy." He smiled, although unhappily. "It's so wonderful to be home. To be with you. Your mother. Everybody."

Emmett sat back. "Sorry I brought it up." But thoughts about the mess—and Jerome's possible involvement in it—didn't fade easily from his mind.

In addition to the billions owed to the tribes, the federal government held approximately four hundred and fifty million dollars in half a million Individual Indian Money accounts. The *mess* Jerome had just referred to stemmed from the fact that BIA records could reconcile no more than one hundred million of those IIM dollars, which had flowed into the bureau from timber, grazing, and mineral royalties due the members of the tribes who'd granted those leases to outside interests. Emmett wasn't overly defensive about his own agency, but the simple truth was that Indian Affairs had always been a bastard child of either the War or Interior Departments, grossly under-funded, given its mandate to enforce the government's agreements with America's aboriginal population. Many tribes had yet to be paid according to the terms of treaties forged two centuries ago, so it'd never been in Congress's interest to give the BIA the means to rectify the nation's negligent treatment of natives.

Suddenly, Jerome said in aggravation, "For years now, royalty payments have been funneled into an accounting system that's so pathetic it can't even track accounts receivable with any degree of certainty."

"Is it fixable?" Emmett asked.

"Yeah, but not with the forty-million-dollar half-measure Congress passed in the form of a new computer system called the Trust Assets and Accounting Management System. Arthur Andersen and Company—"

"The big accounting firm?" Emmett interjected, just to slow his friend down. Jerome was talking too fast for a *Nuhmuhnuh.*

"Right. They were brought in to evaluate how TAAMS was doing. Not well. Piss-poor, a matter of fact. But then Arthur Anderson got in their own hot water over the Enron scandal, and their audit got tossed in the shit-can."

He was right. It was a mess. A fiscal black hole. Nothing to think about on a day when the southern plains were a vibrant green with late spring and the sun warmed rather than burned. Emmett only hoped that Crowe hadn't personally gone astray in any of this. He reached across the center console and gave his friend another half-hug. "Let it go, Jerome. Like you wanted. At least for today."

"Right." Again, a dejected smile. "Let it go."

5

≈≈≈

COWBOY POLO WAS related to traditional polo in the same way country and western was like classical music. The object in both sports was still to whack a round object through the other team's goal. *But that was about the end of the similarity,* Emmett observed as Jerome Crowe and he took the end of a bench in the grandstands of the Lawton Rodeo Arena. Cowboy polo was played on trampled dirt mixed with the powdered feces of cattle and horses. The small wooden ball was replaced by a rubber one larger than a basketball. The mallet looked like an old shoe sole stapled to the end of a cane pole. English riding attire was replaced by Western shirts and Levi's, although for safety, Stetsons were replaced by helmets with face guards.

The first chukker, or fifteen-minute period, was already underway. Even though Emmett had played the game as a youth, the dust-shrouded arena looked like bedlam to him. A bar fight on horseback, with mallets smacking flesh and bone as often as the ball. Lawton was playing Duncan, a town thirty miles to the east, and there was no score so far. Not for lack of trying. Some of the mounts were already lathered, and the riders were only slightly less sweat-soaked.

Jerome fanned himself with the program until his nicotine hunger nagged him again. Then his fat cheeks sucked to life yet another Marlboro. His obesity aside, the man was killing himself with cigarettes. In the old days, native people hadn't used tobacco recreationally. The Europeans had come up with that idiocy. To most tribes, smoke was sacred, something to purify the supplicant and loft prayers up into the sky.

A lean Duncan rider snatched the ball from an unwary Lawton player, turned his quarter horse on a dime, and dashed for the nearby goal. Almost effortlessly, he whacked the ball through the barrels, scoring. Then, as he rode past the stands, he dropped down behind the far side of his mount in a neat disappearing act. Reappearing, he stood in the stirrups and gave the Comanche war cry.

Emmett picked the program up off the bench and glanced over the Duncan team roster. "Had to be Royce," he said to Jerome.

Sometimes in the evenings at St. Benedict's, Emmett and the other boys, especially the Comanches, would sneak the mission's horses out of the stable and ride into the open country west of the school with their bows and arrows. There, beyond prying white eyes, they'd practice the two things a youth had to master before he could join a war party. The first was to drop alongside his mount and shoot an arrow from behind the animal's chest. The second and even more difficult feat was to lean down off a pony's back at a dead gallop and seize a fallen comrade from the ground, swing him up before you, and dash to safety. All the boys practiced this time and again by pulling clumps of sorghum out of the field, but only Royce Eschiti managed to do the real thing. To his own astonishment, Royce plucked Emmett flat off the ground and swung him up onto the withers of his horse. Afterward, he spurned all compliments by explaining in his morose way: "It was only a game this time."

He'd been a quiet boy, quiet to the point of seeming sullen, and cursed with a festering acne the nuns blamed on either swiping sugar out of the commissary or self-abuse. Royce arrived later at the mission than Jerome and even Emmett, and his first day in class was marked by a terrible humiliation. The stress of leaving home, being shorn and outfitted in stiff new denims, the change in diet—all conspired to upset his bowels. He had a noisy accident during roll call, partly because of the suddenness of the attack and partly because he'd been too reticent to ask Sister to be excused.

The referee blew his whistle, and possession of the ball changed. "You recognized his face?" Crowe asked.

"No, not behind the guard. His riding. Nobody but Royce rides like that. What's he doing?"

Jerome's crushed his half-smoked cigarette with the toe of one of his patent-leather dress shoes. "Supervised release from McAlester State Prison."

"Hell," Emmett said, truly disappointed. "Convicted of what?"

"Killing his father." Jerome lit up again. "This happened seven or eight years ago. I was back in D.C., but I heard about it through the grapevine. He pled guilty and did his time."

Emmett looked back at Royce, who was in the thick of a fray of whooshing mallets and reeling horses. Murder made you see a man differently, no matter how many other good memories you had of him. "Was he drunk at the time?"

"I'd imagine. Though he doesn't need to drink to go into one of his rages."

"Did he shoot the old man?"

"I almost wish. No, a butcher's knife. Cut him up prodigiously." Jerome sighed. "He rents a room in Duncan, but stays down in Walters with Wendell Padduhpony most the time. I think Royce is going down the Peyote Road to cure his drinking and temper. . . ." Despite his Yale education, Crowe pronounced the name of the hallucinogenic mescal cactus in the Oklahoman way, *pee-yote*, dropping the Spanish *ey* for a long *e*. In one of the most controversial facets of Quanah Parker's controversial life, Emmett's forebear had adopted the use of peyote from other tribes. This was during the misery of the early reservation period, when the *Nuhmuhnuh* had been forced to give up their free and nomadic life. As with tobacco, the use of peyote had been for spiritual purposes, not casual.

"Well," Emmett said, "I'd still like to say hello to him after the match. You know his people would take it as a snub if I didn't."

"You go on ahead," Jerome said.

"Without you?"

"Royce never cared much for me. Thinks I look down on him."

"Then quit looking down on him and come along."

*   *   *

Duncan won by two goals.

Jerome and Emmett found Royce Eschiti in a corral off the arena. He was brushing down his horse. Except it wasn't his horse, the parolee explained right off in a manner suggesting that Emmett and he had parted company just a few hours in the past, not more than twenty years ago. It warped Emmett's sense of time. "One of the boys in Duncan lets me use his horse," Royce said in a shy but gravelly voice. "I used to have one, Emmett, but I lost most everything."

"Well, you still got your riding skills."

Royce stared at the hoof-churned dirt. The acne had left his face a deep corrugation of overlapping scars, but his eyes seemed clear—and sober.

Then it hit Emmett. Royce felt hesitant about embracing him, a cop. Comanches always hugged. So he made the first move and opened his arms. "*Kima, Pabi.*" Come, Brother.

Awkwardly receiving the embrace, Royce said, "Didn't make your honor dance."

"That's all right."

"I don't go out much nights. They got a habit of sneaking up and biting me . . ."

Emmett wondered if he'd slashed his father to death at night.

"The president was at your dance?" Royce asked with slight disbelief.

"Yes," Emmett said, "he must've figured it's time to kiss and make up with Indians."

Jerome piped in: "Dagen Kirsch pulled the strings to make it happen."

With mention of Dagen, Royce looked sharply at Crowe, but after a moment, he reached into his shirt pocket for a pack of Lucky Strikes. It was empty. Jerome shook out a Marlboro menthol, which Eschiti sniffed suspiciously before letting Crowe light it for him.

Emmett asked, "You still roughnecking?"

"There ain't much drilling these days," Royce said. "Oil boom's over, and some say it's never coming back. But I'll get by. . . ." He paused as if trying to come up with something a bit more encouraging about his future. When he couldn't, Emmett broke off the air of hopelessness—the air that hangs around many ex-cons—with a good-bye and a parting hug. He and Jerome hadn't gone more than a few strides before Royce stopped them. "Emmett . . . ?"

"Yeah?"

"Wendell's kind of sore you two didn't get to talk last night. I'm heading back to Walters in a couple minutes. You want to follow me . . . ?"

Emmett hesitated. It was Friday night, and Dagen Kirsch had given him her cell phone number. He was tempted to use it. But there really was no choice. Once publicly advised, he couldn't ignore the displeasure of an elder as influential as Wendell Padduhpony. He couldn't beg off going to Walters, no matter how inconvenient. "Glad to," he finally said. "You mind taking me, Jerome?"

Crowe was trapped, too. "Not at all."

And so this was developing into a typical *Nuhmuhnuh* day. One destination bled into another, hugs given in farewell proved to be only the first of many offered in parting. And an intricate web of relationships and obligations closed around Emmett.

He could tell that Jerome was irritated tailing Royce's dark-green GMC pickup at fifty miles an hour. Jerome liked to speed over the rolling prairie. In their love of movement, the People had been undaunted by distance. It'd been nothing to gallop off on raids and hunts covering a thousand miles in a few weeks. That way of life had been threatened by the slaughter of the buffalo, and so it was in June 1874 that the Comanche, with their Kiowa and Southern Cheyenne allies, attacked the white hunters in their base camp along the upper Canadian River, so called because two French Canadian brothers "discovered" it—to the astonishment of the native population, who for thousands of years had apparently failed to recognize it as a river and give it a name of their own. The camp was at Adobe Walls, so called because it was the ruin of a former trading post. The attack went poorly, mostly because of the big buffalo guns used by the whites. Eschiti, a Comanche *puhakut,* or medicine man, had prophesied invulnerability to bullets and a quick victory, but Indian valor was no match for the long-range guns. Howea, a respected warrior, fell wounded, as the song sung at last night's dance recounted, and Quanah had dashed through the gunfire to rescue him.

Royce was a descendent of both Eschiti and Howea. It didn't matter that the battle of Adobe Walls had occurred deep in the past. The descendents of Howea owed a moral debt to the descendents of Quanah Parker. As far as anyone could tell, it had never been repaid. That is what Royce had referred to as a boy when he'd reminded the others that his lifting Emmett up onto the withers of his horse was only a game.

Until now, Emmett hadn't thought of that debt in years.

A shadow fell over the Cadillac, and he looked off to the west. A large thunderhead was drifting ponderously toward the northeast and had blotted out the sun. He'd just faced forward again when Jerome pulled especially hard on what must have been his tenth cigarette since they'd left his mother's house, and announced, "I'm ready."

Emmett yawned. "Ready for what?"

"To tell you what's going on at work."

"Okay."

But at that moment, Royce led the way off I-44 and onto State Route 53. Jerome followed the pickup through the half-light created by the thundercloud's shadow. "You know about the class action suit against the Bureau over the unreconciled accounts?" Before Emmett could answer, Jerome muttered crossly, "Of course you do. Anyway, I drew the shitty assignment to slap together the game plan for the government's defense against the Indian plaintiffs. When I say 'slap together,' I mean it. A shoe-string budget and one clerk to help me. Plus, every mucky-muck at Interior phoning me at all hours of the day and night for updates. Updates on what? A mess everybody ignored for two centuries—until it was too goddamned big and expensive to handle within our lifetimes?"

"So what'd you do?" Emmett asked.

"Got the hell out of headquarters. Went out into the field, ostensibly to do some background on the allegations, but mostly I just wanted to catch my breath and think. I rented a convertible, toured our offices. It was nice. Late spring, like now, so I put the top down. It was nice 'til I hit the Anadarko Agency."

"When was this?"

"A year ago—late May, early June."

During the time that Emmett had been away from his home base at the Phoenix area office on assignment inside the Navajo Nation, investigating the murder of a tribal cop and his wife. With Anna Turnipseed, who had yet to call him from her own home base in Las Vegas. *Don't think about her.* "So what happened in Anadarko?"

Bizarrely, Jerome switched on his radio to a rock station. Loud. "Can I trust you with something . . . ?" He raised his voice just enough to be heard. "Can I really trust you like I've never had to trust you before?"

"Are you worried about being bugged?"

Jerome nodded.

Emmett turned off the radio. "Your info's out of date. With the new audio technology, techies can filter out a nuclear bomb blast to hear our conversation. Just tell me what you've got to say."

Royce's pickup had accelerated, and Jerome laid on the gas to catch up. "They're having trouble reconciling their accounts."

"You sure?"

"Reasonably."

"Don't make any accusations you can't prove."

"That's why I'm keeping it all under my hat until an informant steps forward."

"Informants seldom step forward, Jerome. You have to develop them. You have to squeeze them."

Apparently, Royce's blinkers weren't working, for he hand-signaled a turn down a long drive lined with locust trees. The spiky boughs dripped with white blossoms, and Emmett powered down his side window, partly to catch the scent and partly to be rid of the tobacco smoke getting thicker and thicker inside the Cadillac.

Jerome slowed to keep back from Royce's dust. "All I'm saying is—I'm close. I'm on to this Cheyenne who might be laundering the money—keep that under your hat, too, until I can confirm it. But I'm close to busting this whole thing wide open. Are you with me when it happens, *Pabi?*"

Emmett began to catch snatches of piano music from the homestead that lay at the end of the drive. "You bust this wide open, we won't know up from down, let alone who's with us."

They'd pulled into the barren yard between an old farmhouse and a barn. Royce parked on one side of a retired U-Haul van, and Jerome took the other. Crowe shut off his engine and stubbed out his latest butt in the ashtray. Emmett thought he might be listening to the piano player, who was good, but then he sighed. "I really shouldn't be involving you in this. It's my cross to bear."

"Keep me informed," Emmett said.

Jerome asked hopefully, "You mean that?"

"Yeah." He patted Jerome's knee. But it bothered him that the attorney had switched horses. Obviously, he'd gone from defending the federal government to aiding the plaintiffs suing it. Which, at the very least, could get him disbarred. There was another explanation to this. It was all a fabrication to make Jerome a martyr in his own eyes. It was a hallmark of some thieves to transform themselves into martyrs when confronted with their crimes, to turn the ignoble into something noble. But Emmett didn't want to decide if his old friend was a thief. Not this afternoon.

The thunderhead had created an early twilight, against which Wendell Padduhpony had lit a single, fly-shit-splattered bulb that dangled over the baby grand he was playing. Emmett recognized Beethoven's *Moonlight Sonata* as he stood in the wide door, flanked by Royce and Jerome. The barn in which Wendell played held no livestock or bales of hay, just pianos in various states of reconditioning. He listened intently to his own playing, not with any visible pleasure in his own skill, which was adequate, but to the quality of the individual tones. All at once, his long fingers reared up off the keyboard. He reached for his tuning hammer on the bench beside him, rose up with a grunt, his long white braids whipping forward, and tightened a piano string until the strike of that individual key satisfied him.

Then Wendell sat back down and continued playing, remarking over the sonata, "Some honor dance—the honoree didn't even bother to stick around. *Haa?*" Yes?

"One more reason the honoree didn't deserve a dance in the first place," Emmett said, stepping inside the barn, speaking to the elder only because the old one had spoken first.

"You got that right," Wendell said, chuckling. His top lip curled up into his large nose when he was amused. But then, despite the chuckle, Emmett realized that he wasn't off the hook yet. "Drove all the way to the complex in that old U-Haul of mine, cedared the president of the United States with the finest red-berry cedar to be had from the Pease River country, and all I got for my efforts was an eight-dollar blanket made in a Juarez sweatshop. And a California orange. Wasn't even sweet."

Emmett had learned this game early. His father had warned him that his people teased hard, sometimes so hard tears flowed. You had to learn how to stand up to teasing. "Sorry to have offended you. Next time I'll buy Florida oranges."

Wendell interrupted his playing to adjust another string. "Come closer."

Emmett and Jerome approached the old man on his left but were careful not to stand behind him. You never stood directly behind a warrior. A decorated warrior like Wendell, a World War II veteran of Merrill's Marauders in Burma, was due his peace and security at all times. Emmett checked his own orientation to the light bulb, for neither did you let your shadow fall on an honored warrior. All these things came back to him as he neared the formidable old man.

"Who won the polo match?" Wendell asked.

"Duncan did, *Toko,*" Royce replied, venturing inside to join Emmett and Jerome. *Toko* was the word for *grandfather;* as in most cases, a blood connection had little to do with its use.

"Good, Duncan was more deserving." He glanced over the tops of his bifocals at three men. "And at least you know how to properly address an elder, *Tuah.*" Son. "Who's that with you?"

"Emmett."

"No, I know Emmett Quanah Parker. Saw him from a distance at his honor dance last night. He never bothered to come up and talk to me, but I saw him. The president of the United States of America saw fit to chat with me, but not Emmett. Who's this other fella?"

"Jerome Crowe, *Toko*," he said for himself.

"Crowe, Crowe . . . Jerome Crowe," the old man muttered as if trying to tickle his memory while he tuned another string. "I used to know a *Kotsoteka* boy named Jerome Crowe, but he ran off years ago and nobody's seen hide nor hair of him since."

"I get back home at least twice a year," Jerome protested. "You know that."

"I know of it. Second-hand. Is the little burg of Walters that far off the beaten track?"

"No, sir," Jerome admitted.

"Don't call me *sir*, son. I work for a living." Wendell set his tuning hammer on the bench, swept off his bifocals and pocketed them in his denim overalls. He looked over the three men with steady brown eyes. By no means was he a spiritual doctor in the customary mold. Like most true geniuses, Wendell, who'd dropped out of the University of Oklahoma an honors student because the curriculum bored him, defied categorization. Whatever, he had the power—*puha* in Shoshonean—to make you feel young and small. And Emmett found it uncanny how an Indian name could come to define the person's mission or place in life, whether or not he himself was aware of it. Padduhpony, which had nothing to do with horses, consisted of the Comanche words for *see* and *water*, meaning a place to cross a river where the bottom can be seen. A fording. So, strangely, Wendell Padduhpony became a person who helped others ford the difficulties in their lives, a kind of native psychiatrist to help the troubled get back on track. Some considered him to be holy, but he himself would probably find that pompous. And dangerous: There was no distinction in the culture between a medicine man and a sorcerer, although Emmett found it impossible to think of Wendell as a witch.

He hugged Emmett first. "Good to have you home. I hope you stay this time."

"Thank you, *Toko*. I'll try."

"Don't try," Wendell said warmly but firmly, "you'll just do it if you know what's good for you."

Next, he embraced Jerome, who gushed, "Goddamn, it's good to see you, old man."

"Don't cuss. It shows fear. And a lack of verbal imagination. Bad traits for an attorney."

Royce doffed his weathered cowboy hat and briefly held on to Wendell as if he were his anchor.

"Let's sit out in the cool air," the old man said. "Nicest hour of the day is coming any minute."

As the four men turned to round the barn, Royce peeled off for the house, as if on an errand. Several lawn chairs, none a match to the others, were arrayed around a fire ring. The dusk was too warm for a fire, but the heap of ashes served as a focus for the gathering. Wendell no sooner eased into his favorite chair than he pointed triumphantly over his shoulder at the full moon rising in the eastern sky, which was partially clear. "See that? That's the Comanche moon. We'll always have the revenge of that moon. That's when they feared us coming."

Wendell was referring to the long-ago days of raiding, when the *Nuhmuhnuh* used moonlit nights to pour out of this country and descend on the ranches of Texas and Mexico.

Royce appeared with sodas for everyone. Tradition was upheld here: The youngest served the others. Eschiti seemed pleased to have this role, his otherwise severe and acne-pitted face softened by a quiet smile. He lowered himself onto a plank set between two cinderblocks and slurped contentedly from a can of Mountain Dew. Emmett tried to see the murderous impulse in the man's eyes, but the curled brim of his Stetson was pulled low over his forehead. Besides, Royce clearly felt at peace here with the old man.

"Tell me something, Emmett," Wendell said.

He sat a little straighter, waiting for the next verbal trap to be sprung.

"How'd you get wounded in the line of duty this time?"

"Caught an ax blade in the chest while trying to free a hostage."

"Who took the hostage—a lumberjack?"

"No, *Toko.*"

"You know," he said to the others, "my dear son, Emmett here, doesn't like law enforcement. Doesn't care a lick for it. What he really likes is going to the hospital. He enjoys the attention."

Everybody chuckled, then Wendell turned to Jerome. "What's this rumor you might be home from Washington for good?"

"For good or bad. I've been suspended."

"Why?" Wendell bluntly asked.

Jerome glanced uneasily at Emmett, then said, "I can't stand by and watch an injustice as if it doesn't concern me."

"*Does* this injustice concern you?"

"I believe so."

"Know or believe?" When Jerome didn't answer quickly enough, Wendell noted, "You remind me of a Baptist fella I saw holding his hand to his forehead. I asked him if he'd hit his head on something, and he said, 'No, actually I bumped my ass but I'm just too good a Baptist to hold it.'"

Again there was laughter, although Jerome didn't join in this time. Wendell drew his attention to a grasshopperlike pump jack out in one of his fields. "I cut the electricity to my own oil well. You know why, *Tuah*?"

"No," Jerome replied.

"I won't stand for being cheated. If you've been referring to this trust fund thing, rest assured—Indian people will deal with it in their own time and in their own way. Believe me, we've survived bigger injustices than this."

Royce was gazing off at the locust-lined drive when the old man murmured an aside to him: "You can't rush waiting, son." Royce looked from the road to a weather-stained teepee that had been pitched halfway to some Osage orange trees along the small creek that wound through Wendell's farm. "And I don't want you to start looking at this as your next drink. Peyote isn't whiskey and it isn't marijuana. It's a key you keep in your pocket until the door is ripe for opening."

Royce hung his head for a few moments, just as he had when chastised by the nuns, but eventually sat up and took another noisy gulp of Mountain Dew.

Off to the west, lightning was now twitching through the veils of rain. The breeze in advance of the storm had risen, but Emmett believed the huge cloud would avoid the farm. As if the old man had willed it that way.

"So many relatives and friends have been passing away," Wendell lamented, "I've got the funeral home on the speed dialer to my cell phone. The true sadness is that most of them never saw their problems. Oh, each of them tasted their own problem, and there's some good in that. The drinker has to drink too much. The smoker has to puff too much. The thief has to steal too much. But if you taste your problem again and again, and somehow can't free yourself, then it's time to *see* it with fresh eyes, and that's not easy. For some of these folks, I suggest the Peyote Road, even though I don't follow it myself. Quanah went down it, and I don't blame him for doing it. His problem was to see how many of the old ways could fit into the new ways. He wanted to carry the power of the Sun and Earth forward into a world of machines and lawyers and store-bought goods, and he felt he needed peyote to see how that might be done. To see how the old medicine could be used to help us survive in a new age."

Looking puzzled, Jerome asked, "If you recommend peyote to others, why don't you use it yourself?"

"Personal preference," Wendell said. "I don't like to surrender control of my faculties to anyone or anything. But I do see the benefit to some folks. Temporarily, mind you, for the peyote man must return to the everyday world and deal with that world as it is. Hopefully, he's got a new insight, a new power."

Royce asked Jerome, "You ever use peyote?"

Crowe shook his head. He'd begun to fidget, perhaps for a cigarette, knowing that Wendell would disapprove. Again, an elder made you feel small. A *puhakut* made you feel blind to the true nature of the world.

When Royce asked the same question of Emmett, who was simply going along with the flow and had no urge to inject his own views into it, Wendell answered for him, "I sincerely doubt it. Emmett's too much like me—he's afraid of being incapacitated, even for a few hours, and that's because the entire purpose of his life has been to watch over others. That's why we all inconvenienced ourselves last night by holding an honor dance for him. We recognize this obsession and thank him for taking it on for us."

Emmett dipped his head in appreciation.

"But make no mistake," Wendell warned, "it's still an obsession. As full of woe as obsessing on that next peyote button."

Headlights had turned up the drive and were glimmering through the trees. Darkness was coming fast now, but Emmett could still see that the lights belonged to a sedan, one equipped with a whip radio antenna. The driver parked away from the other vehicles in the yard, then killed his engine and stepped out. It was Michael Mangas. The FBI agent was wearing Levi's and a shirt with mother-of-pearl buttons that shone through the twilight like cat eyes.

Royce whistled for his attention, and Mangas started toward the ring. He was halfway there when his stride shortened and he turned cautious-looking. Emmett sensed that the man had just recognized Jerome and him. Everyone rose to receive his perfunctory embrace.

"Want a sodie, Michael?" Royce asked.

"No thanks, Jeralyn and I just gorged ourselves at Ryan's Buffet in town."

They no sooner sat again than Wendell stretched his legs out and drawled, "You all know, the Comanche killed more whites than any other tribe in North America. There's no accurate count simply because this happened over four centuries and in some of the most remote country the Creator devised. But I'd say we killed the invaders in the tens of thousands. Now, in the last half of the nineteenth century, the Chiricahua Apache—led by Goyathlay, better known by his stage name, Geronimo—killed maybe a hundred *taibos*. If that. And, for knocking off a measly hundred whites, the Chiricahua are held up to be the most warlike tribe in history. Well, let me tell you, Geronimo was a piker."

Emmett watched Mangas take this ribbing in his direction with a good-natured smirk. His Comanche blood knew what this was all about—besting your friends. Mangas was also Apache, and his Chiricahua blood showed in his squat, almost toadlike build and nearly lipless mouth. This heritage wasn't to be confused with the Plains Apache, who'd roamed the hills and grasslands between the Rio Grande and the southern extent of the Comancheria until forced onto a reservation in 1876 with the Comanche and Kiowa. The FBI agent was half Ft. Sill Apache, the Chiricahua of southeast Arizona and northern Mexico who'd been imprisoned on the post after Geronimo's capture.

"In case you don't know," Wendell went on mercilessly, "*Goyathlay* means *the Yawner*. I think that gives you an idea of what scintillating company Geronimo was. Quanah entertained him on several occasions in a manner befitting the war chief of another tribe, but his guest arrived late, was drunk and fell asleep early." He winked at Mangas, who scanned the drive coming in off the highway. No sign of another vehicle.

"Excuse me a moment," the FBI agent said, rising and making for his car again. He ducked inside and used his radio. Emmett could see him clasping the microphone. Then he returned and said, "Something's come up, Wendell. Can you explain for me?"

"Go," the old man said curtly.

Mangas shook hands all around, instead of embracing, then drove off. As soon as he was out of earshot, Wendell said, "Looks like we got somebody else holding his head because he's too good a Baptist to hold his ass."

Twenty minutes later, Mangas's purpose in coming to the farm at all was explained by the arrival of a cadaverous old man in a battered Datsun pickup. The moon was bright in the still cloudless east, but he held a flashlight beam to the ground as he and his young drummer walked. They didn't divert on their beeline to the teepee. Neither tossed a passing wave to the other men. They just entered the tent. Emmett had recognized the old man right off. He was a Road Man, part Comanche and part Delaware, but a full-fledged member of the Native American Church and thus legally allowed to dispense peyote as a sacrament.

It was now obvious. There was nothing illegal in any of this, according to the Native American Religious Freedom Act, but Mangas hadn't been comfortable revealing his peyote use, particularly to another federal cop. So he'd left as soon as he could.

Royce politely excused himself and joined the Road Man inside the teepee.

Emmett felt a hand on his shoulder. It was Jerome's, and he said, "I've just been invited to join in. Want to take my car and come back in the morning?"

Emmett was debating whether or not to do that when Wendell demanded, "No, Emmett's staying. He can phone his mama on my cell phone and let her know he's all right. He's going to sit out here in the moonlight and pass the time with me. He's going to relearn what time is all about." Then, as soon as they were alone, the old man said with a mysterious self-satisfaction, "If you don't know the way back, one will be found for you."

"What do you mean, *Toko*?"

But Wendell just smirked.

On I-44, Michael Mangas drove into a curtain of rain. It beat against his windshield like fists and swamped his wiper blades. A violent Midwest downpour, which added to his unease. First, Emmett Parker and Jerome Crowe had barged in on tonight's special peyote ceremony, and now he had to keep a watchful eye on the darkened skies for tornadoes. He flicked on news radio, backed off on the gas and listened with his full attention for several minutes. In that time, there were no warnings for Comanche County, although a small twister was skipping around Lake Eufaula, far to the east. All the danger seemed to be on that side of the state.

Comanche and Apache. Comanche-che.

Todd's baby laughter echoed around inside the bucar. Aeons ago, Michael had sprawled on their sofa, holding the infant over him, watching for drops of drool and such, and tried to familiarize his son with his ancestry. *Comanche-che.* The combination word made Todd giggle. But Jeralyn was Caddo. That made Todd a *Coman-do-che.* More gales of laughter that now stabbed Michael in the heart.

Esikwitu. That's what the Comanche called Ft. Sill Apache. *Gray turds.*

Like most people of mixed native blood, Michael felt the tug of both tribes, often in the same moment. Even though he was enrolled with BIA as a Comanche and served as Keeper of the Pipe with their Thunder Dogs Society, he sometimes felt more *Esikwitu* than *Nuhmuhnuh*. Like tonight at Wendell's farm. He preferred to be alone, which wasn't a Comanche trait. He liked the loneliness of a long and arduous hunt. Alone. And his last name, although the Spanish word for *sleeves*, had been inspired by an eastern Chiricahua chief, *Mangas Coloradas. Red Sleeves,* alleged by whites to have been that color because they dripped with their blood.

Coman-do-che.

Todd's baby laughter flew at him again as an oncoming tractor-trailer splashed past in a blaze of watery headlights. The giggling faded as the radio newscaster mentioned the body found last Friday afternoon in Lake Lawtonka. The autopsy had been performed by the Comanche County medical examiner, but the findings had been sealed. At Michael's suggestion. Law enforcement—regardless of which agency that would wind up with this case—knew too little about the floater to issue anything that might unwittingly help the guilty evade capture.

The rain let up, and Michael relaxed a little.

He tried to apply his mind to the riddle of a possible Indian victim tied to a cross and pitched from some yet undetermined point into the reservoir.

But Todd's baby laughter wouldn't let him go tonight.

Jeralyn had slid into chronic depression. Sometimes he envied her. Depression, however numbing, was a circuit breaker. Under enough pressure, it short-circuited the anger. And that's what Michael mostly felt. He was chronically angry. It shut out every other emotion. The only way he could turn off this roaring furnace was to throw himself completely into his work.

Or use peyote.

He switched off the radio. No tornadoes were being spawned locally out in the darkness.

He found little consolation in telling himself that Down syndrome had sentenced Todd to a life that was less than complete. Somehow, Jeralyn and Michael, acting together with a singleness of purpose that was lacking in all other aspects of their lives, had filled that void for Todd. At least, they'd felt that they had. Now that, too, was missing, their shared purpose in life. Stolen by a couple of militant crackers with a crackpot ideology. *Hijo de papá.* Gone. *Daddy's boy.*

Anger.

And it was to peyote Michael had turned in the hope of seeing beyond that anger. He had no affection for drugs. But in the vibrant, colorful and utterly astonishing universe opened up by that homely little cactus bud, he hoped to embrace something larger than his own anger. Something so all-encompassing that it would put that April 1995 morning in perspective.

And Michael could go on with his life in relative peace.

Now Parker and Crowe had delayed that quest.

Michael had never much cared for Emmett, and he'd been warned by a Department of the Interior bigwig that Crowe was under investigation for possible involvement in the trust funds embezzlement. *Stealing from your own goddamned bureau.* The distance between that and blowing up buildings wasn't far in Michael's mind. There was a great and terrible commonality to evil.

His cell phone rang. "Hello."

"Agent Mangas?" The perfectly modulated voice was Dr. Hawzeepa's. Again, needless formality.

"Speaking. Silas?"

"Yes. We've got a positive ID on the victim," the medical examiner said. "Through fingerprints."

"That was fast." Even though Michael had seen to it that a supervisor out of the Oklahoma City field office heading to D.C. headquarters had carried in his luggage the two epidermises of the hands with him on his flight this morning. It had taken the FBI lab only a few hours to come up with the ID.

Dr. Hawzeepa explained, "An exemplar card for the prints was already on file with you folks. Our victim was a federal employee."

"Here in Oklahoma?"

"Uh, no." The examiner paused. "Take a deep breath. . . ."

6

THE TELLER AT the First Central Bank in Kingfisher, Oklahoma, was daydreaming out the front windows when a large white-and-silver motor home glided into view and parked across the street. It was a slow morning, and she had time to watch the middle-aged couple lock up their Winnebago and walk hand in hand over to the bank. They used the crosswalk, and the teller liked that. Monday, June twenty-first, had dawned hot and clear, and the couple was dressed for the first taste of summer—straw hats, aloha shirts and Bermuda shorts. The teller envied them. The Chocpoyas were retired, earlier than the teller could ever imagine for herself. They'd sold their home near Lawton and begun to roam the country "like gypsies," as Mr. Chocpoya had explained, swimming and kayaking wherever they pleased like a couple of kids.

She knew them by name because two days ago they'd come in and opened a joint checking account.

Mr. Chocpoya swung back the bank glass door for his wife, waved at the teller, then turned and walked off as if he had an errand down the street. He looked more Indian than she did, and she looked plenty Indian, especially with the turquoise earrings she was wearing again today.

Mrs. Chocpoya threaded through the ropes, even though there was no was waiting in line ahead of her. In her five years at the bank, the teller had become something of a student of human nature. At first, she'd been on the lookout for robbers, but the bank had been robbed only once during that period and she'd been out sick that day. No, she just liked to observe people and see how their personalities were revealed by what they did and said. Mrs. Chocpoya was a woman who cheerfully followed the rules. She was in her early fifties with smooth skin of a light brown cast and bright, smiling eyes. There was a time when she must have been exceptionally pretty. Instantly, the teller had liked her.

"Morning, honey," she now said, placing her oversized handbag on the counter. "Wonder if you can cash a government check for me."

"Social Security, Mrs. Chocpoya?"

"Now come on, dear." She tapped the back of the teller's hand in mild reproach. "Do I look that old . . . ?" The teller started to apologize, but Mrs. Chocpoya cut her short with a laugh. "I know you didn't mean anything by it. And call me Mary." She spread a check and a deposit slip on the countertop. "Finally, my Indian money came."

"Indian money?"

"My granddaddy left me a couple oil wells on the land he got when they busted up the reservations here in Oklahoma."

"Oh." The maker was the Anadarko Agency of the Bureau of Indian Affairs. There was nothing unusual in this. The teller cashed BIA checks all the time. But this one was different. It was for $19,983.12. "I'll have to okay this with the manager, Mary, but I should tell you she might put a hold on it."

"No problem, dear. We're not going anywhere. Earl's set us up out at the RV park on Canton Lake. Snow's gone now, so we don't have to keep one step ahead of it."

The teller excused herself and took the check and deposit slip to the manager at her desk and explained the situation. She shook her head and whispered so only the teller could hear: "Naturally, she wants at least five thousand in cash right away. She's Indian."

"What d'you mean, ma'am?"

"Mark my words—it'll wind up in a casino before the week is done."

Then, because of the size of the check and the fact that there was more fraud on government checks than personal ones, the manager took the precaution of phoning the BIA office in Anadarko to make sure they genuinely had the funds to back it up. They did. In the amount specified. They also confirmed Mary's date of birth: December 5, 1952. The manager decided not to put a hold on it, particularly because Mrs. Chocpoya wasn't taking out the full nineteen thousand and change, and the teller returned to the woman with the good news. But there were two last conditions. "Mary, what's your tribal enrollment number?"

Mrs. Chocpoya rattled it off. Perfectly, according to the slip of paper the manager had given the teller. "Great, thank you. Everything looks okay."

The woman was delighted. But not with the second condition the manager had put on the transaction: a thumb print.

"You sure that's needed, dear?"

"I'm afraid so, Mary. Because of the amount, we have to be careful." Mrs. Chocpoya visibly pouted, so the teller added, "You wouldn't want somebody to steal *your* money, would you?"

"I suppose not."

"Now, how'd you like the five thousand? In hundreds?"

The twenty-first of June began much as the twenty-first of May had for Emmett. He slept in until ten, mostly to shorten the day as much as he could, then showered and padded out to his mother's kitchen. She was at the table, pasting the article about the President's appearance at Emmett's honor dance into a scrapbook. She had started this book upon his graduation from OSU and included everything she could find about his law enforcement career up to the present. He'd never had any desire to leaf through it, although he realized he should be touched that somebody cared enough about his personal history to compile it.

She rose out of her chair. "I'll make you some fresh coffee."

"Sit down, Mama. What's in the pot will do fine."

Still, she got up to serve him. He accepted a cup from her, leaned against the sink cabinet and watched her. She poured herself what little remained in the carafe, then reached into a ready bowl for a few pecans and tried to crush them between her arthritic hands.

"Let me," Emmett said. He quickly pulverized them between his palms and dropped the crumbs into her cup.

"*Udah.*" *Thanks.*

Pecans in coffee.

Old tastes died hard. With the confinement of the *Nuhmuhnuh* on a reservation in 1876, reliance on buffalo and the wild greens of the lush grassland was replaced by a dole from the Indian Agency at Fort Cobb. Coffee was included. The People had sampled it with cream, but the agency provided none. So they learned to substitute crushed pecans, and many elders—like Celia and Wendell Padduhpony—still preferred them. The agency had also distributed rice, which was tossed out onto the roads leading away from Ft. Cobb. The tribes of the southern plains had no experience with "swamp seed" and believed they'd been given desiccated maggots by the stingy Indian agent.

Jerome Crowe called to Emmett from the front screen door.

"You know the way," he responded.

But, for some reason, Jerome asked for Emmett to come out to him. Of the past fortnight, Crowe had spent a week of it in Washington, D.C., meeting with his own legal counsel to discuss any action the BIA might take against him. He'd flown back to Lawton looking drawn and exhausted, then closeted himself in the local Marriott. This was only the second time he'd gone out since his return—one evening, the two of them had driven to Ft. Sill to visit the post cemetery and sprinkle cedar over the graves of Quanah Parker; his mother, Naudah; and his sister, Topsannah. As they drove away, Jerome pointed out the stately house where Emmett's first ex-wife was now living with her Army officer husband. The windows had been lit, but a sharp and unexpected pang of loneliness had kept Emmett from looking too hard for Christine.

Approaching the screen door, he now saw why Jerome didn't want to come inside. He was agitated, and Celia Parker didn't allow smoking inside her home. He gave Emmett a wan smile as he exhaled smoke through his nose. "Come on out a minute." His Cadillac was parked along the curb.

"For a drive?"

"No, just a chat."

"Let me grab a shirt and my shoes." Emmett was bare-chested and didn't feel like parading his scars in front of the neighborhood, especially the newest one that was still a deep purple.

"Don't bother. This'll just take a second."

The cement walkway was hot under Emmett's socks, so he stepped off onto the grass.

Jerome was beginning to lose weight. But not in a healthy way. Although he was still portly, stress was sucking both the fat and vitality out of him, and he seemed to getting by solely on nerves. His eyes had that brittle and frenetic look the accused take on. All the accused except the psychopaths. They seemed to relish the spotlight. Whatever he had done or not done, Crowe was no psychopath. "What's wrong?"

Jerome dropped his voice. "The question should be—*what's right?*" He smiled, but again there seemed to be no feeling in it. Emmett doubted that he'd slept in days. "Mark this date, Emmett—June twenty-first."

"Why?"

"Because this is the day you and I are going to blow the lid off the trust fund fiasco." Jerome waited, wild-eyed, for Emmett's reaction.

He had none. He had no intention of getting in the middle of the fiasco. He was on convalescent leave, and even though time was dragging for him, he knew better than to wade into an investigation that made the JFK assassination seem simple.

"Say something," Jerome insisted.

"When's the last time you slept and ate?"

"I can sleep and eat all I want when this is settled."

"And you *personally* are going to settle it."

"No, not personally." Jerome lowered his voice even more and said almost gleefully, "I've finally got one."

"An informant?"

"*Haa, haa, haa!*" *Yes, yes, yes.* "I've got the mother of all Deep Throats."

"Does she admit personal involvement?"

"He. And yes, he's had a change of heart. He wants to talk to us—"

"Us?"

"Yeah, I told him about you. He'd already read about you in the papers and thinks he can deal with you. He's going to phone me back this afternoon so we can work out the details for a meeting."

There was the sound of footsteps on the sidewalk. Jerome's big, sweaty face swung around to take in an old Latino man, who took no note of the two younger men. Even so, Crowe waited until he was out of earshot.

"This informant phoned you?"

"Yeah. He's called repeatedly."

"No, I mean, he contacted you out of the blue?"

"I don't catch your drift."

"You didn't develop him in any way? Didn't have to turn him?"

Jerome shrugged his shoulders. "He phoned me a couple days ago at the Marriott. Out of the blue, like you say."

"How'd he know you're staying there?"

"I don't know. Does that mean anything?"

"He is local?"

"I get the feeling."

"Indian?"

"Maybe, it hasn't come up yet."

"Has he identified himself?"

"Not yet, but he promised he will—when push gets to shove."

And if this was legitimate, Emmett mused, things would swiftly go from push to shove.

"Will you go with me, Em? I don't know how to handle an informant, especially on a first contact. You do. I'm counting on your help."

Emmett was distracted by a crow. It had flapped down to perch on the telephone pole behind the house.

Jerome gave him a gentle sock on the arm. "What's the problem here, *Pabi–noyos?*" Testicles.

"*Uh thine,*" Emmett shot back at him. *Your butt.* The Comanche equivalent of *yo mama.* They both smiled, grudgingly, boys again for a split second. Then Emmett relented. "Okay, when your snitch phones again and suggests the location for the meet—you change it. We don't want this to go down on his home turf."

"Got it," Jerome said, clearly relieved. "If it makes you feel any better, we've got protection."

"What do you mean?"

"When I was back in D.C., I met with Dagen about all this. She'll help us any way she can."

Emmett rolled his eyes. "Dagen Kirsch is a career politician. If and when this hits the media, her way of helping will be to deny that she ever knew us."

"That's not fair, Emmett. Not after all the nice things she said about you."

He glanced away, suspecting that Dagen had shared with Jerome what had happened between them that night on the mission grounds. Inevitably, sex complicated everything. "Phone me here at the house," he said, backing up the walkway, "as soon as he makes contact again. I'll be waiting."

"Okay." Then Jerome added fondly, "I knew I could count on you."

In the kitchen, his mother had put away the scrapbook and was doing her bills. "What'd Jerome want?"

"Absolution."

"Then he should see a priest."

"My sentiments exactly, Mama." Emmett found his cup, but the coffee was now cold. He swilled it down anyway, for the caffeine. Suddenly, after months of inactivity, he needed a clear head. And Jerome needed protecting. That was the only reason he would get involved, even minimally. To steer the snitch clear of Jerome and get him under the thumbs of an experienced handler.

"Who do you know in Alaska?" Celia asked.

"A couple folks. Why, you want to take a cruise or something?" She'd mentioned this before.

"Not now. So you phoned one of these friends?"

He saw that she was clasping her phone bill. "From here, recently?"

"Yes."

"Nobody, Mama. I don't think I've phoned anybody up there in years." He slipped the bill from her grasp. And there it was, dated May 16, a call with a seven-minute duration to the 907 area code, specifically—Wales, Alaska. Emmett could not recall having ever been there, or even where it was in the vast state. "It's a mistake. Tell the phone company. If you have any trouble, I'll handle it."

She nodded and went back to making out her bills.

Emmett was in the guest bedroom, throwing on a shirt, when the phone rang. His mother called for him to pick it up and he grabbed the extension in the living room. Jerome already?

No, it was Michael Mangas. Frowning, Emmett steeled himself for another awkward conversation, but he had no idea how awkward until the FBI agent asked, "You know where my office is here in town?"

"Same place it's always been?"

"Yes. We have to talk."

Something in Mangas's strained tone of voice made Emmett ask, "Tribal or other business?"

"Other."

Emmett ground his teeth together, thinking—*What the hell have you gotten me into, Jerome?* It now seemed more than likely that the FBI was tailing Crowe. "What time?"

"One o'clock okay?"

"I'll be there."

The stenographer waiting inside Mangas's office with the agent didn't surprise Emmett, but the presence of the supervisor of Internal Affairs from the BIA's Albuquerque Central Office West did take him aback. Don Andreas was Paiute, originally from somewhere in California, Emmett recollected. He looked plump but weathered, like an overripe cactus pear.

There were handshakes all around, an offer of coffee he declined, and then things got down to business. Mangas identified everybody for the record—without specifying the purpose of this little get-together. On a positive note, no Miranda warning was given, but Emmett reminded himself to remain vigilant for the turning point in the coming session when he might want legal counsel.

He felt a cramp in the most heavily damaged muscle of his chest, but like a batter who's been hit with a pitch, he didn't deign to touch it. His palms were sweaty, but he resisted wiping them on his Levi's, as well.

Mangas kept a neat office, blandly federal but for the paintings of warrior-dancers by Doc Tate Nevaquaya, a Comanche artist, and the famous photograph of a glowering Geronimo. The clan resemblance was unmistakable in the FBI agent's gloomy face, making Emmett wonder how much of temperament is due to genetics. It was said that the typical Apache laughed only when he saw someone being injured or suffering some catastrophe.

Mangas's voice brought him back to the moment. "Emmett, how many years have you been with the BIA?"

"Fourteen." He glanced at the female stenographer, whose plum-colored fingernails had clicked into action.

"Not all of those were in Phoenix, were they?"

"No, six months on an undercover detail in South Dakota, followed by a two-year stint at the Anadarko Area Office. Then I was transferred to Phoenix."

"And, for the record, prior to all that, you and I worked together at the Oklahoma City Police Department—right?"

Emmett didn't see how that was even remotely relevant, but he agreed with Mangas, who went on without referring to their frosty relations arising from that shared time.

"In what capacity have you served the BIA, Emmett?"

"As a criminal investigator."

"The entire time?"

"Yes."

"In any special area of expertise?"

"All our investigators are generalists." For the first time, Don Andreas piped up. "Parker has a talent for homicide investigation, which we put to good use when the need arose."

"Right," Mangas said impatiently, "but, Emmett, did you ever have occasion to investigate any embezzlement cases?"

"Yes."

"Describe them."

"Tribal funds embezzled by tribal leaders, mostly. A couple wire frauds, where federal grant distributions wound up in an individual's personal bank account."

"Individual," the agent echoed, as if he'd hit upon something.

"Yeah, what about it?"

"Did you work any cases involving Individual Indian Money accounts?"

Emmett paused. So here it was. He felt a curious and brief sense of relief. Curious because he knew now that this had to do with Jerome Crowe, despite the presence of his own Internal Affairs officer. Brief, because it now came home hard that his friend was in trouble. Emmett looked back and forth between Mangas and Andreas, trying to gauge who had the greater interest in all this, but both men were doing a decent job of disguising their feelings. "Yes, I investigated an IIM case."

"When was this?" Mangas asked.

"Six, seven years ago." Emmett stared out the window—unexpectedly, his memory was failing him. Six months ago, he would've have recalled precisely. He blamed his injury and long lay-off.

"Where was this?"

Emmett exhaled. "Where was what?"

"Where'd the offense occur?"

"Phoenix, the Ft. Apache Reservation and the town of Show Low just north of the rez."

"How were all these locales involved?"

"Basically, there were three co-conspirators. An Apache living on the rez with access to tribal records. A white BIA employee in disbursements. And a relative of the BIA inside-man—she worked at the bank in Show Low. The money came from timber royalties due individual Apaches. The guy on the rez would identify recently deceased members of the tribe who were owed these monies. He'd alert the guy in the agency office, who'd intercept the funds and pay out to the dead recipient—except to a general delivery address in Show Low. Then the Apache would pick up those checks at the post office in town and cash them with the connivance of the teller, who was in on the scam and accepted bogus IDs."

Mangas nodded. "Then you've got a pretty clear idea of how these cases work?"

Emmett slowed down. For some reason, Mangas was playing dumb. Surely, he'd investigated his own scams out of this very office. "A fair idea," Emmett finally said.

"Walk me through the process, if you don't mind."

Emmett decided to play dumb, too. "Process?"

"The money trail in one of these things."

"Funds are held in the U.S. Treasury until checks are cut for individuals or tribes by the agency on the basis of royalty payments received in the general fund."

"How's the individual identified in all this?"

"Social Security and tribal enrollment numbers to begin with, then the assignment of an account number."

Mangas turned to Andreas. "Does a red flag go up in the event of an address change to an IIM account holder?"

The Internal Affairs man's sepia-colored face darkened a shade more. "It's in the remedial plan, but the entire system is still being revamped."

Emmett glanced at the wall clock. Already one-thirty, and so far no mention of Jerome. Even indirectly. He was tempted to roll the dice and ask Mangas if this had anything do with Crowe. But that would reveal prior knowledge, and there was still the possibility, however dim, that this had nothing to do with Jerome.

Mangas leaned back in his swivel chair and interlaced his hands behind his neck. "You've gone on temporary duty details quite a few times through the years, haven't you?"

"I've had my share."

Andreas made a stab at helping him: "Parker's always in demand. That's why he deserves a good long rest."

Mangas pressed, "Tell me about your detail to Alaska in 1991."

Again, Emmett paused, this time with the queasy sense that the ground had just shifted beneath him. It had. From Arizona to Alaska in the time it'd taken Mangas to ease back in his chair. He asked himself if Jerome had ever been on temporary detail to the forty-ninth state, but also sensed that too long a delay would make it look as if he was being creative with his answer. "I was sent to assist the FBI, your Fairbanks head resident, with a homicide investigation. A native girl."

"In Fairbanks itself?"

"No," Emmett replied, "an Athapascan village a couple hundred miles to the west of Fairbanks. We were flown in and out by a bush pilot. Had it wrapped up in a couple days. The girl had been raped and murdered by a cousin."

"This village wasn't near the Seward Peninsula, was it?"

Emmett cracked a smile, although his heart was pounding. "It wasn't near anything, as far as I could tell."

"Understood." Mangas smiled back at him. At least, his lipless mouth seemed to be smiling again. "What about your detail up there in 1996?"

"Not much to it. Keep the peace between the local Eskimos and the oil workers at Prudhoe Bay."

Mangas sat up. "Eskimos, you say?"

"Yeah."

"But this, too, was nowhere near Seward Peninsula?"

Emmett met his gaze. "What's so special about Seward Peninsula?"

The agent broke eye contact first and swiveled toward Andreas. "That's all I have for now. I appreciate you both coming on such short notice."

Emmett thought about challenging the Keeper of the Pipe of the Thunder Dogs. He sensed that Mangas had come within an eyelash of Mirandizing him but had decided not to cross that bridge too soon. Emmett had faced the same quandary with suspects countless times—having enough to interrogate but not nearly enough to advise them that they had the right to legal counsel in the face of their possible loss of freedom.

And now he wasn't going to stick around and waste his time trying to get answers out of Mangas and Andreas. They had questions for him, not answers, and those questions had zeroed in on a finger of tundra that thrust out into the Bering Strait.

7

P ARKER WAS NO sooner gone from Michael Mangas's office than Don Andreas said, "I want to see this thing for myself." Doubt was written all over his broad Paiute face.

Typical rabbit-choker, Michael thought, *naturally distrustful.*

Rabbit-choker was slang for a member of one of the tribes of the Great Basin, who'd driven rabbits into brush enclosures in much the same way the plains Indians had stampeded buffalo over blind cliffs. Michael didn't like having uncharitable thoughts about a brother cop, but neither had he wanted Andreas at the interview. But his own superior, the special-agent–in-charge of the Oklahoma City field office, had insisted: *The potential's too great for bad feelings to erupt between our two agencies, so you can't freeze out the BIA, blah . . . blah . . . blah.*

Michael reached for his phone. "Let's see what I can arrange, Don." Maybe it would be good for the BIA to see *the thing.* Only then did it become real.

Fifteen minutes later, they were admitted to the refrigeration unit of the morgue. Dr. Hawzeepa couldn't tear himself away from other duties, but he'd left word that the FBI agent and BIA cop were to be shown the corpse, which had been patched and sewn back together after the autopsy. Hawzeepa didn't want to release the body to the family until all its evidentiary potential had been exhausted.

The morgue attendant rolled back the tray and unzipped the body bag, letting out some fetid air despite the chill. Then the attendant withdrew, leaving Michael and Andreas alone with the victim who'd been found tied to a wooden cross jammed in the water gate at Lake Lawtonka.

He was no longer a John Doe.

Obviously, Andreas had seen grisly death before. But this was different. It was horrific because it made absolutely no sense. After several long seconds, he said, "Go through it all again."

The Anchorage field office of the FBI had dispatched an agent to the westernmost tip of the North American continent to develop the information Michael now reiterated:

"The victim's name was Calvin Ushuk. Federal jurisdiction had been established: Ushuk was an Inupiut Eskimo of a group that called themselves the Kingikmiut—"

"What does *Kingikmiut* mean?" Andreas interrupted, continuing to run his eyes over the milky, bloated corpse.

"People of the High Place," Michael explained. "That's because their main village sits at the base of a mountain overlooking the Bering Strait. . . . *In English, that village was called Wales. It was situated on Cape Prince of Wales at the very tip of the Seward Peninsula. Ushuk, an Air Force veteran with a military occupation of meteorological technician, had been employed by the U.S. Weather Service since 1995."*

"He worked there in Wales?" Andreas asked.

"No, at the weather station on Little Diomede Island."

"Where's that?"

"Twenty miles west of Wales," Michael replied. The possible significance here was that this mesalike speck of rock was only two miles from Big Diomede Island, the easternmost extension of Russia. He decided not to acquaint Andreas with this geographic tidbit. For the time being. He and Parker were co-workers, and despite the fact Internal Affairs men were often pariahs in their own agencies, Michael didn't want him to alert Parker to any of his speculations. Bureau might prove to be thicker than water.

Andreas asked, "How'd Ushuk get over to this island . . . boat?"

"No, though he kept a kayak on Little Diomede for his own recreation.

Weather Service personnel who don't live full-time in the only village on the island are helicoptered over. When there's no fog. Little Diomede's fogged in a lot. Usually, these workers put in two weeks on site with one week off."

"And where was Ushuk when he got that phone call on the morning of May sixteenth?"

"At home in Wales with his wife. It was the middle of the night there. She told the agent from Anchorage she didn't know who was on the other end of the line—"

"Line?" the BIA man interrupted.

"Well, satellite connection. There are no phone lines into Wales. Whatever—Ushuk wouldn't tell her who he was talking to. He was upset. She saw that much. Next morning, he took the Bering Air flight to Nome. We pieced together his itinerary from there. Nome to Anchorage. Overnight at the Sheraton—"

"Is it pricey?"

"I'd guess," Michael answered, slightly interested that Andreas was trying to cast some light in the same dark corners he had. According to the Anchorage agent, Ushuk was the most visibly prosperous *Kingikmiut* in Wales—biggest house, owned one of the few vehicles in town, a Hummer SUV, and more assets were cropping up as the investigation gathered steam. "On to Seattle the next morning, the eighteenth. He arrived late that night in Oklahoma City. The lead flight attendant on the Sea-Tac-Will Rogers run remembers Ushuk deplaning. That's where we lose track of him—strolling on into the terminal. We've got nothing on him anywhere beyond the airport."

"Somebody met him," Andreas said knowingly.

Yes, and his name is Emmett Quanah Parker. But Michael didn't say that aloud. He let Andreas mull over the only shred of evidence suggesting that Parker had been the party to pick up the wayward Eskimo at Will Rogers World Airport: The long-distance call placed from his mother's house in Lawton to Ushuk's satellite phone in Wales, Alaska, two days prior.

Andreas glanced up from the body. "What got you looking into the Parkers' phone records?"

"Informant."

"Reliable?"

"Somewhat," Michael said wryly. "U.S. Customs. Their people were already plowing through Ushuk's phone records and emails in search of smuggling links. He made frequent trips to Anchorage, often under the cover of Weather Service errands."

Andreas shook his head. "I can't believe Parker is tangled up in any-thing like that."

Can't believe or don't want to believe? But Michael let Andreas stew in the looming scandal his bureau faced if Parker was indeed *tangled up*. It was coming at a time when momentum was growing in Congress to turn over all Indian criminal matters to the FBI, thus scrapping the BIA's law enforce-ment division. "How did an Eskimo wind up four thousand miles from home, stuck in the outlet of an Oklahoma dam?"

"Airplane," Michael said, deadpan. He was beginning to enjoy An-dreas's discomfort.

The man looked at the corpse as if not focusing on it. "I grew up on the California–Nevada border," he said, his voice far away. "Place called Fish Lake Valley. Big pools fed by underground springs. When my grandma was a little girl, she and her folks were camped in the mountains above the val-ley. There was a creek up there that flowed into a hole in the ground. Grandma was washing greens in her mother's favorite basket when all of a sudden it washed down the creek and went into the hole. Honest to God—years later, that basket floated up into one of the big pools in the valley. This kind of reminds me of that . . . know what I mean?"

"Yeah. Surprising sometimes what bubbles up out of somebody you think you know—like Parker."

"I was referring to the victim." Andreas turned from the tray and started for the exit.

Michael fell in alongside him.

Andreas said nothing more until they were out in the parking lot. "Em-mett Parker is the biggest malcontent in the BIA. He's also our best investi-gator. He's relentless. And I sure as hell can't see him doing anything that sick—" He jerked his thumb back toward the morgue, indicating Ushuk's remains. "—no matter how fed up he is with our outfit or anything else."

Relentless. Michael had always seen Emmett as arrogant. But he tucked away this new description for future reference. *Relentless.* It was a word many had applied to Mangas himself.

Andreas unlocked the door to his rental car. "I think Emmett deserves the chance to clear himself on the lie box."

Michael shrugged. "You think he'll go for it?"

"No harm in asking. I'll give him a day to settle down. No doubt, we just pissed him off. Maybe after a sleepless night, the box will look like a good option to him."

"Fine with me," Michael said.

"In the meantime, what's your next step?"

"I'll put our polygraph examiner in Oklahoma City on standby and wait for your call."

For the first time since his arrival in Lawton this morning, Andreas looked pleased. "Good." He got inside the car and headed for the interstate, leaving Michael to watch him drive off. Michael had just fibbed to the BIA man. He was doing a great deal more than *just waiting*. For starters, he'd borrowed one of the resident FBI agents from Elk City, a town sixty miles to the northwest. His name was Dustin Ramsey and he had just finished his first office—or rookie—assignment in Boston, so it was unlikely Emmett Parker had ever met him. That could be useful, for at this very minute, Special Agent Ramsey was tailing Parker.

Emmett pulled into the parking lot of the public library and rushed inside to the reference desk. He asked where he could find a North American atlas, and the clerk pointed. He spread the oversized tome on a table and consulted the index for Wales, Alaska. Following the coordinates given, his forefingers zeroed in on the town. On the tip of the Seward Peninsula. The surrounding area was shaded brown, indicating that it was an Indian reservation. Inupiat Eskimo, most likely. Across sixty miles of Bering Strait lay Siberia. Russia.

He snapped shut the atlas and left.

Driving home, he used the time to calm down enough to speak to his mother in a tone that didn't sound like an interrogation. Instantly, she sensed that something was very wrong, so he broke his own momentum and went to the refrigerator for some iced tea. "Mama, do you know any Eskimos?"

"How would I know any people like that?"

"Do you have any friends who know Eskimos who might've called from here?"

"No. What is it, Emmett?"

"Mind getting me your phone bill?"

"Is that it?" She rose from the kitchen table. "Is the phone company giving you trouble about that call?"

Good, she'd just given him the cover story he needed to pursue this without scaring her to death. "Yeah, Mama."

"Things were better when we didn't have telephones."

"Tell me about it."

She dug the bill out of a drawer, and he examined the information on the statement about the call to Wales, Alaska. Allegedly, it'd been made from this house on May 16 at 4:32 A.M. Still dark then, and when he himself had still had been in bed, given his recent habit of sleeping in. His mother rose early, but he had no reason to doubt her claim that she hadn't made the call. Even accidentally. And an accidental call made by an aged woman would never have been enough to trip off the interrogation he'd just endured in Mangas's office. Also, his mother would not have conversed seven minutes—the duration of the call—with a complete stranger.

Assuming that the recipient of the call had been a stranger.

Emmett went to the wall phone and dialed a number from memory, one of many he'd mentally filed away for investigative purposes. It was to a phone company supervisor in Phoenix. "Yeah, Juanita," he said casually, as if he were still on the job, "Emmett Parker from BIA law enforcement. Do me a favor?"

"Anytime."

"Can you get me the customer's name off a listing for an Alaska number?"

"Go ahead."

He gave her the number, then listened to her tap it out on her keyboard.

"Okay," she said, "a satellite phone in the names of Calvin and Irene Us . . . Ush . . . wow, I've never seen one like this."

"Spell it."

"U-s-h-u-k."

"Thanks, as always." He hung up, thought a moment. That had been the unmentionable during the interrogation—the name of either Calvin or Irene Ushuk. This had everything to do with one or both of them.

"Back in a minute, Mama." Emmett went outside into the sultry mid-afternoon heat. His head was spinning. His wound had left him chronically tired, too tired for something like this. But he knew he'd be unable to rest until he had some answers. There were two ways the call could have been made from the Parker residence in west Lawton, Oklahoma. One would have been to force entry into the house at 4:32 in the morning. Possible, but unlikely. Despite his exhaustion, Emmett relied on a potion of even his sleeping mind to be ever vigilant. He would've awakened at the slightest noise, other than his mother's familiar tread on the creaking floors. The second alternative would have involved the use of phone company gear, like a lineman's test set. Shading his eyes against the high sun, he looked up and traced the drop line from the side of the house up to the pole-mounted terminal. Stepping closer, he inspected the pole for signs of recent damage, most noticeably scars left in the creosoted wood by a lineman's cleated boots. Nothing. Still, someone who knew what he was doing could have located the Parker line among the two dozen others of the aerial distribution cable at this juncture. Or the tap-in could have been made even farther from the house, at the cross-connect terminal off the aerial branch feeder. That would have been more complicated, possibly requiring computer access to phone company data.

But he knew from past cases that all of this could be done.

And there was virtually no way for him to prove that the call to Wales, Alaska, had been made from *outside* his mother's house.

And that made him feel even more fatigued. He went back inside.

His mother asked, "What were you looking for outside?"

"Just checking to see if the line is damaged. It's okay. I'm going to lie down a bit."

That got her worrying. "You feeling all right?"

"Tired, Mama."

He was startled awake by a light touch on his shoulder. It was his mother. In silhouette, for it was now dark. "Emmett, sorry to wake you."

"What time is it?"

"Around nine-thirty."

That was consistent with the thin strips of purplish sky that showed alongside the window shade.

"Jerome phoned," she went on.

Emmett sat up in bed. "When?"

"Just a couple minutes ago."

He hadn't heard the ring. "Is he going to phone back?"

"I don't think so. But he left a message. He wants you to meet him up at Mt. Scott right away. . . ." No doubt, Jerome meant the overlook on the summit, but Emmett wished that he'd had the chance to question Crowe about his choice of location for his first face-to-face contact with the informant who'd help them *blow the lid off the trust fund fiasco.* He even might have urged Jerome to postpone the meeting until they could find out exactly what Mangas and Andreas knew. Now, deprived of direct communication, Emmett had no choice but to go up into the Wichita Mountains—or leave Jerome hanging out to dry. All informants were potentially dangerous, something Crowe might not fully appreciate.

"Jerome said something queer."

"How's that, Mama?"

"He said for you not to bring the heat with you tonight. What've you got to do with the weather?"

Rising, Emmett smiled. He wouldn't explain to her that Jerome was telling him to leave any weapons at home. But it also troubled Emmett. Jerome had no reason to say that, so it meant the demand had come from the informant, who might pat down Emmett. It was a demand he'd get around by stowing his .357 magnum in the trunk. "Can I borrow your car?"

"Are you going to be late?"

"No."

"You going to see Kitty Toppah?"

"Not tonight." He'd delayed retrieving his own personal car from Phoenix for too long now. The problem was that it was one more admission he'd never return to work. He had left this afternoon's interrogation with the feeling that, if Mangas and Andreas had their way, his career was indeed finished.

Speeding west along State Route 49 in his mother's old Dodge, Emmett caught flashes to the south. He couldn't hear the detonations over the engine noise but knew them to be artillery bursts. It'd been in the newspaper. For the next two nights, the Army would be conducting night exercises on its live-fire ranges along the northern fringe of Ft. Sill. The post commander had begged for the public's toleration of the thunderlike rumblings until two o'clock on each of these mornings.

Emmett went past the first turn-off to Lake Lawtonka.

He was fuzzy-headed enough from his long nap to woolgather, even though he tried to focus on his imminent meeting with Crowe's informant. Weeks ago, there'd been a news report of a body found stuck in the water gate at Lawtonka—and nothing about it since. Had the floater been Ushuk? Emmett struggled to think this through. But his mind wouldn't focus, and he found himself remembering a trip to Lawtonka long ago, a school picnic for both boys and girls shepherded by Father Jurgen. There'd been no change facilities along the shore in those days, so Father had had the boys huddle around and shield him with their towels while he changed into his swimsuit. They waited while he shed his black suit and briefs. Then, on Emmett's signal, the boys scattered, leaving the old priest standing alone in his scrawny nudity, bawling at them in outrage.

Emmett smiled at the memory.

The lake had lacked change facilities in those days, but some privacy had been available out in the oaks. There, Emmett had been exposed to Dagen Kirsch's precocious sexual appetite for the first time. On that outing, with his head stuffed full of the consequences of carnal sin, he'd stopped short of satisfying her advances, leaving both of them half-dressed and hot. Afterward, she hadn't spoken to him for the remainder of the year. And even then, in his callow youth, he'd come away with a caution he realized could be used by all native peoples: *Covet not that which you don't truly want.*

Headlights showed in the rearview mirror.

The vehicle was about a mile behind, keeping pace. No other cars were in sight on Duhringe Pass, the gateway to the Wichita Mountains. Emmett slowed down and believed the headlights slowed as well.

Paranoia?

He tried to shake his head clear. He'd been tempted to stop at a drive-through for coffee on his way out of Lawton, but his mother had given him the urgent sense of Jerome's message. So he'd barreled up the interstate that split the sprawling Army post, without delay.

Lights appeared below. They were to the resort community of Medicine Park. The spill of those lights was just bright enough to let him shut off his own headlamps and still follow the white line. Almost instantly, the vehicle behind picked up speed.

Shit.

He was being followed. It was now obvious. The only question remaining was who. Jerome's informant? The informant's accomplice? Somebody else who had reason to be wary?

Coasting so he wouldn't have to tap his brakes and show red lights to the rear, Emmett veered off onto the last side street into Medicine Park. He wound up one of the ravines lined with river rock cottages, then made a U-turn as soon as he felt his brake lamps wouldn't be spotted. He crept back up to Route 49 and waited.

A Crown Victoria sedan rocketed past, doing at least eighty miles an hour. Emmett had only a fleeting glimpse of the driver. Male. Short hair.

Still running without lights, Emmett began shadowing his shadower.

The driver of the Crown Victoria soon outdistanced him, as his mother's Dodge was already beginning to overheat on the climb out of Medicine Park. No matter: The driver didn't take the turn-off to the Mt. Scott overlook. What did that mean? He didn't realize Jerome was already up there? Or was it his job simply to seal off the highway to the west?

Emmett finally switched on his low beams and started up the winding road to the summit. He'd shut off the air-conditioner some minutes ago and now rolled down his side window. Crickets were singing out in the spring grass. Their primitive chant of lust was even louder than the pinging of the motor. Off in the distance shone small clusters of lights, marking Chickasha and Anadarko.

He wondered if his tail had come to the conclusion that the highway ahead of him was empty of the old Dodge. If so, he'd already turned around. Still, Emmett had a jump of several minutes on him, hopefully enough for him to find Jerome and get him off the mountain.

Despite the relevance or irrelevance of Calvin Ushuk, and his own alleged call to the Alaskan native, Emmett believed that the purpose of this afternoon's chitchat at Mangas's office had more to do with Jerome Crowe than himself. As soon as they were safely off Mt. Scott, Emmett intended to ask Jerome how Ushuk figured in all this. If anybody knew, Jerome did.

It was time for answers.

Emmett checked behind: no headlights yet.

Fine with me.

As he neared the summit, he could see the blackjack oaks rocking. Here, fifteen hundred feet above the surrounding prairie, which was still giving off the day's heat, the mountain was windswept. Not exactly refreshing, but it did cool Emmett's sweaty skin as it poured through his open window.

Jerome's Cadillac had the big lot to itself. "Good," Emmett whispered. The car was parked close to the overlook railing, framed by the glow given off by Anadarko. Jerome wasn't visible behind the steering wheel.

Emmett stopped directly behind the Caddy, kept his headlights on it, and got out. He called, *"Pabi?"*

No answer.

Something was banging. From the far side of the lot. A door, perhaps.

Emmett kept his attention on the interior of Crowe's car. The key was still in the ignition, but there was no sign of the man. Pivoting, he took in the entire lot, especially the two chemical toilets across the asphalt from him. The door to one of them had been left unlatched, and it was banging on the wind gusts. Midway to the toilets something glistened wetly on the pavement.

Emmett went to the spot and knelt. He dipped a finger into the small black pool. It came away red.

This time, he didn't call out for Jerome.

Rushing back to his mother's Dodge, he backed around and boosted the beams to high as he sped toward the toilets. As he came up on them, he had glimpses of Crowe slumped on the seat in one of the units as the wind tossed the door back and forth. His head and right shoulder were jammed against the side wall, his trousers and boxers bunched around his ankles.

Emmett stopped and rushed from the car. He flung back the flapping door so violently he wrenched it off its flimsy hinges. Jerome's blood-covered fists had closed around something at his midriff. A knife handle. Emmett thought he might already be dead, but Jerome gave a sudden shudder and then blinked sleepily into the Dodge's headlights. *"Pabi . . . ?"* he asked weakly.

"Here, Brother." Emmett debated whether or not to take out the knife. It might be the only thing keeping him from hemorrhaging to death. "Can you feel the blade?"

Jerome chuckled miserably. "Oh yeah, it's . . . it's still cutting me with each breath I take."

That settled it. Emmett would back out the knife. But first he wanted an ambulance to be on the way from Lawton. "Where's your cell phone?"

"Car, I think. Console."

"Did you see who?"

Jerome shook his head, and Emmett decided not to waste a second more. He returned to the Dodge, unlocked the trunk and took out his revolver. Judging from the biggest bloodstain, Jerome had been attacked in the middle of the lot and then for some reason had staggered to the toilet. Next, Emmett went to the Cadillac and killed the dome light so he wouldn't be illuminated as he ransacked the storage compartment, the glove compartment and finally the spaces under the front seats.

No cell phone.

He backed out of the car and listened to the night. Nothing but the wind ruffling the oak leaves. And Jerome gasping for breath.

As he sprinted back to the toilets, Emmett tucked his .357 in the front of his waistband and stripped off his shirt to fold it into a compress.

Jerome's trousers and shoes and the fiberglass floor all around him were awash in blood. Gazing drowsily up at Emmett, he asked, "Find it?"

"No, so I'm going to take out the knife, then drive you down the mountain to Medicine Park. We can get help there, okay?"

Jerome chuckled again. "Helluva a place to die—ain't it, *Pabi?* A fucking toilet?"

"You're not going to die."

"Light a cigarette for me."

"Later."

"There is no later."

Emmett said, "Relax your hands." Jerome had a white-knuckled grip on the knife handle.

"Can't. Oh God, I can't. *Hail Mary, full of—*"

"Let go!"

"Don't touch me. Just let me be."

Emmett slapped his face. Jerome grunted in protest, but released the hilt. Emmett grasped it but hesitated. The blood felt warm and greasy. More of it was flowing out of Crowe's gut every second.

"Remember that time in class Royce Eschiti shit his pants?"

"Quiet," Emmett said, steeling himself to yank out the blade. Once it was out, he would ease Jerome out onto ground and apply the compress. However, the belly was a poor place to apply direct pressure. There were no hard underlying structures against which to pinch a severed artery. Should he leave the knife where it was? Either way, it was all a terrible gamble.

"I can really sympathize with Royce now. As soon as I was struck, I felt myself losing control of the works. Barely made it here onto the seat." A soft laugh turned into a retch, but he quickly controlled it. "Well, this is the place for a piece of shit to wind up, *Pabi.* And you have no idea what a shit I've been these past years."

"Was there another car in the lot when you got here?"

"No, nothing. I thought I was alone."

"You're not alone now."

"Thanks, Brother," Jerome said with a tender smile. There was little color left in his face.

"Clench your teeth for a minute." Emmett didn't want him to bite his own tongue. Jerome obeyed, and Emmett slowly and sickeningly drew the knife toward him—straight out, so he wouldn't create any more tissue damage. Jerome screamed in agony. As Emmett continued to pull, a car accelerated across the lot toward him and headlights joined his own on the toilet. The attacker coming back to finish the job? Emmett had no choice but to ignore the threat as he took out the blade—a wickedly long butcher's knife. The blade was at least ten inches in length. Just the thing to stick in a fat man to reach his vitals.

Still screaming, Jerome fell forward off the commode, knocking Emmett back with his huge bulk. As they fell together out onto the asphalt, Emmett reached for his revolver with his left hand while still clutching the knife in his right. The handle was sticky with congealing blood. He was training his .357 on the driver's side of the blazing headlights when a male voice barked for him to freeze.

Emmett had little doubt that voice belonged to Jerome's attacker, but he couldn't make out the man through the glare as he bawled, "You freeze!"

"Drop your weapons!"

"I'm not dropping anything. I'm a federal officer!"

"Me, too!" the voice responded, sounding rattled. "Do exactly what I say or I'll shoot!"

Emmett glanced at Jerome. He'd come to rest with his butt riding high and the side of his face mashed against the pavement. His eyes were open but had glazed over.

He was gone.

Crying out in rage, Emmett dropped the knife so he could grasp his revolver in both hands.

"Freeze, Parker!" the voice warned, almost hysterically now.

That did it. Jerome had told his informant who would be joining them on Mt. Scott. Emmett fired once, high, to keep the man's head down as he himself rolled out of the confluence of the two sets of headlamps. The man returned fire, a rapid semi-auto volley that sent bullets sparking against the asphalt and crunching into the toilet housings. He'd parked alongside the Dodge, and Emmett would have to charge right into his muzzle in order to retrieve his mother's car.

Staying low, he instead ran for Jerome's Cadillac. He spun around once to fire again. To keep his attacker off balance. But the man had already ducked behind his Crown Victoria.

Emmett went around to the opposite side of the Cadillac and knelt, using the car for cover. Now he too had a fortress. But a throaty blast from across the lot was followed by a spray of pebbled glass that passed over his head. A shotgun round had taken out the Caddy's side windows.

He was facing a shotgun, plus a semiautomatic pistol. That meant, with only four cartridges remaining, he was badly outgunned. He opened the passenger door and crawled across the seats, keeping his head down all the while. There was another blast, and more shotgun pellets thudded into the Cadillac. He turned the key. Resting his revolver on a floor mat, he shifted the automatic transmission into drive, then used his left hand to spin the steering wheel and his right hand to gun the gas. Blindly, he swerved the big car around and headed for the lot exit. More scattergun pellets struck the car, blowing out the rear window and peppering him with glass.

At last, he sat up and swung his legs around to operate the pedals. The front right tire pounded over a curb, but he didn't overcorrect. Nor did he turn on the running lights as he came down the mountain.

He picked up his revolver and nestled it between his legs. "Jesus!" he bellowed from the shock of it all. "Jesus Christ!"

8

AN INTERROGATION AT just the right moment could ratchet up an investigation like nothing else. And it was the rare suspect who, immediately afterward, could resist trying to repair the damage revealed to him by his interrogators. So it was no surprise to Michael when Dustin Ramsey, the Elk City agent he'd borrowed, reported via scrambled communications that Emmett Parker had left his mother's house in Lawton and was speeding westward along Route 49 toward the Wichita Mountains. Parker probably suspected that his mom's phone line was being tapped and the house itself bugged.

Untrue.

So far, Michael had gone out of his way not to offend BIA law enforcement, and he'd come down lighter on Parker than he would have any other suspect. He wanted the man's superiors to see his guilt for themselves. It was the only way to prevent a row between the agencies, which were already at odds over who should be the alpha crime-buster in Indian Country.

Summoned out of the Thunder Dogs' pipe ceremony to usher in the summer season, Michael now retraced Parker and Ramsey's route up to Duhringe Pass, then beyond, anxious for the young agent to report in again. He was convinced of one thing: The BIA investigator had gone out into the hot prairie night to fix something. To meet someone, to warn or even silence that person. And so Parker might soon tip his hand, and by morning, everything could be cleared up.

Contrary to the popular expectation, cops didn't make the best crooks. Most often, they were reckless, maybe owing to the belief that they had the system figured out. Contempt for the system made them careless.

Michael's radio crackled to life. It was Ramsey: "I've located the subject again." The agent had lost contact with Parker some minutes before.

Michael reached for his mike. "What's your location?"

"Mt. Scott viewpoint."

"I'm not far behind," Michael transmitted. "Hang soft 'til I can join you."

"Too late—I'm already on him. Two vehicles, dispatch, both with Oklahoma plates—" But before Ramsey gave the dispatcher the license numbers, he interrupted himself in an excited voice, "My God—he's stabbed somebody. There's blood all over the damn place!"

"Back off, Ramsey," Mangas ordered. "Do nothing 'til I get up there. ETA of about five now." Then he told the dispatcher to put out an urgent call for help. He wanted to know which units with allied agencies were in position to back the twenty-six-year-old agent, who was now more alone than he'd ever been before.

Michael turned on his siren. There was no other traffic on the highway, but he hoped Parker would hear it on the mountain and realize that Ramsey wasn't his only problem.

Dispatch advised that Comanche County Sheriff's Office was sending a patrol car from Cache. That was the closest backup. Michael was much nearer. He punched the accelerator and watched the speedometer needle bump around the one-hundred mark. Bugs splattered wetly against the windshield, but he resisted the urge to run the wipers—that would only smear the goo.

Ramsey's shrill voice set Michael's teeth on edge again: "Shots fired! Shots fired!"

"*Icoño*," Michael swore to himself. This was exactly why he'd wanted Ramsey to stand off and wait. While a corrupt cop wasn't always adept at covering his tracks, he could kill without hesitation. From his first day at the academy, a cop was conditioned to equate use of his weapon with survival.

That didn't change simply because he'd switched sides. And Parker was no virgin when it came to killing. His personnel jackets with both Oklahoma City P.D. and the BIA included numerous lethal force reviews.

Michael keyed his mike. "Answer when you can, Ramsey. What's your status?"

Silence came over the airways.

Michael was near Medicine Park when a car whooshed past, eastbound. It was blacked out.

Ramsey finally reported, "Suspect has fled the scene in the late model Cad. I think he turned east on forty-nine. I'm in pursuit!"

"Make that two of us, *compadre*," Michael muttered to himself as he whipped around and gave chase.

Emmett first suspected that a tire was losing air when the Cadillac's steering turned sluggish and began pulling toward the center line. Probably one of the shotgun pellets had penetrated it. And now, east of Medicine Park, he had no choice but to use his headlights. The humidity was dampening the starlight, and the night swallowed up the highway ahead of him. Added to that was a coating of smashed insects on the windshield.

A loud pop made him flinch. The tire had blown.

He decelerated but didn't touch the brakes for fear of losing control. The hub cap skipped on ahead of him as he slowed, the bare wheel rims grinding into the roadway.

He veered off onto the shoulder, grabbed his .357 and bailed out of the car.

Running, he knew only that he had to get away.

For minutes, he'd not wanted to admit something to himself. It was just too confusing, too awful. But now, he was almost sure of it. He'd faced a cop back there at the overlook. Under other circumstances, he might be tempted to surrender at the first opportunity and hope to clear this all up in the safety of a police facility with legal counsel present. But his mind had been busy reconstructing the seconds prior to his arrival up at the overlook. The only scenario that made sense was the one of that cop stabbing Jerome. Then, seeing headlights coming up the mountain, the son of a bitch had left

Crowe to bleed to death and driven down to a dirt side road, of which there were several, and waited for Emmett to pass before closing on the viewpoint again to finish off the two of them.

So Emmett saw no chance of survival unless he got out of the area. If and when he sought law enforcement help, it'd be from his own agency, possibly Don Andreas, even though he saw the irony in that: It was the Internal Affairs supervisor's job to investigate his own people, not get them out of scrapes.

Any port in a storm.

He jogged along the shoulder of the highway until high beams rounded a bend and flashed over him. Cutting down the embankment, he headed toward a clump of oaks. He was halfway across the grassy slope to the trees when he heard a squeal of brakes. As he glanced back at the roadway, a spotlight reached across the night and fastened onto him.

Emmett kept running, his shadow stretching out in front of him. His lungs, especially his recently injured one, were on fire, and his breaths were coming in sour, explosive bursts. He was getting sick to his stomach, but dared not stop.

A voice rolled out to him, amplified by public address. "Stop, Emmett. This is Michael Mangas. I have a carbine, and I will use it."

Emmett halted and braced his hands on his knees. He had to vomit. There was no other choice. Finishing, he turned and peered up into the powerful beam.

"Drop your handgun, Emmett," the Lawton agent ordered.

It was tucked in his waistband again. He didn't reach for it, but neither did he drop it. "Not until I get some answers!" he shouted back at Mangas.

"Answers to what?"

"Who was that in the Crown Vic on the mountain? Who killed Jerome!"

A long pause followed, then: "Are you telling me you killed Jerome Crowe? If that's what you have to say, Emmett, I'm listening. Drop your weapon, and let's talk."

So that was it.

Mangas had already made up his mind what the theme of that little talk would be—a confession to stabbing Jerome. And Emmett Parker was the only confessor on the menu tonight. Did that mean Mangas was in on this? With no witnesses other than his fellow FBI agent, he might make sure Emmett did not survive long enough for outside law enforcement backups to arrive on the scene.

Emmett heard the crack of the carbine and was already diving when the bullet thudded into the ground just feet from him. He gave up any idea of trying to reach the oaks—the copse of trees would become an isolated trap. Instead, he rose again and began skirting the hill.

All the while, he choked on the taste of bile and fought the need to stop and throw up again.

The spotlight played around him, never quite fixing on him again as he descended the southeast slope of the Wichita Range and crawled under the barbed-wire fence that marked the boundary of the Ft. Sill Military Reservation.

All was dark beyond.

Michael knew that there would be only one chance to capture Emmett Parker swiftly and cheaply. He switched off all the lights on his vehicle so he wouldn't illuminate himself, seized his flashlight and portable radio, and followed the man on foot. He bounded down the road embankment and reached the sloping grassland beyond. From there, he transmitted on his Handie-Talkie: "Units and stations, this is Special Agent Mangas of the FBI. I'm in foot pursuit of Emmett Parker. Off route forty-nine east of the pass and down into the Medicine Creek drainage. Break . . ." The break in the transmission was more for him to catch his breath than to let dispatch catch up with their dictation. "Continuing—Parker is an Indian male adult, about forty years old, seventy-four inches, one hundred and seventy pounds, black and brown. Break . . ." Michael knelt and ran his flash-light beam over an expanse of open ground, looking for tracks. He was sure Parker had passed this way, which was still soft from the recent rains, but there was no sign of him. "I need a hard target search of the northeast part of Ft. Sill. Road checkpoints in all direction ten miles from this location. This is broken terrain, so he's doing no more four miles an hour. Be advised, Parker is armed with at least a revolver and has already proven he'll use it to evade capture."

Kill him before he kills you, Michael thought to add. But didn't. He already sensed that if anybody shot Parker dead, it would be Michael Mangas.

There were times when Emmett had no choice but to stop. His healing chest wound was burning so badly he had to clasp his hands over it and wait for the fire to subside. And it took all of his willpower to hold his breath even momentarily to listen. Twice, he thought he heard Mangas coming down the slope after him. But wasn't sure. Antelope and deer roamed part of the vast post.

He stumbled on through the night.

His options flitted through his oxygen-starved brain.

Keep running and be overtaken.

That was the pathetic truth of it. Mangas was bound to be in better condition. At some point, despite his resolve, Emmett sensed that his body would fail him. If that happened, leaving the highway would have been a big mistake. Safe from prying eyes, particularly those of Comanche County deputies, Mangas would simply roll an exhausted Emmett on his back and execute him. Later, he could claim that Parker had gone down resisting.

Halt somewhere and ambush the agent.

That provided some hope, but only temporarily. Killing Mangas would whip the FBI into a frenzy, launching a massive and determined manhunt and ultimately decreasing Emmett's chances to explain himself.

He had to get away, no matter what. He had to buy himself time.

But time seemed to have expired when suddenly a flashlight beam split the night and rippled over the grass around Emmett. He dropped and drew his revolver, tried to hold down his loud gasps for breath.

The light quickly went out, but Mangas's voice came from the high ground above, steady and calm. Mangas had always been steady and calm, even when threatened by bigger and meaner boys at the Ft. Sill Indian School. A streak of cold ran through his heart, and maybe that's why they'd never been close. He had a chronic air of calculation swirling around him. "I know where you're lying, Emmett. . . ."

He wasn't sure if Mangas's meaning was literal or figurative, but still he scrambled on his elbows and knees a few yards from where he'd been hiding.

"Give it up, *Pabi*—please."

Emmett didn't quite know what to think of a man who'd just tried to shoot him calling him *brother*. It came over him with a heavy sense of dread that, in the blink of an eye, his world had shifted in a fundamental and inalterable way. Nothing would be as uncomplicated as it'd once been. And Jerome Crowe was dead. Emmett had to choke down an unexpected sob. Jerome was *dead*. But, all the while, the tactical side of his mind coolly went about the business of fixing Mangas's location while improving his own. The agent would not have hailed him unless he himself had cover. Cover was different from concealment. It could stop a bullet. Grass was not cover, and grass was all Emmett had.

He reared up slightly for a quick look around. He no sooner lowered himself again than Mangas said from the direction of a dark hulk Emmett had just noticed upslope of him: "Whatever you did, Emmett, don't make it worse. I'll help you any way the law allows, okay?"

Emmett ignored the offer as he peered over the top of the grass again.

There were several dark hulks scattered around the shallow basin in which Mangas and he found themselves. Tubes projected from a few up into the sky at forty-five degree angles. Tanks. The shapes without tubes were probably armored personnel carriers. Military junk towed up here to serve as targets.

Emmett decided to make use of one of the armored vehicles as cover. First, he would speak. Then, not waiting for Mangas's reply, he would dash for the nearest APC. Scrambling to his feet, he cried, "I did not kill Jerome . . . !"

"I'm listening. Stay put and let's talk. Don't run . . . don't run, Emmett!"

He expected Mangas's flashlight to wink on and his carbine to bark. He did not expect a faint but strange noise like the hissing of a spray paint can and then a massive, dirty-orange fireball to erupt up out of the ground off to his left. The hot concussion swept his legs out from under him, and as he fell he saw red fragments flying through the air around him. A second explosion, or maybe it was several blasts in quick succession, made him hunker his head down into his shoulders and shut his eyes. There was a short, rapid increase in air pressure, then more detonations, more searing heat.

When the salvo was finished, he slowly opened his eyes. His body was limp with fatigue, but unhurt. His ears were ringing, and he barely heard Mangas shouting, "You okay? Are you hit . . . ?"

His answer was to get up and stagger toward the APC. A pall of dust and smoke now concealed him. He had just emerged from the densest part of it when, far off, miles to the southeast, he noticed a string of orange pinpricks. They quickly went out and made no impression on him—until he realized that they were distant muzzle flashes. The next salvo was only seconds away from landing all around him. He was still yards shy of the APC, but he threw himself to the ground, cupped his hands to his ears and opened his mouth.

These artillery rounds struck farther up the slope, closer to Mangas, which gave Emmett hope that the agent had been hit—until the man's voice drifted down to him again. However, this time he didn't seem to be talking to Emmett. He was talking over a radio. That was it. He was telling his dispatcher to get a hold of the Army, to get them to cease fire at once.

Still prone, Emmett gazed up at the far-off battery of big guns. It would takes minutes for FBI dispatch to raise the Army, and perhaps minutes more for them to notify the battery. Those were all the minutes he needed.

Lunging forward, half crawling, he reached the APC. But he lingered next to its protective bulk for only a second before continuing across open ground. And he went down again only after he saw the muzzle flashes and counted to three.

These explosions were so widely scattered he made up his mind to keep moving—away from Mangas. It seemed like a bad gamble as glowing fragments sizzled all around him.

But he kept running.

Finally, he reached the edge of some scrub woods, and collapsed face-first to the rocky ground. The scene behind him was a confusion of dust and smoke through which the armored vehicles slowly emerged. He spotted neither Mangas nor his flashlight among them.

But it was too soon to rest.

Emmett rose again and thrashed his way deeper into the woods.

9

As dawn slowly brightened outside, the basement window became a viewpoint on a life Emmett had walked away from almost two decades before. A middle-aged U.S. Army colonel with Asian features stepped from the big house along Ft. Sill's officers' row. At curbside, he took stock of the morning, the epitome of self-assurance in his natty uniform as his eyes roved the pink sky for all the pleasant possibilities the day held for him. A staff car promptly appeared and whisked him away.

Emmett realized that, in a sense, this man had taken his place in the world.

An hour later, a Comanche woman in her late thirties, with dashes of gray in her hair he found stylish, herded two little girls, twins, seven or eight years of age, out to the family SUV in the driveway. This expanse of concrete ran right up to the basement window.

Mother and daughters were bickering about something.

After the harrowing night, Emmett found the argument reassuring for all its normalcy and was disappointed when their voices were cut short by the firing up of the engine of the Nissan Pathfinder.

The woman drove her children down the street, probably toward school. An ordinary Monday morning.

For everybody except Emmett Parker.

Her name, presumed from the placard he'd located out front of the house two hours before daylight, was Mrs. P. Chin. He had met her at the Indian mission, a black-haired girl from Stephens County who was more handsome than pretty, more driven than most to make something of herself. She'd liked to draw and make clothes in school, and in the three years Emmett and Christine were married, she'd been single-minded in her determination to become a fashion designer. He wondered if, now given the right man, she contented herself with caring for her husband and girls. He also wondered if some lack in Emmett Parker had spawned that fiery ambition of hers back then.

As soon as the Nissan was out of sight, Emmett climbed down off the steamer trunk on which he'd stood to look out the window. He returned to the dirty laundry heaped before the washer and drier on which he'd slept poorly for an hour before Colonel Chin's closing the front door awakened him. He lay down again, surrounded by the unfamiliar smells of a family that was not his own. He could not detect the Christine he had known in any of these smells. Different soaps and perfumes from when they'd lived together. After his trek across the live-fire range, his own clothes were a torn and stinking mess. He wanted to wash them, but expected Christine to come back shortly.

He'd just drifted off when a sound sat him up.

A vehicle was cruising ever so slowly down the street. He knew the sound well from his years as a patrolman.

He shot to his feet, igniting another fit of coughing that had dogged him most of the night. Fighting it behind his fist, he crossed the shadowy basement and again mounted the steamer trunk. He showed no more of his face than he had to. A Department of Defense police car was creeping past, the two cops carefully looking over each and every stately house. He flinched back behind the edge of the window and waited for the sound to recede.

It did, but all too slowly.

Twenty minutes later, Christine parked in the driveway and headed inside, walking just past the window on her way to the front stoop. Emmett was tempted to beckon to her through the glass but decided against it. The last thing he wanted to do was frighten her, but he had no idea how to alert her to his presence without scaring her.

He sat on the trunk to think.

Soon, the basement door creaked open. Light from above fanned down the wooden stairs, split by a human shadow that began descending toward him. Legs appeared, then the entire woman, holding a full laundry basket before her. He watched her come down, unable to speak. He couldn't think of anything to say, anything to explain his busting in on her life like this. He was still waiting for the words to come when she caught sight of him from the corner of her eye.

Gasping, she dropped the basket.

"Christine," he said, rising, "it's Emmett."

A long moment passed in wide-eyed silence before she asked, "What're you doing here . . . ?" He was about to stammer that he needed her help, that he'd had no other choice than to approach her, when she answered her own question. "*You're* the reason the security level got bumped up this morning."

"I'm the reason," he admitted, then coughed again. It now rumbled deep in his chest. "Are the gates locked down?"

"No, but the guards are going through all the cars." She reached up and pulled the chain to a light fixture, apparently so she could see him clearer. She still colored her long fingernails with maroon polish. He'd had no idea how bad he looked until she winced. "What *happened* to you?"

"Got caught in an artillery barrage last night."

"How could you be so stupid?"

"I just was."

"Well, the brave die young," she said, "and the stupid are lucky." It was something of a Comanche axiom. Her tone was casual and slightly mocking, as befit a *Nuhmuhnuh* woman, but he watched her appraising the situation. He'd brought danger to her doorstep, and she had to think of her family, foremost. He expected no less of her.

"Listen, Christine—"

"Shut up and wait here." With that, she went up the stairs and closed the door behind her.

Sinking back down onto the trunk, he told himself that the ice had been broken. A milestone. But remembering their unhappy past, she had no reason to risk anything for him. He felt helpless, even more helpless than he had at three this morning when he'd come up with this desperate idea. While he'd successfully crossed the length of Ft. Sill and evaded motor patrols and a Blackhawk helicopter sent out to find him, he knew he had little if no hope of getting off the post on foot. Not with perimeter security at its highest level in months. His last reserves of energy were used up, and one especially hard fit of coughing left the taste of blood in his mouth. That's when he'd seen no choice other than to break into Colonel and Mrs. Chin's basement. There, at their laundry sink, he had his first drink of water after hours of clawing through scrub woods.

What if she'd gone upstairs to phone the Department of Defense police?

As much as this suspicion made him want to bolt, he had to sleep. Soon. He had to win her trust if only long enough for him to sink down on that pile of soiled laundry and sleep. He told himself that turning him in wasn't the Comanche thing to do. Starting with the early reservation period, you never handed over a brother or a sister to white law, which was severe and often incomprehensible, even if you disagreed with what the offender had done.

But he was also dealing with an ex-wife, and the risk in that transcended culture.

The door above creaked open again.

She came down, but with a more halting step this time, as if she'd made up her mind about something and didn't want to break it to him.

But then Emmett saw that he had it wrong. She was merely carrying a tray. On it was a plate of fry bread, a glass of orange juice and a cup of coffee. "Still black?" she asked, setting the tray on his lap.

"Yeah, thanks." He drained the cup of coffee in a few gulps and wanted more, but she'd already sat across from him on an old hardback chair.

"How'd you get inside?" she asked.

Emmett nodded at the basement window. "Unlatched. I wouldn't leave it that way in the future."

She gave him a fleeting smile. A strong face, as he fondly remembered, nicely proportioned and honest. Yet, her eyes were nervous. For him or be-cause of him? He had never wanted to crash back into her life, and he'd al-ways respected his ex-wives' privacy. But last night had taken away all his polite choices.

"Peter likes fry bread now with his breakfast," she said as if trying to sound conversational. "Mama says I'll make a *Nuhmuhnuh* of him yet." Then it seemed to hit her that this wasn't the sort of thing to say a Co-manche former husband.

Before she could apologize, Emmett said, "How is your mother?"

"Fine. Papa passed away, but mama's fine."

He dipped his head respectfully, then told her in his slightly stilted Co-manche that he was glad she was happy, that he had seen her girls and they were beautiful.

But it was clear she wanted to keep the conversation in English. "I was going to name of one of them Leah. But then changed my mind."

He kept a poker face while he chewed. Leah had been the name they'd decided on, if they'd ever had a girl. He'd wolfed down all the bread. He could eat three times that portion, but each request he made of her shamed him. He had never known he could feel so awkward. Now he knew what shy people felt like.

"What did you do, Emmett?" she blurted. "I read about your honor dance in the paper. I can't imagine—"

"They're going to say I killed Jerome."

"Jerome Crowe's dead?"

"Yes. Last night on Mt. Scott."

Tears glimmered in her eyes. Like all the girls at the mission, she'd been fond of Jerome. But then, her rigorous self-discipline took hold and her eyes cleared as she asked incredulously, "Why would you ever kill Jerome?"

"I didn't." He couldn't help but add, "You've got to believe me."

She said nothing, but he could see that she was hovering somewhere between belief and disbelief. And his mind was too fuzzy to come up with convincing explanations, even for himself. "I'm just asking for a couple hours of sleep. That's all. Then I'll go. There are people with the FBI who

don't want me to talk. I'll get in touch with my own folks at BIA law enforcement and settle this that way. I just need some rest first, Chris."

She went on staring at him in silence.

"Say something," he begged.

Sighing, she heaved herself up out of the chair and went to a shelf clut-
tered with camping gear. She removed a sleeping bag and Styrofoam pad,
unrolled both on the cement floor and gestured at the impromptu bed. "You
have to be gone by the time Peter gets home at five-thirty. And I've got to
go out before that. I want you gone when I get back. *Unha nu naksu-pana
inu?*" *Do you understand me?* A more emphatic inflection than his mother
had given to the same words to Mary Chocpoya.

"I'll be gone," he promised, although leaving the basement while it was
still light increased his chances of being caught. Still, he was relieved that
she'd spoken to him in Comanche.

"*Udah,*" she said coolly. *Thanks.*

He reclined and shut his eyes.

As Jerome died once again in that portable toilet, he reached out with a
bloody hand and touched Emmett's shoulder. He jolted awake, breath seiz-
ing in his throat and eyes flickering around in search of the slasher who'd
come and gone before he himself had ever arrived atop the mountain.

Christine had turned on the light again and was gazing down at him.

"Are you going now?" he asked.

"Not quite yet."

"What time is it?" His voice was dry.

"Three-thirty." She handed him a Coke in the can. His skinned and
swollen fingers had trouble with the pull-tab, so she helped him. Watching
her, he sensed that her mood had shifted during the time he'd slept. She'd
had hours and hours in which to dredge up the past and massage it to her
taste. Captives of the *Nuhmuhnuh* invariably reported that the women
were to be feared more than the men. "Somebody told me you have somebody. Is that so?"

Anna Turnipseed, she meant. He drained half the can before he tackled her question. "No."

"Somebody said you were getting ready to marry again."

"Your somebody got it wrong. Marriage wasn't on the table."

"Then there was somebody."

"Until recently," he said. This felt like a locker room interview after a crushing defeat, and it irked him that she was beginning to find the situation interesting.

"You ever think about us?"

"Us?"

"What happened to us?" she clarified. Not sounding nostalgic in the least.

"I try not to."

"Why not?"

He laughed helplessly, which brought a look to her face he remembered quite well. *All I need—an ex-wife to flame on me just when I need her help.* "I know I failed you, Chris."

"And how'd you fail me, Emmett?"

He tried to sit up, but his left shoulder and chest muscles were agonizingly stiff.

"Do you know why, Emmett?"

He could now visualize her pacing and fuming upstairs while he slept, revisiting all the old hurts. At forty-one, he knew what the problem was. They should have had this discussion years ago, on the night they split up for good. He, especially he, should have resolved all this then, instead of letting it dangle in the mental breezes of decades. Everything deserved its season, even bitterness.

"*Time,*" she flung at him when he failed to respond.

The second person recently to accuse him of abusing time. Wendell Padduhpony had been the other. That evening on his farm, with a thundercloud in the western sky and a full moon rising in the east, while Royce and Jerome ingested peyote in the Road Man's tent, Wendell had kept their conversation focused on the subject of time. He'd accused Emmett of having *gone white* in his concept of time. Time to white people was something to be crammed with obligations and chores. To simply experience life was held to be a waste of time. To focus on relationships was a detour away from success.

"The job, Chris," he finally said, "The P.D. took over my life. If I could go back, I'd do things differently. But I can't."

"You know the difference between Peter and you?" Her pause wasn't long enough for him to answer. "The Army tries to take over his life, too. But he *makes the time* for me and the girls."

Emmett's gaze gravitated toward the window as he tried to think of just the right thing to say, not to justify his failure but to take responsibility for it. But the magnitude of that failure, and all the others, including his most recent one with Anna Turnipseed, made his tongue feel heavy. He wanted nothing more than to storm out of this basement—and leave off things with Christine where they'd safely if not comfortably been until now: on the courthouse steps in Oklahoma City. He was still staring off through the window when fangs appeared behind the pane of glass.

A German shepherd was barking at him.

Emmett started to roll for the shadows when Christine told him, hushed, "Stay still." She flicked off the light, scooped an armful of clothes up off the laundry pile and covered him. Shifting slightly, he peered out as a military policeman, with a pistol in one hand and the dog's lead in the other, crouched down into the window frame. He'd spotted at least Christine, for he ordered the shepherd to settle down and tapped on the glass with a knuckle.

She stepped up onto the trunk, as Emmett had earlier, and unlatched the window so she could speak to the MP, who asked, "Is everything okay, Mrs. Chin?"

"Yes. What's going on?"

"There's a fugitive loose on the post, ma'am. And we've tracked him to this neighborhood. Are all your doors and windows secure?"

"I think so, Sergeant."

"Why don't you make sure while I stand by here?"

"Very well."

Emmett could hear Christine hurrying upstairs. One thought occupied his dry-mouthed wait for her return. Had Michael Mangas recalled that one of Emmett's exes had remarried an Army officer and presently lived on the post? *Maybe not, hopefully not.* Mangas had gone to the Ft. Sill Indian School, not the mission near Anadarko where Emmett had met and fallen in love with Christine. On the other hand, he knew most members of the tribe still living in and around Lawton, and one glaring thing lent credence to the FBI agent guessing Emmett might turn to his first wife: An MP was squatting on his heels with weapon drawn outside her house.

If this was not enough, he recalled something unpleasant. During a fight in their final bitter months together, Christine had promised him *one day you'll get yours.*

Had that day arrived?

But she returned to the basement and told the MP that all her doors and windows were locked. *Bless her.*

Still, he didn't budge. "Would you feel comfortable if my dog and I went through the house for you?"

"There's no need," she said. "Somebody's been home all the while, and the colonel will be back soon."

"As you wish, ma'am." The MP sergeant rose, then strode away from the window—after glancing over the interior of her Nissan Pathfinder.

Christine left the window open.

Emmett sat up and exhaled.

"Wait here," she said with a new resolve in her voice. She went outside and, inexplicably, started up the SUV. She pulled out of the driveway, but only a car-length before turning around and backing up until the tailgate was within four feet of the window.

At last, he understood. When she came down the stairs again, he said, "I can't thank you—"

"Don't try." She yanked a dusty quilt off one of the camping-gear shelves. Yet, over the next several seconds, a change came over her, and when she spoke again her tone was softer, making him suspect that after all these years she'd finally taken her piece out of him and was satisfied. "There's something different about you. I don't know if you're really sorry, but you're sad. Sad like you finally know what it's like to be crushed." End of topic. "I'm going to put this quilt in the back of my Pathfinder. As soon as I go into the house again, crawl inside and cover yourself. I'll pull the cargo cover and close the tailgate. Got it?"

"Yes." He resisted thanking her again.

"Remember that trip we took to Europe?" she asked.

"Of course."

"That's mostly how I remember you. On that trip. Everything turns to shit when I think about you here in Oklahoma. You and Oklahoma were never meant for each other." Then, once more, she trekked up the stairs.

Welcome home.

As he waited, crouched on top of the steamer trunk, he heard the phone ring upstairs. But she let it ring. She went outside and dumped the quilt in the back of the SUV. Then she stood there, surveying the street with a wrapped present under her arm. He watched her, noticed the thin sweat on her upper lip. But her body English told him that the MP and his dog were no longer in sight. She deposited the present on the front passenger seat and strolled back inside the house.

Instantly, Emmett grasped the transom post and began to muscle himself up over the window frame, which was open to the hot afternoon. His chest wound sent fingers of lightning through his brain, but he held on to the transom long enough to swing his legs outside. From there, he planted his shoes on the pavement and did a painful limbo-dance maneuver until his head was clear of the opening. Without taking a glance up or down officers' row, he scrambled into the cargo area, kept as low as he could and unfurled the quilt over himself. Despite the open rear hatch, the interior of the SUV was sweltering. Sweating like crazy under the quilt, he listened for Christine to come out.

Nothing.

From down the block came barking. The German shepherd? And if so, had the police dog caught his scent?

The cargo cover was extended with a snap, making him jump. Then the tailgate was slammed shut.

Christine got behind the wheel and started the motor. And more importantly, the air conditioner, although it was some minutes before the coolness worked its way back to him. By then, he was drenched in sweat. "I'll pick up my girls at the post elementary school," she said from up front. "They're invited to a birthday party in town. We'll go out through the main gate. I'll drop off the twins at the party and drive to the Indian hospital. I'll park and go inside . . ." She braked and tapped her horn. Didn't explain as she sped up. ". . . to see a sick friend. I'll park around back, close to the old school. Don't say anything unless you object."

He didn't. A good enough plan. He was familiar with the grounds of the now-abandoned Ft. Sill Indian School. They were screened from the eastern edge of Lawton by the woods along Cache Creek.

The Pathfinder stopped, one door and then another swung open, letting in the heat again, and Emmett could hear children's voices. A happy babble of them that was reduced to two as doors were shut and Christine drove away from the school. She identified her daughters for him: "How was school, Beth and Maryanne?"

"Fine, Mom."

"Okay." As in the case of most siblings, one personality was more positive than the other. The latter groused about a spelling quiz slated for tomorrow, then cut herself off and asked anxiously, "Did you remember the present?"

"It's up here with me," the other responded.

He listened for hints of the girl Christine in their voices, but the inflections weren't hers. Perhaps they took more after their father. Strange, to meet the children—however awkwardly—of someone you had loved.

They hadn't gone far when Christine slowed and then stopped altogether. "Would you look at this line?" she complained, alerting him to the logjam at the gatehouse exit.

His stomach knotted for the coming wait.

"There's a killer on the post," one of the twins reported enthusiastically.

Christine asked, "How do you know that?"

"A policeman came to our school and stayed all day."

"He stabbed a guy up on Mt. Scott," the other told Christine.

Silence, but for the whirring of the air-conditioner fans. Emmett tried to imagine Christine's face as this detail sank in. Was she having second thoughts, particularly with her two girls in the car? What was she thinking?

"Mama, something stinks in here."

Emmett froze. His last shower had been yesterday morning.

Christine laughed, unconcerned. "Oh, don't mind it. I gave our gardener, Mr. Gomez, a lift to the PX." Yet, Emmett heard how her tone at the end of the fib drifted off into worry.

One of the girls had noticed, too. "What's wrong, Mama?"

"Nothing. Why do you ask?"

"You don't look happy."

"Maybe I'm not. You can't be happy all the time."

This one, obviously the little clairvoyant in the family, persisted: "What are you thinking about?"

"Something sad, Beth."

"Like what?"

"Oh, a story about Quanah Parker I heard once."

"I know who Quanah Parker was."

"Shut up, Maryanne," Beth said. "Everybody knows who Quanah Parker was. Our class went to his grave in the cemetery."

Emmett smiled beneath the quilt. But it faded as the SUV inched forward only to stop again.

"What was the story about Quanah, Mama?"

"Oh," Christine said, "when the Army killed most of our horses at Palo Duro, the People had to come in off the plains. They couldn't ride to hunt the few buffalo that were left—"

"Mama did a painting of the Army killing the horses," Beth explained to Maryanne.

"I know that."

Christine quashed their little argument by going on in the same melancholy voice, "Quanah and the Antelope Eaters were the last to come in. That's because they'd been smart about hiding the few horses they had left. As he rode with his children toward the fort, he told them that soon he'd be separated from them. The soldiers would take him from his family and they might not see him for a long, long time. . . ." She paused as she drove a few yards and braked again, making progress toward the gatehouse. He had never let her see his revolver in the basement. He'd stuffed it in his sock and fastened it to his ankle with some twine he'd found on the workbench. And now he didn't even want to think about a confrontation with the Department of Defense police that might make him draw his .357.

She'd put the safety of her children in his hands.

"Quanah's children didn't understand why the Army would take him away," Christine went on. She was good storyteller. The knack ran in her family. "So Quanah told them how it was different with war chiefs. The Army thought the war chiefs were bad men. They didn't understand—"

"Mama, is Daddy a war chief?"

"Yes, Maryanne. The Army didn't understand the People turned to a war chief to protect them. That was his job. Not to make trouble, but to protect his family and friends. So Quanah told his children how the Army would lock him up in the stockade when they got there. Maybe, they wouldn't be allowed to see him."

"Ever again?" Beth asked, her voice cracking.

"Maybe. Some of the war chiefs were being sent far away to Florida. So maybe never again. What would you do if you might never see your daddy again . . . ?"

Troubled silence as the twins considered Quanah's plight. Then snuffling. One of them was crying. No doubt, Beth, as the sounds seemed to be coming from the far front.

There was a whine as Christine powered down her window. "Afternoon, ma'am," a businesslike male voice said. "May I see your post identification, please?"

"Sure, Officer."

A shadow flickered past the seam between the cargo cover and the side window over Emmett: He surmised that a second cop was wending his way around the vehicle, examining everything in plain sight. No indication that a dog was working with them. Emmett had closed his right fist around his revolver grips. He didn't know what he might do in the coming moments, but he couldn't let go of his .357. If he did, he would wind up in Mangas's grasp. Inevitably, he would wind up like Jerome.

"What's wrong with the little girl?" the first officer asked.

"Oh," Christine said, "we're late for a birthday party."

"I'm sorry, little lady. Ma'am, who's your husband?"

"Colonel Chin. With the Judge Advocate's office."

A voice just outside the rear window from Emmett said, "Ma'am, you mind popping the rear hatch so I can have a look inside?"

A scenario ran through Emmett's mind in flickering-fast images. Lunging at the officer as soon as he opened the tailgate, disarming him on the fly, running for the gate. Not a good scenario. And it still could imperil Christine and her girls if other guards opened fire on him.

The first officer said, "Never mind, Walt. Thank you, Mrs. Chin."

Christine did nothing for a maddening second, then drove on.

Emmett let go of his revolver. His fist was still so tight he had to shake the feeling back into it.

Christine was speeding onto the interstate toward town when Beth asked, "We're not late to the party, Mama. I wasn't crying on account of the party."

"I know, honey." Even Christine seemed stymied for the moment.

"What happened to Quanah?" Maryanne asked.

"Well, when they reached the fort, his daughters got so scared the soldiers would take him away, they clung to him and cried and cried. The soldiers tried to pull the girls off him, but that only made them hold on to him harder and harder. But the soldiers were human beings, too, for in the end, the crying touched their hearts and they let Quanah stay with his family. We call this story *'Quanah Is Saved by His Daughters' Tears.'*" At last, the tension broke in her voice and she added, relieved, "That's what was making me feel sad. Just an old story."

Still hidden by the cargo cover, Emmett flipped a corner of the quilt off his face and inhaled the air-conditioned coolness.

Christine had had everything right—except the issue of orchestration.

Quanah had coached his daughters to carry on in this way when they reached the fort. He'd known how to get around the U.S. Army, even on his most powerless day.

With another long night awaiting him, he tried to draw inspiration from that.

10

MICHAEL WAS AWAKE by three-thirty, lying beside his wife in the pre-dawn quiet of their Lawton home, pretending for her sake that he was still sleeping. He suspected that she, too, was awake but didn't want to rouse him. Sleep was precious to both of them, a highly selective form of amnesia in which the brain skipped over life-shifting realities and let the past go on uninterrupted. In an hour or so, Todd, who was an early riser, would get out of bed and go to the bathroom. The toilet would flush, and his day would begin. Michael was still close enough to sleep to find this plausible. The Murrah Federal Building had never gone down in fire and smoke, and Todd would be waiting for him out in the kitchen, as he had every morning before he moved to the home in Oklahoma City.

Yet, Michael's slowly-waking mind was already coming to terms with the 1995 collapse.

Jeralyn's was not, for she murmured something in Caddoan, her native tongue. Murmured as a mother would to her child. That was the tone, and it pained Michael.

The Caddos had their own way to deal with grief. An agricultural people from the Red River country that extended all the way to Louisiana, they held a series of funerary feasts on the tribal dance grounds near Binger. The first for Todd had come six days after his body was found in the rubble. Michael had been too numb to recall much of it now. Then Todd's death was memorialized one, two and three years thereafter. The last feast stuck in his mind better than the others, although Jeralyn and he had had to personally prepare all of them. That which was not consumed was buried atop the remains of the ceremonial cooking fire. For Todd to partake of. That's what the Caddos believed. Michael recalled the plop of each piece of cold fry bread as he tossed it onto the muddy bed of ashes. Todd had been very fond of fry bread. Then a tribal holy man, a large and gentle soul, commanded all present to put aside their tears and rejoice that Todd Mangas was in a better place.

Apparently, in sleep, Jeralyn had forgotten that commandment from Todd's last feast.

Michael trusted that his son was in a better place. Not from any religious conviction. But from peyote. He had been there.

Like many cops, Michael had gotten his bachelors degree late, information systems with a minor in criminal justice at Lawton's Cameron University. But he had liked philosophy much more than computer science. Especially Plato, who said something to the effect that the idea in the mind is more true than material objects the eye sees. To Michael, peyote was not an hallucinogen. He'd come to rely on the cactus bud not because it let him escape into hallucination but because it cracked a hidden door on that truer reality, a universe of heightened color and dimension in which Todd still existed, in which father and son could still interact.

Something vibrated against his hip bone. His pager.

Before retiring, he'd clipped his FBI pager to the elastic waistband of his pajama bottoms and put it on vibration-alert so as not to disturb Jeralyn. He now eased out of bed and shut the door behind him. He kept his clothes and service weapon in the hall closet, all so she might go on dreaming.

He read his pager: The summons was from Ramsey, the agent from Elk City who was staying at the Marriott in town with the task force assembled to nab Parker. The shootout with the fugitive had rattled the kid. But he'd quickly recovered his nerve. He just needed some mentoring to mature as an agent, but mentoring was in short supply in the competitive white world.

Michael grabbed his cell phone from the charger in the kitchen.

Ramsey sounded wide awake. And excited. "One of your taps just paid off."

"Which one?" Michael asked, although he'd already guessed.

"Wendell Padduhpony's phone."

Of all the phone taps he'd requested yesterday, this one had agonized Michael the most. A grasp at straws to reconnect with Parker before the trail got cold. First, Michael had gotten court permission to tape Celia Parker's line, then those of other relations. Finally, as the hour grew late and the Army sweeps on the post continued to come up empty-handed, he hounded the judge for one more tap—Wendell's phone. After all the things Michael had told the elder in confidence, it felt like betraying the old man. But the FBI agent within Michael had gone ahead with this betrayal, realizing that Parker would turn to Wendell in his desperation, as he himself had done.

"What was said?" he asked Ramsey.

"We're waiting for you to tell us from the tape. It sounded like Comanche."

"Are you sure it was Parker?"

"Yes. Same voice I heard up on Mt. Scott."

"Could Oklahoma Bell pinpoint the line he used?"

"A pay phone outside the hall at the Comanche Reformed Church."

Michael thought only a second. "All right, wake up the boys and get them ready to roll in ten minutes. Long guns and whatever night vision gear we've got. Then advise Lawton P.D. and the S.O. to yank anybody they've got patrolling the east-side. Keep them out. I promise there will be hell to pay if they screw this up."

"You want us to hit the church right away?"

"No. Just stand by 'til I get there."

"See you in ten." Ramsey disconnected.

Michael hurried into the spare bathroom. Unlike many Comanches and Apaches who bore the blood of captive Mexicans, he'd never had much of a beard. He skipped shaving but smoothed down his hair with water and his comb. The mirror reminded him of something he'd forgotten: The bandage on the side of his neck where a piece of shrapnel had nicked him the night before last. He grinned and shook his head at the thought of Parker running through a firestorm of hot metal to escape arrest. Things like this amused him, and he wasn't even sure why. Jeralyn said it was the Chiricahua in him. But he wasn't amused to think of how many others Parker might have murdered over the years in addition to the Eskimo, Calvin Ushuk, and his own closest boyhood friend, Jerome Crowe.

Today might tell.

Michael quickly dressed but lingered at the closet door a moment, cradling his pistol in his hands and studying it. Life was full of unpleasant ironies. Two weeks ago, he had invited Parker to join the Thunder Dogs Society. As Keeper of the Pipe, Michael had held out that pipe to him in brotherhood. Now, in the next few hours, he might have to kill the same man.

Michael slipped his 9mm into his belt holster.

Seven minutes later, he was riding the elevator in the Marriott to the second floor, where the FBI had rented an entire wing and set up a command post in the Quanah Parker Conference Room. All the agents were assembled in the CP, doing their best to empty the coffee urn. Ramsey handed Michael a steaming cup. "Let's hear that tape, Dustin."

Ramsey motioned to a sleepy-eyed technician, who played it for Michael. Definitely a Comanche exchange between Parker and Wendell. Emmett made a reference to Mt. Scott: *pia toya*, the big mountain. And *nakwu soo kuni*, east Lawton. There was much more, but it was obviously coded, veiled references to things familiar only to Parker and Padduhpony. Sadly, Wendell's tone sounded helpful, a grandfather helping his grandson. Not even an errant grandson.

"That's enough," Michael told the techie. He had all he needed, given the time constraints. "Listen up, people—we knew Parker had to sleep sometime. Now we know where."

"At the Yellow Mission?" Weeks, one of his Lawton agents, asked.

"Don't bet on it. Parker made his call from the Comanche Reformed Church, better known as the Yellow Mission," Michael explained to the out-of-town agents. "We'll let the S.O. check that out. But I'm going to gamble he's holed up across the interstate on the grounds of the Ft. Sill Indian School."

"Potential hostages?" the leader of one of two tactical teams, a hawk-nosed female, asked.

"Negative," Michael replied, "the school's been closed for years. However, the Indian Health Service hospital next door is still up and running. Evacuation is not an option, so I want the facility secured behind the perimeter we clamp around the school. I'm familiar with the grounds, so I'll lead the insertion team."

The female agent tried again. "But—"

"Butts are what we've got to get moving. Our intelligence is now thirty minutes old. Old intelligence and old fish have a lot in common. . . ." The agents began taking their long guns and equipment off a table at the back. "Remember, people—this is a high-risk felony takedown. Nothing less. You are not dealing with a fellow law enforcement officer. You are dealing with an armed and determined suspect who now stands accused of two homicides. Do not hesitate to drop him, if the need arises, because Parker will not hesitate to drop you. Good luck." On the way out the door, he lowered his voice to Ramsey, "Alert the state police and sheriff's office to stop any U-Haul vans that approach the old school."

"Pardon?"

"I want Wendell Padduhpony detained if he tries to reach Parker. Let's move."

Yesterday afternoon, as Christine had pulled into the Indian hospital parking lot, Emmett had been tempted to ask her to call his mother and tell her that he was well. Everything would be fine in the end. But his ex-wife had already risked so much for him—her marriage and even the safety of her little girls—he couldn't bring himself to do it. Besides, he had no doubt now that the FBI was tapping his mother's line. So, minutes ago, he'd asked Wendell in his halting Comanche to personally convey that message to Celia.

Emmett's call from the Yellow Mission had been brief and to the point. Wendell was given every opportunity to refuse him help. He didn't. And although he referred to the accusations being made against Emmett on television and in the newspapers, he passed no judgment on them. *Kutseena haitsu* was staying the night with him in Walters, and he would send this *coyote-friend* to fetch Emmett where I-44 bridged Cache Creek. The place was at the western border of the abandoned school, and he agreed. In an hour, then. The most emotional moment had come at the end of the conversation, when he tried to thank Wendell. He got choked up, but the elder just laughed and said, "Don't get all maudlin on me, *Tuah*. You're not home free yet."

Emmett then dashed back across the interstate to the school and hid in the mouth of the tubular fire escape on the administration building. His brother Malcolm and he had been caught sliding down it. One of numerous violations that eventually led to their expulsion from the BIA institution and transfer to the Catholic mission.

The Ft. Sill Indian School was much as he remembered it: tan brick buildings perched on a grassy knoll above Cache Creek, and his waking moments during the night were filled with memories as he kept checking the quadrangle. Hobo football—a chaotic variation on the sport, played with a rag ball—on that quad in summer and fall, sledding in winter where the grass sloped down to the street. Sobbing at night in the dorms, especially from the new arrivals who'd been shorn and uniformed that day. Navajo kids, especially, took losing their traditional hair and dress hard. He visualized a young Jerome Crowe as one of those boys, sitting rigidly in the barber's chair, trying to ignore his severed locks tumbling to the floor. But that was absurd. Jerome had never gone to school here. His death was coloring Emmett's every thought.

But it was too soon for grief. Too soon for anything except finding a way out of this trap.

He pressed the glow button on his wristwatch. It was a quarter past four. Time to move again. To a place from which he could see the interstate bridge over the creek.

Sliding out of the metal tube, he cut across the dark and ghostly campus. He kept below the brow of the knoll as he jogged so the hospital lights wouldn't backdrop him.

Roadblocks.

Thirty hours had now passed since he'd given Mangas the slip in the artillery barrage. The FBI agent would've ordered roadblocks along key arteries, maybe even on I-44, although Emmett had seen nothing tonight to indicate that traffic was being backed up by vehicle searches. But certainly, there were blocks on lesser roads leading out of Lawton.

Don't get ahead of yourself.

He still had to get down to Cache Creek without being spotted. The FBI, S.O. and Army would have set up surveillance teams. He was less than a mile outside Ft. Sill, and the Department of Defense police and MPs wouldn't restrict their observation to the post. Some of them would have night vision gear, and their helicopter was probably equipped with an infrared scanner that would pick up the heat of his sweaty body.

His pursuers had a dozen ways to locate him.

So he'd move down to the creek only at the last possible second—when his ride arrived on the bridge above. That way, even if spotted, he had half a chance of escaping by vehicle.

Half a chance. Even that's probably optimistic.

He knelt behind a lone tree and watched the headlights on the interstate. Some traffic, but not much. Sooner or later, he expected an old GMC pickup to veer off onto the shoulder of the northbound lanes near the bridge. Seeing that, he'd run down to the creek and then up the embankment to the waiting truck.

Royce Eschiti would be behind the wheel. Only he fit Wendell's description of a *coyote-friend.* Somebody with a coyote's willful nature and a checkered past. An ex-convict. And, if there'd been any doubt remaining, Emmett had only to remember that the name Eschiti itself was derived from the words for coyote and droppings. *Coyote turd.* Thankfully, this wasn't widely known, for something had been lost in the translation from generation to generation. In Quanah's era, there had been nothing particularly derisive in the name. Shit was an acceptable part of life. It still was.

You're drifting, you're drifting.

His mind would no longer stay fastened to one thing. It had to. He had to keep focused.

Poor Royce.

Eschiti was on parole. Aiding and abetting a fleeing homicide suspect could land him back in the slammer. And in that Emmett realized something. He'd lost an essential freedom: the right to pick and choose the help offered him. He had lost one of the cornerstones of self-pride. As with Christine, he had to impose on others.

A sedan took the exit just north of the hospital, well within the off-ramp speed limit. He thought nothing of it, scarcely noticed it, until about one minute later another sedan got off the interstate there at the same speed. Emmett lit up his watch face and began timing. A minute later, another sedan took the exit.

Suddenly, he hoped that Royce wouldn't show up on the bridge.

All bets were off. Mangas was making blanket taps. And it was now clear they included Wendell's phone.

Emmett turned and melted back into the buildings.

As always, it took longer than expected to throw a cordon around the search area. The trouble, and inevitably there was trouble, came along Cache Creek. One of two field office agents posted down there stumbled into the stream, which was running high this time of year, and had to be rescued by his partner. While all of this was being played out over the radio, Michael waited with the insertion team in a field north of the Indian hospital.

The only positive news to be transmitted during this time came from the sheriff's department: Their SWAT team had cleared the Yellow Mission and come up with no sign of Parker. Michael asked for their identification technician to dust the surfaces of the pay phone there for latent fingerprints—this evidence would lend credence to Emmett's having made the call to Wendell, should voice print analysis of the tape prove inconclusive, as it often did.

Eight minutes later, the school was finally sealed off.

In his bucar, Michael led a van down the frontage road to the hospital. The van contained one of the two SWAT teams out of Oklahoma City. The agents who'd secured the medical facility had the staff draw all the window blinds and turn off the floodlights shining down on the lot, so the two FBI vehicles parked in near darkness. Michael reached up and switched off his dome light before bailing out.

Immediately, he drew his 9mm and looked all around. He grasped his flashlight but didn't turn it on. The half-moon had set, but he could see well enough by the stars.

It would be like Parker to strike first, unexpectedly, while the insertion team was still organizing itself. So Michael brusquely waved off the team leader, who wanted a whispered conference about God-knew-what, and started for the nearest building, the old dining hall. The smell came back to him as he inserted the key into the rusty door lock—disinfectant and stale food. English only spoken. He had the keys to most of the federal properties in the area, but now wondered if he'd brought along the right master.

The lock was rusty from disuse.

The tumblers finally turned, and he nudged back the door to let the team scouts enter first. Through a small window of chicken-wired glass, he watched them working down the corridor that had once been thronged with his classmates, mostly from the plains tribes, but with Indians from all over the West. Their voices reached out to him across the years, but not fondly. He had never been happy here, even though it was only a few miles from his parents' home in west Lawton. Maybe the homesickness of so many around him had been infectious.

The scouts, wearing night vision goggles, worked in darkness. The rest of the team followed. Michael, who had no goggles, trailed the rear guard at a safe distance so as not to bump into him. Their boots crackled over broken crockery. The school had been vandalized since its closure and never really cleaned up.

A voice came through the earpiece to his Handie-Talkie: one of the soaked agents on the south end. He had movement coming at him through the trees from the direction of the big building. The old administration building, he probably meant. Michael acknowledged, then snapped his fingers, trying unsuccessfully to get the attention of the rear guard. By now, the entire team had filed into the kitchen and was searching it.

Michael knew he couldn't delay. Parker would be gone again in the blink of an eye.

Backtracking, he used his flashlight to find the old footpath across the quad, through the overgrown bushes and stone memorials to long-ago classes. Just before the knoll fell away to the south there was a row of darkened bungalows in which school staff had once resided. Parker wouldn't be so foolish as to hole up in one of them. He knew that his only chance was in staying on the move.

Thumbing off his light, Michael ignored the cottages as he ran toward the creek, slowing for a few seconds to finally advise everyone by radio that he was in foot pursuit.

He came to the woods through which Cache Creek meandered, sluggishly most of the year but roiling high and noisy now. These were the same, dense, thorny woods where, in the fall, Emmett, Malcolm, Michael and the other boys had fought wars with the baseball-sized fruits of the osage orange trees—*bo-dark* trees, as Jeralyn called them, in her fractured Caddo-French for *bois d'arc*, wood of the bow. Somehow, it'd been voted that Michael was Geronimo and Emmett was Quanah, and the animosity between the two chiefs was rekindled when Emmett hit Michael squarely in the head with one of the hard fruits. From there, the two boys had resorted to fists.

Michael dropped his gait to a walk as he slipped silently through the spiky branches.

Headlights flickered through the trees.

When they slowed and then stopped along Cache Road, Emmett knew what was happening. Mangas was throwing a cordon around the school grounds. Exactly what Emmett himself would do, if the shoe were on the other foot. Reaching the interstate bridge on the west side of the campus was now out of the question. Too much open ground to cover.

So he struck south, where the rolling countryside was thickly wooded, but avoided the dirt lane that dipped down to the creek. It was still soft from the spring rains, and the tracks he left would be deep and distinct. Instead, he kept to the trees, mostly osage orange saplings. The thorns ripped at his face and bare arms, but he kept pushing through the undergrowth. These cuts were nothing compared to the pain his five-month-old chest wound gave him. He could feel rib cartilage tearing with each breath, and he was sure those gasping breaths could be heard fifty yards away. That's where he figured at least two FBI agents were hunkered down, waiting for him to ford the creek and scramble up the road embankment on its far side.

Emmett halted. He'd caught a new noise to the rear.

What now?

Straining to pick it up again, he tried to hold his breath. But he was just too starved for air. He sucked down a lungful and starting coughing. The grips to his .357 were slick in his sweaty palm. He'd removed it from his makeshift ankle holster of sock and twine on the promise to himself that he'd use his last four rounds only for covering fire. In case the agents opened up on him first. But what if the threat came at him out of the blue? What if he had no choice but to drop his attacker?

Damn Michael Mangas. Damn him for dragging other cops into this!

Trying to control his coughing, Emmett had taken three stumbling steps toward the creek when a familiar voice echoed at him from behind: "We've got you hemmed in, Parker!" It was Mangas.

Emmett looked skyward. Had the chopper spotted him with its infrared? The heat-seeking scanner cut through foliage; night vision goggles didn't. But he saw no sign of the Blackhawk, heard no rotors strumming the air. Gambling that the agents didn't yet have him in their gun sights, he kept plodding toward the creek.

"Emmett," Mangas went on, "think of your mother!"

He froze on those words.

They had killed Jerome. They'd tried to kill him. But it had never really occurred to him they'd threaten his mother. Wasn't that what Mangas was saying? In all the wars the *Nuhmuhnuh* had known, their families had been in play. He had to remember that now.

Fuck that son of a bitch!

Emmett spun around and started back, crashing through the dead branches on the woodland floor, mindless of the racket he was making as he ran. He was going to put a bullet in Mangas's head here and now. He was going to end it tonight.

Again, Mangas called to him: "She has to be worried sick. Don't do this to her, Emmett. Sing out, and I'll come to you. I won't let anybody else get close to you . . . no itchy trigger fingers . . . all right?"

Emmett stopped again and spat blood. The salty taste of blood was left on his tongue.

Seemingly, Mangas had just softened his threat against Celia Parker. But he had also urged Emmett surrender to him. Personally. Was that so there'd be no witnesses to the execution? And Mangas had not ordered Emmett to throw down his revolver. He wanted Parker's dead fist to be found wrapped around the grips of the weapon he'd refused to throw down.

Think . . . think!

Emmett ran a hand over his damp hair. *Don't play into Mangas's trap.* The FBI agent might have taken months, even years to put this all together. And, in the space of a few reckless seconds, Emmett could put the frosting on that plan for him. *Slow down.* Get out of the area, rest, collect your wits and piece together the next move. He felt the middle of his chest. His heart galloped and twitched like it wanted to get out of his rib cage. He took more deep breaths, trying to calm it. His biggest fear was that his body would give out before he could clear his name. But in that he had a reason to push on no matter what. Death now would be ignominious.

He headed south once more. Toward Cache Creek. There might be a crack in the perimeter the FBI had thrown around him, one seam Mangas might not know about. During their last year at the BIA school, Emmett and his younger brother, Malcolm, had run away, repeatedly. None of these escapes would've been possible without their secret passageway into the heart of Lawton.

Emmett broke from the trees.

He'd reached the water's edge. He scanned Cache Road from behind a large stump but couldn't pick out the agents posted along this flank. Waiting wouldn't help. With each passing second, the cordon grew tighter and stronger. And he had the sense that Mangas was pressing him from behind again. He pocketed his revolver, waded out into the swift shallows and lay down. The current carried him along, faster than he wanted, so he dragged his fingers along the muddy bottom. The cool water felt good, and he wanted to linger in it, gather his strength in its liquid comfort.

But there was no time.

He had to find the outlet to a storm drain that ran from central Lawton to Cache Creek. If it still existed. It could have been abandoned, like the school, and left to collapse in on itself.

The moon was down and there was little starlight. His eyes ached from so many hours of looking out for danger.

Suddenly, he dug in his heels and resisted the current: A black and circular shadow showed in the embankment. But at the same time over the burbling of the creek came the unmistakable clack of a cartridge being chambered in a rifle. Emmett ducked his head under the surface and let the flow sweep him up against the next bend. There, he reached out of the water and seized a clump of grass. He didn't stand. Instead, he pulled himself up onto the bank by slithering on his belly and keeping the side of his face flush to the muddy ground.

Out in the woods, a human voice was murmuring. As if quietly transmitting over a Handie-Talkie. Mangas. He was nearing the creek. And perhaps he, not Emmett, had spooked the agent waiting on the roadbed above to ready his assault rifle.

Emmett had to make use of this slight confusion. Without a moment's delay.

He crawled up to the storm drain's outlet. Some foul-smelling water trickled from it. But, worse than that, the opening was now grated. Someone had welded iron bars over it, probably after enough runaways from the BIA school had made use of the pipe to get into town. He yanked on the bars, hoping for rust to have weakened them over the years.

But they held firm.

He was on the verge of turning away when he realized that the upper end of one of the bars had been pried downward, almost bent double, leaving a space. A tight one, but a space.

God bless the little miscreant who'd found a way to do this.

But at that instant a beam of light stretched out over the water and swept along the sloping face of the embankment.

"See anything, Michael?" a voice asked from above.

Then Mangas hushed from directly behind the glare of the flashlight he held, "Quiet—he went into the creek right here."

"Want me to call the dogs?"

"Quiet, for shit sake!" Mangas hissed.

The beam passed over Emmett, but he stayed huddled at the base of the outlet, arms thrown over his head and eyes shut so they wouldn't reflect the light. As soon as it had swept past him, he rose and jammed his upper body into the opening. He could squeeze inside no farther than his chest, which throbbed under the pressure of the bars. He exhaled, forced every bit of air out of his lungs until dizziness came over him and his ears began to ring. Only then could he writhe and wriggle the rest of the way inside.

He felt safe within the four-foot diameter of that darkened tube.

But only briefly.

Two yards on, the drain was blocked by a logjam from base to top. He explored it with his hands. Mostly driftwood and refuse, glued together with silt that was still moist from the last rains. He clawed at the uppermost part of it, tearing away branches one by one, pausing only to feel with a fumbling hand to test the size of the opening he was creating.

Progress was slow.

Behind him, outside, he could hear someone splashing across the creek. Mangas, probably, fording to this side.

Again, Emmett thrust himself into another small opening and scuttled forward. The jagged ends of broken branches snagged his already torn undershirt, but he pushed on, shoving the loose debris before him until it abruptly fell away.

He'd reached another cavity. He slid down into it. The blackness was almost total. But only momentarily. Then a faint light winked onto his back. It broke over the top of the logjam, flickering through the opening he'd just dug. He could hear excited shouting outside.

Bending at the waist to keep from bumping his head, Emmett ran blindly into the darkness before him. The air was cool but stale. His wet clothes squished at his armpits and crotch. He tripped over a sand bar, bounded up again and kept splashing forward.

By now, Mangas would be arranging for the main storm drain to be sealed off. It originated downtown, close to the movie theater, more than a mile away. But the tributary pipes that fed it were too narrow to crawl through, most only fifteen-inches in diameter. The agent would raise the P.D. by radio and the police would raise the city engineer, who'd provide the manhunt with the exact locale of each and every egress. A cop would be waiting at each of those portals, weapon drawn. And the FBI might pump chemical agents, such as tear gas, into the system. Even nonlethal agents became lethal in confined spaces: These gasses simply displaced the oxygen and suffocated you to death. Mangas would know that. There were ways for him to make sure Emmett never saw the sun rise—tactics an unsuspecting grand jury would buy as being justifiable.

It was almost a curse to know what was coming next. It robbed Emmett of hope.

All at once, the air smelled fresh. Full of the prairie night above.

Emmett backtracked to the spot where the freshness had first sifted down over him. He peered up through a circular opening, through which a lone star shone. It was a standpipe, a vertical shaft that allowed the drain, if blocked by things such as brush dams, to overflow without bursting. He didn't recall it from any of his boyhood excursions down here, but the precaution could have been added long after Malcolm and he had moved on to St. Benedict's.

Close. I'm still too close to Cache Road.

He was tempted to hurry along the drain. Find a way out farther from Mangas and half the Oklahoma City field office, which no doubt had come down to reinforce him. But there might be no such exit.

Handholds had been welded onto one side of the standpipe to let workmen climb in and out. He pried his revolver from his pocket, cracked the cylinder to drain off as much water as he could from the barrel. Modern ammunition was crimped tightly where the bullet fit into the brass hull, and he trusted that his four last rounds would fire, as long as the barrel wasn't obstructed. He tucked the .357 in his waistband so it would be ready when he emerged into the night again.

Then he started climbing.

As he neared the top of the pipe, a loud whine made him hunker back down several rungs and wait. A Blackhawk helicopter streaked overhead, lights blinking.

Dammit! Emmett started coughing, and the sound was amplified by the pipe. He beat his chest with a fist to stop.

He'd been dancing between the rain drops for a day and a half now. The chopper was just one more raindrop. Mangas would have requested it to trace the length of the storm drain, casting its infrared sensors downward to catch Emmett on the run through the deserted streets of pre-dawn Lawton. It also meant that, from this point on, he was dead meat if he tried to make his way through the woods and across the open fields. Escape by foot was no longer possible.

The Blackhawk veered off toward town, and its whine faded into the distance.

Emmett clambered the rest of the way to the top of the pipe and gazed out. A sedan was parked on this side of the embankment, previously blocked from his view by the road itself. A silhouetted figure stood with rifle at port arms in the middle of lanes, facing the creek to the north. Emmett believed him to be the agent who'd called out to Mangas. He was dressed in ninja garb—SWAT uniform, but no bulky night-vision goggles were visible around his face.

Using the holds on the outer surface of the standpipe, Emmett slowly and quietly descended to the ground. He eased into the knee-deep grass and watched the man for the slightest hint that he'd heard something to his back.

No.

And to prove it, the rifle-toting agent stepped to the far shoulder of the road and began conversing with somebody below. Probably Mangas. Their words were unintelligible to Emmett, but the tone was urgent.

He rolled away from the pipe. Apparently, the SWAT agent was oblivious to its import, but Mangas would understand as soon as he noticed it. Emmett stayed prone, motionless. Headlights were coming down the road from the direction of the interstate. The vehicle gradually slowed to a stop, and another FBI ninja, a female—judging from her wide hips, bailed out. She'd extinguished the lights but left the motor running. She consulted briefly with the other agent, then jogged down the far embankment and out of sight.

Emmett crawled toward Cache Road. It would have been easier, psychologically, to head into the prairie behind him, but that would only delay the inevitable. The chopper would catch him if remained on foot. His sole remaining hope was to escape by vehicle, weave among the other drivers who were already beginning to throng the interstate toward work.

Dawn was pinking up the eastern horizon.

He quit crawling and found himself staring at the agent over the sights of his .357. A little voice asked him how the hell he had arrived at this moment—thinking about carjacking the FBI at gunpoint? *Don't think . . . just get away.* But the voice reminded him that the agent was undoubtedly wearing a Kevlar bullet-resistant vest. That, plus his assault rifle, would give him the confidence to fight back. *Can I drop him from behind? Can I honestly do that to a cop?*

Then, clearly and distinctly, Mangas shouted for the agent to bring him a tire iron. Of course. He was thirty or forty pounds heavier than Emmett. He was having trouble squeezing through the grate. The agent popped the trunk to the female ninja's bucar, found the iron and rushed it down the slope.

Emmett stood on rubbery knees a moment, hyperventilating. He lowered his revolver to his side and ran to the car. He had to take a few moments to steady his hand before he could turn the key in the ignition.

11

≈≈≈

UNDER THE WATCHFUL eye of her manager, the teller at the Benton County Savings and Loan in Bentonville, Arkansas, counted out the money for Agnes Snowbird. A little over eight thousand dollars in crisp new bills. At first, there had been the usual awkwardness over the amount of the BIA royalty check and the fact that the Snowbirds were new to this resort community in the foothills of the Ozark Mountains. But as soon as the manager had okayed the transaction, the teller turned congenial. Was Snowbird an Indian name? Yes, Agnes explained, Cherokee, the name of an ancestral village. And wasn't it ironic? The Snowbirds were indeed snowbirds, chasing the warm weather. She thanked the teller, swung by the manager's desk to thank her as well, then walked out. With no haste in her step. They watched you as you left, looking for an eagerness to be gone. That was a dead giveaway, so Agnes did the complete opposite. In full view of the windows, she lingered on the sidewalk and took the measure of the day. Hot and muggy. Not even noon yet.

Maybe later, when they returned to the RV park on Beaver Lake, she'd inflate her little kayak and go for a paddle in the shade of the tree-lined shore.

Finally, she continued across the street to the white-and-silver Winnebago. The generator was running to power the two air-conditioners on the roof, so it was cool inside. Seated at the kitchenette table, her husband was on his cell phone with somebody. As soon as he mumbled a few terse words in reply to something, she could tell whom. "That isn't the goddamn point. . . ." A pause followed in which her husband listened, massaging his big paunch as if his belly had begun to churn on him. She took the cash from her over-sized handbag and fanned the bills in front of his worried face, hoping to brighten his mood.

But he waved her off.

"Yeah, I understand how all this has to be sequenced in advance," he went on to the caller, his tone gradually turning more argumentative, "but originally we weren't going to hit Louisiana 'til late October. You have any idea what that bayou country is like in summer? What's wrong with Colorado and New Mexico? We could work from Pueblo down to Santa Fe cool as cucumbers and not have to have to beat the mosquitoes off with baseball bats while we did it—" He glanced at her and shook his head in frustration with the caller. "You're not listening. Why the rush to Louisiana now? That heat down there makes me sick. I'm from up north. I can take heat but not that kind of heat."

She took off her turquoise earrings and went to the refrigerator for a diet Sprite. By the time she got back to the table, her husband's voice had raised a notch. "I *know* we're not the only team in the field. Is that some kind of threat? Don't threaten me, Hola. I don't take threats kindly—"

Another listening pause.

"All right," he finally said, his lower jaw quivering slightly as it did when he was really pissed off, "as long as we're putting everything on the table today, how about giving us a fairer cut? I think twenty percent is more like what we deserve for everything we do."

She could tell by her husband's look that the caller had said no.

"Then screw you. If it's still ten percent, we're headed to Colorado. Put together something fast for, say . . ." He raised his elbows off the travel atlas he'd spread over the table and consulted it. ". . . for Amarillo and then Pueblo at least three weeks later . . ." Abruptly, he handed the cell to her. "The son of a bitch wants to talk to you."

She accepted the phone with unease. The caller's high-pitched voice and condescending tone made her skin crawl. Still, she managed to say evenly, "Yes, Hola." She had never really understood what his name meant. When, during their first phone conversation ten years ago, she had asked him to spell it, she thought he was calling himself the Spanish word for *hello*, except he pronounced the *H*.

"Talk some sense into him," Hola said. "This is a very bad time for him to turn contrary."

"I'm sorry, but he wears the pants in this family."

"Not as far as I'm concerned, dear. Women are much better than men at this business. Females tend to trust females, so I've always valued you more."

Even his compliments gave her the creeps. She'd never met him face-to-face, but she imagined he smirked as he talked. "I think we should head to Colorado," she said.

Silence.

It would've frightened her a little, except that her husband gave her a thumbs-up.

Finally, Hola said, "Very well, I'll arrange something for the two of you in Amarillo." He disconnected without another word.

"It's Amarillo," she said, handing the phone back to her husband. It was one of those fancy jobs with a scrambler for security, just like the cops had.

He dropped it into his shirt pocket and borrowed a sip from her can of Sprite. "You just have to know how to talk to that pencil-necked geek."

He, too, had never met Hola in person, but that's how she imagined him as well. Thin and geeky. Plus Indian. She had little doubt he was Indian.

"Also, we're going to take out twenty percent before we make the drop tomorrow. Let's see how he handles that."

Michael hadn't slept in two days. And, as he sped north on I-44 with Don Andreas of BIA Internal Affairs beside him in his car, he realized that he had no clear idea what hour it was. The sun, muted by a gray sheet of overcast that had yet to swirl apart into individual thunderstorm cells, was no help.

Neither was the dashboard clock. He had switched on his headlights and the digital screen had faded to black. But sometimes it was a comfort not to know the time.

Andreas had been thinking out loud for some minutes. "And how the devil did he avoid your roadblocks . . . ?"

Emmett Parker, he meant.

Once again, Michael relived trudging up the Cache Road embankment two dawns ago with the female agent out of Oklahoma City—and hearing her gasp. *Ooops.* Her bucar was missing. From that *ooops* and an admission from the shame-faced agent, Michael swiftly put it together—how Parker had exited the storm drain from the standpipe just west of the road, found her bucar with the keys in the ignition and the motor running, and driven off with the audacity he'd shown repeatedly throughout his career.

It had made Michael laugh. Something that had astonished his fellow agents, whites who didn't understand that a clever adversary deserved a laugh. "I ordered roadblocks ten miles from the scene," he told Andreas. "Parker ditched the bucar and found other transportation at mile nine."

"A motorcycle, you said?"

"Dirt bike. Used by a Mexican laborer to irrigate a big tract of sorghum. By the time Parker putt-putted across that field, he was way outside our roadblocks. He dumped the bike, probably hiked into the little burg of Sterling and hot-wired a Ford pickup, which was reported stolen yesterday evening—"

"And recovered by the airport cops on the BOLO you put out," Andreas finished for him. A Be-On-the-Look-Out. "We got time for lunch?"

Ah, so that's what time it is. Noonish. "Let's have a look at the recovery first." Lunch could wait. Mangas had no appetite, and Parker's trail was growing colder by the second. Maybe something left inside the cab of that truck would put him back on the scent. He took the get-off for Will Rogers World Airport and wound around toward the control tower, which was now partly obscured by light rainfall. The only thing Parker had left behind so far was a consensus among law enforcement that he'd somehow managed to board a flight.

Clever.

An experienced detective, he'd known that canvassing a major airport ate up investigative man-hours like nothing else. Instead of spreading his manpower throughout the surrounding countryside, where it belonged, the special-agent-in-charge of the Oklahoma City office—who now headed the task force—was focusing on the airport staff. As of yet, none of those interviews had yielded a single confirmed sighting of Parker. The agents were now working the stowaway angle, another dead horse.

"You know," Andreas said on a jaw-clicking yawn, "I can accept Emmett stealing a couple cars and a bike."

"I can't," Michael said. "Tack on three more felonies, as far as I'm concerned."

The BIA man glanced at the bandage on Michael's neck. "What I still don't get is why he crossed that artillery range under fire the other night when even an ant wouldn't crawl out of its hole."

"Desperation."

"Pardon?"

"Get ready for the possibility Parker's been involved in more crap than we know about. We haven't even scratched the surface yet. . . ." The FBI had indeed scratched the surface, starting with a search of Jerome Crowe's room at the Lawton Marriott. Convenient because that's where the agents on the task force were staying as well. The result was more than $33,000 in hundred dollar bills in a briefcase. But Michael would share none of this with the BIA. At least, not this soon. Sometimes, the best way to obscure what you knew was an overview. "I've got a feeling Crowe was the embezzler, Ushuk—our floater—the courier, and Parker the enforcer." He decided that kept it sketchy enough.

But Andreas asked, "Ushuk was courier to what?"

"Not sure. *To where* is more like the question that needs answering. Siberia, maybe."

"How'd that go down?"

"That'll be determined far above my pay grade," Michael answered, deciding it was time to dole out a bit more info. "Our Anchorage office is sending agents to Little Diomede again, as we speak. Remember, Customs was already leaning on Ushuk to explain his kayak trips to Big Diomede. That's

Russian territory. He claimed cultural reasons, but nobody was buying it. They also think he was close to cracking under the pressure when he got that mystery call."

"So, based on phone company records, you're assuming Emmett told Ushuk to come down to the lower forty-eight—and whacked him?"

"Something like that." Michael flashed his credentials to the parking attendant, and the gate arm went up for him to enter long-term parking.

"I just don't buy it," Andreas said.

Michael didn't care. If the BIA man didn't buy it after only Parker's latent fingerprints had been found on the butcher knife that had slashed Crowe, he never would.

"Why kill Ushuk so . . . so *weirdly*?"

The word gave Michael pause. He'd finally gotten a look at the rough-hewn timber cross to which the Inuit had been lashed. Missing from the police inventory report was mention of a rawhide string wrapped around the cross-beam. Attached to it was something a white evidence technician might see no significance in: the broken-off stub to a quill. At one point, an eagle plume had been fastened to the cross and allowed to dangle in the wind. When a *puhakut* turned to witchcraft, he dug a mock grave beneath the ornament and prayed for the death of his victim. When the feather fell into the little grave, the curse was complete.

For reasons he wasn't ready to defend, Michael had the feeling this Comanche touch was contrived.

He could see the Evidence Response Team van at the far end of the row, but he braked just beyond the guard shack so Andreas and he would have a few more moments of privacy. "Explain what you mean by *weirdly*."

"I mean, why tie this guy to a cross and dump him in a reservoir? Doing something like that is *mental*. Emmett's been called a lot of things, but not mental."

Michael already had an argument for that. "The night of his honor dance, I asked him to join our dancing society, the Thunder Dogs. He said, *I'm not ready right now.*"

"So?"

"He said he didn't feel up to the obligations."

"Understandable. Five months ago in Syracuse, some maniac planted an ax in his chest. He's still on the mend."

"I don't think he was referring to that. He said he didn't feel *right* about joining. I don't think Parker felt clean and worthy enough to join us. At least one part of his conscience is still functioning." Michael could tell that Andreas wasn't convinced, but the man let it slide.

"Okay, Mangas, for argument's sake—Emmett offed Ushuk six weeks ago and then Crowe last Monday night. Why Jerome? Why his old buddy from school?"

"Desperation," Michael repeated, driving forward again.

"Over what?" Andreas was beginning to sound irked.

Good. Andreas deserved to be irked. One of his men was running amok throughout Oklahoma. "We don't know yet," Michael replied. "But whatever Parker had going, it was starting to unravel on him. And the only way he saw out was to eliminate those who can testify against him. He knows that sooner or later he'll be captured, so he's busy clearing the decks for his day in court."

"Is that your read on all this?" Andreas asked.

"That's my read."

"And you're sure your agent out of Elk City identified himself to Emmett as a Feeb up on that mountain . . . ?"

Parking behind the crime scene van, Michael tried not to fault Andreas for defending Parker in little ways, such as this. Even though the man was an Internal Affairs supervisor, he would feel some loyalty for his former investigator. But you had to watch your personal loyalties as carefully as your emotions. Three days ago, he had included Wendell Padduhpony in his own circle of unquestioned loyalty.

Now he'd watch the old man and see how far he would go to help Parker.

Emmett began cutting off his hair with a paring knife. He'd bought it along with some shave cream, a disposable razor and a cellophane-wrapped ham sandwich at the convenience store around the corner. He'd also taken the precaution of lining the bathroom sink with newspaper: Days from now, he didn't want an FBI evidence technician to unscrew the trap out of this sink and discover that Emmett had altered his appearance. He knew that slight changes in manner, posture, filling one's space with more or less presence—all were more persuasive than overt disguises. But he felt the need for a dramatic change, as least until he could get off the southern plains, where he was widely known.

The motel catered to migrant workers, and he'd put on a Mexican accent to rent this room. With cash. He was down to ten dollars and some change, after his purchases. His credit cards were worse than worthless. Without a doubt, the FBI had his account numbers red-flagged. Any use would prompt a rapid response from the closest available law enforcement.

He sliced off his hair with firm strokes.

Mourning. This used to be a mourning practice. What have I lost that warrants a sense of mourning? His familiar life, he supposed. He might not connect with normalcy again for years, if ever. *Don't dwell on that. Just look for any light at the end of the tunnel.* He went on hacking off his hair. Emmett Parker had become a burden to himself. He was leaving Emmett behind, replacing him with a fierce-looking stranger who'd pass through dangers as if he were invisible. Invisibility was the best thing to have when the entire world seemed to be searching for you. It was even more valuable than strength.

A knock made him jump—and nick himself with the paring knife. A drop of blood rolled down the side of his face.

Don't overreact. There was no phone in the cheap room, so maybe the manager or housekeeping had some trivial chore to do.

Emmett tossed the knife into the paper-lined sink and crept out to the main room. He took his revolver from the nightstand drawer.

No phone and no peephole in the door.

He went to the vinyl drapes and parted an edge, ever so slightly, to look out. The man who had knocked wasn't wholly visible. Just the curvature of his muscular back and his faded Levi's where they wrinkled over his cowboy boots. Emmett scanned the scattered buildings and handful of vehicles across U.S. Route 287 for signs of the perimeter law enforcement might have thrown around the neighborhood.

He glanced back toward the bathroom. There was no way out there. Even a chimp couldn't clamber through the tiny window.

He waited for a key to turn the lock. None did.

"Who is it?" he finally demanded, still sounding Mexican.

The answer was silence.

Emmett shifted the revolver to his left hand and jerked open the door. He reached outside with his right hand for the intruder, seized him by the shift-front and pulled him inside. The intruder flinched as the muzzle of Emmett's .357 pressed against his temple—he was now a human shield who'd make any other cops on the entry team think twice about opening fire. Emmett found himself staring into the acne-scarred face of Royce Eschiti.

"*Pabi,*" the man muttered with a wry smile, "you look like shit."

Emmett kicked the door shut and patted down Royce for weapons. He was clean. "How'd you find me here?" Here was the small town of Quanah, seven miles inside Texas from the Oklahoma border and named in honor of his great-grandfather.

"Wendell."

Wrong answer. Emmett hadn't talked to Padduhpony since that FBI-tapped call from the pay phone at Yellow Mission, nor would he anytime soon. He used the revolver to motion Eschiti into the solitary hardback chair at the table. He sat stone-faced while Emmett cracked the door for a peek outside. No movement. Yet.

Think. Not with your heart but with your head!

He turned and ripped open Royce's shirt. Buttons flew like popcorn, and the man protested as Emmett flipped up his undershirt, "Hey . . . !"

"Sit still, Royce, and do exactly what I say."

No wire was taped to his chest. Meaning only that any transmitting device he wore was not immediately apparent. Royce growled in a low and ugly voice, "Why're you breaking my balls like this?"

Eschiti was on parole. Mangas could have coerced him to help them take down Emmett. It was probably the safest way to do it for his own people: use the parolee to find out Parker's emotional state, how heavily armed he was, even if other conspirators were involved.

Emmett realized that he himself would do the same thing in a heartbeat. Furthermore, Mangas and Eschiti were fellow peyote men.

He had kept the door slightly ajar. At the merest flicker of movement outside, he would put Royce between himself and the threat. It seemed impossible that the man had located him in Quanah, Texas, on his own.

Or was it?

Mentally, he retraced his trail here, trying to figure out where he'd given himself away. After abandoning the Ford pickup in the long-term parking lot at Will Rogers, Emmett had walked west from the airport. He'd found a freight train loaded with sugar beets waiting on a siding. With his bare hands, he dug a pit for himself in the bulbs and rode that train south to Wichita Falls, jumped it in the switching yard there for another headed west, an empty coal freight bound for the Colorado mines. West, he needed to get west. But then, in the switching yard near Quanah, the locomotive uncoupled the coal cars on a siding and departed east. He waited. Any of his friends who might help him in his current straits were farther west: his fellow investigators in Phoenix and Anna Turnipseed in Las Vegas. But the empty coal cars remained on the siding, and eventually, after hours of fruitless waiting, hungry and sleepless, he hoofed it into Quanah.

Emmett shut the outer door, motioned for Royce to stand, and jammed the chair under the knob. Minutes had passed uneventfully, and no rescue had been mounted for Royce, or at least Mangas had not made his presence known.

All this counted in Eschiti's favor, but Emmett wasn't ready to call the encounter a reunion.

He gestured for Royce to lead the way into the bathroom, then put down the commode lid for him. Eschiti understood without asking that he was to sit. He stared sullenly up at Emmett, who tucked his revolver in a back pocket of his Levi's. Finally, keeping one eye on the entry door through the mirror, he picked up the paring knife again and resumed cutting off big fistfuls of hair. No matter what happened in the coming minutes, he wouldn't get far with a head that looked as if he had the mange. "How long have you been in town?" he asked Eschiti.

"Since last night."

"You came in your pickup?"

"Course. Slept in it, too."

Emmett moistened a washcloth with cool water and washed the blood off his scalp. Still, when he lathered up his scalp, the shave cream was streaked with a frothy pink. "I need the truth and fast, Royce—how'd you find me?"

"Like I said—Wendell."

"I never told him I was headed this way," Emmett said, running the disposable razor over his scalp to remove the stubble. "I didn't even know myself I was coming through here. Have Mangas or any other feds come to Wendell's farm in the last few days?"

One button had survived Emmett's savaging of Eschiti's shirt front, and the man now slowly fastened it with his heavily calloused fingers before he shook his head.

"Did Wendell tell you I'd told him I'd be coming through Quanah?"

Eschiti's eyes shifted evasively. "No."

"Then how'd he know?"

"Dream."

Emmett lowered the razor from his head. *Careful. Don't disrespect that old man, even if you doubt Eschiti's word.* "What kind of dream?"

"Quanah Parker came to him and said you'd be riding his train into Quanah soon. . . ."

Emmett listened with greater interest. His great-grandfather had had several business concerns in this area, including the Quanah, Acme and Pacific Railroad. From raiding Texas ranches to investing in a Texas railroad—that had been the span of Quanah's life. And Royce had mentioned this dream as matter-of-factly as a weather report. "Go on."

"Quanah said you were in bad trouble, but he'd get you to safety as long as you took the time to honor his mother."

Naudah, or Cynthia Parker.

How could any of this be true? Yet, Wendell did not have idle dreams.

Still, was Emmett willing to trust his life to the dreams of an old man? He tapped a dollop of stubble-peppered shave cream onto the newspaper, then looked at Eschiti, troubled by a new thought. As Jerome squatted, dying, in that portable toilet atop Mt. Scott, he'd only shaken his head in reply to Emmett's question about who had stabbed him. But what had he said of Royce that afternoon at the polo match? *He doesn't need to drink to go into one of his rages.* Such volatile rages that he'd murdered his own father. With a knife. "You didn't care much for Jerome, did you?"

"No," Eschiti admitted. "Never did. I saw through all that sweetness and light stuff. He was just another stuck-up lawyer, as far as I was concerned. Even when he was a kid, he was a lawyer, spreading on the grease."

"Was this motel in Wendell's dream?"

"No."

"Then how'd you find me?"

"I waited outside the Medicine Mound Depot Restaurant for it to open up this morning, thinking to ask if anybody'd seen you. But then I remembered it don't open for breakfast. Wasn't too much longer after, I saw you walking into town from the tracks."

"Why didn't you contact me right off?"

"You know I'm on supervised release. I wanted to make sure you weren't going to be busted any minute. You know what'd happen to me if I was caught rubbing elbows with a fleeing felon . . . so I just wanted to make sure the coast was clear."

"Think I'm a felon?"

The man shrugged, indifferently.

Emmett wiped the remaining lather off his head with the hand towel. When he glanced back, Eschiti was frowning deeply at him. "You don't have a clue what I'm doing here, do you?"

Emmett didn't answer.

"And you're treating me like a con, *Pabi.* Jerome treated me like a dummy, but you're treating me like a con. It's funny how when an Indian becomes a cop he turns more *taibo* than the whitest cop. Damn but what if you ain't looking at me with white eyes."

Emmett dropped the towel and jerked Eschiti to his feet. The man's arms felt strong and wiry in his grasp and he knew he'd have a hard time taking him. But he was still on the verge of swinging when the man said in a smoldering voice, "Don't get me going, Emmett. You don't want to see me when I get going. And remember—I'm the only fool who rode back for you."

Emmett let go of Eschiti, who strolled out of the bathroom. "My truck's out back of this dump," he said over his shoulder. "Key's in the ignition. Drive down to Copper Breaks and leave the pickup in the lot. You'll know which way to head from the breaks."

"Where are you going?" Emmett demanded.

"I can use a drink."

Then Eschiti was out the door, slamming it behind him.

Emmett let him go, even though the true test of Eschiti's loyalty was now only minutes away. Mangas, if he had his hooks in Royce, might have ordered him to loan Emmett the old pickup so he could be apprehended down the highway, removed from any potential hostages at the motel.

He shifted the revolver from his back pocket to the front waistband of his Levi's and draped his T-shirt over it. Then he moistened a washcloth from the hot water tap and used it to wipe down all the surfaces he touched inside the room. Finally, he bundled up the dirty towel in the newspaper that had trapped his hair and took it outside with him into the late morning sun. As promised, Eschiti's GMC rattletrap was parked behind the motel. He looked around for any sign that he was being watched by cops. There was none. Neither was Eschiti was anywhere to be seen.

The key was as worn as an old copper penny. Emmett turned it, and the engine grumbled to life.

Copper Breaks State Park, he figured, was about twelve miles south of Quanah.

12

THANKFULLY, THE SUMMONS was to the Baymont Inn and not the Marriott. Although the FBI task force had been scaled back in the last day on the assumption that Parker had flown the coop, several out-of-town agents were still bunking at the Marriott, and Michael didn't want his peers to know about this meeting. He parked his car a block down 40th Street and walked toward the three-story motel under a clearing sky. He had to remind himself that he was in his hometown of Lawton, that the heights looming in the west were the Wichita Mountains and not the blue-green hills of Maryland—so strong was the sense that he was revisiting the most secretive year of his life.

Inside the inn, the open doors of the elevator awaited him. He hesitated, ever so briefly, but then tapped the button that was marked with a three. His skin was moist, not from the late-afternoon heat, which was only moderately humid after the rains that had drenched I-44 all the way back from the airport, but from an old familiar expectation. It was alive in him again. The feel of that other place, an apartment in Silver Spring, a suburb of Washington, D.C. It'd also been on a third floor. He reached Room 336, wiped his palm on his trouser leg and knocked. He almost expected the door to swing open on that other place.

Close enough—it swung back on Dagen Kirsch.

She looked a bit paler than usual, but smiled and gave him a peck on the cheek. He stepped inside. It was a suite with a whirlpool, which brought back even more memories. A whirlpool had been one of the few luxuries she'd permitted herself in her otherwise barren apartment back east—stress had always been her demon, she'd claimed, and the hot and bubbling waters were a tonic to her.

"Thanks for coming, Michael."

He mumbled something in return, but a few seconds later he was unable to recall what, exactly. The past and the present had fused into a sensory crush: the glint of her platinum hair under the soft lighting, her perfume, her feathery touch on his arm. She had a light touch, before passion took over. She led him to a sunken portion of the suite in which two small couches and an easy chair were arranged. He took the chair. "When'd you get in?" he heard himself asking, as if his voice belonged to somebody else, a nervous stranger.

"Late last night," she replied.

"Why didn't you go home to Anadarko?" It was half the distance from the airport.

"I wanted to see you. And I wasn't sure how you'd feel about dropping by my place."

He nodded, even though all of this was rife with layers of meaning. Echoes of old promises. Worries of discovery.

Her gaze fixed on the carpet in front of her bare feet as she seemed to think of broaching something. A resumption of how things had been left off eight years ago? He told himself that he didn't want that. It'd complicated his already paper-thin marriage. Yet, he did want it. Desire was like any other drug. Mind- and mood-altering.

"Michael," she finally said, her eyes flashing up at him, "did you have any evidence—any inkling at all—that Emmett was involved in what he apparently was . . . ?" She shook her head in frustration. "I didn't say that well." She exhaled, wearily. "I've taken a leave of absence because I have to come up with some answers about Emmett."

"For whom?"

"My boss."

"The president?"

A quick smile at his naïveté about the inner workings of the White House. "I'm one of his special advisers, but technically I report to the chief of staff. He—and that really means the president, too—wants to know how it came to pass we publicly honored a law enforcement officer who's now suspected of . . ." Killing Jerome Crowe. She couldn't make herself say it.

So that was it. This was not a summons to renew things. She could indeed live without him. He told himself that was all for the best. For her. For him. For his wife. But all at once he felt like a sucked orange. Nothing but hollow pith inside.

"This couldn't have happened at a worse time for me," she added, her eyes clouding.

"Why?"

"Don't you see? *I* suggested to the president that he drop by Emmett's honor dance."

Despite his feelings for her, the interrogator within him took over. "I understand, though I can't see why you'd be held to account. What I mean—why is now a worse time than any other for this to happen?"

She gave him a calculating stare for a moment. "Can you keep something under your hat, Michael?"

"I don't wear hats except when I dance," he quipped, but it fell flat on her worry. "Yes, I can keep a confidence." It hurt a little that she questioned that.

"There's a movement underfoot to make me national chairwoman. It's in its preliminary stages, but I've got growing support at the highest levels."

"Chairwoman of the *whole* party?"

"The *whole damned* party."

"Good for you, Dagen," he said vacuously. She'd always dreamed of something big like this. At one time, her sights had been set on the vice presidency, an ambition that had proved beyond her reach. But he had to admit that heading the party might be within her grasp, given her fund-raising skills. As best he comprehended, it was her job within the White House to forecast the effect of policy on political contributions and oversee polls.

"It's not good, Michael. Not now. Jerome's gone, and Emmett might have done it. It's like this mess fell right out of the sky on top of me. Out of nowhere." She began to cry.

He stayed in the chair, feeling lame. She had been very fond of Jerome, although she'd assured Michael that Crowe had never learned of their affair. Finally, awkwardly, he rose and went to her on the couch. He gently drew her face against his chest. "I don't think anybody, including the president, is blaming you, Dagen."

"Sweet, but not true, Michael." She disengaged herself from him and went for a box of tissues on the bar, leaving him to feel as if she hadn't wanted his embrace. She blew her nose, then took the chair he'd just vacated. "What the hell is going on, Michael?" she asked, no longer crying. "What's behind all this?"

He paused. Her questions sounded simple enough. But they weren't. In effect, she was asking him to brief the president. That was the FBI director's job, not a lowly agent's in Lawton, Oklahoma. There was another pitfall in this for Michael. Dagen had liked Jerome Crowe. What if he now confided in her that Jerome might have been Emmett's co-conspirator in the embezzlement scheme? It was possible that she'd try to block this tack in order to save her late friend's name. A call from the president to the director could do that in a minute. "Agents all over the West are working to put the pieces together," he finally hedged. "We don't have a clear picture yet. But you can tell your boss that prior to last Monday night on Mt. Scott, there was no sign to me or his own supervisors with the BIA that Parker was capable of this sort of thing." He hesitated, then added, "Are you familiar with the Thunder Dog Society?"

"Of course. Aren't you the head guy, the pipe keeper?"

"Yes. Well, the night of the honor dance I asked Parker to join. It's a privilege and an honor. Not a right."

"So you trusted him enough for that?"

"Yes."

As the import of that sank in, she brightened immeasurably. "What did Emmett say?"

"He declined."

"Why?"

"He didn't say." Untrue. And Michael had only told Don Andreas what Parker had truly said because he worked Internal Affairs for BIA and had to be persuaded with every possible argument that Emmett was dirty. Most decidedly, a Thunder Dogs matter was none of Dagen's concern. Michael now hoped that she wouldn't make an end-run to Andreas as well. He doubted it. BIA law enforcement didn't trust her after her tenure as a deputy to the assistant secretary of the Interior with oversight over them. And it was no secret that she was in the camp that favored the FBI handling of all criminal cases in Indian Country. Michael knew that his influence had put her squarely in that camp: She'd worked for the Interior during their affair.

"These pieces your people are working on . . ." Her voice trailed off as she visibly speculated.

"Yeah?"

"What are they?"

"We're trying to find out who might have helped Parker tap into the trust funds loop."

Her eyes had now cleared. "It'll be hard to prove that Emmett, assigned to law enforcement and not finance, had access to IIM and other trust funds . . . wouldn't it?"

True. And that's where Jerome Crowe had come in. As the BIA attorney charged with putting together the government's defense against the Indian plaintiffs who were alleging gross mismanagement, he'd had plenty of access to strategic points in the disbursement process. The proof of that might be the more than $33,000 in cash found in Crowe's room at the Marriott. But, again, for the time being, Michael wanted Dagen and her superiors to think of Jerome as only a homicide victim. He'd reveal the man's role in all this when the evidence was rock-solid. "We're not ruling out co-conspirators and accomplices, Dagen. We're not ruling out anything. We're at a very early stage."

"Which was Calvin Ushuk?" she asked.

Michael took a moment to make sure his expression remained blank. "Pardon?"

"Which do you think Ushuk was—a co-conspirator or an accomplice?"

Suddenly, he wished that he'd never come. He'd been had. She was working both ends of the pipeline for her superiors. Her incredibly powerful superiors. In the last day, finally, Ushuk's Inupiat identity had been given to the media by Dr. Hawzeepa, but Dagen's question inferred that she had knowledge of the call placed from Celia Parker's residence in Lawton to Ushuk's satellite phone in Alaska. Again, Andreas might have told her. But Michael doubted it. This bit of privileged information had come from the FBI director. He'd bet six months' salary on it.

"I don't have that information," he said coolly, letting her know that she'd stepped over the line. "I'll have to refer you to our public affairs people."

Her severe look crumbled. "I'm sorry, Michael. I'm not trying to pry. It's just that I'm under the gun here. They want answers. Like why you didn't capture Emmett when you had the chance? These are decent people, but they don't really understand how law enforcement works."

"Do you?"

"I try, Michael. You know I've always been on your side." Rising, she headed back to the wet bar. "Gin and tonic?"

He checked his wristwatch. It was close enough to five, even though he had no intention of calling it a day—as always, there was simply too much to do. "Please."

Having broken the tension, she quietly went about making them drinks. She preferred whiskey sours or white wine. He didn't care for wine but had liked drinking it with her in her whirlpool. He liked watching her pale, graceful hands at work. Jeralyn had attractive hands in a different way. Strong and supple-looking. Perhaps a genetic inheritance from the earthen mounds her Caddoan ancestors had built in antiquity.

The seeds of Dagen's and his affair were to be found in the Special Olympics. Todd had been a participant, so the Oklahoma committee had cajoled Michael into becoming the state representative to the national office— he already had to make periodic trips to D.C. on FBI business. As if her job with Interior wasn't hectic enough, Dagen had been cajoled into serving as an assistant to the national head of the Special Olympics. They became friends, and she confided to him that she resented always being assistant to someone important, forever being relegated to the number two slot. Months before things got rolling between them, an FBI friend of Michael's, a Seattle agent of Yakima ancestry, warned him that she had a thing for Indian men. He never asked the agent if that interest had included him. But then came the Murrah blast, and Michael ignored the warning. Sometimes, he believed that only their affair and peyote had kept him in one piece during the year that followed.

She now handed him his gin and tonic and sat beside him. "Cheers."

They clicked their glasses together.

"How's Jeralyn?" she asked casually.

"Sad but hanging in there." He always found her concern for his wife a bit odd. He supposed that it violated his sense of propriety. As Dagen had never even come close to pressing him for a divorce, he thought the subject of his wife should have been taboo.

"What about you, Michael—sad but hanging in there, too?"

"Yes," he said, "that's about it."

And then, just when he believed the conversation had turned entirely personal, she reached for his hand and implored with eyes that had turned damp again, "Michael, please—tell the president's chief of staff what you just told me about Emmett and the Thunder Dogs. I can have him phone you under an assumed name at work. I wouldn't ask unless I really need your help. Please, please . . ."

Emmett trudged through a landscape of red and green bluffs dotted with mesquite and juniper. These trees were not tall, but the sun was low enough in the west to cast long shadows off them. To his left, the red waters of the Pease River sheeted past on their way to the Gulf of Mexico.

He walked as if in a dream, thinking about a dream.

Can a holy man's dream side-track a string of coal cars within spitting-distance of a town named after your great-grandfather? Is the modern world still answerable to *Nuhmuhnuh* beliefs? Emmett wasn't sure. And that, he supposed, was the price of modernity. Not knowing. Several generations back, there would have been no doubt of the cause-and-effect between Wendell's dream and that locomotive engineer uncoupling the empty coal cars near Quanah, Texas. Deep down, whites were no different, at least those who believed prayer could divert a hurricane or subside a flood.

Two hours and five miles ago, Emmett had left Royce Eschiti's pickup in the visitor center parking lot at Copper Breaks and struck out across country. And prior to that, he'd waited inside the hot cab of the truck, for what, he knew not—Wendell in his U-Haul piano mover, maybe, though by now the old man would have little doubt he was being watched by the FBI. Emmett also kept an eye out for cops of any sort. But after an hour, nobody significant—friend nor foe—showed, so he went inside the visitor center. The displays were devoted to Comanche culture. He paid scant attention to the blown-up photographs. Most were familiar to him, and he had to split his attention between the female ranger at the reception desk and the entryway, through which at any moment the purpose of this rendezvous might become evident. He was pretending to be absorbed with one particular reproduction when it hit him.

"Of course," he whispered.

He walked directly out of the building. And kept walking past Royce's pickup, over the highway bridge and onto the shelving banks along the south side of the Pease. The rangeland was raw and thorny. It tore up the street shoes he'd been wearing ever since the night of Jerome's murder.

Eventually, he reached a stand of native pecan trees. He was nearing the spot where the photograph that hung in the visitor center had been taken. Even in those days, the late 1890s, this range had been grassier and more open. A century of over-grazing had let the mesquite and beavertail cactus grow rampant, species not favored by cattle. Yet, Emmett guessed that the same screen of pecans had lined the Pease the day in 1860 a mixed force of U.S. Army regulars and Texas Rangers fell upon a large Comanche supply camp pitched just north of the river. Although, it'd been autumn then, and the leaves had probably turned.

Finding an open space among the pecans, Emmett gazed in that direction now. He could imagine the smoke-stained teepees of the *Nuhmuhnuh* standing over there—women, children and a few old men going about their routines, unaware of the approaching danger. Naudah, or Cynthia Ann Parker, had camped with Topsannah, her daughter, on this, the south side of the

Pease. Emmett's great-great-grandmother was unaware of the impending massacre on the north bank until the first gunshots rolled across to her. It became a bloody, one-sided slaughter because most of the warriors—including Peta Nocona, her husband, and Quanah, her teenage son—were out hunting. Naudah grabbed Topsannah and leaped onto a horse's back. Perhaps she had galloped right past where Emmett now stood. Her flight had been in vain. The Rangers ran her down and returned her to her white relatives.

"Me no Cinee no more," she told them. She wanted to go home to her Comanche family. The consuming purpose of her remaining time had been to get back to the Comancheria. She did return, eventually, but only in death. Years later, Quanah brought the bodies of his mother and sister back to Oklahoma. He also marked Naudah's final encampment as a free woman with an iron stake, lest he forget where it had been, lest he forget her face the last time he'd seen it along the Pease. Sometime in the 1890s, he returned with his entire family, his many wives and children, to show them where Naudah had been recaptured. A photographer was hired to record the occasion for posterity, producing the photo Emmett had noticed in the visitor center at Copper Breaks.

Emmett cautiously broke from the pecan forest and began winding through some hackberry saplings toward where he believed the stake to be. It was difficult to find. On purpose. These lands, once the very heart of the Comancheria, now belonged to a white rancher. Yet, he was married to a *Nuhmuhnuh* woman, and the two of them guarded this site by keeping it inconspicuous. Somewhere among these hackberries, Quanah's stake still jutted a few inches out of the earth.

Somewhere.

Emmett stopped to listen. He felt the need to listen.

There was no wind, and this stretch of river was running deep but silent in its muddy bed. The sun had gone, although its last light was being reflected by a golden thunderhead far to the northeast. The rangeland around Emmett was gray with twilight.

A horse nickered out in the growth.

Sliding his revolver out of his waistband, he crept toward the place from which the sound had come.

He hadn't gone far when something white caught the corner of his eye. He spun that way but kept the muzzle of his weapon pointed at the ground. Immediately, he was glad that he had: His mother was standing with her back to him about thirty yards away. She was wearing the same white beaded dress she'd worn the night of his honor dance. As always, she was hunched with age. But she was clasping her hands before her in a nervous way that tightened the pit of Emmett's stomach.

Quanah's stake was visible nearby, and he wondered if his mother had been positioned near it to draw him in.

This time, the unseen horse snorted instead of nickered. The animal had smelled Emmett, something anyone who knew horses would quickly realize.

He backtracked, walking on the outer soles of his shoes to hold down the noise. Just as he'd been taught as a boy by his father—*don't slap the ground with the flats of your feet when you're stalking game.*

What was the game now? Who had placed his mother next to the stake on the south bank of the Pease?

The horse was hidden somewhere off to Emmett's and his mother's left. He'd halted and was slowly pivoting that way when a figure came into view. A tall and straight-backed man loomed in Emmett's sight—he couldn't recall having drawn down on him. But he had. The man was dressed all in black, even his bowler hat was black, from which two long gray braids dangled down to his chest. Wendell Padduhpony looked somber but also vaguely amused as he said, "Shoot me, *Tuah,* and I can die knowing at least one thing . . ."

"What's that?" Emmett finally had to ask.

"You killed Jerome, too."

After a moment, Emmett lowered his .357 and concealed it again.

"Thought so," Wendell said, closing the distance between them and smothering Emmett in an embrace. "Sorry to lead you around with blinders on, but the FBI's been on me like flies on manure. I'd imagine right at this moment a couple of 'em are shadowing poor Royce around Quanah, trying to skin him out of his parole." He let go of Emmett and nudged him toward Celia. "Go on. Give your mama a kiss before she dies of a broken heart."

Emmett ran.

His approaching footfalls startled her. But, as she wheeled toward him, her look of fright swiftly became one of joy. He held her and said so only they could hear, "*Sukwaittu,* Mama." *Love.*

She started to repeat the word but then broke down and wept. Emmett had never heard anything quite as painful, for she did not cry easily, but that pain was commingled with the relief of having her close at hand and safe. She didn't weep for long. Leaning back, she held him at an arm's length and asked, "Why, Emmett—what'd you do to your hair? You look like a heller."

A laugh escaped him.

"What's so funny?"

"Nothing, Mama. Absolutely nothing." He held her tight again, but she pushed him back a step. "They say you murdered Jerome. That can't be true."

"It isn't."

"Good, because you'd never do anything like that unless I told you."

He came close to laughing again. "Exactly."

The summer he was thirteen, she rented a room in a government project, a tenement in Lawton, for the three of them until his brother Malcolm and he returned to the mission in fall. One stifling night, they were awakened by a ruckus. The ex-husband of the Kickapoo woman who lived next to them had shown up drunk and was trying to beat down the door to get at her. Although Emmett could not have weighed more than a hundred and ten pounds, Celia showed no hesitation as she ordered him, "Go stop him." Stepping out onto the concrete stoop, he saw that the man was very large. He needed something to equalize that disadvantage, and the only thing at hand was a claw hammer Malcolm and he had used that day to pop caps on the steps because they couldn't afford a cap pistol. He grabbed the hammer, went slowly down the steps and approached the neighboring stoop. The man staggered hugely over him, surprised by the thin but adamant voice commanding him to quit and go away. "And if I don't, *muchacho,* what you going to do about it?" Emmett brought the hammer down on the man's right foot with all his might. Then he braced for a beating in turn. Instead, incredibly, the man hopped down off the stoop and screamed profanities in Spanish all the way out to the street, where he drove off.

A *Nuhmuhnuh* mother could urge violence, but only as long as it was under her direction. "What are you going to do about all this?" Celia now asked.

At last, Emmett answered her. "I'm not sure, Mama. I'm headed west, though. I've got friends out there who might help me."

"Not so fast." Wendell had joined them. "You've got friends in Oklahoma who *will* help you."

Emmett looked over at the old man. "How'd you know to find me in Quanah?"

"Part dream and part good old horse sense. I figured you'd steer clear of the roads and take to the rails. Most trains headed west are made up of empty coal cars. I worked for the railroad after the war. Just a year or so, but long enough to realize that empty cars are lighter than full ones, so they shunt them off on onto the Quanah siding 'til they got a string worth hauling to Colorado. That's the rational explanation . . ." Wendell gave him a sly smile. "You want the real one, too?"

Emmett smiled. "No thank you, *Toko*. Royce already told me." Then his smile went out. "I've got to get away from this country for a while."

"Agreed," Wendell said, "but only for a while. And not far. It got where you didn't have time to be *Nuhmuhnuh*. Now you've got no choice. You've got to go back to being Comanche just to stay one step ahead of the pack that's after you."

"That may be harder than you think."

"No, it isn't. First, you have to straighten yourself out. Catch your breath and get in tune with your country. The plains will protect you, if you let 'em. Meanwhile, maybe I can talk some sense into Michael Mangas."

"And where am I supposed to disappear while you have a heart-to-heart with the son of a bitch who set me up?"

"Language, Emmett," his mother cautioned him.

"Yeah, language . . ." Thinking, Wendell tugged at the black kerchief around his throat. "I've got an idea or two." He gave a birdlike whistle, and hooves started thudding toward them out from the hackberries. Two horses, not just one, appeared. The first was a handsome bay quarter horse, saddled, and the second, a Morgan-mix, was packing gear. The bay was led by the reins by an old woman. Her name was Frankie Acheson, and she had to be pushing ninety. She halted the string of two horses and asked Emmett, "*Unha numu tekwaPeyu?*" *Do you speak Comanche?*

He thought he might be dealing with Alzheimer's until she winked at her own jest and hugged him. "*Ma ruawe,* Emmett." *Hello.*

"Hello, *Kaku.*" *Grandmother.*

Her husband's family had been on this range even before the Comanche had been completely removed from it. Bob Acheson's great-great-grandfather had ridden with the Texas Rangers the day Cynthia Parker was recaptured. In the course of several fights, he'd killed six warriors. Yet Bob had married Frankie and settled into respecting tribal ways. He was custodian of the recapture site and refused entry and guide service to all non-Comanche, especially historians and anthropologists, who wanted to put this exquisitely painful moment of *Quahada* history under a magnifying glass.

Wendell glanced down at Emmett's ruined oxfords, then turned for the packhorse and took a pair of worn but serviceable cowboy boots from a pannier. "Bob and Frankie were hoping these might fit," he said, handing them to Emmett.

They did. "*Udah.* Excuse us a second." Then he motioned for Wendell to follow him over to the river's edge. He chucked in his shoes with a splash. "I don't want the Achesons involved in this."

"They won't be."

"The hell they aren't—you've got them abetting my flight!"

Wendell arched his back as if he'd been slapped. "What'd you just say to me?"

Swiftly, Emmett dropped his gaze to the ground.

The old man went on in a low, tremulous voice, "You're talking to your elder. You're talking to the man is who is laboring day and night to save you from yourself. Never speak to me like that again. This is just why you've got to get your head right again. You're a loose cannon. Sore at anything and everything." He extended a forefinger and came within a half inch of poking Emmett with it. Still, static electricity bridged the gap between them with a crackle. "You've grabbed your lance and your shield and you're galloping off into the sunset with no idea who to fight. How to fight. And whether you like it or not, Michael Mangas is the answer to all this, so you better figure out some way to communicate with him." Then he finished with an even harsher tone: "Understood, *Tuah*?"

His face darkening with shame, Emmett saw that his mother and Frankie were watching them with concern. Celia was twisting her rosary beads in her hand.

Wendell ordered with a sweep of his arm, "Stand to my left."

In his agitation, Emmett had taken the position to the elder's right, inadvertently disrespecting him. He shifted around, then nodded, indicating that he'd calmed down.

"What happened up on Mt. Scott?" the old man demanded.

"That day, Jerome told me that he had an informant who could bust the trust fund scandal wide open."

"You believed him?"

"I believe that's what he believed. Enough for him to arrange a meeting with the snitch. He asked me to be there to help him out."

"And you agreed?"

"Of course."

"Go on."

"This was midday, and the location for the meeting hadn't been set. I warned Jerome to tell the snitch we'd choose the place, but then while I was taking a nap, he left a message with mother for me to meet him up on Mt. Scott right away. So I had no chance to case the area first, like I'd wanted." Emmett paused. "I got there just after Jerome had been stabbed."

"See anybody?"

"No. Even Jerome didn't get a good look at the bastard who stuck him. He told me that just before he died. On the way up there, I was tailed by the FBI. I lost him past Medicine Park, but he drove up on me and Jerome just as I was pulling the knife out of his belly."

Wendell had shut his eyes, but his pupils were visible dancing back and forth beneath the lids, as if he had the ability to transport himself to the actual event. "That was Ramsey," he said, looking at Emmett again, "the agent out of Elk City."

"How do you know his name?"

"It was in the papers."

"And you've had no contact with Mangas since this began?"

"None."

"I don't give a damn if the agent's name is Cheops," Emmett said angrily, "he never identified himself as a federal officer—and he was looking for any damned excuse he could to blow holes in me."

"Why don't you let me tell Michael just that?"

"Don't say a word to him. Promise me. You've already put yourself at risk by organizing this little rendezvous—you, the Achesons, and Royce, too. Please promise me, *Toko*."

Wendell chuckled. "We're all born at risk, *Tuah*. All born to die. What matters is how we deal with fate. After all you've been through, haven't you figured that out yet?"

"I can't accept those horses."

"You've got to. And that's on greater authority than mine."

"What if the FBI finds Bob's brands on them?"

"There are no brands on them. No lip tattoos either. They're as unmarked as the day they slipped wet from their mothers."

"What authority?" Emmett asked.

But had Wendell started back to the women. After a second, Emmett followed.

"Frankie and Bob have offered to take in Celia 'til this all blows over," the old man said.

Emmett was moved. But his first impulse was to decline. But could he? The Acheson homestead stood on a bluff overlooking the entire river valley between Copper Breaks and the town or Rayland. His mother now understood the danger, and their place would give her a good vantage from which to see trouble coming. There was no obvious familial connection between Celia and Frankie, so it could be a long time, if ever, before Mangas cast his gaze in this direction.

He turned to the aged woman and embraced her. That was how he accepted.

Wendell laughed. "Don't this beat the devil? Yonder's a ranch we tried to put to the torch to a dozen times in the old days, and now it's home to one *Nuhmuhnuh* woman and about to become refuge to another!" Then, still laughing, he ambled back to the packhorse and dipped into one of the panniers. He removed a pair of chaps and a duster, and then took a piece of paper from one of the pockets of the light overcoat. "I can't be with you, son, so I jotted down a couple instructions."

"Instructions for what?"

"You'll see when you get there."

"Get where?"

"The Palo Duro. And then you're to leave by way of Adobe Walls."

The Palo Duro was a network of canyons in the desert badlands to the west of them. It was virtually invisible until you rode up on it. Adobe Walls, of course, was the site of the last big battle with the buffalo hunters. "Why should I do any of this?"

"Are you going to argue with my dream?" Wendell handed him the riding gear and paper. "It helped me find you, right? Besides, in it, Quanah told me you should go to the Palo Duro and then north through Adobe Walls. So I don't know why. You can ask him, if you get the chance. All I know is that he doesn't think you should go far from home. Most of the time, all our *puha* is concentrated at home." Our *power*. "Everybody gather round . . ." Then Wendell sprinkled cedar sprigs over the hallowed ground near the iron stake and had them join hands.

As Royce had mentioned as a condition of the dream, the old man paid homage to Naudah, honoring her for her grace and courage and fidelity to the Comanche way of life. Being *Nuhmuhnuh* was not a simple matter of blood, and she'd proved that. Death had denied her a reunion with those she loved, so Wendell beseeched her to do all she could to help spare her descendent, Emmett, the pain of mother-and-son separation she and Quanah had known.

"May the Blessed Virgin shine through Naudah," said Celia when Wendell had finished, her eyes glistening, "and guide my son back to me."

13

"**P**OOLAW," THE BANK teller said. "That's an unusual name."

"*Kiowa*," Gladys Poolaw said, smiling but also glancing at the clock on the wall. She'd planned the transaction late in the day on a Friday to take advantage of the crush of patrons, but not so late that the Anadarko Agency of the BIA would be closed and unable to confirm that the $9,612 oil royalty check was backed by funds. It was ten minutes to five.

"Okay, here we go." The teller began counting out the cash.

Gladys pretended to be disinterested. She even yawned and gazed off while bill after bill piled up on the counter. She pretended as if money meant nothing to her. *Wouldn't that be nice?* At last it was done. Gladys thanked the teller and left at her usual unhurried pace.

The white-and-silver Winnebago was parked down the block and along a side street. The modest skyline of Amarillo, Texas, showed above it, the windows of the high-rises bronzed by the setting sun. Not much of a downtown, especially when compared to a true megalopolis like New York or Los Angeles, but it loomed out of a flat plain and seemed bigger for it.

The door was unlocked, as expected, but the coach was silent. She paused in the step well. Life in a motor home was a life on springs, so you were always aware of the movements, however slight, of those you shared the space with. But now, the Winnebago was completely still.

She called out her husband's name.

There was no response.

All right, then. He was off gallivanting somewhere in the neighborhood. It'd been moronic of him to leave the door unlocked, given the expensive photographic development equipment crammed in the rear bedroom, which served as their darkroom. Reluctantly, they had removed the queen-size bed in there to make space for it all and slept on the sofa fold-down up front. Her husband could be so careless. He'd been careless over the phone with Hola, bossing around the geek like that, refusing to go down to Louisiana in the heat of summer. She'd had second thoughts about that, even though she'd stuck up for her husband at the time.

But, apparently, Hola had caved in to their little rebellion, for the next sequence of checks they picked up at the central Oklahoma drop site near Will Rogers World Airport was readily cashed in the Texas panhandle, Colorado and then New Mexico. Just as her husband had insisted.

Maybe that's how to treat the bastard.

Gladys took off her turquoise earrings and went to the refrigerator for something to drink. She grabbed a diet Sprite, then returned to the table to sip and rest and wait for his return.

Long ago, when the two of them had worked eight-to-five for Kodak in Rochester, New York, they'd dreamed of a life like this, traveling at whim, no permanent home to tie them down. But lately, she'd begun to miss having a real address, a place to plant a few flowers, a piece of solid ground under her feet. As far as whim, they had to keep a definite schedule or Hola went ballistic on them. It was tiresome to document and juggle a score of identities in a given year. She now knew that every way of life had its hidden stresses, and she was growing weary of vagabonding.

After a few minutes, she had to pee.

She rose from the table and went to lavatory in the rear of the coach. It would be wonderful to have a full-sized bathroom once again, a proper tub instead of just a shower stall. She hiked up her skirt, lowered her panties and sat on the commode. As she waited for the trickle to start, she examined her thighs and calves. They'd grown chunky over these past years. Once, they'd been shapely. Hollywood shapely.

Pat . . . pat . . . pat . . .

The spout was dripping in the stall.

Everything was so compact inside the lavatory she could remain seated while she reached out to roll back the shower door. Even before it began to slide, she noticed the dark shape behind the pebbled glass. As soon as the door fully opened, she screamed. She slid off the seat and onto her knees, her panties dangling around her ankles. Still screaming, she covered her ears with her hands and shut her eyes.

Then she went quiet. Instinct took over and told her to be quiet.

After a few seconds, she forced herself to turn her face toward the impossible sight again—just to convince herself that it was real.

It was all too real.

She toppled sideways out of the lavatory and crawled the length of the coach on her elbows and knees. She could no longer scream. Instead, she vomited, and Sprite shot out her nose. Groping with a trembling hand, she unlatched the door and tumbled outside onto the sidewalk. She couldn't rise, her legs were too weak, so she scooted backward on her buttocks until she found herself cowering against the front of a beauty salon that had gone out of business.

She sat there, frozen to the spot, her eyes wide with horror as they beheld the Winnebago.

Eventually, a thought burned through her shock. The beast might still be around, the monster who'd hung her husband by the neck with one of their own towels to the showerhead and left a big-handled knife in his gut. *He wants me, too!*

That got her moving again.

Rising, she looked up and down the street. It was a seedy neighborhood of mostly failed businesses, and no pedestrians were in sight. It didn't matter. There was no help for her. She could never turn to strangers for help, least of all the cops.

She had to help herself.

She inched back up to the open door of the Winnebago. Whimpering, she darted inside and across the kitchenette for the pantry. Standing on her tiptoes, she fumbled inside the highest pull-out tray for a nickel-plated .38 special revolver. Once and only once, her husband had committed a robbery with it, but that'd been years ago, and since then he'd never worked up the nerve for another heist. It wasn't his style of crime. But now she rejoiced as her palm closed around the wooden grip—it was strange to feel such a burst of joy in the midst of her terror.

But then that thin joy vanished as she realized: The beast might still be *inside* the Winnebago.

Clenching the .38 in both hands, she advanced deeper into the motor home. She'd taken no more than a few steps when there were voices to her back. She wheeled around and aimed the gun into the faces of two black teenagers, who were peeking inside the yawning door as if looking for something to steal. Catching sight of the revolver, the youths disappeared in a blink, and she quickly slammed the door.

Then she stared down the length of the coach at the back.

The folding door to rear bedroom was shut.

She had to clear that space. There was no other choice. She had to regain control of her home and then drive away. Only then could she figure out what to do next.

She tried to ignore the nightmare vision of her husband slumped off the showerhead, but the corner of her eye filled with red. She would have never believed that a single human could hold so much blood. For the first time, it sank in that he was clad only in a polo shirt and his jockey shorts. He'd probably been caught unaware, taking a nap.

Swallowing down an up-swell of bile, she kept moving toward the closed door.

She stepped over her shoes and panties, left in a jumble on the hallway floor just outside the lavatory.

They'd sealed the back bedroom against all light, and now the promise of the darkness waiting there terrified her. But the flat rays of the sun were streaming through the kitchenette window behind her as she nudged open the folding door.

Nobody.

But it was possible somebody could be crouching inside the cloth-paneled film-drying cabinet. Her hand was shaking so badly she could barely take hold of the zipper.

Again, nobody.

Her gaze fell on the makings of Gladys Poolaw. Scraps still lay on the guillotine trimmer from her own photograph she'd reduced to fit into the prescribed place in a Texas driver's license. The developing baths were still filled with their solutions.

The ringing of a cell phone made her jump.

Her husband's. There was no mistaking the jingle: *We're in the money, we're in the money* . . .

Coming from the bathroom.

The sound petrified her, but she knew she had to answer. Somehow, the way out of this would be revealed to her if only she answered the phone, and the anxiety of not knowing what to do next tortured her worse than anything else.

The problem was that her husband always put it in his shirt pocket, even when he napped.

She turned for the bathroom. As she stepped inside, she closed her eyes as tightly as she could. She believed it would be easier to do this blind. She reached high, far higher than his savaged belly. Something helped her: the sense that this gore-splattered thing was no longer her husband. Her fingertips felt his nose, then his chin and finally located his shirt pocket. She grabbed the phone as if fishing it out of flames and ran for the kitchenette.

Only there did she open her eyes again. *"Hello . . ."*

"I trust my point's been well taken," the voice on the other end of the connection said. Hola.

She wanted to rant against him. She wanted to do this with a white-hot anger, but her own voice sounded weak and shuddery to her as she whispered, "Yes . . ." She'd never even seen his face. If only if she had a face to despise, she might feel stronger. But she begged, "Please don't kill me."

"I'll consider it," Hola said in a sensible tone that came close to infuriating her. Only close. "Get behind the steering wheel. A right turn will put you on Business Forty. Go west until I tell you otherwise . . ." The revolver. She no longer held it. She must have set it down to unzip the film-drying sleeve. She was pivoting for the dark room when he barked over the airwaves, "Listen, you stupid cunt—don't you realize I've got you in sight at this very second!"

She broke into loud, pathetic sobs.

"Stop it! Stop it right now and get behind the wheel!"

This time she obeyed. She started the engine and strapped herself into the seat—all the while looking straight ahead. He was out there somewhere in the grim neighborhood, but now she didn't want to see him. She choked down one last sob and shifted the automatic transmission into drive while still holding the phone against her ear. The big coach lumbered forward.

A horn brayed at her.

She braked, and her husband's body thudded against the fiberglass of the shower stall.

"What was that horn all about?" Hola demanded.

A car had swerved around her. "I . . . I pulled out without checking my mirror."

"Concentrate, concentrate!"

She put on her signal and turned right. Again, a thud came from the shower. In addition to the smell of blood, she caught the sour stink of the developing fluids, which had spilled. The sun had sunk halfway into the featureless western horizon, but its light was still dazzling. She let go of the wheel and flipped down the visor, drifting over the yellow line in the process. She expected Hola to scold her, but he didn't. Checking her side mirror, she looked for him in the cars that were streaming out of downtown at rush hour, but none of the drivers fit the mental impression she'd formed of him over the years.

"Soon you'll come to Route Three-thirty-five. Turn left and head toward Canyon. Head south."

She tried to say *all right*, but her mouth was now too parched for words.

Again, as she turned, her husband swung on his garrote. That dull sound was driving her out of her mind.

She tried not to think too far ahead. She tried to think no farther than Canyon, a small city that was the gateway to Palo Duro Canyon State Park. There, or somewhere close by, would Hola kill her as well? She couldn't recall when, but the can of Sprite had slid off the table and rolled forward to come to rest against the convenience console between the front seats. Most of the soda had spilled, but once again she let go of the wheel and reached down for can. Enough Sprite was left inside it to wet her tongue and give her voice. "I told him we should do what you say and go down to Louisiana," she lied, all in a rush as she tossed the empty can behind her. "I told him, but he just wouldn't listen. You weren't going to take that lying down."

"Is that what you think killed him?"

She didn't know how to answer that.

"Listen, he's dead because of duplication."

"*Duplication?*" she echoed hollowly.

"Yeah, that's when two people can do the same job. You eliminate one of them in the interest of efficiency." Hola paused. "Okay, you should be coming up on Ranch Road Two-two-one-nine. Turn right."

"Right?" she questioned. That would take her away from Canyon.

"Yeah, right—west. Just do it."

"I will, I will." And she did a few seconds later, directly toward the final hazy glow of the vanished sun. Within minutes, he directed her south again. The darkness was full when, on his orders, she took a dirt road that wound around the north end of Buffalo Lake National Wildlife Refuge. The shoreline was thick with reeds, and somehow the sight of this rank growth made her plead again over the phone, "Please don't do anything to me. I don't want to be left out here in this awful place. I told him. I *told* him."

"Relax, I'm going to let you live for the time being. You're my best little check casher. You're moving up in the firm. We're downsizing, but you're moving up. First, however, you have to dispose of your duplicate."

"*How?*" she moaned. "He's so much heavier than me. I don't think I can drag him out of the coach."

"You'll find a way. Just think of me, dear, as you do it. You had no idea what kind of hacker I truly am. But now you know. How very well you know."

The white soldiers sent their Tonkawa scouts down into the Palo Duro first that daybreak on September 26, 1874. Colonel Ranald Mackenzie was seiz-

ing upon a rare opportunity in the Red River War: The *Quahada* Comanche—with their Arapaho, Kiowa and Southern Cheyenne allies—were
camped for a length of three miles along the headwaters of the Red River.
He knew where the renegades were, and they had no idea he was coming, or
at least that he was so near. Mackenzie's Tonkawa scouts found a narrow
game trail that coursed down the steep walls of the canyon. They were almost
to the bottom when an Indian lookout shouted the alarm. The Tonkawas
shot him dead, and the lopsided fight was on. Mackenzie had brought thirteen companies of cavalry and infantry with him. The renegades, especially
the *Quahada*, fought a desperate rear guard action to give their women and
children time to assemble their ponies—which their band alone had taken
the precaution of hiding—and scramble up blind draws off the main canyon
to escape onto the plain above. Eventually, these warriors, or what remained
of them after a withering fire from the soldiers, fled along the river, closely
pursued by the cavalry. The troopers gave up the chase only when night fell.

The die was cast that day in the Palo Duro. The last free Indians of the
southern plains had lost the means to sustain their nomadic lives. The foodstuffs, teepees and weapons could have been replaced. But not the nearly fifteen hundred ponies they left in the canyon for Mackenzie to seize. Without
them, buffalo-hunting and raiding over long distances were impossible. And
it wasn't long before even the *Quahada* band, led by Quanah, rode their few
remaining and exhausted thunder dogs into captivity at Ft. Sill. The modern
world began for the People.

Mackenzie let his Tonkawa scouts choose three hundred fifty ponies.
The rest had been shot by his men.

Emmett stirred the coals of the small fire he had built in one of the
draws used by his ancestors to flee the main brunt of Mackenzie's attack. He
hadn't built the fire to warm himself; the July night was already torrid. Nor
had he built it to cook his food. On Wendell Padduhpony's written instructions, Emmett had not eaten or drunk anything in four days. He now took a
small cloth pouch from one of the saddlebags. He spread the drawstring and
sniffed the contents. Inside were the dried, scalelike leaves of the red-berry
cedar. The best, in the opinion of most *Nuhmuhnuh*, grew in the Pease
River country Emmett had left eight days ago.

He took a generous pinch of cedar and dropped it into a tin coffee cup he'd already set on a hot rock beside the embers. The fragrant smoke trickled skyward, and he leaned into it, cupped his right hand and washed his face with it, anointed his arms and chest, cleansed himself.

You will hear things, Wendell's hand-scrawled missive advised. *But don't let them obsess you.*

His first sleepless night down here in the Palo Duro, Emmett had been confused by a low rumbling sound vaguely like distant thunder. Eventually, he realized that it came from hooves beating the bottomland. Ponies. Not just a few ponies, but hundreds of them. And they had a rhythm in their skittish movement, the single-minded dance of flocks and herds darting back and forth in peril. Then he imagined that he heard gunfire. Only imagined because he knew that the ponies had not been killed here. They'd been herded twenty miles away to Tule Canyon, so this was not even the ground that resonated with the sounds of that massacre.

If ghosts existed, that's all they were. Resonations of the past.

The second night of sleep deprivation—for Wendell insisted that Emmett not sleep for the three nights contained within these four days—he suddenly snapped out a reverie that was perilously close to dozing. He definitely heard a distant gunshot. One gunshot in the Texas night was easy to dismiss, maybe high school boys riddling traffic signs with bullets along a rural road. But this solitary shot was followed by more, and then whole volleys of them, so many they sounded like hail popping against a metal roof.

Through this, he heard ponies screaming.

Do not listen to the thunder dogs screaming, Wendell had further counseled. *Get beyond it. Pray. Wait for power to express itself in you.*

The sound diminished with the coming of day, then let up entirely, and Emmett thought he was beyond it.

But when night fell on his third day in the sun-baked draw, the ponies started up again, dancing and screaming. Emmett felt close to losing his mind as it went on and on, and might have—had not a blood-red sun finally lit up the east with day just when he was at the limits of his endurance.

Metaphysical razzle-dazzle didn't suit the Comanche temperament, and Wendell confirmed this by allowing for other possibilities: *This might be nothing more than the power of the subconscious, for I believe the subconscious to be the most powerful ghost of all. But that portion of the mind is no less real than anything else, so you're not off the hook.*

And now, as Emmett tried to clarify his mind with cedar smoke and prayer, the ponies were at it again. His people had used the Palo Duro as a sanctuary for as long as they'd been in this country, and he now unabashedly begged any lingering spirits who'd chosen to make this their abode after death—*calm your ponies.*

But it didn't work. The horrible shrieking continued. Accompanied by the wild drumming of hooves. Always, that death dance.

He glanced off toward Bob Acheson's two horses. They were quietly grazing, cropping the nubs of the grass carpeting the slope below the spring Emmett had located for them. Two votes for the screams residing entirely inside Emmett's subconscious. Weren't animals supposed to be far more prescient than humans?

Get beyond it.

Emmett sprinkled more cedar into the tin cup. More smoke. More anointing. And then, finally, he began trembling. Not in fear, although he had a premonition that something was on the verge of making its presence known. No, he was shaking from a chill, as something cold and powerful sifted through his body.

Not long after, he heard a clatter of rocks in the draw above him—someone was coming. Heavy footfalls were descending toward him.

Emmett prepared himself for God only knew what. Perhaps one of the bogeymen of his childhood, even a *piamupit,* a huge and cannibalistic owl whose bones the whites said came from ancient reptiles. Any Comanche child knew better.

He could smell the dust raised by the footfalls, which were quite near now. He expected Quanah Parker. Everything Royce and Wendell had told him about the dream had prepared him to meet his great-grandfather. He struggled to clear his mind so he would worthy of the visitation.

A shape appeared just beyond the throw of the firelight. It broke from the shadows and eased down across the fire from Emmett as if there was nothing peculiar in this man's returning so vividly from the dead. Father Jurgen didn't speak, and in those timeless minutes Emmett stopped trembling. He was no longer cold.

"You, *Tuah*, are dear to me," the old priest finally said over the continuing cries of the frightened ponies. His voice was not as Emmett recalled. It was now strangely Indian, somewhat like Wendell's. "But let me criticize you."

Emmett lowered his head in assent.

"You must make yourself clear. You seldom bother to do this, and it makes trouble for you. I don't know if it's conceit or stubbornness. But make the effort." He scowled. "Now clean up that filthy mess in the shower room." Then the priest rose in his brittle way, joints cracking as they had in life, and vanished up the draw.

The ponies were silent.

For hours, Emmett waited for them to start up again.

They didn't, and from that slowly came a heightened sense of peace. He felt as if he'd slipped over some hidden boundary in time and was safely tucked away in a dimension before the slaughter of the ponies, before the existence of the BIA, before his divorces, before Jerome Crowe's murder, before his own current predicament. Before everything bad in the world.

He was safe because he'd willed himself to be safe.

He was also sleepy. More sleepy than he'd been all these days and nights.

He reached for a canteen. Not to drink. He poured some water into his palm and splashed his face. When that didn't work to rouse him, he took hold of a live coal and grasped it as long as it took for the burst of pain to strike his brain. Then, alert again, he sucked thoughtfully on the scorched bit of flesh.

Wendell—the college dropout, the tuner of old pianos, Emmett's unsolicited benefactor—had written in conclusion: *A vision is where the world comes together for you. It's a solution that pops into the mind, not preconceived. You've got to eliminate food, water and sleep as distractions. You've got to feel safe and then strive for an uncluttered mind. You aren't trying to alter the mind. You're trying to raise its natural efficiency to root out a so-*

lution. Through inattention, you've wound up on the wrong side of your-
self. So don't be surprised if you must turn around and fight the mirror
image of yourself.

Now sleep.

At last, Emmett slumped against the ground.

14

B ARBARA, THE SECOND hurricane of the season, struck the Mexican coast just south of the border city of Matamoros and gradually weakened over land. But weakened was a relative term, for as the storm died, much of northeast Mexico and west Texas received between eight and eleven inches of rain. The panhandle counties of Deaf Smith, Potter and Randall got about nine, which was in the moderate range, but those inches came in the space of a few hours. And so, those counties were now federal disaster areas, littered with the carcasses of drowned livestock.

The Secretary of Agriculture was due in from Washington this afternoon, but Michael had already grabbed the only available U.S. government chopper in the area, an Air National Guard H-60 from Reese Air Force Base outside Lubbock. As the pilot flew through swirling gray fluff, Mangas expected his own Washington headquarters to order him to return to Reese as soon as possible and turn the helicopter over to Agriculture.

Until then, he and Dustin Ramsey out of the Elk City office would continue to search the rolling plains and desert canyons around Amarillo. Ramsey had taken one rain-streaked window in the cabin, and Michael the other. The grasslands had already been burned brown by the summer sun, but the storm had touched them up with patches of pale green. At least temporarily, until the searing heat returned. Flash floods had swollen the Red and Canadian rivers, catching as many as two thousand head of cattle by surprise. They now lay dead along the muddy banks.

But Michael wasn't interested in livestock losses.

He was looking for the killer who'd left a body behind in this country. A floater, to be more precise, and the second floater of the past six weeks, including Calvin Ushuk of Wales, Alaska. A male corpse lashed to a rude timber cross with nylon ropes knotted similarly to Ushuk's bindings. Also with the remnant of an eagle quill tied with rawhide to the crossbeam.

This new body might have gone undiscovered for months if not for Hurricane Barbara. Tierra Blanca Creek boiled down into Buffalo Lake, which soon overlapped its own banks. The rising waters floated the corpse above the cattails that had ensnared it for at least a week, according to a preliminary forensic examination. The autopsy wasn't slated until tomorrow, but a few things were obvious: The marks around the male victim's throat left by some sort of ligature, biting trauma to the tongue and petechial hemorrhages, or tiny blood clots, to the inner eyelids—all signs of strangulation. Yet, only the post mortem could determine if the cause of death had been asphyxial or from bleeding. There was a ghastly cut across the abdomen, which made him the second victim in the past month to have been stabbed below the midriff. The first, of course, had been Jerome Crowe. This victim appeared to be American Indian, as well, although the chance he might be native was not enough to save Michael from viewing this case over the shoulder of the Randall County sheriff and the Texas Bureau of Investigations. However, the fact that Buffalo Lake was a national wildlife refuge did give the FBI a jurisdictional toehold.

Michael suddenly frowned as he watched below.

This was their third sweep over the pond-dotted lowlands southwest of Amarillo. He decided that further searching here would be fruitless.

Going forward to the cockpit, he asked the pilot to head north of Amarillo, for it was here that something that almost defied coincidence had come into play.

The pilot gave a helmeted nod and banked sharply, making Michael return to the cabin along a sloping deck.

It was north of Amarillo two days ago that a Potter County deputy sheriff had been hunkered down on a ridge with a spotting scope. He was staking out that portion of the range south of the Canadian River in the hope of catching some cattle rustlers, who'd been plaguing the local ranches. At dusk, two horses caught his eye in the distance. One was a bay saddle horse, the other a black packhorse. Riding the bay was a male subject, possibly Indian, decidedly bald, for the last bit of sunlight glinted off his pate— Michael had counted on Parker to change his appearance. All too quickly, the sun was shrouded by a curtain of rain, and, within minutes, the deputy had to run through a hailstorm for his own four-wheel-drive, which he'd concealed behind the brow of the ridge. He didn't follow up on the sighting and recalled it only when the FBI issued a request for any information related to the floater in Buffalo Lake, no matter how seemingly remote the connection.

Can this be dismissed as coincidence? A floater is found and then, within days, Michael has the first plausible brush with Parker since he slipped the FBI perimeter along Cache Creek in a bucar. A sighting less than forty miles from Buffalo Lake.

The Canadian River came into view. It looked like a fat, rust-colored snake wriggling across the prairie. Rivers were natural barriers, particularly when in flood, so he ducked forward again to ask the pilot to sweep up and down the river.

Returning to the cabin, he caught Ramsey yawning. The agent didn't care for this country. He probably yearned for the day when he was reassigned to a big flagship office somewhere in the east. Michael had always dreaded that possibility for himself, and thankfully the FBI had seen political advantage in keeping a Comanche-Chiricahua agent in Lawton.

"Cows, cows, cows," Ramsey griped over the whine of the engine.

Michael didn't correct the citified agent that cows were the mature females of the genus *Bos* and mostly what he was seeing were dead steers. Herefords, dappled red and white. Angus, as black as coal. Charolais, cream-colored.

But then a spot of reddish-brown caught his eye, a color called *bay* when applied to horses.

He rushed into the cockpit and nearly shouted at the pilot, "Set us down anywhere you can close to the river!"

As soon as they touched down, Ramsey started to follow Michael out of the cabin. But Mangas stopped him cold. "Got your H.T.?" His Handie-Talkie, or portable radio.

"Yeah, why?"

"Continue to search the river with the pilot. Tell him to work downstream."

"Why?"

"Just do it." Michael leaped down onto the soggy ground and jogged clear of the main rotor. The chopper lifted off, nose-heavy, and headed down the river. Mangas was glad to hear the deafening noise recede but, immediately, he regretted having forgotten his hiking boots in the trunk of his car. His street shoes squished through the brick-red mud as he made his way down to the Canadian.

The river was still running full and swift, but it'd been running even fuller and swifter when it swept the legs out from under the quarter horse he now beheld. A quality mount half-entombed in a fresh slab of mud. One eye glared back at Michael in death. The left rear leg was broken and nearly bent double. That was the result of the sheer weight of the rampaging water. The poor animal had tumbled down the river bed, snapping at least one leg and conceivably losing its saddle.

And conceivably losing its rider.

Michael slogged out onto the shelf—and sank to his knees. Still, he continued over to the horse at the risk of losing his shoes and brushed away the muck, searching for a brand.

None.

Almost as expected. Parker would be too clever to leave behind a horse that could be traced back to its owner.

Ramsey's voice squawked from his radio, and Michael took the H.T. from his windbreaker pocket. "Go ahead."

"There's something—something manmade—in the mud down from you."

"How far?"

"Two, three hundred yards, maybe."

Michael found Ramsey's exactitude irritating. "How do you know the object's manmade?"

"It has sparkles on it."

"Do you see any other horses?" The bald rider had also had a black packhorse with him.

"No, just more cows."

"Copy." Michael slogged up the bank to firmer ground and started downriver. A grim satisfaction made him smile. The Canadian might have wrapped up this case for him. Emmett Parker might have died along the stretch of river, although there could be a fly in the ointment about that: Often, the bodies of flash-flood victims were never found.

The chopper pilot was standing off so Michael wouldn't be buffeted by his rotor wash. Considerate of him.

"You're close," Ramsey transmitted.

"Which way?"

"To your left."

Then Michael saw it at the water's edge, and recognized the object right off. A saddlebag with decorative *conchas* on the flap, medallions fashioned from silver pesos, usually by Navajo craftsmen. Several yards of silt stood between him and the bag. He trusted his luck, hoping that he wouldn't sink in up to his armpits, and plodded for it.

The mud wobbled underfoot but held him.

Saddlebags came in pairs, but this was a single. A ragged tear in the leather told him the story: The force of the flood had split the bags. He opened the flap and poured some brown water out before examining the contents. Within was a tin cup, fire-blackened on both the outside and the inside. He found that odd. Usually, a camp cup was only blackened on the outside. But then this anomaly was explained by something Michael found jammed in the very bottom of the saddlebag—a sodden cloth pouch with a drawstring. Filled with sacred cedar. There was a logo on the pouch: an eagle's head surrounded by the words EAGLE TRADING COMPANY—ANADARKO, OKLAHOMA.

Also inside was a crow-feather amulet. Something a *puhakut* would give a ward for his protection.

Michael radioed, "Ramsey?"

"What do you have?"

"Reason enough to roust the Potter County Search and Rescue unit. I want ground teams searching every inch of both banks of this river all the way down to Lake Meredith. And then I want boats with grappling hooks to drag the bottom of the lake."

"For what purpose?"

"Closure," Michael replied, sprinkling the cedar from the bag over the water, as if blessing it. Water was sacred, and there was a good chance it'd done justice here. It had indicted, tried and executed the guilty.

He was about to pitch the feather amulet into the river, too—when something made him pocket it.

Dustin Ramsey had grown up in New Hampshire, but had gone to Boston College, where he majored in accounting. He hadn't especially liked accounting, but all the other possible career choices had left him with even less enthusiasm. He'd never dreamed of becoming a cop, much less an FBI agent, but in his senior year he received a flyer urging accounting majors to join the bureau. It had never occurred to him that his degree might lead to something adventurous. His first year as an agent with the Boston field office took some of the luster off of that, but not all of it. And he'd especially liked the camaraderie. The common interest among the rookie agents was professional sports, so it was natural when they started a football pool. As football season wound down, they began a basketball pool, and then shifted their focus to baseball. Like all addictions, even seemingly harmless ones, gambling requires bigger and bigger doses to give the user a kick. In this case, the doses were cash, and before anybody really comprehended how far they'd gone, the pool for the World Series exceeded five thousand dollars. That much money attracts attention, and the pool was busted by the ASAC, the assistant special-agent-in-charge. The other accounting major in the group, who ran the pool off his work computer and took ten percent of the proceeds for his efforts, got a four bagger—in FBI-speak, disciplinary action in the forms of censure, transfer, suspension and probation.

Ramsey got just censure and transfer to Elk City, Oklahoma, a city of ten thousand, smack dab in the middle of the nowhere.

Ramsey now turned off I-40 onto Broadway Avenue.

Broadway.

Since Boston probably didn't want him back, Ramsey's office of preference was New York City. That meant he'd requested transfer there. But the censure didn't help his cause. So he was stuck in Oklahoma, where the towns were built low to the ground as if cringing in fear of tornados. They were also drab, making him miss a New England charm he hadn't appreciated until it was behind him. There were no major league sports teams in the state, and so far he'd stayed neutral about the rivalry between the University of Oklahoma and Oklahoma State. He detested fried okra and grits, two dishes every acquaintance here thrust on him with a culinary vengeance.

In short, Oklahoma was purgatory to Dustin Ramsey.

His dash clock read ten after two, but he had one final chore before he could crash. He had to swing by his office and drop his Handie-Talkie into its charger so the batteries would be ready for the next summons by Michael Mangas at some ungodly hour. At first, it had seemed kind of cool: working with a guy who looked just like Geronimo. But then it hit Ramsey that the head Lawton agent was asking him to do jobs he didn't want to offload on his own subordinates.

Like assist with the search near Amarillo today.

Finally, the radio call had come in for the Air National Guard helicopter to return to Reese AFB and pick up the Secretary of Agriculture for his own sweep of the disaster area. Ramsey expected Mangas to kick him loose. No such luck. He insisted that Ramsey accompany him back out to the Canadian River and uphold the FBI's interests at the sheriff's command post. The hours dragged on, and the only thing to interrupt the boredom was a ball of snakes, flushed from their den by the flood waters, bobbing down the river.

It had given Ramsey the heebie-jeebies.

As day turned into night and the Coleman lanterns at the CP were lit, Ramsey reminded himself that he would be relieved when Parker's body was finally discovered. The exchange of gunshots with the BIA investigator on top of Mt. Scott had been Ramsey's first shooting incident, but the usual rookie elation over coming through such an incident unscathed was clouded by all the wild fear he'd felt and the fact that he'd faced another federal officer. Even though he was now a renegade, Parker was a legend in cop circles.

Possibly a dead legend.

By eleven o'clock tonight, no body had been found in either the river or the lake, and the search was suspended, to be followed up by a scaled-down effort in the morning. At last, Mangas freed Ramsey to return home to Elk City. He sped through the warm, misty night, fighting spells of drowsiness so strong he had to roll down his window several times and sing college fight songs at the top of his lungs.

Now, all he had to do was drop off his radio for charging.

Ramsey parked in the rear lot. He grabbed his keys and the H.T., then made for the employee entrance. It was locked, as expected. He secured the door behind him, in case he was delayed longer than expected inside his office by some messages.

Stepping into the elevator car, he pressed the third-floor button. The doors whisked shut, but the car seemed to drop, not rise. After a second, it stopped altogether. Ramsey checked the control panel: The right button was lit, yet the level light showed "B." *Basement*. Repeatedly, he jiggled the three button. Nothing happened, so he tried to open the doors.

Again, nothing.

A wisp of air crossed the back of his neck as if another opening had formed somewhere in the car.

Then he felt a soft tapping against both sides of his neck. Instinctively, he tried to bat the objects away—boots, shin-high boots, for Ramsey's groping hands closed around a pair of human shins. Shins to powerful legs, for before the agent could glance up at his attacker, the man bashed him against the back wall of the car. Everything went gray, and his ears rang.

When Ramsey had his senses again, he was lying on his back against the floor, staring up with bleared eyes at an open panel in the ceiling.

He attempted to rise, but then felt a knee pressing into his throat. A double image swam in circles above him, then slowly coalesced into a single figure, that of a large Indian man. His head was completely bald, but for some salt-and-pepper stubble. Recognition of the man could wait, for Ramsey realized that he had been relieved of his pistol. The man was holding it on him. From his first day at the academy, it had been drummed into him to never lose possession of his service weapon. It was an agent's biggest night-mare—quite literally, for often Ramsey had dreamed of his 9mm being ripped from his grasp.

But now, he was undeniably awake.

"Stay where you are," Emmett Parker said.

That's who it was. Parker. Keeping Ramsey's pistol trained on him, the fugitive rose and gave a fierce yank on the handrail at the back of the car. The agent thought the man might be looking for an impromptu club, but then he seized Ramsey by the belt and rolled him on his side to remove his handcuffs from their carrying case. Ramsey understood that these were his last few moments to mount any resistance. Yet, he continued to sprawl limp on the floor and comply as Parker clapped one of the bracelets onto Ram-sey's right wrist, threaded the chain behind the rail and then attached the other cuff to the agent's left wrist.

He felt a curious relief that resistance was now probably futile. Mo-mentarily, he had foreseen personal glory coming his way if he somehow managed to take down the fugitive. But now, that vision seemed vain and stupid.

Still, Ramsey needed to regain some of his dignity. "Why don't we move someplace more comfortable, like my office, and talk?" he suggested.

"No way," Parker said, relieving the agent of his H.T. and cell phone. He pocketed both. The fugitive had immediately seen behind the ruse: A charge of false imprisonment could be bumped up to full-blown kidnapping if movement, even from room to room, was involved. Finally, Parker sat down and began holding Ramsey's pistol more loosely. "We can talk right here. So let's go over that night up on Mt. Scott."

"Okay," Ramsey said, licking his lips.

"Did you tell Mangas you properly identified yourself to me?"

The agent hesitated. He was terrified that the wrong thing might trip Parker off. So far, the man seemed to be in control of himself. But that could change in a heartbeat. "I'm nearly positive I identified myself as an FBI agent."

"Not what I asked you," Parker said icily.

"Yes," Ramsey admitted, "that's what I told Mangas."

"Let's see how that jibes with reality."

"I don't understand."

"Just listen." Parker had his own handgun, a revolver, showing above the fly of his torn and mud-caked Levi's. "You tailed me westbound on Route Forty-nine. I ditched you in Medicine Park and drove on my lonesome up to the overlook on Mt. Scott. I found Jerome Crowe dying in a Porta-potty, a butcher's knife still stuck in his gut. With me so far?"

Ramsey nodded.

"Crowe didn't get a good look at his assailant, but whoever the bastard was, he'd just left the parking lot. The knife was still cutting Crowe. Internally. So I saw no choice but to remove it. That's when you showed up at the overlook. Either for the first time that evening or the second. Which was it, Ramsey?"

"The first," he said emphatically.

Parker smiled in a way that chilled him. "All right, let's proceed on that basis for the time being. You show up for the first time in a blaze of high beams. That's all I could see—the glare of headlights. You told me to freeze. Hate to differ with your version of the events, but that's all you said. And I'll take that to the polygraph. For all I knew, I was facing the son of a bitch who'd just mortally wounded one of my best friends. So I told you to freeze. Does all this sound new to you?"

Ramsey knew better than to try to answer. Parker's eyes were now simmering with rage.

"Next," the man went on, "you told me to drop my weapons. Plural. Meaning the revolver and the knife, correct?"

"Yes," Ramsey replied.

"I said I wasn't dropping anything. *'I'm a federal officer,'* I said. And you responded, *'Me, too. Do exactly what I say or I'll shoot.'* Then you failed to specify what I should do, as if you'd never undertaken a felony takedown in your entire life." Parker grinned, but there was no humor in it. "*Me, too.* Less than a ringing endorsement for authenticity, and I believe that at this point in my future trial—if I live to trial—my attorney will get a laugh from the jury as he repeats your stirring declaration of agency."

"You fired first," Ramsey said, angry now at being unnecessarily humiliated. And ashamed by how soaked with perspiration he was. It was pouring off him.

"I did. After wasting precious seconds exchanging niceties with you, I watched my friend die. Then you shouted, *'Freeze, Parker!'* A memorable moment, for this was the first time you referred to me by name. As far as I knew, only Crowe and the nameless informant we planned to meet up there knew I was on the way from Lawton. Referring to me as Parker put you at the top of the list for nameless informants. I was also exposed out there in the parking lot, so I fired once, high, to keep your head down while I rolled for cover. You fired back. A lot more than once. And not high, because bullets were striking the pavement all around me. You also opened up with your shotgun as I made every effort to decline further combat and get the hell out of there. I was no further threat to you, but you riddled Crowe's Cadillac with buckshot as I drove away."

"I've got nothing to apologize for," Ramsey said, his voice firm for the first time.

"Oh, I don't expect you to apologize. All I expect is for you to put my words down on paper. Accurately record this interview for posterity, even if you contest everything I've said. Think you can do that, Ramsey?"

The agent fired back at him, "And if I don't?"

"I'll know you were showing up at the overlook for the second time that evening. And do what I think fit."

Posterity. The agent sensed a ray of hope. Parker's request inferred a next time, a future—however limited—for Dustin Ramsey. He wasn't prepared to quash that hope for himself. "Okay," he finally said, "I'll file a report."

"Good."

"Mind if I sit up?"

"Not at all, just point your legs away from me."

Ramsey complied. Once he was sitting, he had a better view of the BIA detective. The man's clothes were caked with dried mud. While he looked exhausted, nothing about him indicated that he was ready to throw in the towel. "So you made it across the Canadian."

Parker smiled faintly. "Is that where you spent the day?"

Ramsey wasn't inclined to share any information about the investigation. The man's smile died. "What does Ushuk have to do with all this?"

"You tell me."

Ramsey didn't see the blow coming. But he felt the back of Parker's hand landing against his cheek. The contact was numbing, and the man's face drew close to the agent's eyes as he growled, "Look, you prissy little fuck, you tried to kill me two weeks ago. Since then, I've been framed and chased out of Dodge. Don't count on my good graces. I'm plum out of good graces. And there's still a damned good chance you killed Crowe, so don't push me."

Ramsey broke eye contact first. He didn't want to, but he heard himself muttering, "Ushuk was under investigation by Customs before you phoned him. . . ." The young agent had interrogated enough people to notice the mental connection Parker visibly made as if for the first time. Either he was a good actor, or he didn't honestly know much about the Eskimo. "Customs wasn't sure what he was smuggling. But they believed he was a smuggler."

Then Parker shook his head in momentary distraction. He really was behaving queerly. Not like he was dissembling, but more like he was snapping bits and pieces of a puzzle together after a lot of confused speculation. "So, Mangas is putting it out that I suckered Ushuk down here so he could be eliminated?"

That was pretty much it. But Ramsey kept mum.

"What was Ushuk's cause of death?" Parker demanded. "The papers never said."

Ramsey hesitated. It wasn't a given that floaters died of drowning, but that wasn't the true reason for his hesitation. There was an opportunity here to learn incriminating details about Parker from the man's own lips, as long as he himself didn't divulge too much. Or too accurately. "Ushuk died of drowning," he lied, for the Eskimo had died of a slit throat. "But there was some antemortem trauma. He'd been beaten around the face and neck." On purpose, the agent glanced at Parker's fists. They were bruised and chapped.

But the fugitive's eyes were boring directly into his. "So all Mangas really has on me is a phone call, presumably from me, placed from my mother's house to Ushuk in Wales, Alaska? Answer me, dammit."

Time for some more evasiveness. Short of getting slapped. "I doubt that's all Michael has. But I'm not the lead investigator, and both of us know he's not an overly communicative guy."

"If an Alaskan Inupiat wound up dead in southwest Oklahoma, we both know this is a nationwide effort. Agents from your Anchorage office had to have flown out to Ushuk's home—" Parker impatiently interrupted himself. "There are three possibilities. One, they found a promising connection between Ushuk and me, something more than an untapped phone call. In that case, Mangas would be grabbing complete strangers to tell them the happy news. Two, the Anchorage guys found a connection between Crowe and Ushuk. If that's true, I'd like to hear about it. Three, none of the above. Which is it, Ramsey?"

He didn't want to admit that it was number three. The agents from Anchorage had found no Oklahoma connection in the Inupiat's life, other than the call placed from Celia Parker's home. There was a lead that defied explanation as of yet, but it pointed toward Siberia, not the American Midwest. Ushuk had kayaked on numerous occasions from his weather station on Little Diomede Island to Big Diomede, which was uninhabited but still frequented by its Russian masters, especially security forces. Anchorage was working on this angle, but Ramsey saw no need to tell Parker. What he felt was a need to salvage his own wounded pride and turn this embarrassing fiasco around. "What do you say you start treating me like a fellow investigator?"

Again, a faint and weary smile. "Oh? And how might I do that?"

"Uncuff me. These things hurt. You can keep my nine-mil for the time being. We go upstairs together. You can call your attorney from my office, and the three of us will sit down to talk."

Chuckling, Parker came to his feet. "I would, Ramsey, but I hate like hell getting your Oklahoma City SWAT team out of bed this early. Don't worry. You won't have long to wait. Folks ought to start arriving at work by seven-thirty or so. It'll take a half hour to roll the maintenance outfit to get the elevator working again. But I figure you'll get your French roast and Danish by eight. Eight-fifteen at the latest."

Then he did something baffling.

Smiling, he tapped the top of Ramsey's head, as if playing tag.

Then, at last, he reached up and grasped the outer edges of the opening in the ceiling. "Don't bother smacking all the buttons like you were. Including the fire alarm. They're all disconnected." Parker hoisted himself out of the car, wincing as if the effort gave him pain. Ramsey would mention that to Mangas.

Standing on top of the car, Parker replaced the ceiling panel and disappeared from sight.

Ramsey was left with the uneasy feeling that the man had gotten what he'd come for.

He wouldn't mention that to Mangas.

He waited half an hour, then began hollering, hoping against hope that an Elk City patrolman might swing through the parking lot and hear him. Before Parker got too far away.

15

"**Y**OU'RE RUNNING LIKE *porra*, Dustin," Michael said irritably. "Punch it, for Chrissake."

"What's *porra?*"

"Snot."

The FBI SWAT team out of Oklahoma City had a one-hour jump on Ramsey and him. The two agents had linked up at the field office downtown so they could continue on to the extreme northeast corner of the state in a single bucar. It was now almost three in the morning, and they were ten miles beyond Tulsa on an I-44 that was empty but for big rigs. Even though they had taken Michael's car, Mangas let Ramsey drive. He needed the time to think. The young agent drove at ninety miles an hour with the blue warning light flashing in the grille, but Michael knew his Ford would do a hundred.

Two mornings ago, Parker had left Ramsey handcuffed to the rail in his office building's elevator. The agent's cell phone had had a life of its own since that time. Once advised, the field office flew in a radio-electronic specialist from Washington to intercept any calls Parker made, but he arrived too late to monitor the first transmission. According to the cellular provider, it'd been made within the Elk City service area to a cell phone with a Maryland area code. The call had been placed about thirty minutes after Parker climbed out of the elevator.

Ramsey now proved that he was mentally going over the same events. He asked out of a silence that had lasted some minutes, "Any luck running down the subscriber to that first number Parker called?"

"No, not yet," Michael answered. He didn't add that he'd purposely kept that number to himself.

Ramsey was still smarting from his hours in the elevator. It was good for him to be ashamed. Shame seasoned you, filled you with the resolve never to be humiliated in the same way again. And he'd screwed up royally. The loss of his Handie-Talkie to Parker had compromised the bureau's primary communication system in the state, rendering it virtually useless in the near term. *Brilliant move,* Michael thought to himself, *but no use crying over spilled milk. Parker hadn't drowned in the Canadian River, no use crying about that as well.*

The second call had been placed yesterday, twenty-eight hours after the first. Transmission quality was too poor to monitor the conversation, no doubt owing to weak batteries, but it had been dialed from a roaming zone to a residential number in Quapaw, Oklahoma, named after a tribe relocated there from the lower Mississippi Valley in the early nineteenth century.

The Quapaw had nothing to do with Michael's decision to call in the SWAT ninjas after a second call had been made to that number nine hours ago. However, a minor historical fact had much to do with his speeding up the interstate in the early morning darkness. In 1873, a rebellious element of a tribe along the eastern California–Oregon border was exiled to the Quapaw Agency in the Indian Territory, later Oklahoma. For the better part of a year they'd kept most of the U.S. Army busy and had even managed to kill a major general. That tribe was the Modoc, and Michael had learned from a memo on Parker's career prepared by Andreas's BIA staff in Albuquerque that Emmett had been partnered on three major cases over the past eighteen months with an FBI agent out of the Las Vegas office. Anna Turnipseed. Her Modoc ancestry could be traced to both the California–Oregon and Oklahoma branches of the tribe.

Michael had met her once before. At a dedication service as two more names were added to the Indian Peace Officers' Memorial at the BIA law enforcement academy in Artesia, New Mexico. A pretty woman, though slightly withdrawn.

But even before Parker had shown up in Elk City, Michael had asked for a tap on Turnipseed's home line, trusting that sooner or later Parker would try to contact the closest person in the world to him. His partner. The Las Vegas office nixed that idea on violation-of-privacy grounds. Next, Michael asked that Turnipseed be told to report any communication from Parker. The denial to this request came from D.C. headquarters: She was on an extended undercover manhunt and her handlers didn't want her distracted by the Parker affair. A matter of her personal safety.

Michael's cell phone rang, and he scooped it up off the console. "Mangas."

"What's your ETA?" It was the female ninja with the SWAT team already surrounding the house near Quapaw. She and Michael had conversed several times over the past hour.

"Just left Vinita," he told her, "so about twenty minutes."

"We think we're getting movement inside. We don't want to wait any longer."

Michael glanced at the dashboard clock: 3:46 A.M. This was the hour to storm a hideout, when the suspect's biorhythm was at its lowest ebb and his mental processes sluggish. He wasn't exactly sure when that was with Parker. Maybe never. But Michael guessed that there was another reason the team wanted to roll now: They'd lost Parker and one of their bucars during the attempted apprehension along Cache Creek two weeks ago. As with Ramsey, embarrassment was a great motivator.

"Go ahead and do it," Michael said reluctantly, for he genuinely wanted to be on the scene. Yet, it'd be held against him if the team delayed entry on his request—and then took casualties from an alerted Parker. He disconnected and told Ramsey, "Keep stepping on it. SWAT's going in."

The agent pressed the gas pedal as far as it would go, but then looked over at Michael, his expression worried in the dash lights. "I've got something I want you to take a look at."

"Like what?"

"A report. I haven't submitted it yet."

"Later."

"Please, Michael."

"Can't this wait?"

"I really need you to take a look now. I've probably already delayed too much."

Michael sighed. "Where is it?"

"My gear bag."

Michael reached around into the backseat and unzipped the bag Ramsey had tossed there in Oklahoma City. On top of his Kevlar body armor was a sheaf of papers. He turned on the high-intensity lamp attached to the console and read the hand-written incident report. Twice. Then he confronted Ramsey: "Why didn't you mention this in the debriefing?"

"I wasn't sure it was appropriate at the time. You and the suits from the field office were mostly interested in how Parker kept asking about Ushuk."

Michael boosted the volume knob to the Motorola. If things went badly in Quapaw in the coming minutes, maintaining radio silence would be superfluous. He started to return Ramsey's report to the bag when he suddenly stopped, bit his lower lip, then folded the pages in quarters and pocketed them in his windbreaker. "You write any of this on your work computer?"

"No, all long-hand at home. Why, what's wrong?"

"And this is the only copy?"

"Yeah, a draft. I wanted to show you first."

"Did it occur to you that—by questioning now that you properly identified yourself up on Mt. Scott—Parker might be manipulating you?"

"Yes."

"Now, I'm asking you again—did you properly ID yourself that night?"

After a moment, Ramsey stammered, "It all happened so fast, Michael. I was right on top of him as soon as I came into the lot. Crowe was covered with blood, and Parker was holding the—"

"*Icoño, icoño, icoño!*" *Crap!* Michael took a moment to simmer down. Every culture had its standard for truth, which was really just the socially accepted gap between reality and interpretation. To whites, a white lie was perfectly acceptable. An Apache hunter incurred no blame if he boasted that he'd killed a bear as long as he'd killed at least a rabbit. But Mangas didn't quite know how to explain this to a kid from New England who was on wafer-thin ice with the bureau. "Dustin, listen—self-doubt about what happened during a few critical seconds is natural. I know that. And certainly Parker knows it. But do you have any idea the spin the BIA will put on your doubt? It can and will be used against you. Do you have any goddamned idea?"

"I'm sorry."

"Route One-thirty-seven is our exit," Michael said more calmly. "Don't miss it. Straight north into Quapaw." Still no radio traffic from the entry team. He took that as a good omen. "Dustin . . ."

"Yeah?"

"If you kept this out of the debriefing, what then made you want to put it down on paper?"

A long pause followed. Michael thought that was all a mortified Ramsey had to say, so he took the shotgun down from the roof rack and fed a cartridge into the chamber in preparation of their arrival at the scene.

But Ramsey finally said, "I promised Parker I'd do it."

Michael believed he understood. For whatever his reasons, Parker had spared Ramsey's life. As bizarre as it probably seemed even to himself, the agent was feeling gratitude. Maybe Emmett had known that might happen—and had wanted to drive a wedge in the FBI team.

God only knew.

Ramsey asked tentatively, "What're you going to do with my report, shit-can it?"

"Hell no. I'd like to retire someday on max benefit instead of handing folks shopping carts at the entrance to Wal-Mart." Michael exhaled. "We'll work this out together. You are to relate everything the fugitive said to you. However, tack on an opinion and conclusion that '*I, Special Agent Dustin Numb Nuts Ramsey, identified myself and it was clear to me during the entire event that Parker knew I was a federal agent.*'"

"Thanks for helping me, man," he said with relief.

"Don't call me *man*."

"Sorry."

"You already said that. And yes, you are." Michael sat back and sighed again. Even though he'd had less than a stellar start with the bureau, Ramsey would probably settle down into a fair agent. It was one of the ironies of this business that the stars at the academy quickly flamed out and many rookie fuck-ups gradually clawed their way up a wobbly ladder to competence. There was one thing that couldn't be denied about Ramsey. He was unflappable. After twice facing the most deadly fugitive Michael had ever known, the young agent hadn't mentioned quitting even once. Something was largely missing in the way the bureau brought along its novices, something that hadn't been missing in Chiricahua culture—an older warrior, a relative if possible, took a youth under his wing and secured his path to full manhood. The old took full responsibility for the young and were not content to stand back and watch them sink or swim.

"Can I ask you something, Michael?"

"What?"

"Why did Parker do what he did to me?"

"Meaning, why didn't he kill you?"

"Yeah."

A good question. Maybe Ramsey had promise as an agent after all—most whites would have just chalked up Parker's nonlethal attack to their own good luck. "I get the feeling he counted coup on you."

"Counted what?"

"Coup." Michael spelled it for him. "A French word for *blow*. Many tribes had a coup stick for this purpose."

"What purpose?"

"You'd gallop up on your enemy during battle and—instead of killing him with an actual weapon—you'd just tap him with your coup stick. To die in battle is honorable. But counting coup on your enemy leaves him alive, so he can wallow in his shame and reflect on the fact he's a worthless lowlife."

That sobered Ramsey for a minute. But then he proved unflappable again. "Can I ask you something else, Michael?"

"Shoot."

"How come you always ask me for help and not one of your own residents?"

"Why, is your boss bitching?" Michael meant the supervising agent at the Elk City office.

"A little, but that's not why I'm asking."

Mangas took a moment. "Part of it's that I can use an unfamiliar face on some of these jobs, like shadowing Parker up to Mt. Scott that night. Part of it is because I trust you to keep your mouth shut."

"Really?"

"No, but it sounded nice, didn't it?"

Michael's call sign came over the radio in a female voice, and he grabbed the microphone. "Go ahead."

"House has been cleared. Subject isn't here."

"You check the attic, basement and storm shelter?"

"Affirmative," the ninja said, sounding miffed he would doubt her.

Michael had half-expected this outcome, but was still disappointed. He would have assumed from the get-go that Parker had promptly ditched Ramsey's cell phone—except for the unexpected Modoc element in the calls that had been made. Two days ago, Ramsey had encountered a haggard and exhausted fugitive who might become increasingly, even atypically, careless as he staggered around Oklahoma in search of help and refuge. Then again, maybe Parker wasn't that bad off. Yet.

Ten minutes later, Michael and Ramsey were standing in the living room of a shantylike house that had been crowded even before the FBI burst inside. There were sleeping bags and bedding rolls on the two greasy-looking sofas and even on the bare, hardwood floor. At least three generations of an extended Modoc-Quapaw family were present.

Right off, Michael demanded to know who among them had been out of the area recently.

Three adolescents, a youth and two girls, admitted to having attended a powwow at the Caddo County fairgrounds near Anadarko. They were cousins and had just returned earlier tonight. Michael had the ninjas keep the threesome separate from each other. He interviewed the boy first in the kitchen. He'd seen enough television to immediately demand the presence of his attorney. Michael doubted that he had a lawyer, but he fobbed the boy off on Ramsey and interviewed the older of the two girls next. A pudgy eighteen year old with a homely-cute face. She was more cooperative than the boy, and when he abruptly asked her where the cell phone was, she trooped compliantly into the bathroom. She used her back to block Michael's view as she removed the lid from the tank of the nonfunctioning toilet and produced a Nokia phone.

Taking it from her, Michael lit up the screen for the number—it was Ramsey's.

Gently nudging her aside, he peered down into the bottom of the dry tank. The cellular had shared space with a Baggie of apparent marijuana. "I'm not interested in that," he said.

She returned in jubilation with him to the kitchen. And couldn't say enough now. Four nights ago, the three kids had been attending the opening ceremonies powwow when an *'old drunk guy'* seated near them in the stands engaged them in conversation.

"Was he Indian?" Michael asked.

"Definitely. But I don't know which tribe."

"How old?"

"Pretty old, like you."

Michael frowned. "This is important—was he bald?"

"I don't know."

"Had he shaved his head?"

"I don't know."

"Why not?"

"He was wearing a fur hat," the girl replied.

"What kind?"

"One of those otter caps."

"Go on."

"He asked us if we wanted to buy a cell phone for ten bucks. So we took him up on it."

"Did you figure it might be stolen?"

"I don't know what we figured," she said remorsefully.

"Did he know you were Modoc?"

"Funny you say that . . ." Her voice trailed off as she seemed to recall.

"Why's it funny?"

"Well, the emcee had just told the crowd all the tribes that had sent dancers, and me and my cousins joked that you never see a Modoc dancer in any of these powwows. That's when this guy got up from where he'd been sitting—"

"Where?"

"A couple rows back. And he came down right next to us."

Michael took a paper from his shirt pocket and unfolded it. A wanted flyer on Parker. "Was this him?"

The girl took her time. "I don't know. This guy looked a lot more wasted. I just don't know. It was kind of dark in the stands, too. All the lights were on the dancers."

Michael put away the flyer. "Does the name Anna Turnipseed mean anything to you?"

She shook her head.

Michael returned to the living room and called for the entire family's attention. "Does anybody remember some folks named Turnipseed living around here?"

A chorus of murmured nos was punctuated by a frail voice. It came from the far corner of the room, where an aged woman sat with her arms around her knees on a chaise lounge cushion that apparently served as her mattress. Michael went to her and knelt respectfully. "What did you say, Grandmother?"

"I remember the Turnipseeds." There wasn't a tooth in her mouth. "The last one left a long, long time ago. His name was Jack Turnipseed. He went off to college in Stillwater but got to drinking and got hisself in bad trouble there, so he went out west to the homeland to start a new life."

"You mean the Modoc homeland in California and Oregon, Grandmother?"

"Yes, that's the place. There's another homeland farther west . . ." She showed her pink gums in a grin. "But it's up in sky. That's where I'm headed soon. The place of the dead."

Michael patted her liver-spotted hand. "Not too soon, I hope." Then, rising, he caught Ramsey's eye and motioned for the agent to follow him outside. Once they were in the yard, he said, "We've been had."

"How?" Ramsey asked.

Michael turned and took in the eastern sky. It was swiftly brightening. "Parker was in the Anadarko area a couple days ago. I doubt he's still there. He sent us on a wild goose chase. Maybe just to test our responses. Probing us."

"Where's he headed?"

"There used to be lots of swamp rabbits in the fields down by Cache Creek."

"I don't understand."

"Listen," Michael said sharply, "and you will. From now on, the most important thing you can do is listen to me." He paused until he felt he had Ramsey's full attention again. "We boys from the Indian school would chase them. A chased swamp rabbit will always run in a circle, even if he doesn't know that he's running in a circle. Everything heads for home when it's in danger."

"You have anybody sitting on his mother's house?"

"Yes, Weeks," Michael replied. "It's been dark. Celia Parker is gone. Nobody will say where." He watched the very top of the sun crest the horizon. "But Parker's not a swamp rabbit, and he's not afraid. So why's he running in a circle? Ft. Sill, Amarillo, Elk City and now Anadarko. A circle."

"You know, he did something really weird in that elevator."

Michael steeled himself for another ground-shaking revelation that, somehow, had been forgotten. "Tell me."

"Right before he climbed out of the elevator, he reached over and tapped the top of my head. Like this . . ." Ramsey demonstrated on Michael. "He didn't have a stick, but was he counting coup on me, like you said?"

"Big time," Michael said, starting back for the car.

16

AN ALABASTER VIRGIN in a pale blue robe shone from her shrine. Emmett watched her from the waist-high corn in which he sprawled, waiting for her to offer counsel. She'd said nothing in the two hours he'd lain here, although he felt that they had something of a working relationship. He'd once labored in these fields surrounding St. Benedict's. He couldn't make out the ruin of the old mission from his hidden vantage. But, if he rose up a little, he could scan the parking lot of the modern church at the front of the property. Vehicles went to and fro on the highway, but none had turned off.

He pulled on a plastic Coke bottle filled with water so the last heat of the day would not dehydrate him.

He'd come early to wait and watch, to size up the yet unidentified person he expected to appear sometime before nightfall. And, more than anything, he needed to make certain that this person came alone, intentionally or not. Every hour or so, he switched on Ramsey's Handie-Talkie, trying to catch any FBI radio traffic, however cryptic, hinting that Mangas and his task force were operating in the Anadarko area. The chatter he overheard sounded routine, although the low battery strength kept his monitoring to a minimum.

Almost three days ago now, as he left Elk City in the predawn darkness, he'd seized an opportunity. It was fleeting, for within hours Ramsey's cellular would be worse than worthless—it'd be a beacon leading Mangas directly to him. The call was a long shot and certainly had its risks, but with each passing day, Emmett realized that he had to make his case to someone before Mangas caught up with him. So he'd dialed a cellular number he recalled from memory. A female voice answered, cottony with sleep. *"Hello?"*

"Good morning."

"Oh, my God." Instantly, Dagen Kirsch sounded wide awake, but still she asked, *"Who is this?"*

"You know."

"My God, where are you?"

He responded to her question with one of his own. *"Are you back in Washington?"*

She hesitated. *"Yes."*

"I don't have long to talk," he went on. *"Will you listen to what I have to say?"*

"Of course." With no hint of accusation in her voice. Just concern.

"I did not kill Jerome."

Silence on the other end.

"You've got to believe me, Dagen, I didn't. I went up to Mt. Scott only because Jerome said he'd developed an informant I should meet—"

"Slow down," she interrupted, although he knew he'd been talking slowly and deliberately. If anything, she probably wanted time to think. *"An informant about what?"*

"The missing trust funds."

"Did you get to meet this person?"

"No."

"Do you know who he or she is?"

"He, but no. I don't. Jerome was all alone and had a butcher knife in his belly when I got to the overlook. Minutes later, just as I took out the knife, Ramsey, an FBI resident from Elk City, drove up. He might've been in the area for some time."

"Are you saying this agent killed Jerome?"

"Look, Dagen—this is what you've got to do for me. Have Interior press for a special counsel, somebody objective to look into this. It's bigger than just me, I'm sure of it now. The counsel's investigators have to question everything Ramsey and Mangas say. Their version will fall apart under scrutiny and the investigators have more than enough leads. Can you do that for me?"

"I . . . I have a close friend. She's highly placed at Justice. Shouldn't I go to her instead of the Interior Department?"

"No, don't—the director of the FBI is also highly placed at Justice, and he'll kill the inquiry to cover his own ass."

Silence. She was afraid to do this. Emmett understood the dangers to her career, the thing she held most dear. He had no choice but to ask. Fighting this single-handedly made it almost impossible for him to clear himself, especially with Mangas stacking the deck against him at every turn. *"Dagen . . . ?"*

Rather than go on vacillating, she changed the subject. *"Where've you been all these days?"*

His mind flashed through his fatiguing route of the past week. The Canadian, where he lost Bob Acheson's bay saddle horse and most of his gear when he was forced by a glint of binoculars on a distant ridge to ford the flood-swollen river when he should have waited. Pushing on another thirty miles, riding bareback on the surviving packhorse, he reached Adobe Walls, the site of the frontier outpost where the *Nuhmuhnuh* fought the buffalo hunters for the last time. Wendell had insisted Emmett leave the Palo Duro by way of the Walls, and the reason for that became clear when he rode down into that grassy and still remote valley: An old Chevy Impala was parked near the monument to the Indian warriors who'd fallen there. The car was covered with several days of dust and registered to a Manuel Gonzalez of Lawton, whom Emmett didn't know. But it was unlocked, and the key was in the ignition. Emmett had no doubt the Impala had been left for him. He released the packhorse into a corral with water, trusting the local rancher would care for it until Emmett could contact Acheson. The Chevy got him to Elk City and beyond, but it'd broken down this morning.

But there was no time to get into all of this with Dagen. Within minutes, FBI soundmen might be scanning the airwaves for this particular cellular. So, he said, *"I've been on the road. On the move."*

"Oh God, Emmett, I don't know what to do."

"I know, I know. This is hard, and I hate asking."

*"It's almost easier for me to go to the President than Justice or even
Interior. . . ."*

That would bypass the FBI director. The idea had crossed Emmett's
mind, but he'd been afraid the request would scare her off. Dagen already
had too much to lose, and Emmett was giving her nothing in return, except
trouble. Now, she herself was offering to play the presidential card. Still, the
lull in the conversation that followed seemed to crackle with uncertainty. *"I
just don't know, Emmett. . . ."*

He couldn't afford to let her off the hook, so he held his tongue.

*"You have to pick your moment with the oval office. You have only so
many shots with the president, and if you hit him at the wrong time with
something difficult . . ."* She sighed again. *"Let me think how to do this. I've
got to be careful about this."*

"I understand, Dagen."

*"And I can't blurt out to the president that I just got off the phone with
you, can I?"*

"No." It struck him that, so far, she hadn't urged him to turn himself in.
This, he knew, was a weathervane. If she asked him to surrender, she believed that he'd murdered Jerome. *"But, just remind the president he knows
me. We worked together."*

"I will, Em. As soon as I can. In the meantime, what do you need?"

"Reliable transportation and some cash," he said offhandedly.

But she surprised him: *"I'll see what I can arrange. There's a friend
who'll keep quiet about this. That, too, is going to take some time."*

He was tempted to warn Dagen that aiding him would make her and
that friend complicit. But he couldn't do it. He needed her help, especially in
regards to transportation. *"How much time?"* he asked.

"I don't know—maybe a few days. Where will you be in, say, three days?"

"I'll phone back with the answer. Do you have caller ID?"

"Yes."

"Well, don't phone this number. It won't be good much longer. Promise."

"I promise."

"You don't mind a collect call, do you?"

She laughed, but then her voice broke. "Oh God, Em, I'm so frightened for you."

"Don't be. I'm managing. All I need is a little more time to turn this around. With time, it's going to crack." He paused. "Who's your friend?"

"I don't want to say over the phone. But I'm sure he'll help."

"Fair enough. Just have him make sure he isn't followed. Good-bye for now."

"Take care, please take care."

This morning, Emmett had used a pay phone to call the same number, although this time it was collect from *Father Jurgen*. A cautious-sounding Dagen told the operator that she'd already donated a substantial amount to the Benedictines' mission program and it wasn't convenient to speak to Father until this evening. Silently, Emmett had congratulated her on her resourcefulness: the mission that evening.

Now, he could hear a vehicle slowing out on the highway. He reared up, slightly. The daylight was nearly gone, but he could see that the car was a white Ford sedan. It turned down the lane that ran alongside the church. The driver was male, judging from his short-haired silhouette. His running lights were on, and as he went past the shrine to the Virgin Emmett saw that the Ford had Oklahoma plates. The driver continued up the drive to the brick rubble of the old mission building and stopped. His lights went out, and a moment later Emmett heard a car door shut. Yet, the driver was screened from view by the overgrown hedges.

Emmett stood and checked the highway. There was traffic, but no other cars slowed for the church. He drew Ramsey's 9mm from the back band of his Levi's and started moving toward the ruin.

After the firefight with Ramsey atop Mt. Scott, Emmett had been left with only four rounds in his revolver. There was no doubt in his mind that the FBI had alerted firearms dealers in the Midwest to be on the lookout for a male Indian adult trying to purchase or steal .357 ammunition. So, late the same morning he'd left the Elk City agent stranded in the elevator, Emmett reluctantly pitched his own revolver into the Washita River from an interstate overpass. He didn't like semiautomatics. Never had. They tended to jam just when you needed them most. But now he had to make do with one.

He found the irrigation ditch that encircled the mission grounds. Thankfully, it was dry. He used its cover to approach the ruin, then dashed across an expanse of grass to the first hedge.

There, he knelt and listened.

Somewhere to the northwest, a cow was lowing, mournfully. But that was all.

A light came on behind him.

Pivoting, he saw that it was to the shrine. The Virgin was now bathed in fluorescent. An automatic timer or had somebody switched the light on from inside the church?

No vehicles were parked in the lot.

Emmett refocused his attention on the white Ford.

Time to find out to whom it belonged.

Parting the foliage with his free hand, he peered at the front steps that once had led up to the ground floor of the main building. A figure was seated on them, smoking a cigarette. The coal winked on and off with each puff. "Come out, come out, wherever you are, *Pabi*," a familiar gravelly voice said in a playful singsong.

Emmett approached by way of the sedan, glancing over the interior to make sure nobody else had hitched a ride here. Then he concealed the pistol again and walked the rest of the way up to Royce Eschiti, who rose unsteadily from the steps and threw an arm around Emmett. He was very drunk, and Emmett used the hug to pat the roughneck down and make sure he wasn't packing a weapon.

Again, Eschiti had dropped unexpectedly into his life, although this time it was at Dagen's invitation, not Wendell's. It made sense: Dagen and he had gone to school here with Royce. But Eschiti wasn't his first choice for help in a pinch.

Then the man revealed that, despite the booze, part of his mind remained keenly aware: "What's wrong, *Pabi?* You going to get rough with this old con again? You already owe me for one shirt, you know."

Emmett disengaged himself. "Who's car?"

Royce touched his forefinger to his lips before lowering his voice. "Dagen's. She keeps it at her apartment in Anadarko for when she flies home from Washington. She phoned for the landlady to give me the keys."

"How'd you get there?"

"My old truck, why?"

"Anybody follow you?"

"Nope." Then he waved conspiratorially for Emmett to follow him to the trunk of the car. He'd forgotten that the lid was popped from inside the car, so Emmett did it for him. The trunk light came on. By the time Emmett returned to the rear of the Ford, Royce had taken a bundle of crisp twenty-dollar bills from a large manila envelope. He fanned them in Emmett's face. "What you think of this? There was a note on the front seat telling me it was hid back here for you. Isn't Dagen great?"

Emmett checked inside the envelope—several thousand dollars, at least. The sight of so much cash didn't elate him. It meant only that, with Dagen in Washington, somebody here in Anadarko had been included in the mix to help him. Somebody he might not trust.

He took the bundle of bills from Royce and returned it to the envelope. He closed the trunk, thankful to be covered by darkness once more. "When'd you start drinking again?"

"Oh, let's see—I'd say just before I missed my last two parole check-ins."

"That means they're looking for you, Royce."

"Well, shit, that's two of us, then!" Eschiti cackled, then suddenly yowled and shook his fist like mad. His filterless Lucky Strike had burned down to his fingers.

Emmett strode for the tallest pile of rubble. It was the only thing resembling a hill from which to scan the surrounding farmland and the houses on the outskirts of town. He would drive away as soon as he felt sure nobody was waiting for Royce and him out on the highway.

Eschiti staggered up the slope of broken bricks behind him and plopped down at his feet. "Where you been since I last seen you in Quanah?"

"All over the place," Emmett replied, running his gaze over the darkened corn. "Palo Duro, even Adobe Walls."

The man gave a shudder. "The Walls is a bad place. Don't tell me nothing about Adobe Walls."

A moment too late, Emmett realized that his mention of the battle site had been careless. There, not only had young Quanah saved Royce's ancestor, Howea, saddling his descendents with a moral debt, but Eschiti—Royce's namesake and a renowned medicine man—had convinced Quanah and the rest of his band he'd concocted an unguent that would repel the .50-caliber bullets of the buffalo hunters. It didn't. Thirteen warriors were killed and many more were wounded, including Quanah.

"What's it feel like, *Pabi*?"

"What?"

"Being on the other side of the law?"

Emmett said nothing. A sheriff's cruiser had pulled into the gas station mini-mart a half mile down the highway. The deputy got out and went inside.

Royce lit another cigarette. "I ain't ragging on you. It's just good for a soul to see things from the other side sometimes. 'Specially a proud soul. That's what peyote does for you. Least, that's what it does for me. Not saying it's for everybody. But it works fine for me, and I ain't even that proud. Mangas is plenty proud, and it works for him, too."

"You seen him lately?"

"Naw. Since this shit started up with you, he won't give me or Wendell the time of day."

"What about my mother? Is she all right?"

"Sure, her and Frankie are making a quilt for you."

"You haven't mentioned to anybody where she is, have you?"

"No way."

"Not even to Dagen?"

"Not even to nobody." Then Royce said sourly, "I know what I owe you, Emmett."

The deputy nonchalantly returned to his car with something in hand, possibly a soda, and drove away, toward town. "When's the last time you saw Wendell?" Emmett asked.

"Other night. He doesn't want me staying down at his place so much 'til this trouble with you blows over." Royce fell silent while Emmett continued to look all around. "Hey, Em, that time you followed me down to Walters, the night of the full moon . . . ?"

"What of it?"

"How come you didn't try the bud like Jerome did?"

"No desire."

"You should, really should. I was just sitting there in the tent, all full of light and colors, when in came my papa. And sat across from me. Can you believe it? I wasn't sure I should talk to him, but Wendell said if I ever got the chance I ought to. . . ." Royce inhaled deeply, and the brightening of his cigarette ember revealed a troubled squint. "Papa said he was sorry. Don't that beat the devil? He said he should've respected me more." But then, Royce added bitterly, "Yeah, right. I sure wish he'd said that when he was living."

Emmett asked, "You know anything about that floater they found in Lake Lawtonka?"

"Only what was on the radio news. An Eskimo." Royce cackled again. "Don't that beat the devil? An Eskimo from Alaska. And now they got another one."

"What do you mean?"

"Another stiff they fished out of Buffalo Lake over in Texas."

Near Amarillo, the panhandle country Emmett had ridden through last week. "Is this one from Alaska, too?"

"Nobody knows yet. Ain't identified. But maybe he is another Eskimo. That would *really* beat the devil, wouldn't it? We'd have Eskimos popping up all over the place." Royce flicked his butt away, before it could burn him. "You ever been to Alaska, *Pabi*?"

"Couple times on the job."

"I never been, job or not. Thought about it. You know, going up there to Prudhoe Bay to the oil fields. Had me a buddy in the joint who went up to Alaska all the time."

Emmett decided to go easier on him. At least Royce had brought him a car and cash, and he'd had neither a half hour ago. "Oil worker?"

"No, he was a mule."

Emmett had to hide his distaste. "You mean he ran drugs up there?"

"No, cash. His drug run was usually from Mexico to Oklahoma City. But he was too smart to get busted transporting, otherwise he would've gone to the federal pen instead of McAlester, and I never would've met him. No, he got sloppy and was peddling right out of his mama's bar in the city."

"What bar?"

"She owns the Powwow Lounge on Reno Avenue, and they shut down her place for a while, even though she had nothing to do with it."

"Wait a minute—you're saying he carried shipments of cash to Alaska as a sideline?"

"Something like that."

"For what purpose, laundering?"

"I guess, Emmett."

"Who'd he do it for?"

"Wouldn't say. Cheyenne. You know how they are. They won't say nothing unless it suits 'em."

Emmett's face turned sharply toward Eschiti. Could this have been the Cheyenne involved in money laundering Jerome Crowe had alluded to? "Where'd he take the money in Alaska?"

"I got no idea." Royce stood, steadied himself, then stretched. "And I sure as hell can't ask him now."

"Why not?"

"He's dead. Hepatitis. The real bad kind. Died in the prison hospital last Christmas eve."

"What was his name?"

"Hold on. I got to piss." Royce clattered down the backside of the pile and disappeared into a thicket of elm saplings that had shot up where the garden outside the vestry had once been.

Something about the missing trust funds had always bothered Emmett:

They never seemed to re-enter the economy. Billions of BIA dollars had vanished over the years, yet it was as if the embezzlers had burned the cash in their fireplaces. Most thieves of this sort couldn't resist going on buying sprees, sales trends that would have been detected by now.

A new thought hit him. "You ever tell anybody else about this guy?"

"Just Jerome and Dagen," Royce said from the saplings.

"When was this?"

"Just before I got released. They came to visit me in the joint. Dagen for moral support, but Crowe just to look down his nose at me."

Neither had ever mentioned this to Emmett.

The moonrise was imminent, but what Eschiti had just said about the Cheyenne glued Emmett to the top of the rubble pile. Had this knowledge cost Crowe his life and was Dagen now in danger as well?

Suddenly, Royce cried out, "You son of bitch . . . !" Emmett had no idea what the drunk was angry about, until the man said even more emphatically, "You just cut me, you lousy son of a bitch!"

Drawing the semiauto, Emmett raced down the far side of the pile and waded into the saplings. Royce wasn't visible. Emmett couldn't find him. Not for nearly half a minute. Then he saw that he was almost on top of the prostrated man. Royce had fallen to the ground and was pawing at his shirt pocket for something. "I'm cut all to shit, *Pabi*," he mumbled, sitting up. Sparks materialized in the air before his dazed-looking face as he clumsily tried to the spin the striker wheel of his butane lighter with his thumb. Emmett grabbed it from him and ran the flame over Royce. He had a defensive gash in his right forearm and an even deeper across in the palm. The arm wasn't bleeding badly, but the hand wound was gushing. And Eschiti was splattering himself with blood as he waved the palm ineffectually back and forth as if trying to cool the burning sensation of the cut.

A few feet away lay a butcher's knife.

Emmett ripped off Royce's shirt buttons, lifted his uninjured left arm out of the sleeve, then twisted the shirt around his right forearm and tied it off around his palm. As a temporary tourniquet. "Did you get a look at him?"

"Freaky-looking bean pole. Am I dreaming?"

"No." Emmett relit the lighter and made sure the worst of the bleeding had been stanched. "What do you mean *freaky?*"

"Head's too big for the rest of him. Like a big old owl or something."

"Did he have a gun?" Emmett asked, rising.

"Don't think so."

"Stay here, Royce. Don't move. Don't make a sound."

"Bullshit. I'm going to kick his ass." But then he slumped back down to the ground.

Emmett ran through the saplings.

Within a few strides, he could hear the attacker moving through the corn ahead of him. Sprinting without regard for the noise he was making.

Emmett dipped down into the ditch and was topping the opposite bank when fireflies blinked out in the field before him. Except the *pftt-pftt-pfft* sounds told him that the blinking was from the muzzle of a sound-suppressed firearm. As he rolled back down into the ditch, one bullet came close enough for him to feel its heat pass by his ear.

Probably believing that he'd finished off Royce, the attacker had then drawn Emmett out here into an ambush.

Rising to a crouch, Parker scrambled up the bank and fired where he believed the attacker lay out in the field. His shots reverberated across the mission grounds.

The bastard had egged Emmett on by making a lot of thrashing. Then he'd had the coolness under pressure to lie down prone and squeeze off several rounds. Fortunately, a sound-suppressor, a baffled tube screwed onto the muzzle, affected accuracy.

But not that much.

For Emmett then heard another faint *pfft*, followed by whisk of a small-caliber bullet right over his head.

He was being backlit.

Turning in exasperation, Emmett saw that the full moon was emerging from the rooftops of the housing development to the east of the mission. But, looking out across the field again, he saw that its light was being absorbed by the dark green of the corn. For all he knew, the attacker could be on the move again.

Royce was drunk. In violation of his parole. With a car and several thousand in cash in the trunk.

Emmett couldn't rely on the man to stay put.

But he wanted to get the son of a bitch who'd just tried to kill him. Maybe even more, he wanted answers.

He was over the bank and out into the field when an unmistakable sound stopped him dead in his tracks. A police siren. Someone in the housing development had heard his shots and phoned in.

Grudgingly, he about-faced and headed back to Royce, who was staggering around the car in a swoon, bare-chested, tripping over his feet but never quite completely losing his balance.

"Steady," Emmett said, helping Eschiti into the front passenger seat of Dagen's sedan.

"You get him?" he asked.

"Not yet." Emmett still had hopes of driving around the far side of the cornfield on the county road there and catching the attacker before he got to his vehicle. Failing that, he had retrieved the butcher knife on the way back to Royce and planned to hold it for latent fingerprints, prints invisible to the naked eye until they were dusted with black powder.

Royce was soaked with blood, which made no sense because the tourniquet seemed to be holding. "Can you wait for stitches long enough for me to run down this bastard?" Emmett asked.

"You bet, *Pabi*." But the trouble with Royce's reply was the fact that blood was trickling from the corners of his mouth.

"Jesus, Royce!"

"What?"

On Eschiti's red-stained left side was a small caliber bullet entry wound, quietly pulsing a few driblets of blood with each beat of his heart. There was no exit wound, so he needed help fast.

"What's wrong, Em?"

"You've been shot. Didn't you know you've been shot?"

"No. Honest to God?"

"Hold your shirt to your side like this . . ." Emmett positioned his hand to the place, for in shock the man probably felt nothing. Then he belted him in. "Hang on, I'm getting you to the hospital."

The siren was close now. Emmett slammed Royce's door to kill the dome light just as the sheriff's cruiser streaked past the church. His brake lights didn't come on, and the deputy continued west to the county road that Emmett had wanted to take to try to catch the attacker. The deputy sped up. Maybe he would have better luck.

Whatever, Emmett accelerated for downtown Anadarko.

17

D R. HAWZEEPA READ the Randall County medical examiner's report on the body found last week in Buffalo Lake. From time to time, his long face showed mild disdain for something the Texas pathologist had dictated. Michael had asked him to drop by his office in Lawton on the way home to talk about the findings on this autopsy, and the man had agreed after one of his typically resistant pauses. "It's all pretty cut and dry," he finally said, glancing up from behind bifocals that magnified his fox-brown pupils. "Is there something here that bothers you?"

"Yes," Michael admitted. He took a sip of coffee. He was back to drinking coffee after midday. He was sleeping no more than three hours a night now, a sure sign that once again his life had been taken over by an investigation. "The cause of death. Was it strangulation or evisceration?"

Dr. Hawzeepa gave one of his aloof smiles. "Either was sufficient to do the job. Petechial hemorrhages to eyelid conjunctivae and tongue trauma indicate that his throat was wrenched quite violently by some sort of cloth ligature. But, also, very little blood was left in the vascular system. So it's a toss up, especially since you don't seem to be privy to the crime scene."

"Why use both means, when one was enough?"

"Chalk that up to all the usual human passions—jealousy, hatred, even love. But I have the feeling this killer was concerned with presentation."

"What do you mean?"

"He or she wanted his work to create an effect."

"In what way?"

"I rather think he or she was trying to impress or frighten somebody," Dr. Hawzeepa explained. "What interests me is the second use of a timber cross, now. Any evaluation on what kind of wood?"

"The forensic botanist says Ushuk's cross was fashioned from bur oak."

"Interesting. Native to the east side of our state, not the west. And the second cross?"

"Still waiting for the same botanist to have a look at it." Michael narrowed his eyes. "You keep saying '*he* or *she.*' Anything make you think a female might be up to this?"

"Can't rule it out. Back to presentation—both victims died as Christ did, hung from a cross and lanced, in a manner of speaking. I believe we now have a motif. This latest victim, what's his name again . . . ?" The examiner quickly leafed through the pages and found it himself. "Regis, Joseph Regis. Slashed across the abdomen. Ushuk's throat was slit. That might be a significant difference."

"Enough to rule out the same killer for both homicides?"

Dr. Hawzeepa paused, his expression unreadable. But then he lowered his voice to a confidential murmur. "I don't think it's unseemly to pass this along to you, Agent Mangas, as long as you're discreet with it . . ."

"Pass what along?"

The examiner hesitated, then said, "I'm sure you are aware Parker and my sister, Ladonna, were married for a few years."

"So . . . ?"

"Well, she once suggested to me that Parker resented his Catholic upbringing. He wouldn't even allow a crucifix inside their house. That may be germane to this case, increasingly so, and it's the only reason I'm now mentioning it to you."

Michael found the man's endless formality tiresome. He wished he would speak less precisely, drop his *gs*, and talk like an Indian. "You want me to share this with the profilers back at Quantico?"

"If you wish. I just thought you should know. A parting thought." Then, just when Michael believed the examiner was going to excuse himself, Dr. Hawzeepa leaned back in his chair again. "Hope I'm not bringing up something unpleasant, but my sister tells me there was bad blood between Parker and you."

"Oh? What'd she say?"

"I'd prefer to hear your side of it. For objectivity's sake."

Michael nodded. Trading information tit for tat was standard in this business. He had just milked Dr. Hawzeepa, and now the milking machine was on the other udder. "Emmett and I were cops together with Oklahoma City P.D.," he began, trying to sound even-handed. "He had a close friend on the department who was also treasurer of the patrolmen's association. I and some others had reason to believe that this guy was skimming funds. I ran for treasurer and won. I was cooperating with the state A.G. in an embezzlement investigation against this officer—when he was killed in the line of duty."

"Unrelated to your case?"

"Yeah, a domestic dispute on the west side of town. Anyway, Emmett reacted emotionally. Protective of his dead buddy's reputation. Understandable, I suppose."

"But still," Dr. Hawzeepa observed, "Parker appeared to condone a possible case of embezzlement, correct?"

"I thought so at the time," Michael said, holding the examiner's eyes for a moment.

"Do you still?"

"Yes."

"I hope I've been of some help, Agent Mangas," Dr. Hawzeepa said, rising.

"You have, thanks."

The examiner was at the door when he turned. "Who was the attorney general you worked with at the time?"

"He's now President of the United States."

Dr. Hawzeepa arched his eyebrows, probably as much surprise as he ever revealed. Then he was gone.

Michael scooped up the Randall County M.E.'s report and locked it away. He hadn't shared the full quart of milk with Dr. Hawzeepa. Joseph Regis was but one of several aliases the victim found in Buffalo Lake had used over an adult life that had included a prison term in New York state for both forgery and wire fraud. As best Michael could tell, his true name was Morris Cornplanter. A member of the Seneca tribe, though he'd never been active in tribal affairs. In the 1980s, he worked for Kodak in Rochester, honing photography skills of later use to his forgery career. He had a common-law wife, possibly part Indian, who had her own long list of AKAs.

Both had dropped out of sight five years ago.

Motifs.

The medical examiner had missed the second emerging motif in all this. The Randall County evidence tech had improperly identified the eagle feather tied to the crossbeam of Morris Cornplanter's cross as a rawhide bootlace. And once again, as with Ushuk's cross, the stub of a quill had gone unnoticed. Was it possible Dr. Hawzeepa had recognized this touch of *Nuhmuhnuh* witchcraft and, for his own reasons, let it slide without mention? As for himself, Michael was beginning to distrust this clue. A hint too much, as if the killer were saying, *Look, I resent Christianity and, by the way, I'm also Comanche.*

Pondering this, Michael swiveled his chair around and turned on the police scanner he kept on a bookshelf behind him. He'd shut it off when the examiner arrived. Now, he again half-listened to the constant stream of law enforcement radio traffic. Most, even the hot calls, were of no interest to him. With repetition, even emergencies seemed dull, and police work was full of repetition. He was waiting for the signal that would tell him that Emmett Quanah Parker was still lurking in either Comanche or Caddo County. He waited with the patience of those radio-telescope technicians who search deep space for signs of intelligent life:

In Lawton, traffic units and a fire ambulance were responding to an injury accident on Gore Boulevard.

A Love's Restaurant had been robbed outside Chickasha.

A Caddo County deputy needed backup in taking down a belligerent drunk.

Endless and meaningless background chatter.

None confirmed what he was beginning to suspect after the Elk City incident: Quite possibly, Parker was re-entering his life in an attempt to clear himself. If that were not the case and vengeance hadn't been Emmett's aim after turning east from the Amarillo area, Dustin Ramsey would be dead.

Michael checked his emails. An agent from the Rochester satellite FBI office had finally responded to Michael's request to find any possible connection between Parker, who'd just completed a case in upstate New York in January, and Morris Cornplanter. The agent noted that the real action in Parker's recent case had centered on the Syracuse office, but he'd checked with the supervising agent there, who was positive Cornplanter hadn't been involved.

A dispatcher's voice broke through Michael's concentration. He wasn't even sure why it had. Something about having a patrol unit responding to Anadarko Municipal Hospital. A horn was blowing in the ambulance bay outside the ER entrance. "So," the patrolman asked sarcastically over the airwaves, "why doesn't somebody go outside and turn it off?"

"Stand-by." The female dispatcher was off the air for only a few seconds. "Be advised, this could have something to do with the subject who showed up at the Indian clinic a few minutes ago, claiming his friend had been shot. The clinic staff told him they're not a trauma unit and directed him to Muni. Also, the S.O. had several reports of shots fired east of town within the last hour."

"Describe the subject," the patrolman said.

"Indian male adult, thirty to forty years, with a shaved head."

"I'm rolling to the hospital."

Michael was up and rolling, too.

"Drop me off any old place, *Pabi*," Royce said deliriously from the passenger seat in Dagen's Ford.

"Sure," Emmett said ironically. "How about inside the phone booth at a gas station?"

"That'll do." Royce's acne-scarred face was pasty-looking in the glare of oncoming headlights. "You already got my truck key?"

"Yes, in my pocket." As far as Emmett could tell, the wound in the man's side had stopped bleeding, but he was sinking fast. "Listen, Royce . . ."

Eschiti's lackluster eyes clicked toward him.

"I'm going to leave you at ER," Emmett went on, running a red light when he saw no cross-traffic.

"ER at the Indian hospital?"

"There's no trauma unit there anymore. Budget cuts. I'm taking you to Anadarko Municipal. The cops will come because of your gunshot, and parole will violate you. But I want you to know that as soon as I get myself cleared, I'll be in there, fighting for you, getting things straightened out. Right now, helping me is a crime—so don't mention us meeting here and last week in Quanah. Do you understand?"

"Just dump me off any dang place. Right here's fine. You don't understand you're not a cop no more. You're on the run. Just like me. You're no better than me."

"I never thought I was, Royce."

"Bullshit. Both you and Jerome did. Next, you'll be saying there's no debt."

"Not after tonight."

Royce's chin had dropped to his chest, but he cast a questioning eye at Emmett. "What you mean?"

"You took a bullet for a Parker. Howea's debt to Quanah for saving him at Adobe Walls is satisfied."

"You speak for all the Parkers?"

"Yes."

"You'll say it at a gathering?"

"I promise. First chance I get."

"Wow." Royce gave him a happy but bloody grin. *"Udah."*

Emmett pulled into the hospital parking lot and sped up to the pneumatic doors of the emergency room foyer. He hit the horn. Yet, as half-expected, no staff showed to help. Glancing back at Royce, he saw that the man had passed out. He checked his pulse at the neck. Weak. But he was still breathing. Emmett reached under the front seat for the tire-changing kit. He dumped out the tools and, carefully so as not to destroy any latent prints on the handle, placed the butcher knife inside. He'd ditched Ramsey's H.T. back on the mission grounds—the batteries had finally given out. Emmett had no way to recharge them. Besides, he believed the FBI had switched frequencies for sensitive traffic by now, and simple possession of the radio was a dead giveaway. He thought about taking the cash out of the trunk. But didn't. There was something wrong about that much money coming his way. He couldn't exactly put his finger on the reason, but the instinct to leave it was strong.

He tapped the horn again. Longer.

No one showed through the doors. If he himself went inside, he might encounter security. Possibly armed security.

He muscled Royce out of the passenger seat and into the driver's side. Gently, he leaned the man's forehead against the pad at the center of the steering wheel. The horn wailed without interruption.

Then Emmett walked away from the hospital. Walked, not ran.

He was just turning the street corner when a P.D. cruiser barreled up to hospital and parked behind Dagen's Ford. Good. For the next several minutes, the cops would fixate on the sedan and Royce. Widening the search would wait until they felt sure the hospital was secure.

At last, Emmett jogged. His lungs burned, but he ignored the pain.

He found Royce's GMC pickup parked down the block from the Dagen's apartment. He was turning the key in the ignition when he noticed that an upstairs window—her bedroom, if he recalled correctly—showed a light. She'd claimed that she was back in Washington, so did she leave a timer on that light in her absence from Anadarko? She seemed the type. Cautious.

Regardless, Emmett had no time to knock on her front door. Like Ramsey's cell phone, the GMC had a brief useful life to him before it became a liability. No more than thirty minutes, and that might be stretching it. During that time, he had to get out of Anadarko and abandon the pickup, preferably somewhere Wendell could later recover it for Royce.

*   *   *

Arriving at the hospital, Michael saw that both a P.D. and an S.O. cruiser were parked behind a white Ford in the ambulance sally port outside ER. He rushed from his bucar and approached the sedan. The driver's door was wide open to the night, and the interior panel was smeared with what appeared to be blood. As were the steering wheel and both front seats. He touched a fingertip to big dollop of it on the nearest floor mat—the drying blood was still viscid to his touch.

The drive from Lawton to Anadarko had eaten up thirty minutes. He had no time to waste on this vehicle, but something made him flip down the sun visor and take out the Oklahoma registration card. The Ford was registered to a Dagen Kirsch of 1310 Pecan Drive, Apartment C, Anadarko.

His face hardening, Michael blew through the doors and nearly ran to the reception desk. He flashed his credentials to the floor nurse and police sergeant who were casually chatting there over coffee. "Who's the victim?"

"He won't say," the sergeant replied, "and he wasn't carrying any ID."

"Extent of injuries?"

The nurse said, "Deep cuts to the right arm and hand. Gunshot wound to his left side. They're prepping him for surgery right now."

Michael turned to the sergeant again. "I need some help to make a hard target search on an apartment here in town. Get it going by phone, not radio."

The sergeant set down his cup of coffee. "Want us to call out our SWAT unit?"

"Not unless they're already camped inside the station. Alert mutual aid to get ready—on my word—to throw up checkpoints at thirty miles."

"Who's the fugitive?"

"I should know that in about ten seconds." Michael continued down the corridor to the operating room. Bursting inside, he halted just past the door and smiled. He couldn't help but smile. Royce Eschiti was lying on the table with an anesthesiologist hovering over his head, preparing to feed him the gas that would take away his obvious pain. "One minute," Michael demanded, showing his creds again, "I need to talk to this man."

"Can't it wait?" the surgeon asked, his mask puffing as he spoke.

"You tell me, doctor. Is a dying declaration in order?"

"No. Not unless you kill him with all the street germs you just traipsed in here."

Michael ignored the surgeon. "Royce, where's Emmett?"

Silence, although Eschiti has turned his face toward Michael and struggled to focus on him.

"Were you with Emmett tonight?"

The man shook his head. "I didn't go to school with you, Mangas." His meaning was clear. He wouldn't talk. He was declaring his loyalty to Parker, with whom he'd gone to St. Benedict's, and the bond he and Michael shared from the peyote tent on Wendell's farm didn't rise to that.

Then the anesthesiologist slipped on the mask, and the surgeon barked for Michael to get out.

Back at the reception desk, he found the sergeant on the phone to his department. Michael interrupted, "The victim's name is Royce Eschiti. The fugitive you asked about is Emmett Parker. He's presently attempting to flee the Anadarko area in Eschiti's older model GMC pickup, dark green in color. I don't know the plate, but have Motor Vehicles cross-index it off his name. Put a guard on the Ford outside until our evidence people get here. Order those checkpoints now and get me some bodies ASAP to hit that apartment. That's the other possibility—Parker's still inside your fair city, holed up and armed. Assemble your people here."

"You ever say please?" the chagrined sergeant asked.

"Seldom."

While the man relayed this jumble of information to his communications center, Michael stepped outside the glass doors for better reception on his cell phone. He raised Ramsey, who, judging from the background noise, was watching a baseball game on TV. "Saddle up, *compadre*."

"What gives?" the Elk City agent asked, chewing on something crunchy.

"Lady luck. Parker was at the hospital in Anadarko thirty minutesa ago."

"Really?"

"I'd bet my paycheck on it. Start rolling this way. As you do that, roust an evidence tech out of the field office and send him to the hospital here to process anything and everything in or on a white Ford sedan parked outside ER. Also, phone state parole. Find out who Royce Eschiti's P.O. is and have him put a hold on him, if there isn't one already. Royce is under the knife right now, but he's a tough bird and I don't want him strolling out of here as soon as he feels up to it."

"Got it," Ramsey said, though Michael could tell he wasn't eager to tangle with Parker again.

More police and the sheriff's unit were arriving in the parking lot. Two detectives bailed out of an unmarked car, strapping on Kevlar body armor over their shirts and ties. A deputy trotted up, clutching an automatic carbine. Michael decided that these three men were all he needed. He didn't want to wait a second more.

"Listen up, people," he announced, "here's the game plan. I have reason to believe Emmett Parker might be inside apartment C, as in Charlie, at Thirteen-ten Pecan Drive. The owner's away, so the potential for hostages is low. As best we know, Parker is armed with a three-fifty-seven wheel gun and a nine-millimeter semiauto. He will use them if confronted. Don't give him the chance he'd never give you. He is no longer a cop. He is a fugitive. You . . ." He pointed at the deputy. ". . . Run around to the back on arrival and cover it with your long gun. Everybody, Parker has access to an older GMC pickup, green in color. Let's do it."

All four of them crammed into Michael's bucar, so Parker wouldn't be tipped off by a parade of law enforcement vehicles coming down Pecan Drive. Michael had to hold down his rising excitement. There was much to sort out. But he was close to paydirt.

Three minutes later, he was standing before Dagen's Kirsch's door.

He tested the knob. Locked.

Then he kicked, splintering the lock through the jamb. The two detectives were right on his heels as he dashed through the door and swept the living room with his flashlight. The kitchen and dining room were so minimally furnished that the first story was swiftly cleared, and Michael charged up the stairs to the darkened second floor while the plainclothes-men covered him from below.

A few moments later, he was glad they had. So they didn't catch the look on his face when he nudged open a half-shut bedroom door on Dagen Kirsch, who was sitting up in bed, her hair tousled and dark circles under her eyes.

18

"ARE YOU ALONE?" Michael asked Dagen, aware that there was no way to avoid the double meaning.

She'd risen from her bed and gone to the closet to fetch a robe. He recalled it—imitation satin, carmine-colored—from their nights together back east. "Yes," she said, eyes on his pistol as she threw the sleek garment over her slim body. "I'm alone."

Still, he ducked through the doorway to check the spare bedroom and the bathroom. Finding no one, he holstered, but then noticed the crawl space to the attic. He went downstairs and sent one of the Anadarko detectives off to the manager's office for a ladder.

Finally, he returned to Dagen's bedroom. "I thought you were back in D.C."

Her big blue eyes flared a little at his suspicious tone, but then she explained with a catch in her voice, "I just flew in to Will Rogers this morning. I'm taking a leave of absence from my job."

He decided to move this discussion to the lower floor, which had already been cleared. On the way down the stairs, he watched her hips sway beneath the robe. Watched with a sharp pang of longing. The personal and professional in his life had just intersected at the point of maximum discomfort.

As soon as they reached the living room, the remaining detective handed Michael his cell phone. "For you."

The P.D. sergeant was on the other end. He'd gone back to his station to coordinate things. "You Code Four there?" he asked, meaning, *Are you all right?*

"Affirmative," Michael said, lapsing into radio jargon. "Don't send any more people this way." He wanted all available law enforcement out and about, searching for Parker. The next few minutes were crucial. After that, the trail would grow cold. Emmett would make sure of it. Michael saw that Dagen had gone on to the kitchen and was going through the motions of making coffee, but he could tell she was listening to every word he said over the phone. "Any luck on that computer cross-index, Sergeant?"

"None. Royce Eschiti isn't the registered owner of anything, let alone a GMC pickup. Also, his driver's license was suspended in the nineties and hasn't been renewed."

Great, Michael thought. "Okay, continue to re-broadcast what vehicle info we have. I'm going to be tied up here a few. Make sure those checkpoints are up and running."

"Got it."

Michael disconnected and tossed the phone back to the detective. Then he sat across the table from Dagen. Her face looked drawn under the strong kitchen light and the dark crescents under her eyes spoke of a string of sleepless nights. The only sound for a few seconds was the *drip-drip* of the coffeemaker. Then a rattling announced the entry of the second detective with an aluminum step ladder. Dagen watched the two men troop up her stairs toward the attic crawl space. "Don't scuff my walls," she warned them. Then she turned on Michael again: "You're scaring me. What's going on?"

"How well do you know Royce Eschiti?"

"Very well. Why? Has something happened to him?"

"You two went to St. Benedict's together, right?"

"You didn't answer me, Michael. Is Royce all right?"

"He'll live."

Strangely, she shut her eyes for a moment. Almost prayerfully. Was she giving thanks? "A few years ago, Jerome Crowe told me Royce was in prison. He'd murdered his father and was doing time at McAlester. I'd always liked Royce . . ." She shook her head as if correcting herself. "No, I'd always felt sorry for him. He was such a lonely boy. I started writing him now and again. To encourage him. Hopefully, change him. If that's possible. And when he got released and was in need of work, any kind of work, I gave him a job, as best I could afford—"

A thump and then a clunk drew her eyes up the stairs. The detectives were now checking out the attic space. Michael would have searched it himself, if he'd even remotely believed that Parker was here. But the man would never let himself get boxed in like this. "What kind of job did you give Royce?" Michael asked to get Dagen back on track.

"Part time. Caretaker of my apartment and car here in Anadarko while I was in Washington. You know, air the place out now and again, sweep the patio and make sure the battery to my car stayed charged. That sort of stuff."

Michael nodded impatiently. "Do you know where your Ford sedan is right this minute?"

"In my space behind the building here."

"No. It's outside ER at Muni hospital. And Royce is inside undergoing surgery for a gunshot wound."

"I don't want to know," she muttered, momentarily shutting her eyes again. "I just don't want to know."

"Why not?"

"I don't want to be disappointed. I invested a lot of time in Royce."

"Did you give him permission to use your car tonight?"

She visibly thought about that, then glanced up at Michael. "If I say no, is he in trouble?"

"Dagen, this is a lot more serious for Royce than a little joyriding. I believe he met Parker tonight."

"Has Emmett been found?" she asked sharply.

"Not yet. We're still looking."

"Certainly, you don't think I—"

"No. We're searching your place like this because it's how we search every place a fugitive might be found."

Suddenly, Dagen rose as if she couldn't sit still. Going to the coffeemaker, she poured two cups, and despite himself he was flattered to see she still remembered he took an Equal with his. "How long is all this going to continue to haunt me?"

"What are you talking about?"

"My association with Emmett." She sat. "I'm close to being fired, Michael, and all because I made a stupid, stupid suggestion to the President, that he swing by a fucking honor dance!" She knew he didn't like it when she swore, but that obviously was the least of her concerns at the minute. "Did the chief of staff ever phone you?"

"No," Michael replied. "I'm sorry."

"Then that's it," she said fatalistically.

"I don't know what's going on with your job, but your boss should realize you can't be held responsible for whatever Parker is mixed up in. Wasn't Emmett vetted prior to the President's appearance?"

"Not really. The President remembered Emmett, and I vouched for him."

"Still, you shouldn't be left holding the bag. That's wrong. You didn't mean—"

"Doesn't matter, Michael. That's how Washington works. Intentions don't mean squat. I'm responsible for something that embarrassed the President, and now all the work I've done, all the financial support I've brought in for him, means nothing. . . ." Her eyes filled with tears. "It's amazing how the past can bite you, isn't it . . . ?"

He added nothing to that. It was true, and now he feared that his past with her could bite him, causing Jeralyn more pain.

"What's wrong, Michael?"

He set his feelings aside. It was time to spring a trap, and one of his Apache grandfathers had taught him the patience never to spring a trap too soon. "Dagen," he said slowly and deliberately, "have you had any recent contact or communication with Emmett Parker?"

Then he waited.

The instant he'd gotten the log on Ramsey's phone traffic, he had recognized the cellular number with the Maryland area code and the Silver Spring prefix.

He didn't care for the lengths she took as she drew the cup up to her lips and drank. Surely, she must have sensed what this pause could do to her credibility. Surely, she felt his gaze hard on her. But then she looked him straight in the eye and said, "Yes, a phone call."

"When was this?"

Without racking her brain, she gave him the date and the approximate time of Parker's call to her, just after he'd humiliated Ramsey.

At that moment, the two detectives came down the stairs with the ladder. One of them had little pink fuzz-balls of fiberglass insulation all over his clothes. "Nothing," he reported.

"I'll be with you outside in a minute," Michael told them, making it clear that he wanted privacy with Dagen. Then, once they were alone again, he pressed, "What was said?"

"Emmett asked me to intervene on his behalf with the President. Remind him that they'd worked together when he was state A.G."

"Did you?"

"No." Then she hid her eyes behind a hand, as if too ashamed to show her tears. "I couldn't bring myself to do it, Michael. My job was already hanging by a thread. I couldn't."

"Did you urge Parker to give himself up?"

Looking at him again, she shook her head.

"Why not?"

"I felt like I was dealing with a paranoid," she answered. "He was so convinced you'd kill him the first chance you got, as you tried up on Mt. Scott—well, I was afraid asking him to give up would set him off. Make him think I'm part of some kind of conspiracy against him."

"He actually said that I was out to kill him?"

"Yes. You, Ramsey, even the FBI director."

Michael sat back. He should have expected that. Parker, like any other felony fugitive, was bound to characterize the effort to apprehend him as a witch hunt. Finally, it was time for the question he genuinely regretted asking. "Dagen, why didn't you report this call?"

"But I did."

"To the FBI?" he asked, skeptically.

"No. Please don't take offense, Michael, but I had my reasons for not going to the bureau. I didn't want agents out of the D.C. office storming into the West Wing to interrogate me. That could've been the last straw. Next thing, I would've been dumping my desk drawers into a cardboard box. Don't you see?"

"Who'd you report Parker's call to?"

"The Secret Service, of course."

"I don't follow you. The FBI has jurisdiction in this, so do state and local enforcement here. What does the Secret—"

"Don't ask me how," she butted in, showing irritation with him for the first time, "but I heard what happened to your poor agent in Elk City, which is—what?—like sixty miles from Taloga and the western White House."

That meant she had a source inside the Justice Department, but he let it slide.

"I'm no psychologist," she went on, heat rising in her face now, "but it seemed to me Emmett was zeroing in on the President as the solution to the mess he's gotten himself in. I wasn't sure how healthy it was, or how it'd turn out. So I went to the White House Detail of the Secret Service, all right?"

Michael took his pen and spiral notepad from his shirt pocket. "Name of the agent you talked to?" he asked, taking his small spiral pad from his shirt pocket.

"Thorsen. Eddy Thorsen. I mean, Ed."

"You have his phone number?"

"I'll do you one better, Michael." She snatched his pen and pad from him and jotted down a dot-gov email address from memory for him. "Satisfied?"

Now, he felt his own face burning. "There's nothing personal in what I'm doing right now."

"Don't be naive, Michael. This is going to get all too personal before it's over. We both know that."

A threat? He couldn't decide. He turned his mind to a new investigative difficulty: The Secret Service refused to discuss security issues with the public and, in the past, had proved to be only slightly more forthcoming with the FBI. He'd once had a close friend in the Oklahoma City office of the service, somebody with whom he could've broached anything. But Michael had lost more than Todd in the Murrah blast.

His cell phone rang. He rose and went into the living room, simply to be out from under Dagen's now accusatory gaze. "Mangas here."

It was one of the evidence technicians out of field office, who began by advising that he'd been working on Dagen's Ford at the hospital for some minutes now. "You aware of the cash in the trunk?"

"What cash?"

"Obviously not," the techie said. "Yeah, there's several thousand in twenties in a manila envelope in the trunk. I want to fume the bills for latents and do the hard count after."

"Take your time," Michael counseled. "Do it right."

"Later."

Ending the call, Michael looked at Dagen. She was now slumped over the table, her face down on her crisscrossed arms. He noticed her hands. They were faintly blue, like skimmed milk. A sign of aging. He feared the consequences of her growing old without an important job to prop up her ego. As far as he knew, she had nothing else. No one else. Ordinarily, he would've tried to persuade an interviewee in her straits to take a polygraph exam. However, she might come off as entirely deceptive if she tried to hide their past affair. He had one more detail to clarify before he could go. "Dagen . . . ?"

"Yes," she said without lifting her head.

"Our technician found a large amount of cash in the trunk of your car. Is it yours?"

"No," she said, sounding as if she'd begun to cry again.

Then the currency had belonged to Parker. A tiny portion of the millions he might have embezzled with Jerome Crowe and brought along tonight to buy Royce's help. The two of them had been flush with money, judging from this stash and the $33,000 found in Crowe's room at the Lawton Marriott.

Quietly, Michael approached Dagen and rested his hand on her back. He wanted to say that he hoped this didn't erase all the good things that had passed between them. But she didn't respond to his touch, and he couldn't bring himself to say again that he was sorry.

So he just went out.

*   *   *

The most frightening thing Fe found about Hola was that she'd never seen his face. She had no real idea what he looked like. Once, at the drop in eastern Oklahoma just south of Lake Eufaula, one of several places he had arranged for leaving the new checks and collecting the lion's share of the cash, she thought she saw him standing back in some chinaberry trees, a strange and willowy creature with braids. Maybe it hadn't been him at all, but that's how she imagined him, judging from the high-pitched voice that had given Morris and her instructions over the years.

Now her husband was gone, and she was totally at Hola's mercy.

Standing at the kitchenette sink in the Winnebago, she applied her makeup, managing with her compact mirror. It was too small for the chore, but she couldn't force herself to go inside the little bathroom unless she absolutely had to go potty. The day after she had left Morris at the lake near Amarillo, she'd scoured and disinfected the shower stall with every cleaning product she could grab off the store shelves. Still, each time she ventured inside the bathroom, she saw his blood. Everywhere. She'd had only two showers in all the days since, and for both of those she'd used the facilities at RV campgrounds.

She set down her compact and poured from a pint of vodka directly into a can of diet Sprite. *What am I coming to? I'm too far gone to use a glass like a lady?*

And once, Fe believed, she'd been a lady. An attractive young lady with lots of suitors, especially in the years she'd spent in Hollywood. She'd almost made it there. *Versatile.* That's what one casting agent had said about her looks. With a Filipino father and a half-Mexican mother, Fe had been convincing as almost any ethnic group, except lily white. She even landed a good supporting role in a low-budget feature that was being shot in upstate New York. But when the financing fell through two weeks into the shoot, she was left stranded in Rochester. The bastard producers didn't even pay off the cast, so she'd had no way to get out of town.

Remembering this, she started to cry. Things had never been easy for her. Why should they start getting better now? She took a mouthful of straight vodka, almost gagged, but the warmth of the liquor going down cut off her tears before she really got going once again.

It was so easy to cry these days.

She'd met Morris in Rochester, at a bar, and this was the result—she rolled her reddened eyes around the inside the Winnebago. Not even a real home, which she wanted now more than anything. Some ground where she could plant some flowers. This was just a box on wheels, its ass-end crammed with photographic equipment. And now, there was absolutely no freedom to this life. A murderous geek was playing her like a marionette, and she had to go wherever he said and do whatever he said.

Louisiana.

He was sending her down to Louisiana, hot and buggy bayou country, just to remind her that he was the boss.

She gave up trying to apply her makeup. She looked bad, and she knew it. You couldn't be scared day-in and day-out without eventually looking like hell. Taking another drink of vodka, she shut her eyes and tried to remember her face as it appeared in an outtake a film editor she'd been dating had given her: a sloe-eyed beauty caught in a loveliness that was artfully out-of-focus.

Then she opened her eyes, checked herself in the mirror and wiped away her tear-smeared mascara with a wad of Kleenex.

Finally, she stepped out into an overcast morning that reminded her of the June gloom in coastal California. She'd give anything, sell anything—including her aching soul—to have just a few of those days again. The illusion that great and wondrous things were just around the corner. That's all you really needed in life to get by, a few pretty illusions.

The only thing awaiting her around this corner was the First Pottawatomie Bank of Shawnee, Oklahoma.

Hola was pushing her toward Louisiana with calculated stop-offs in Oklahoma and Arkansas en route. There was no use trying to run away. She'd already tested him, as much as she dared, by deviating slightly from the proscribed route to Shawnee, and he'd called her immediately on the scrambled cellular. Somehow, he could track her every movement. He'd watched her as she had pulled out of Amarillo with Morris thudding back and forth against the shower walls. Dashing for freedom was impossible. Defiance was deadly. Morris had defied him about going to Louisiana—and wound up dead.

Still, she wanted to kill Hola. Badly. But she also knew that she'd never have the nerve.

Her ankle turned on a crack in the sidewalk, and she spun around as if to scold the imperfection in the cement surface—only to see that there was none.

I'm falling to pieces . . . falling to pieces.

The interior of the bank had an echoing sense of unreality to it. However, she had the presence of mind to pick out the least experienced-looking teller and then stall before entering the velvet ropes so that she, of all the other customers lined up, would get the young woman.

Fortunately, it worked out that way. "Good morning," the teller said pleasantly.

For an instant, Fe's mind froze and she couldn't think of anything to say, even something trivial. In a suffocating silence, she took out her Oklahoma driver's license and spread the BIA check on the counter. "Do you have an account with us, Ms. Cornstalk?"

Oh my God. Fe couldn't recall if she'd done that in the past few days or only now imagined that she had. All the banks of the past decade were blurring into one inside her frazzled brain. "I think so. Least I used to."

The girl hadn't looked at the amount of the check yet. "Pauline Cornstalk—I'll check. That's a nice last name."

"It's Shawnee," Fe explained.

"Shawnee Indian?"

Fe nodded. It was horrible: She couldn't muster the small talk that usually came so effortlessly to her.

"From around here?"

"That's right." She could feel sweat erupt on her upper lip, and a drop of it rolled icily down between her breasts as well.

"Why," the teller observed, "today you're wearing the same pretty peach dress you wore for your driver's license photo. Must be one of your favorites."

Fe looked down at herself and then at the photo, aghast. It was the same dress. Not only the same dress, a stain—from the bourbon-laced coffee she'd had for breakfast—appeared on both. And then she saw something that almost made her jump out of her skin. She'd set her handbag on the counter, and the grips of Morris's little revolver were clearly visible inside. How had she been so stupid as to bring the gun into the bank? She now carried it in public because of Hola—but had never meant to bring it inside here.

Insanely, it crossed her mind to shoot her way out, if it got to that.

Fortunately, the teller was focusing on the amount of the check. "I'll have to clear this with the manager, Ms. Corn stalk, even if you have a current account. It shouldn't take long—"

"No," Fe said, grabbing her bag off the counter and closing its drawstring. Realizing that she'd sounded too sharp, she tried to soften her tone with a sickly smile. "I'm not feeling so good, sweetie."

"You know, you don't look all that well, ma'am."

"Flu. Think I've got a touch of the flu. I'll come back later."

19

EMMETT WAS QUIETLY babbling to himself when an Oklahoma City P.D. patrol car pulled alongside him. There were two white officers inside it. The driver kept pace with Emmett while his partner, riding shotgun, powered down his window and hailed him: "Hey, Rasta-man."

Emmett went on babbling down the sidewalk, though his pulse had kicked up.

"Hey, I'm talking to you," the cop said with more edge to his voice.

Emmett halted and pirouetted toward the cruiser. Then, slowly and theatrically, he spread his ragged black overcoat like bat wings, as if he'd been conditioned by countless police shakedowns to show on demand that he was carrying no weapons. But he was concealing a weapon—Ramsey's 9mm.

Both cops laughed at him.

Emmett didn't join in. He waited for them to get out of the air-conditioned car and pat him down. He was filthy from weeks on the run now. He stank, even to himself. And in the two days since leaving Anadarko, he'd put bits and pieces of a costume together by raiding the Dumpsters behind thrift shops. He wore a black overcoat that made him sweat enough to keep surprisingly cool. A knit cap with Rastafarian colors to cover his cropped hair, which he was now letting grow back. And Elton John sunglasses.

Emmett could see it in their faces. The cops were debating whether or not this human derelict was worth checking out. Last week, in the Palo Duro, he'd cached his wallet and BIA credentials, so he could only be identified by fingerprints. But he wasn't about to stop packing the pistol, not with Mangas and the FBI still gunning for him. Careful not to turn his head and telegraph any intent to flee, he mentally recalled the city block he'd just come up. Back fifty or sixty yards, a culvert ran under the street and down to the north branch of the Canadian River. There, he could shed the coat and dive in. But any hope of doing that meant he had to run before the cops patted him down. They would almost certainly shoot at him if they discovered the handgun.

The cop riding shotgun took a toothpick out of its cellophane wrapper and tucked it in the corner of his mouth, all the while keeping his eyes on Emmett. "You can put your arms down, Rasta-man." He was still wondering if he should haul his lard ass out of his comfortable bucket seat, put on his gloves and search a piece of bedraggled human filth in the late afternoon heat. Even if vagrants had warrants, they were for chicken-shit charges, like petty theft and trespassing.

The cop was in his thirties. He obviously wasn't a slick-sleeved rookie, but he wasn't an old salt either, so Emmett wasn't sure where his attitude registered on the scale between gung-ho-ness and indifference. "What do you have to say for yourself . . . ?" the patrolman challenged, as if he needed a bit of street sass to get up his enthusiasm for the shakedown.

But Emmett gaped at him and said, "Born to die, mon."

"No shit," the cop said, then languidly waved for his partner to drive on.

Emmett took a deep breath and continued along the street, invisible again. Reno Avenue is where you came to be invisible. The city had cleaned up the district considerably since his own days here as a cop. But stretches of the avenue still bore the stamp of generations of Indians who'd drifted here to haunt the sidewalks and alleys, panhandling and pilfering and checking the coin returns in pay phones for change. Eventually, they were swept up and carried off by the avenue's existential vertigo in which down felt like up. They became invisible.

Emmett had come here to hide in plain sight, and apparently the tactic had just worked.

For the time being.

He stepped inside the Powwow Lounge. Immediately, he took off the sunglasses, but the interior was still very dark. A cue ball cracked, scattering a triangle of balls. In the dim cast of the green-shaded light over the table, he could make out the players, two Indian biker types. More figures were prostrated in the booths against the far wall: The management didn't discourage problem drinkers from making themselves at home. These emaciated wraiths would come around soon enough and buy another drink.

The management stood waiting behind the bar, a woman in her seventies with permed white hair and a bulbous nose.

Emmett took a stool before her, and she studied him as if looking for something familiar in his face. He didn't recall her from his days with the P.D. here, but there was always the chance she remembered him. "What'll it be?" she asked.

"What tribe are you?" he asked, flat out.

"Who's asking?"

He ignored her question. "Bet I can guess your tribe in your own tongue."

"That'd be a first." She folded her arms over her age-flattened breasts. "Try."

"*Tsetschestahase.*" Southern Cheyenne.

Her eyes crinkled with suspicion, but then she laughed. A hard-bitten laugh. "Now what you expect, a free beer?"

"No, ma'am, a free Coke." Not exactly an Indian woman you'd call grandmother.

"What the hell, I'll spot you one." She reached down into the cooler for the can. "That was too easy. You Cheyenne?"

Emmett shook his head.

"Didn't really think so," she said. "Arapaho?"

"No, I'm beyond all that. It don't mean nothing to me no more."

"Beyond your own blood?"

"Sure, what'd being Indian ever get me?"

She gave him his Coke. "Don't home mean something to you?"

"Just got back. I'll tell you in a couple weeks, if I last."

"Where you been?"

"Los Angeles, mostly."

The old woman made a face. "I tried to live out there once. Too many Chinks. They own all the little markets, jabbering like monkeys. And too many gangs. I saw 'em beat a man to death there. It was just ugly."

Emmett sipped his Coke, and she left her station behind the bar to collect the empties off the booth tables. Beer bottles clinked, but the sleeping drunks didn't stir. Emmett couldn't imagine that they were dreaming. A place like this sucked the dreams right out of you.

The door swung open, letting in a burst of sunlight through which a ferretlike little man flickered over to the old woman. He opened an overcoat, not unlike Emmett's, and began unloading unopened packages of cold cuts onto the table before her. "Five bucks in trade, okay?"

"Not today."

The shoplifter scooped up his goods and left, showing no disappointment. There were many bars along Reno Avenue.

The sight of cold cuts reminded Emmett that he hadn't eaten since yesterday, some sweet corn he'd picked right out of a field near the truck stop where he hoped to find a ride into the city. Yet, he was now drawing a kind of strength, an unexpected high, from his hunger.

The old woman returned to her place behind the bar, but he didn't try to engage her in more conversation. He had to come on slow and easy to her. Otherwise, she'd think he was a cop. Cops always got to the point too swiftly. He hunched over his Coke as if it were an honest-to-God drink, thinking, once again going over the calculus that had sprung from the other night at the mission.

Could the attacker have been Special Agent Ramsey? For a second time, a butcher knife had been left at the scene. And, on that first occasion up atop Mt. Scott, Ramsey had been in the neighborhood. Emmett considered

Ramsey for a few minutes, then shook his head. *No,* all his instincts about the agent told him *no.* Royce Eschiti's assailant had been a cold-blooded creature with the predatory guts to interrupt his flight in order to lie in wait for Emmett. That took a rare kind of courage Ramsey probably lacked.

But there was a contradictory issue.

The sound-suppressor, or silencer as it was inaccurately called by the public, had been professional grade, not some homemade job. It had reduced the muzzle report to a whisper while not throwing off the accuracy—judging from the bullets that had come within inches of Emmett's head. Could someone have drawn it out of a government arsenal? Or had a veteran agent, like Michael Mangas, acquired one when it had still been relatively easy to get one?

The old Cheyenne woman wagged a finger in Emmett's face. "I seen you before someplace. I know it."

He smiled, playing hard to get. This jaded old broad had to be played perfectly, otherwise he'd walk out of this dive with nothing to show for it but a Coke.

Who to blame for the fiasco at the mission? Royce, who'd been so drunk he wouldn't have known if he was being tailed by a circus parade? Or Dagen Kirsch? In trying to cover all the bases perfectly for Emmett, had she let the cat out of the bag to Mangas? Or had she done so on purpose?

Who to blame . . . who not to blame?

"You want another Coke?" the woman said. "This one won't be free."

"I wouldn't expect it."

"What brought you in here?"

"I heard about it from somebody."

"Who?"

"My brother."

She popped another can for him. "Who's that?"

"Royce Eschiti."

"Ah," she cackled, wagging her finger at him again, "I knew it—*Komantcia!*" Mildly derogatory, it was an old Ute term that roughly meant *he who wants to fight me all the time,* which became *Comanche* on Spanish tongues. The Ute and the Southern Cheyenne had been neighbors on the Colorado borderlands.

Emmett offered his hand. "John Eschiti."

"Glenda Bowstring." She shook like a man, squeezing firmly. "How is Royce? Ain't seem him forever."

"Just got out of McAlester."

"That's good."

"But they got him again. The cops. Shot him up the other night down in Anadarko and put him in the hospital just because they say he violated his parole."

"That's bad," she said with precisely the same inflection. "They looking for you, too?" Not a polite thing for a bartender on Reno Avenue to ask, so she was genuinely curious, suspicious even, about why he—a nondrinker—had come to the Powwow Lounge. "They after you?"

"Maybe. I got out of there before I found out for sure. Made it here, but I got the feeling anywhere in Oklahoma ain't far enough."

"Who you talking about, Anadarko cops?"

Emmett didn't really want to connect himself in any way to the FBI, but he also wanted to see how she would react. "No, feds."

"Ah, you can't fight the government," she noted. "They're too big a company. My folks had a nice little place up in Blaine, but the government took our water. They're either taking Indian water or damming water on top of us, like they done to them Creeks over in Eufaula." Another flash of sunlight came through the front door, and she went over to meet a young couple. The skinny man had a weak and dissipated face marked by some scraggly whiskers. The woman, barely out of her teens, was plump but pretty. She wore red hot pants, which meant she was peddling her ass out on Reno Avenue—under the supervision of her man and despite the fact she was holding a squalling infant. Emmett had almost forgotten how sick at heart the streets could make you feel.

Glenda Bowstring took the baby from her and returned to the bar, where she took a bottle of formula and two beers from the refrigerator case.

"Your grandkid?" Emmett asked.

"No," she said, hushing the infant with the bottle, "but this little guy would be dead if it wasn't for me." She flicked her chin toward the couple. "This Coke's free too if you take these beers over to 'em."

Emmett carried the bottles over to the booth where the couple had settled in. They each mumbled thanks, but avoided his gaze. As he slid back onto his stool, Glenda swayed the baby in her arms and said, "How come you acting like you don't know Royce and my Timothy was in McAlester together?"

Emmett shrugged. "Didn't know if prison was a sore subject with you."

"I'm seventy-six and been a barkeep forty of those years. Ain't no such thing as a sore subject to me, John Eschiti, and you been dying to ask me something ever since you walked in this place."

"Fair enough." Emmett took a swig of Coke. "Royce mentioned Tim got himself a sweet job up in Alaska for a while."

A far-off look drifted over Glenda's eyes as she went on rocking the baby in her arms. "He used to say, '*Got to fly up there and feed the bear, Mama.*'"

"What bear?" Emmett asked.

"Hell if I know," she said crossly. "I don't know what kind of bears they got up there. Why you so keen on Alaska?"

"I wouldn't mind making myself scare in a place like that for a while." Emmett decided to go on pretending that Timothy Bowstring's ferrying cash had been some form of legitimate employment. "He ever mention the name of the company or his boss up there?"

"No," Glenda said flatly.

And Emmett believed the subject was closed.

But, as soon as the baby was done with his bottle, the old woman opened a side door and inclined her head for Emmett to follow her into the room beyond. These were her personal quarters, grandma-neat with doilies on the furniture. It was all remarkably wholesome, except for the stale odors of cigarette smoke and beer that wafted in from the bar. Keeping an eye on the cash register through the door, she opened a closet for Emmett and told him to take a cardboard box off of the top shelf.

He brought it down—and immediately realized what it was.

The return address was a post office box in McAlester, one he recognized as belonging to the state prison there. These were Timothy Bow-string's belongings, the few possessions to have followed him from the county jail that held him prior to sentencing and the even fewer possessions he'd acquired inside the joint before hepatitis caught up with him.

"Go ahead," Glenda urged, "open it."

Emmett hadn't wanted to appear too eager. The box seemed funerary to him.

He removed the civilian clothing first and laid the washed and pressed articles on the table. The old woman watched him with cold, brooding eyes, yet her hold on the baby was tender. She even absently kissed his cheek once. The contrast between aged and fresh new skin was striking. Emmett tried not to think where this child would be twenty years from now. Proba-bly out front in one of the booths, emptied of all his dreams.

He set aside some toiletries, resolved to examine them more carefully only if he came up blank with all the rest. There were some books. One Em-mett himself had once owned, *A Guide to the Indian Tribes of Oklahoma*. The rest were lurid paperbacks. At the very bottom, nested in a red ban-danna, was a small address book.

"You mind?" he asked.

Glenda glanced from the book to the cash register. "I already said, go ahead."

He thumbed through each and every page, checking both the names and the numbers. No entry for Royce Eschiti, but that made sense. They'd been in McAlester together. Emmett also looked to see if Mangas, Ramsey or even Dagen Kirsch were included. They weren't. He recognized none of Bowstring's acquaintances, and there were no entries under the letter *U*. At the public library in Norman, yesterday, he'd gone through the back issues of the newspapers to learn more about Calvin Ushuk, the Inupiat weather-man who, somehow, had been blown far from his Seward Peninsula home to Lake Lawtonka. He now asked Glenda, "Tim ever mention a buddy up in Alaska named Calvin?"

"He never mentioned nobody from up there."

"You're sure he never talked about a Calvin Ushuk?"

"Yes."

Emmett got all the way to *W* before the Alaska area code—907—leapt out at him. But there was no name beside the number. Just the ten digits. Trying not to show his excitement, he committed them to memory, then began going through the books. Cons often used them as repositories for notes and mementoes. He was halfway through the last volume, the guide to Oklahoma tribes, when he noticed a dot on the map of the Indian Territory, circa 1860s, in a central portion termed "unassigned lands." In pencil. Beside it were the notations *35.361N* and *97.380W*. Also in pencil. Emmett estimated the dot to lie about twenty miles southwest of modern Oklahoma City's downtown.

He realized that the old woman was staring at him, breathing shallowly through slightly parted lips. "What if something comes of this?" she asked.

"Comes of what?"

"Whatever you're looking for in Timothy's things."

"I don't catch your drift, Glenda."

"If something good comes out of this for you, what you going to share with me?"

Again, he knew he couldn't come off as too easy. "What if I don't?"

"It could get ugly," she said, without batting an eye, then kissed the baby again.

Don Andreas of the BIA didn't like to receive packages. In an age of terrorism, especially bioterrorism, they were a royal pain, especially those that came unsolicited and with addresses he didn't recognize. And so it was when his secretary entered his Albuquerque office with a concerned look and a nervous grasp on a four-by-ten-by-fifteen box. No oily substances, such as those given off by some explosives, had leaked through the plain brown paper wrapping, but he didn't give the box an exploratory shake. The return address, lacking the name of an individual or business, was a P.O. box in Norman, Oklahoma. Andreas recognized Norman to be the home of the University of Oklahoma, but he knew no one there. Never had.

Sighing, he told his secretary that he was on his way to the U.S. Veterans Medical Center in town. He wanted her to phone ahead to the radiology department to tell them he wanted the usual procedures for a package scan.

Then he headed for the parking lot, holding the box with care.

Driving through Albuquerque's busy streets, Andreas tried to hold down his unease and irritation by thinking of his home in eastern California. He used memories of home to control his stress, and heading up Internal Affairs entailed far more stress than he'd ever bargained for. The most pleasant thing about New Mexico to him was its resemblance to the homeland the *Numa*, the Paiute. Same cottonwoods lining the rivers and creeks. Same backdrop of pinyon-juniper clad mountains. But this was foreign territory, and all tribes seemed a bit strange to him, except his own. And working IA, constantly looking into the misdeeds of his fellow BIA cops, added another layer to his sense of alienation.

It was now summer, and he longed to be home with his own people, sitting under a brush arbor and enjoying the sage-scented warmth.

But that wasn't possible. He had a job to do.

The rooms and corridors of the radiology wing of the vet's hospital had been evacuated for his arrival. He strode into the X-ray room. The technician, used to this chore for area law enforcement, examined the exterior surfaces of the box, set it on the padded top of the medical table and swung the X-ray tube into position. She motioned for Andreas to step into the viewing area.

Within a minute, it was evident that the box contained no explosives, no substances resembling anthrax. There was the unresolved issue of some kind of soft container, possibly a vinyl pouch. But it was the object within the pouch—a knife with a long blade—that made Andreas hurry from the lead-protected space to the corridor, hitting his speed dialer for the Albuquerque field office of the FBI along the way.

He had little doubt who the sender had been.

Andreas was patched through to the evidence techie, who promised to meet him here at the hospital. *On neutral ground,* Andreas thought to himself. Disconnecting, he returned to the X-ray technician, told her it was safe for everyone to resume their normal duties. He also asked for a room in which the FBI man and he could open the package.

Waiting in that room, he sat on a stool and reflected on the box in his hands.

It was strange how quickly, almost effortlessly, trust in an individual you'd worked with could be eroded. Ten, maybe eleven years ago, Emmett Parker had saved Andreas's hide. He readily admitted that. In those days, Andreas had been a uniformed BIA sergeant assigned to an Apache reservation in southern New Mexico. A feud between two Mescalero families escalated to gunplay, and Andreas was caught in the middle with no backup. The closest federal help happened to be a BIA dick named Parker who was in Lordsburg on an unrelated case. The investigator commandeered a Cessna at the local airport and had the pilot land him on a straight stretch of highway just outside the tribal capital. Parker then jogged the last mile to the scene of the confrontation.

Andreas hadn't forgotten that during these past weeks Parker had been a fugitive.

But he also had to admit to himself that he'd never really liked Emmett. There was an unknowable quality to him, and he could be brutally short with people. And quick-tempered, resorting to his fists more frequently than some thought appropriate. The Comanche and the Paiute shared the same language group, Shoshonean, and might even have been the same tribe in the distant past. But that did nothing to make Andreas feel close to Emmett Parker.

The door swung back, and a red-headed man with a camera hanging around his neck entered the room. The FBI techie set down his evidence kit and asked, "What you got, Don?"

Andreas hesitated. It wasn't that he hadn't already made up his mind to share this with the allied agency. He just didn't like the eagerness in the man's face. The old hue and cry for BIA law enforcement to be disbanded was being raised by the FBI's clique in Congress, and in sharing this discovery, Andreas felt as if he were aiding his enemy. But there was really no choice. And he certainly didn't want an accusation later that he'd tampered with evidence in an effort to protect Parker. Emmett was beyond protection. "I've got a knife inside this box, according to X-ray. I have reason to believe Emmett Parker might've sent it to me."

The techie smirked. "What kind of nitwit homicide suspect mails in his own evidence?"

Andreas had no retort other than silence. Occasionally, the FBI got low marks when it came to interagency sensitivity, and the Paiute retort was silence. You punished bad behavior with a moment of silence. "I'm not going to read anything into it, yet," he finally said, setting the box on the exam table. "I just want you on hand to witness the opening and help preserve the evidence."

There were flashes as the techie photographed the exterior of the undisturbed box from several angles. "Let's do it." He took Latex gloves from his kit and put them on before unwrapping the brown paper in careful stages, pausing to take digital shots of each major fold and taping. With the box revealed, he flattened the square of paper and examined it. "We can get somebody out of the Oklahoma City field office to check the surveillance camera at the Norman post office."

Andreas had already noted how the sender had affixed two priority stamps on the package that was obviously less than a pound, thus avoiding the need to show his face at the counter.

Finally, the FBI man opened the box, removing what indeed proved to be a soft vinyl pouch of some sort. He was unzipping it when a scrap of paper fluttered out.

Andreas picked it up off the table by holding the edges of the note. A note to him in a familiar scrawl: *Don: Use all poss. technology to lift any latents off this. Believe unsub wore gloves during attack, but maybe he was careless with prior handling. Will contact you later with name of victim. EQP.*

Unsub was an abbreviation for *unknown subject.*

The techie had read the note over Andreas's shoulder. "Damned helpful of him," he commented.

Then he removed the knife. Parker had carefully protected it from rubbing against the felt lining of the pouch, and the techie had to remove a second layer of brown paper. Paper and not anything resembling plastic, which was explained as soon as the knife was bared. Blade, hilt and handle were covered with dried blood. Plastic created a hothouse effect which could leave blood evidence worthless.

Andreas set down the note and excused himself.

He needed air.

It had occurred to him that Parker might be gloating. He might now be sick enough to take pleasure from taunting his own agency.

Going out into the hot and still desert morning, Andreas gazed off at Sandia Peak, trying to take comfort from its resemblance to the mountains of home. He told himself that Parker would not have mailed him the weapon used to eviscerate the victim who'd been found floating in a Texas lake.

He just wouldn't do that.

But Don Andreas had been disappointed in his fellow cops before. And that spoiled the view.

20

I T WAS CALLED *dry cleaning.*

That harmless-sounding term, which brought back memories for Emmett of taking his uniforms into a little Korean place on the west side of Oklahoma City, also referred to the methods used to detect surveillance. For the last hour, Emmett had the sense he was being dry-cleaned by someone who knew what he was doing. There were no signs that anyone other than himself was in the abandoned oil field. There was no visible movement under the waning moon. No sounds other than crickets and the jetliners coming and going from Will Rogers World Airport five miles to the east.

But Emmett sensed a presence closing on him.

He lay atop a rusted derrick, eighty feet off the ground, holding a pair of pawn-shop binoculars to his eyes. As soon as darkness had fallen each of the last three nights, he'd climbed up here to glass the countryside between the airport and the farming community of Wheatland. Timothy Bowstring's map coordinates, penciled in his guide to Oklahoma tribes, had led Emmett to this spot.

He scuttled around so he could watch the dirt lane winding out of the north off State Route 152 through a sea of sorghum. Most of the surrounding fields were lying fallow before the winter wheat planting in fall. Except for the sorghum, which was chest-high. He himself had parked at the end of that field, behind a vacant farmhouse two miles away. He had wheels again, a 1975 Buick he'd hot-wired off a used-car lot in Oklahoma City. To start a newer vehicle without the key was beyond his skill as a car thief. However, when he spotted another Buick of the same year and model in a Moore wrecking yard, he wasted no time swapping the license plates. That way, the Buick he'd taken could be identified only by its vehicle identification number, which appeared in tiny digits and letters on the dashboard and a hidden location on the engine block.

Taken, he thought. *How quickly "stolen" becomes "taken" in the mind of the thief.*

It was probably much the same for the embezzlers who were diverting the trust funds to their own use. He wasn't sure when, exactly, he'd come to the conclusion that several persons were involved. But each of them had made the moral shift he himself was now being forced to make, although no doubt they'd done so with fewer pangs of conscience. It was called the *fraud triangle: need, opportunity and rationalization.* Restricted opportunity made embezzlement an insider's crime. At least one individual in the conspiracy had to be a BIA insider.

Had that been Jerome Crowe?

No, Emmett wanted to believe, not the Jerome he'd known most of his life. Why would Crowe have invited him to probe the trust fund scandal by joining him atop Mt. Scott? Why would he have claimed to be on the verge of cracking the decades-old mystery? If he'd been involved in the scam, he wouldn't have wanted Emmett anywhere close to the operation. Whatever his appetite for expensive things, Jerome simply hadn't been that devious. Or pathological.

The insider could also be with a federal agency other than the BIA. Even the FBI. Someone who had worked closely enough with Indian Affairs to know the ins and outs of the royalty system.

Emmett lit up the dial on his wristwatch. It was almost ten o'clock. Once again, he was coming up empty-handed.

The moonlight showed the pump jacks scattered out in the fields. They looked like huge grasshoppers, grazing. Emmett scanned all around them in

search of a human figure. But, deep down, he knew that the presence out
there wouldn't show himself until he'd checked out the site. For all his brash
violence, this was a cautious creature.

Emmett shifted around again, this time searching westward with the
binoculars.

He supposed that he was hungry and tired, but he felt neither. A discovery had energized him once again. It had sustained him these long
nights on the derrick and the even longer days inside the sweltering oil tank
across the field. Coming here was not a wild goose chase. He'd known that
as soon as he checked the Alaska phone directory in the Norman public library. The number in Timothy Bowstring's address book was to the U.S.
Weather Service facility on Little Diomede Island.

According to the newspapers, Calvin Ushuk had worked at that weather
station.

Emmett was stretching—when he froze.

What's this . . . what's this?

A dim, reddish light below caught his eye. He crept out to the edge of the
platform and peered down. A human figure was shuffling around the base of
the derrick, searching the ground for foot tracks with a red-lens flashlight.
Emmett guessed that the figure was male, although he didn't have a clear
enough view to tell for sure. A large head topping a slender body.

At nightfall, before climbing up the long ladder to the platform, Emmett had brushed out his foot tracks with a willow branch.

Now, he asked himself how well he'd done this.

Well enough, for the figure quit checking the earth around the derrick
base. He walked across an open area to a Christmas tree, a conical array of
control valves used to prevent a black gusher. Producing a wrench from the
weed-choked clutter around the tubing head, he began loosening the nuts
on the master gate valve. Like most youth in the area, Emmett had done casual labor for an oil company and was familiar with most of the equipment.

What use was a decrepit Christmas tree to anyone?

Emmett glanced up at the moon. It was directly overhead, so he wasn't
being backlit by the thin crescent.

The figure lowered the freed valve plate onto the cement casing and picked up something Emmett hadn't noticed before. Whatever it was, the pliant object required rolling up before it could be stuffed into the exposed valves. Quickly now, the figure re-fastened the plate and uprooted a green tumbleweed. This he used as Emmett had the willow branch: to erase his foot impressions. He walked backward into the sorghum, sweeping away any evidence of his passing. Then he was gone from sight.

Patience.

Emmett reminded himself to be patient. This wasn't a simple matter of catching just one fish. He was after the whole school, and only by learning its size and make-up did he have any chance of unraveling the conspiracy.

He'd already guessed the relevance of this oil field. It was the site for a dead drop, where money could be left by one person and picked up by another. Without requiring the two to meet. Ever. The fact it was close to the airport meant that the next individual to appear to pick up the object inside the Christmas tree would be Timothy Bowstring's replacement, who would soon board a flight to wherever. It also meant that this person was farther down the food-chain in the scheme than the figure who'd just vanished into the sorghum.

Changing his mind, Emmett decided not to wait for the courier to show.

He climbed down off the derrick and started north after the figure.

Michael found Ramsey close to dozing in his chair outside the ICU cubicle at Anadarko Municipal Hospital. Michael had left the young agent in charge of the detail to guard the prisoner. Technically, Royce Eschiti was being held as a federal material witness, although the distinction could be conveniently blurred in the event his attorney bitched, as Royce had violated his state parole. In short, he was going nowhere until the FBI got some answers.

"What's up?" Ramsey asked sleepily.

Michael didn't have time to tell the agent about the phone call he'd gotten an hour ago from Don Andreas in Albuquerque. He urgently wanted a go at Eschiti while he was still coherent: Michael had phoned ahead and begged the attending physician to hold off Eschiti's nightly dose of painkillers until he had a chance to talk to him. "I'll fill you in later, *compadre*. What's Eschiti been like today?"

"Same. Quiet, pissed off. Much like you."

"Anything notable happen?"

"Nope." Ramsey yawned. "Except for some old Indian guy."

"What old Indian guy?"

"I don't know. Receptionist told me he came to the front desk about two hours ago, asking to see Eschiti. She told him no visitors, and he went away. You happen to catch the score for the Cardinals game?"

"No." Michael pushed through the door into the muted light of ICU. He no sooner headed for Royce's bed at the end of the row than the duty nurse cut him off. "I'll be brief," he promised. "I need some information. I wouldn't even bug him unless somebody's life was hanging in the balance."

The nurse vacillated, but then stepped out of his way and went back to her station. It struck Michael as odd that he'd just referred to Parker. He could think of no one else's life that was in immediate jeopardy.

From bed, Eschiti watched his approach with resentful eyes.

Michael sat beside him and took a moment so he wouldn't appear to be too eager. Then he gave the Miranda warning to the captive. Eschiti, as expected, gave no response other than to go on glaring—which Michael took as a waiver. "I'm only going to ask you one question, Royce. This isn't a trick. You'll see that. All I want is the truth." Michael paused, waiting for the man to dip his head or show one iota of cooperation. He didn't. "Was it Emmett Parker who stabbed and shot you?"

Royce smiled. With surprise, it seemed. *"Kee."* No.

"You willing to submit to polygraph on that?"

"Thought you had just one question."

"You're right," Michael apologized. "I'm sorry. I just broke my own rules." He'd instructed all the personnel on the guard detail to treat Eschiti with kid gloves, hoping that he might come around of his own accord. Threatening him with an inevitable return to prison would only make him clam up. Royce had been around the block many times before, and threats were only apt to irk him. "I trust you, but there are others who might not."

"They don't count," the prisoner said. "You're asking me, and I just told you. Emmett had nothing to do with me getting hurt. Matter of fact, he saved my ass. I'm telling you that as a *Nuhmuhnuh*."

Michael kept a poker face. Unwittingly or not, Royce had just confirmed that Parker had been with him that night last week. He'd just strengthened the argument to hold him as a material witness. Michael rose. "I believe you."

In the corridor, he filled Ramsey in, as promised, then hurried out to his bucar.

Sliding in behind the wheel, he vowed to drive directly back to Lawton. Home and his wife, a few hours of sleep, and then back on the hunt for Parker. But he paused to switch on the dome light and re-read the hard copy of an email that had arrived earlier in the evening. It was from Special Agent Ed Thorsen of the Secret Service's White House detail. He reiterated what Dagen Kirsch had told Michael. Almost verbatim. She had indeed reported Parker's call to her. And then submitted to the lie box, clearing her of both criminal involvement and any job-related impropriety. Thorsen offered no apology for having failed to pass this information on to the FBI, and even had the balls to ask Michael if he thought Parker represented a threat to the President, should he and the first lady return to the western White House anytime soon.

"*Culo*," Michael muttered as he started to turn the key. *Ass.*

But then he noticed a former U-Haul van parked in the back of the lot.

He thought a moment, then leaned over and took out something he'd been storing in the glove compartment, before stepping from his car.

Slowly, he approached the van, music from a radio reaching out to him. Haydn, he believed. Wendell Padduhpony had insisted that, while completing his degree at Cameron, Michael take a music appreciation course. *White music is the only redeeming element of their culture.*

The old man was seated behind the wheel, his side window open to the night. His long braids were draped over his yet powerful-looking chest, and he stared steadily over the tops of his bifocals at Michael.

Mangas made sure that his shadow, cast by one of the lot lights, didn't fall upon the elder. "Good evening, *Toko*."

"Evening." Wendell didn't call him *Tuah. Son.*

From that, Michael realized that things were now different between them. "You here to see Royce?"

"Yes. If you've got no objection."

Michael had to consider that. It could lead to a lot of trouble. Something was going unstated here: The FBI had tapped Wendell's phone, and no doubt he now realized that. The conversation between the elder and Parker had been in Comanche, so nobody with the bureau was fully aware of its content, something Michael had used to protect his mentor. But the air between the two men was still heavy with a sense of betrayal. "All right," Michael finally said, his heart in his throat, "I'll take you in to see Royce, but an agent will have to be present while you two talk."

Not him. Ramsey. The thought of eavesdropping on Wendell and Royce was too much for Michael to bear. *Don't ask, don't tell.* That was the recipe for any continuation of their relationship.

Wendell turned off the radio, grabbed his black bowler off the front seat and got out of his van. As they strolled toward the hospital building, Michael said as casually as he could, "Are you familiar with the practice of dangling an eagle feather over the mock grave of an intended victim?"

"Of course," Wendell said, eyes forward.

"Do you know anybody who does that?"

"Not anymore. It's the kind of thing you'd read about in a book." Then the old man added, "Sometimes we get a little too hung up on being *Nuh-muhnuh.*"

"How's that?"

"You remember the old saying, '*With no enemies to fight, we become weak and effeminate?*'"

"Yes."

"Well, I can add something to that: '*With no enemies to fight, we Comanche fight each other.*'" Wendell paused. "Chase somebody into a hall of mirrors, and it's yourself you wind up chasing. But sooner or later, one way or another, this is going to end, and you'll find yourself right back where you were when the Murrah went down."

Michael said nothing to that. It was true. He feared the day when this hunt ended. Crushing routine would take over his life once again, and routine was the breeding ground for grief. There had been no time for peyote these past weeks, and without the bud, lacking this nonstop manhunt to distract him, Michael knew his world would turn sad and ordinary around him. And, earlier this evening, when he'd learned from Don Andreas that Parker had actually *mailed* in the knife that might have been used either to gut Morris Cornplanter or slash Royce, or both—Michael had suddenly realized that this pursuit was as confused and ambiguous as everything else in life.

Just outside the hospital entrance, he said, "Stop, please." As soon as Wendell halted, Michael handed him the crow-feather amulet. "I found this along the Canadian River. Figured you might know who it belongs to."

This time, the silence bristled between them.

But finally, Wendell said, "I've done nothing I wouldn't do for you, *Tuah*."

"I want to believe that."

"Then believe it," the old man said tartly, turning for the door.

Inside, Michael arranged for Ramsey to monitor the visitation, then took his leave.

After all this, he was too agitated to go home to Jeralyn. She was no company these days, and after the cold confrontation with Wendell, Michael felt alone in a new and crushing way. He needed comfort tonight.

So, fifteen minutes later, it didn't seem wrong to him that he was standing at Dagen's door. The hour was eleven, and he had no right to be here. When he remembered his wife, it was unthinkable to be here. But his heart quickened when the porch light came on and she opened the door.

There was no invitation to enter. He just stepped past her. The half-circles under her eyes were darker. Her skin was flushed, and when she spoke, it was clear that she was a bit drunk. "I knew you'd come back," she said.

"I'm back," he said pathetically as he sank into an easy chair. It smacked of weakness. Insurmountable weakness.

She leaned over him to kiss his forehead. Then, still upside-down, she found his lips, and he tasted a whiskey sour. He went along with it because he hoped he would yet feel the life-sustaining thrill that she'd once given him.

"Don't ever mistrust me again, Michael," she whispered, close in his ear.

Emmett hadn't gone far into the sorghum when he realized that the figure had doubled back. He caught a rustling noise off to one side, someone slipping through the leafy stalks. The man was returning to the oil field. It made no sense until Emmett noticed what the figure apparently had: high beams coming along a farming road out of the south. Making for the derrick at low speed as if the driver was watching for danger. Emmett could track the figure's return by his stirring of the seed-heads as he ran, bent over. Emmett followed, holding Ramsey's 9mm down at his side.

The car, a Mazda sedan, stopped near where he remembered the Christmas tree to be. The driver shut off the engine but kept on the headlights. They fanned out over the sorghum, still now that the figure had gone to ground.

Emmett dropped, too.

Crawling forward, he reached a place just back from the edge of the field through which he had a narrow glimpse of the driver. He wasn't sure where the figure was hiding, but it seemed obvious that he, too, was focused on the driver, who was busy unfastening the cover to the master gate valve. He was caught in the blinding glare of his own headlights, but Emmett had the sense he was a large blond man in a baggy suit. He smoked a cigarette as he worked, taking puffs between turns on the wrench. Finally, he was able to reach inside the valve and draw out the object the figure had left there only minutes ago. He unfurled a vest used by drug couriers to strap drugs to their upper bodies. Except this one held cash. The blond man—his hair glinted like frost in the beams—took a sheaf of currency from one of the slotted pockets and ran his thumb through the bills with an air of satisfaction.

But his satisfaction was short-lived.

A high voice behind him said, "You're a day early."

Startled, the blond man spun around, dropping the vest. His right hand darted instinctively toward the part in his coat, but the voice warned, "Keep your hands where I can see them."

The blond man obeyed.

Emmett wanted to shift positions so he could fully see the figure, but he couldn't move without rattling the sorghum stalks.

"I said *you're early*," the voice repeated.

"That is correct," the blond man said, holding his hands up, slightly, in glum compliance. "I was told to cancel my reservation with the airline and hire a private jet. A much earlier departure. Minutes from now, really. So I must get going."

Emmett ran the accent through his mental catalogue of them—and came up with Slavic.

"Not so fast, Goldilocks," the voice said.

As the two men went on talking, Emmett backed down the row he'd just advanced along. Obviously, the blond man was a mule. Maybe he'd even taken Timothy Bowstring's place. But something was wrong. His showing too early to collect the cash worried the figure. Enough so for him to negate the purpose of a dead drop—avoiding face-to-face contact—and to return here to confront the courier he'd probably never even met. Something was missing in this conspiracy. Trust. And how had Calvin Ushuk's murder figured in that lack?

Giving the men a wide berth, Emmett slowly made his way around them. The sorghum leaves cut the high beams into dappled light and shadow he found disorienting. Like swimming through a kelp forest. By the time he reached the derrick, the men were arguing, loudly. "You are never to deviate from the plan," the figure cried. "Never!"

His back was to Emmett and he was standing outside the limit of the headlights, but for the first time he saw that the rail-thin figure had knotted his long hair atop his head, making his head seem much larger than it was. This was how an Indian man arranged his hair when not wearing braids. He was Indian. He sounded Indian.

The blond man said, "You have no right to tell me how to do my job."

"You wouldn't have a job without me, you dumb shit. I make it all happen. If I didn't program this every step of the way, you'd be back home scratching body lice and sucking up beet soup!"

"Fuck your mother," the blond man snarled back at him. He scooped the vest up off the ground and dusted it off.

Emmett checked the license plate to the Mazda—and saw at once that the number didn't matter. There was a green Enterprise Rental sticker on the trunk lid.

The blond man began checking all the pockets. "If this is going to be the last shipment for a while, it better be a good one."

"Yes," the Indian said chillingly, "so good I think I'll keep it for myself."
With that he produced a pistol. A tubular object was fixed to the barrel, a
sound-suppressor.

"Are you out of your mind?" the blond man gasped.

"Hardly."

"Do you have any idea what this will bring?"

"With mathematical clarity. Ergo, why wait for tomorrow to solve what
I can solve today . . . ?" *Pfft . . . pfft . . . pfft.* Three little spurts of dust appeared on the front of the blond man's coat. He drew his own semiautomatic, but the impulse to return fire was lost in his dying brain and he fell,
not to rise again.

The Indian ambled over and gave him a kick in the ribs.

The Slavic man gurgled.

It might have been no more than air forced out of his lifeless lungs by
the kick, but the gunman took no chances. He pumped two more rounds
into his face.

Emmett was aiming Ramsey's pistol squarely at the Indian's back—
when his forefinger eased off the trigger. He wanted to punish this cold-
blooded execution. But he no longer carried a badge, and his biggest duty
was to himself. Self-preservation made him sidle behind one of the metal
legs of the derrick, even as he cried, "Freeze!" He didn't say *Freeze, police!*
Cops didn't work felony takedowns alone, and the man would quickly sur-
mise that.

The Indian grabbed the vest and rolled behind the car. Again, Emmett
refrained from firing. His shots were not sound-suppressed, and the last
thing he needed were Oklahoma County deputies showing up.

The man asked from behind the Mazda, "Who the hell are you?"

"I was Ivan's bodyguard. Until a minute ago."

Silence, then: "You've got to be shitting me."

"How do you think he got his gun? You can't get a gun on board a flight
these days."

"Balls! What right did they have to hire somebody on my freaking
turf? That takes balls." More than outraged, the Indian sounded bewildered.
And high-strung. He seemed too tightly wrapped for this kind of work, al-

though his pathological willingness to murder at the drop of a hat had probably gotten him by.

"I don't argue with work. It's hard to come by." Emmett crouched, wondering if he could skip a shot under the Mazda if needed. But the Indian had
positioned himself behind the right front tire, with the engine block giving
him additional protection. "You serious about keeping the cash?" Emmett
asked.

"What of it?"

"I could make some major points with the bosses if I got the money
aboard that private jet on time. It could make up for you offing this poor
bastard."

The Indian chuckled. "You're an idiot. His own people ordered this. He
was skimming. That meant less for them . . ." Somehow, Emmett suspected
this to be untrue. Whatever, these people were careening off one another in
a popcorn machine of distrust. "Where were you when Ivan drove up?"

Emmett smiled to himself: The Indian had bought it. He believed
Emmett had known him. "I was lying across the backseat. He said to
cover him."

"Well, you did a helluva job covering him. 'Tween us, I wouldn't mention this gig in the future. Yessiree, I'd keep Ivan's name off your resume."
Definite Oklahoma accent, which registered as no accent to Emmett's ears.
But with thirty-eight federally recognized tribes in the state, telling which
one was impossible. "You need a ride to the airport?"

"No, thanks," Emmett replied.

The Indian gave a full-throated laugh. "My, oh my." But then all was
quiet—before the Mazda's engine was gunned to life. He shouted over the
scream of acceleration, "Suit yourself, Parker!"

Emmett trained the pistol on the driver's-side window, but the Indian
didn't sit up until he was well out of range. He sped down the dirt lane into
the south, the passenger door still ajar and flapping. Walking out from under the derrick, Emmett watched his tail-lights grow small on the fallow
fields.

21

ICHAEL HAD BEEN to the site of the Murrah Federal Building in
downtown Oklahoma City many, many times. Most of the visita-
tions had been in the sleepless, gut-wrenching days immediately
following the April 1995 explosion, when he used his credentials to join in
the rubble-turning search for his son, Todd. Family members were supposed
to have been excluded, for their own sake. He'd also come to the site on peyote. In the teepee on Wendell's farm, he'd been transported to the smoldering ruin, where he found Todd patiently trying to sweep away the massive
pile of wreckage with his push-broom. Michael explained to his son that
such an effort was useless. Endless. And Todd, finally free of the syndrome
that had imprisoned him in perpetual juvenility, said in a clear and bright
voice, "I know, Daddy. It's like grief. Useless and endless."

But never until now had he visited the site in person at night.

He left his bucar on Harvey Avenue and ambled along the chain-link
fence studded with messages and gifts from well-wishers. He'd never cared
for these touches. Some of the mementoes, especially the teddy bears,
seemed carnival-like to him. Yet, this distraction was left behind as he entered the memorial proper, where the Gates of Time became visible. They
did appeal to his sense of propriety. These monoliths were separated by a

long, shallow reflecting pool that was beautifully lit tonight. The gate astride Robinson Avenue had 9:01 on it. On this, the west side of the pool, the Harvey Avenue gate showed 9:03. In-between was the empty space roughly defining the ends of the destroyed building. And in-between was the defining minute of Michael's life: 9:02.

To the south was the Field of Empty Chairs. Each chair was made of bronze with a glass base. Again, Michael had never seen them at night and was pleasantly surprised by the glows shining from the inside the glass. As if the chairs were inhabited by spirits. Big chairs for the adults, small ones for the children. He'd not felt quite right about Todd getting a big chair, for he'd never been a true adult.

A National Park Service ranger was explaining the arrangement of the chairs to a group of tourists, who were quiet and respectful, especially the Japanese, who probably understood ground zeroes better than most. The chairs were arrayed in correlation to the blast's point of origin, the spot where the rental truck packed with explosives had been left by Timothy McVeigh on NW Fourth Street, and the floors of the building on which the deceased had worked or been in day care.

Michael approved of the lecture, but he found he couldn't bear to hear it. It sounded objective, like history, and there was nothing objective about this to him.

He walked on without pausing to pick out his son's chair. Todd's body had been found sandwiched in the squashed space between the fourth floor, where he'd been buffing a freshly waxed corridor, and the fifth floor. The last time Michael had seen Todd's chair, a crow had been roosting on its back. Crows were the enemies of owls, and owls were emblematic of death. But the omen had not felt like a triumph over death to Michael.

Vengeance is mine.

It'd been the only biblical citation Michael, a member of the Native American Church married to a Catholic, had managed to recall during the nationally televised memorial service attended by the President and his wife. The Clintons offered words of comfort to Jeralyn and him that were now lost in the daze of that day.

Vengeance is mine, I will repay, says the Lord.

Michael passed through the 9:03 Gate of Time and out onto Robinson Avenue.

Disappointingly, McVeigh's execution had done little for him. He had marked the moment, but with a tepid satisfaction. It was as if Todd's murder had only awakened a wider appetite. A voracious need to punish the wicked that went far beyond McVeigh and Nichols and any others who might have plotted with them. But wasn't Michael, an adulterer, to be counted among the wicked? And according to Paul in the same passage from Romans: *Beloved, never avenge yourselves, but leave it to the wrath of God.* Sometimes he believed that the Murrah Building had made him a better cop. Sometimes he felt that it'd left him a worse one. And most often, he believed that God had run out of wrath.

He turned right onto NW Fifth Street. Not far was the group home in which Todd had lived his last year. Michael could never bring himself to go there.

Halfway down the block, he found the address he was seeking. A venerable old home that had been converted into apartments in the 1950s and then reconditioned back into a single dwelling as part of its post-blast renovation. He had phoned ahead, and the woman he'd contacted answered the buzzer outside the locked entry door. "Good evening," she said. Kiowa women could be tall, stately and very pretty. Ladonna Hawzeepa was all of those things, and somehow the streaks of gray at her temples only enhanced the effect. "You must be Special Agent Mangas."

"Call me Michael."

She offered her hand. "Ladonna."

"Thanks for seeing me. I didn't mention it over the phone, but we met years ago at a Fraternal Order of Police function. I worked for the P.D. back then."

"With Emmett?"

"Yes," he replied.

"I apologize for not remembering. Are you friends with my brother?"

Michael decided not to stretch it. He and the Comanche County medical examiner had never been close. "The doctor and I went to the Ft. Sill school together." Then he asked, "Did you go there as well?"

"No, times had changed. I went to the public schools in Lawton."

Halfway houses always reminded Michael of college dormitories for the jaded. He got a lot of knowing smirks from the women sitting around the large living room as they glanced away from the TV to watch Ladonna and him pass. Suspicious of everything, the parolees probably thought their night supervisor was receiving a gentleman caller. Ladonna was unfazed as she led Michael down a hallway to a tidy office. She offered to make some coffee, but he declined. After visiting the memorial, it would already be hard enough to sleep tonight.

They sat.

On the wall was a painting by Harvey Pratt, a Cheyenne artist Michael admired. They chitchatted about Pratt's work for a few minutes, but then Ladonna said, "I guess I expected this sooner or later."

"Pardon?"

"I haven't seen Emmett in years. The last time was by accident. We bumped into each other at the airport in Denver. Connecting flights. A few minutes talking about this and that. Then we went our separate ways." She had a nice dignity about her. She wasn't overly formal like her brother, just dignified, which she softened at just the right moments with a quick and appealing smile.

"No, no," Michael hastened to say, "this has nothing to do with anything like that, Ladonna. I assumed you've had no contact."

She waited with a patient look for him to explain why he was here, then.

"I'm trying to understand Emmett better," Michael finally said.

"So you can catch him."

"Yes. Before he does any more harm to himself or others."

For a few seconds, her look was unreadable. Akin to her brother's. But then she shook her head ever so slightly and said, "Go on."

"Emmett is Roman Catholic, correct?"

"He was raised Catholic," she clarified.

"Did he practice his faith while you two were married?"

"Not really."

"Not even as a Comanche Catholic?" Michael asked.

Her smile said that she understood the distinction. He was asking if

Parker was a Christian with a traditional native overlay. It wasn't a simple question. Few Indians he knew were Christians in the European sense, and he suspected that many whites had forgotten how their own Nordic culture had altered the Middle Eastern faith originally brought to them by Hellenistic Jews. "I don't know how to answer that, Michael. Other than religion was never a priority to him."

"What about Comanche religion? Did he keep things of power around the house?"

"Other than the usual medicine pouch?"

"Yes." Every *Nuhmuhnuh* man kept one, including Michael.

"No," she replied, swift on the uptake that he was intimating witchcraft. "Absolutely nothing like that."

"Sorry," Michael apologized. "I'm sure this is difficult. So personal."

"I don't mind the personal part. It's just difficult." She took a moment. "Emmett is the kind of ex you think a great deal about. Do you know what I mean?"

"Not sure that I do."

"I was married before. But I think about Emmett more. Maybe because it's harder to pin him down, like you're trying to do right now. The failure of our marriage is more difficult to understand because he's a good person. We're both good people. And there are times I miss him very much."

Michael didn't like this turn in the conversation. He didn't need another endorsement for Parker's character. "What did Emmett have to say about his Catholic upbringing?"

"This and that—"

"Did he refuse to let you hang a crucifix in your home?"

"No, no—that's not quite right. He refused to hang a crucifix over our bed."

"Why?"

"I think it made him uncomfortable." And then she blushed. "You know, Jesus looking down on us. Or something like that. It was just Emmett."

"Did he have an interest in religious art?"

"No."

"Woodworking?"

"No."

"Please go on with what you were about to say, Ladonna."

"Just that—his mother's very devout and that kind of amused him. Except at Easter, when she made him go to mass with her. I think he found the nuns at the mission heavy-handed."

"And the priest . . . what was his name?"

"Father Jurgen," Ladonna replied. "It was a love-hate thing. Talking to others who went to the mission, Father rode Emmett harder than anybody. But of all the boys, he felt Emmett had the makings of a good priest." She laughed. Lovely teeth.

"What?"

"Oh, I understand what Father saw in him, but the mental picture still tickles me—Emmett in a cassock."

"What did the priest see in the boy?"

"Single-minded dedication."

"To what?"

"Certainly not the church."

"Then what?"

"It became the cop thing later. That's where it led him. I'm not trying to belittle this. You know it's about—doing the job right. Getting the baddies, no matter what the cost. You must know what I'm talking about. It becomes an obsession. Em went over the top with it, proving himself, and we wound up with no life together."

Ordinarily, this was a worthless question, the answer was so predictable. But Michael had a hunch that this bright woman had not and would not deceive herself about Emmett Parker. "Do you believe he's done the things he's accused of?"

"No," she said without the slightest hesitation.

"What makes you so sure?"

"Ego would never let him go bad. He'd see corruption and betrayal as human weaknesses." She smiled again, faintly. "And weakness is what Emmett fears above all else."

*　　*　　*

Emmett crouched behind a boxwood hedge in the muggy dark as a police cruiser pulled into the compound of the Anadarko Agency of the BIA. A spotlight came on, illuminating the side of the main building and, indirectly, the female patrol officer behind the wheel who'd just switched it on. Emmett had been gripping Ramsey's pistol, but catching the young woman's palely lit face made him lay the weapon on the ground. She was half his age. She braved the night to protect others. She was his sister, and it sickened him to think of having to shoot her.

Be careful . . . be careful . . . don't stumble into that emotional mine-field.

The patrolwoman completed her slow circle around the building. The spotlight went out and she accelerated off toward the next facility on her list. Whether she realized it or not, she was making her rounds on a schedule. It was now almost three A.M., and she'd checked the doors and windows to the agency twice previously, around eleven and then at two o'clock. But Emmett wasn't ready to put his faith in her apparent predictability. As an Oklahoma City patrolman, he had sometimes made his building checks with a lockstep regularity, only to suddenly double back on the same structure after a few minutes. This tactic had netted him a commercial burglar, a once-in-fourteen-years occurrence for the average cop. He had done it in less than three years.

He picked up the pistol, but didn't budge. He'd already waited more than four hours, casing the building, and would wait a few minutes more. After an undercover assignment in South Dakota, he had begun his official BIA career here in Anadarko, although that now seemed two lifetimes ago. Not here in the agency office, which was more committed to seeing that treaty obligations were honored, especially resource royalty payments. Rather, he'd been based with law enforcement staff at the area office, about a mile distant. But he'd come here often enough, and he could now visualize his younger self bounding across the lot and through the employee entrance in a double-breasted blazer so badly out of fashion now it made him smirk.

But his smirk died as he recalled the Indian last night in the oil field.

What had he said to the blond foreigner he called Goldilocks before gunning him down? *If I didn't program this every step of the way, you'd be back home scratching body lice and sucking up beet soup!*

Program.

The contemporary-sounding verb was what had brought Emmett back to Anadarko, despite the fact that the cops here had his mugshot emblazoned on their memories. But the risk was worth it, all because the Indian last night had known who he was. The man had recognized Emmett's voice. And the conspiracy, for all the signs that it was unraveling into internecine homicide, saw value in keeping Emmett at large. Otherwise, the Indian would have tried to finish him off, as he had so ably the blond Slav. In fact, the conspirators probably saw Emmett as a useful distraction, running legitimate law enforcement ragged while they went about their own business.

Emmett had made no attempt to conceal the corpse. He hadn't even gone near it. Such a misstep would have left a bounty of evidence to implicate him in another death he'd had nothing to do with. Besides, it might be helpful for the sheriff's office to find the body for themselves.

No, his first priority had been to get away from there and turn the tables on the conspiracy, to study them as they'd obviously studied him. But one thing was crystal clear—neither the Indian nor the Slav had struck him as FBI types, even FBI informants. They were seasoned criminals, both of them.

He lit up his watch dial. Nine minutes had elapsed since the patrolwoman had driven away. At last, he was willing to gamble that she wasn't returning anytime soon.

Rising from behind the hedge, he put away the pistol and donned a pair of neoprene gloves. Then he crossed the parking lot to the rear door of the building. Reaching up, he unscrewed the bulb in the light fixture over it. State-of-the-art security had long since outdistanced his technical skills. But there was nothing state-of-the-art about the Bureau of Indian Affairs. Given its mandate to oversee the welfare of more than two million Americans who'd listed themselves in the last census as Indian, the bureau's budget was pathetically inadequate. Once the bastard child of the War Department and now the bastard child of the Department of the Interior, the BIA was last in line for military surplus and cast-off equipment.

So Emmett bet that security hadn't been upgraded at the Anadarko Agency since he'd last been here. Breaking out a keychain penlite to inspect the door, he wasn't disappointed. It had a sensor that set off the alarm when a circuit was closed by any after-hours opening. Easy to bypass, which Emmett did by depressing the sensor with a thin metal strip. Then he jimmied open the latch with a pocket knife.

He stood there, holding the door open.

Years ago, there had been some discussion about putting photoelectric cells inside the entrances of all BIA facilities in the area as a backup security measure. Remembering this on his way in from the place where he'd parked the Buick, he scraped some lime dust off the sideline of the high school football field. He now took a handful of this fine white powder and flung it in front of him. The dust vanished into the darkness. As often happened with discussions for improvement in the BIA, no light beam sensors had been installed.

Dim glows came from the screensavers, but he ignored the desktop computers on his way to the records room. He doubted that his user ID and password worked anymore. Besides, the bureau was a paper-redundant operation.

Yet, the old records room was now the coffee room.

Irritated, he advanced down the corridor. What had formerly been the conference room was crammed with file cabinets.

An hour and a half later, he had one scrap of useful information. Just one. But it would be significant, should this ever go to trial. If and when he survived to enjoy the safety of some distant criminal proceeding. It concerned Mary Chocpoya, his mother's friend who'd railed against the BIA for sending her a mineral royalty check in the amount of two dollars and twelve cents—after the pump jack on her property brought oil to the surface day and night. That piddling check had been cashed in Lawton on June second of last year. However, according to the records, this June, and a week prior to that morning in his mother's kitchen, Mary had cashed a check for $19,983.12 at a bank in Kingfisher, Oklahoma. The phone log for the same date confirmed that the bank had phoned the agency for verification.

This discovery about Mary only confirmed what Emmett already knew.

An apparatus for wholesale fraud was in place. He needed to find its human gears and wheels.

The files were of no help in that regard.

He looked for anything on paper related to minority contractors and found nothing.

He hurried out to the main room. He'd just sat down before a computer when a blinding light washed from right to left. He wasn't sure if it had passed directly over him, but he stayed on his hands and knees behind the desk.

Damn.

The spot swept back to the center of the room and held fast to a portrait of the President on the back wall. Had the female cop confused the portrait for a real person? Or had she caught a fleeting glimpse of Emmett as he dropped to the floor?

The light shifted away, but still his heart was pounding. It only meant she'd opened the car door to which the spot was attached. He crawled low to the carpet to a place from which he could see her. She strolled across a bank of windows, sliding her nightstick into the ring on her Sam Browne belt and taking out her flashlight. She examined the glass along the way for breakage.

She was headed for the door.

If she nudged it, even a little, she'd realize that it was unlocked and the sensor had been by-passed.

Emmett started to draw Ramsey's semiautomatic from his waistband. But he couldn't do it. He promised himself that he'd use the 9mm only to bluff his way past her. Still, he knew that firing a gun wasn't always a consciously deliberate choice. Sometimes, the survival instinct took over—ask any number of convicts serving time for manslaughter.

Go away . . . go away . . . go away.

She inspected the door. Closely. But didn't give it a push.

Emmett knew why. Decrepit alarm systems were prone to going off without good cause, and there was nothing quite as galling as hanging around a parking lot in the middle of the night, missing your breaks, waiting for an employee to be rousted out of bed to switch off an audible alarm that had woken the entire neighborhood.

So the patrolwoman didn't touch the door.

Instead, she ran her flashlight around the big room, forcing Emmett down again.

Then her light went out, the boot heels clipped over the pavement, and she drove off.

Emmett hugged the carpet a full ten minutes more before rising.

A sweater hung on the back of the swivel chair he'd briefly sat in. He settled back in and draped it over the monitor and his head as a light shield. Then he brought the screen to life.

And hesitated.

The problem wasn't familiarity with the BIA's computer network. It had frustrated him and his fellow employees for more than a decade, drawing the complaint that these were the only steam-driven PC towers in existence. The problem was with his user ID. What would happen if he tried now to log in? Had he been blocked from the system? Or worse—would he tip off some remote auditing site to his presence in the Anadarko Agency?

"Well," he whispered to himself, "things can't get much worse than they are now."

Like hell they can't, he realized as he logged in.

His icons came up. He hadn't been locked out of the nationwide system. Yet, as always, because he'd been posted in Phoenix, his password gave him limited and indirect access to the Anadarko data base. He fed three components into the balky search engine: "I.T. Outsourcing" combined with "Minority Contractors" and "Midwest Region."

Minutes later, as Emmett perspired under the sweater, the screen began to fill with the alphabetized names of firms. None meant anything special to him, and he was almost to the end of the list when one leaped out at him: *YaholaWare.* He clicked on the name to bring up the firm's address.

22

A FEW AGENTS greeted Michael from their desks, but he gave them no more than nods as he passed through the bull pen area of the Oklahoma City field office. Besides, they had their own excitement this afternoon: A spiral of turkey vultures, hanging high in the morning sky, had drawn the Oklahoma County Sheriff's Department to a dead body in a defunct oil field five miles west of the airport. Papers on the D.B. tentatively identified him as an energy resources attaché from the Russian consulate in Houston.

On any other day, Michael would have been interested.

But not today.

Nor was he interested in chatting with the agent who, as a favor, had screened the surveillance videos for the Norman post office. And come up with no sighting of Parker. As expected.

Michael took the elevator to the basement, where the evidence staff had a small lab. The computer specialist roosted on a stool before a workbench strewn with gutted computer components. He was bald, white and disinterested in small talk, which suited Michael fine. Wires were attached to a motherboard as if it were a human brain being artificially kept alive. It came from the computer Emmett Parker had used last night in the Anadarko

Agency. Not that Michael hadn't had the devil of a time learning that—and hours after Parker had logged on with his user ID and password of *teekwa!*, the Comanche command for *talk!*. Michael had asked Don Andreas not to block Parker from any of the communication and information systems he had freely used right up to the moment he'd gone on the lam. They were red-flagged, meaning any attempted use would be reported to the FBI. Instantly. That's the way it was supposed to have worked. Yet, the night-shift Internet technologist at BIA headquarters in Washington had simply noted in his duty log Parker's log-on, and it wasn't until two hours ago that a sheepish Don Andreas phoned Michael to confess that his I.T. folks had dropped the ball.

Mangas then had this FBI techie rush down to the Anadarko Agency to seize the computer Parker had used this morning.

"What do you have?" Michael asked impatiently.

The man held up a hand that he didn't want to be disturbed. A second later, he tossed Michael a look that said he didn't like anyone standing over his shoulder as well.

Michael retreated a few steps and resisted the urge to pace. What had Parker been looking for? Progress on the investigation against him? As a precaution to that happening, Andreas had promised not to enter his case files on this into any of the BIA databases. And Michael had no reason to believe Parker could hack his way into the FBI's heavily fire-walled system.

"Okay," the bald techie said at last, "come here." He tapped his screen. "I checked the firewall, and this appears to be what he was after."

Michael asked, "What are all these Web sites?"

"Let's find out."

Five minutes later, the techie had the apparent answer: The sites were to I.T. companies that had outsourced for federal agencies in the Midwest. Minority-owned companies. What use had Parker found in this? Had he been seeking a way inside the Anadarko database so he could embezzle more funds? That made no sense. For if he and Jerome had embezzled millions over the years, this was something they would've done long ago. Unless the unknown party who'd been handling the technology side of the scam for them had dropped out, voluntarily or involuntarily, and Parker now needed a new I.T. person. He tried to recall if Morris Cornplanter, the Seneca ex-con found tied to a cross and dumped in Buffalo Lake, had had a computer background. Nothing exceptional came to mind. He'd worked mostly in photography prior to turning to fraud. "Find me something on this firm," Michael specified.

"YaholaWare?"

"Just do it. Has to be in or around Muskogee."

"How'd you know that?"

Michael didn't bother to explain that *Yahola* was a Creek Indian word, and the Creeks' own name from their tribe was the *Muskogee*. "Ever had dealings with this company?"

"None," the techie replied. "Never even heard of them. A flash in the pan, probably. Let's see . . ." He found an article in the BIA's inhouse newsletter, mentioning that ten years ago YaholaWare had been contracted to update the computer system for the region comprised by Kansas, Oklahoma and Texas.

"Where's the name of the person doing business as YaholaWare?" Michael asked.

"Got me. Looks to me like it's been expunged, somehow."

Michael had been leaning into the screen and now stood straight. Two hours ago, he hadn't bothered to throw a ring around Anadarko. Trusting that Parker was long gone after breaking and entering the agency office, Michael did no more than advise the local P.D. and S.O. to be extra vigilant. But this was different. For the first time, he had some idea where the fugitive was *headed*, not just where he had been.

He rushed out of the lab and impatiently rode the elevator to the main floor. Unable to contain himself, he burst in on the special-agent-in-charge, who was meeting with his staff. "If we get rolling right now and don't screw the pooch again," he announced, "we've got half a shot of taking Parker down in the next few hours."

The SAC finally broke the long silence that followed. "Well, Michael, fucking nice to see you, too."

*   *   *

You didn't get a minor in anthropology from Oklahoma State University without learning about the gods of the Indian Territory. In a sense, they weren't the deities of Oklahoma, as the Indian Territory was renamed when it passed into the hands of white settlers. All but a few tribes—the Comanche was an exception—weren't indigenous to this country and had been exiled here from the East. First to be plunked down on the wooded fringe of the southern plains were the Five Civilized Tribes—the Choctaw, Chickasaw, Creek, Cherokee and Seminole. Civilized because they'd adopted Christianity and constitutional forms of government. Their high degree of acculturation didn't spare them from forced relocation, something not lost on the far less civilized and nomadic *Nuhmuhnuh.*

Despite having taken the Jesus Road to please their new landlords, many of these people, especially the Creeks, held in secret to their old deities. Whites called them Creeks because their *talwas,* or agricultural settlements, had clung to waterways in northern Georgia and Alabama.

They called themselves the *Muskogee.*

In the stress and turmoil of being uprooted, many Creeks looked to *Yahola.* He was a male god who lived in the sky without the comfort of a female god. If properly petitioned, this moody and ethereal loner could give you physical stamina, good health, razor-sharp reason and the ability to see the future. Helping Spirits, such as *Yahola,* didn't easily correspond to anything in Western mythology, except perhaps guardian angels. Wingless angels who taught you secretive rites and eerie curing songs.

Emmett had come to Muskogee seeking *Yahola.*

He walked down Okmulgee Street under a sky milky with heat. He'd never been overly fond of this city of forty thousand. With all the problems of modern life, including drugs, it wasn't the redneck paradise described in the Merle Haggard song.

Midstride, Emmett pivoted and ducked into a pet store.

He had no interest in the place and found the smell of animal urine unpleasant. But it got him off the sidewalk long enough for a sedan to speed past. It was headed in the direction from which he'd just come. Seconds before, he'd caught the blue light in its grille blinking at him through the heat waves rising off the asphalt.

"May I help you?" the clerk asked. White and apparently not well disposed toward Indian vagrant types.

Emmett continued to watch the sedan until it was out of sight. "Do you have any weasels?"

"No, nothing like that."

"Get some." He went back out onto the sidewalk with a new urgency in his step. The Muskogee satellite office of the FBI employed probably a dozen agents, and he believed that he'd just seen two of them headed down the boulevard at sixty miles an hour. But he told himself that he'd expected no less. There were many reasons for a bucar to speed through a summer afternoon, foremost bank robbery, but he knew in his gut that he'd tripped this off by using the BIA computer last night.

Some things were inevitable. He just had to stay ahead of them.

If the agents were responding to the address given for YaholaWare on its Web site, they'd find a newly established pizza joint. Before that, it'd been a used bookstore, and before that, a Democratic Party campaign headquarters. Nobody he'd queried recalled it being a computer business. But Emmett was relying on the fact that often your competitors will keep closer tabs on you than your friends. So he'd torn the computer service and repair page from the *Yellow Book* and now walked into Fredericksen's Computer World.

A scrawny kid turned away from showing a woman a PC. "Help you?"

"I'm looking for a buddy of mine. We went through certification together."

"You mean Fred?"

"Who's Fred?"

"The owner. He's in the back."

"Mind getting him?"

"Uh, okay," the kid said as if it entailed a hike of several miles.

Emmett glanced out the front window just as a P.D. unit sped by. The opposite direction the bucar had gone. Things were humming. A search was on. But he made himself calm down. It might not be for him, and even if it was, he would manage. He'd parked the heisted Buick on a side street, but either way this was a reminder it was high time to swap vehicles again.

Fred appeared, wiping his grimy hands on the front of his Grateful Dead T-shirt. Old Merle would have been proud of this denizen of Muskogee, Oklahoma, U.S.A., what with his waist-long gray ponytail and his vapid hippie smile. "Do I know you?"

"Doubt it," Emmett said. "I'm looking for this Indian guy I went to I.T. training with. Braids, tall, thin—"

"Eli Cusseta," Fred said without batting an eye. "You say you're friends?"

"Well, we got along pretty good. Why d'you ask?"

"Most people looking for Cusseta want their money back."

"What money?"

"The cash he conned them into investing in his business. You're not a cop, are you?"

"Not in this lifetime," Emmett replied. "What was Eli's business called?"

"YaholaWare."

Bingo, but Emmett kept an indifferent expression as he said, "I'm not involved in nothing with Eli. Just passing through town and wanted to get together for a beer."

Fred studied Emmett's face a few seconds more, as if looking for sincerity, then said, "Promise me you won't break his legs. I'd feel bad if I told you where he is and you did something like that."

"Wouldn't dream of it. Do you know where he is?"

"No, but come along." Fred inclined his head for Emmett to follow him to the workshop in the back. "Couple months ago, a city cop came round asking about him. But I don't tell cops shit." While the man punched in a number on his wall phone, Emmett positioned himself so he could keep an eye on the glass front door and street beyond. In quiet undertones, Fred chatted with somebody he obviously knew well, asking if he'd seen the *Creek Geek*. There were three or four minutes of *uh-huhing*, which was finally ended with a quick *thanks*. Hanging up, Fred said, "This buddy of mine saw Eli down near Eufaula back in April."

"The town or the lake?" Emmett asked.

"My buddy saw him gassing up a big Chris Craft at Brush Hill Landing."

"Does he have a new business down that way?"

"I've just told you all I know."

"Appreciate you taking the time, hoss," Emmett said.

"Hey," Fred chuckled, "it's a relief to finally meet somebody who don't want to kill old Eli."

Emmett walked back out through the showroom. The kid was going on in his relentless monotone about gigabytes and such to the woman. Emmett's mind was already skipping ahead to the swelling in the Canadian River known as Lake Eufaula as he pushed through the front door.

And nearly collided with Michael Mangas.

It was no simple task to blanket even a fairly small city like Muskogee. At any given time, less than a third of the combined strength of city cops, deputies and highway patrolmen were on duty. And, with their wide-ranging investigations, less than half the special agents assigned to an FBI satellite office could be found there on a single afternoon, especially at the height of the vacation season. So, as Michael Mangas sped from Oklahoma City to Muskogee, he kept phoning the supervising agent there to muster every available cop, regardless of jurisdiction, to seal off and begin searching the area. Even the Oklahoma Department of Fish and Game was pressed into the effort.

However, Michael kept the primary target to himself. He wanted to hit YaholaWare in person, before some first-office agent with a tattoo hidden under his button-down shirt screwed up the best chance they had yet to take down Parker.

Arriving in Muskogee at four-thirty, he had no one to blame but himself when he saw that the computer store was now Buck's Pizza Palace. The need for absolute security had cost him time. He checked the entire neighborhood for YaholaWare, just in case the BIA database had the address wrong. No sign of it. Only then did he meet with the local supervising agent and a captain from Muskogee P.D. in a grocery store parking lot.

Having been waiting outside in the late afternoon heat for some minutes, the head agent and the captain, a thickset black man in uniform, were sweating profusely. When Michael began to explain to them the relevance of YaholaWare in this, the captain butted in that it was long gone. A pizza place now, he noted needlessly. Needless until the captain added that his niece worked there.

"Can you trust her with something confidential?" Michael asked.

The man looked slightly offended. "She's a fine girl."

"Ask her if an Indian male adult, about forty years old, six-two, medium build, shaved or short hair, came in anytime recently and asked about the old computer shop."

The captain broke out a cell phone and stepped aside so Michael and the agent could go on talking in normal voices. "I want your people to stake out the pizza restaurant in case we beat Parker here. He's bound to be skittish, so they better know how to hide themselves like white on rice. Use your scrambled phone. Everyone use their phones from now on. He snatched one of our H.T.s a few weeks ago, and God only knows if he still has it."

"Didn't he snatch one of our cell phones, too?"

"Yeah, but we recovered it in Quapaw."

"What was Parker doing in Quapaw?"

"He wasn't, and I don't have time to explain."

The agent went to his bucar for his bureau-issued phone, which he'd left in his blazer pocket.

The captain returned to Michael with an excited look. "My niece says a subject fitting your description came in about thirty minutes ago." The man couldn't help but grin. "He asked where the computer store went."

Michael took a moment. To calm himself. To do the right thing under pressure. Random searches were useless. Worse than useless, for law enforcement assets were never more visible than when they were jumping from place to place, blindly searching. To search everything was to search nothing.

Computers.

This was narrowing down to computers.

Michael turned to the captain and asked for his help in canvassing the PC stores and Internet service providers in town. In less than a minute, they were speeding down the main drag, Michael following the captain's unmarked car in his own vehicle. He'd left it to the supervising agent to call in the half-hour-old sighting of Parker so it could be passed on to all area law enforcement. By cell phone only. Cops who didn't have cells were to use pay phones.

Parker wasn't going to slip away this time.

They were a quarter-mile along Okmulgee Street when the captain double-parked, leaving an open space at curbside for Michael. He took it and joined the captain on the sidewalk. The man gestured with his sweat-soaked handkerchief at a sign a couple stores down: Fredericksen's Computer World.

They walked toward it in silence, Michael taking a slight lead even though the captain had longer legs. Certainly not short Apache legs. Michael was almost to the door when a tall figure emerged from the computer store and nearly bumped chests with him. Emmett Parker's face instantaneously registered, but with an air of unreality to Michael, as if this were a peyote experience so real he'd somehow forgotten he was inside the teepee down on Wendell's farm.

Michael's pistol was out—with no memory that he'd drawn it from his belt holster.

Parker had a weapon out, too, Michael realized in the same instant he lunged to the side.

He was ready to shoot.

He knew he had every reason to shoot. But the captain, large and beefy and sweat-drenched, materialized in his sight picture, getting in the way and blotting out any sign of Parker.

"Freeze, *Pabi!*" somebody screamed. "*Freeze!*"

Belatedly, Michael realized that it was he who was screaming. Everything turned into a slow dance, as if everyone were moving through molasses instead of air. Mangas waved his pistol back and forth, clutching it in both hands and waiting for Parker to reappear from behind the captain. Just a piece of Parker. It was all he needed.

But that wasn't going to happen anytime soon.

Twice, the captain pawed at his clamshell holster before it occurred to him that Parker had taken his sidearm. Then his face turned an ashen shade of sickly brown and he slowly, ever so slowly, raised his forearms over his head.

Michael went to a knee. He braced his aim and carefully prepared to take the only target he'd probably have—a slice of Emmett's torso visible under one of the hostage's arms or a peek at the fugitive's head over the cop's shoulder. But Parker was making good use of the man's bulk, showing as little of himself as possible. He shouted for the captain to back up with him toward the double-parked car.

No fool, the man complied, sweat trickling off his scalp and down his face, making his eyelids twitch.

"Don't do this, *Pabi!*" Michael was surprised by the pleading in his own voice. And his effortless use of the word *brother* on a man he'd been prepared to kill for weeks.

One of the guns must have been jammed in the small of the captain's back, for he was arching it. Parker and he stopped shuffling backward. They'd reached the unmarked police car, and Emmett unlatched the door. "Keys!" he cried.

"In the ignition," the captain said, squinting up into the sun as if praying.

The smart play would be for Parker to take the cop with him. The man was his ticket out of Muskogee.

But he didn't do that.

Unlatching the passenger-side door, he gave the captain a kick that sent him rolling against a storefront. Michael fired twice as soon as the large man fell clear, even though Parker had dived headlong across the front seats. As his spent bullet casings tinkled against the sidewalk, Michael felt a glimmer of hope that he'd hit him at least once. But he saw no blood, no damage to the window glass or sheet metal of the car, and then the engine thundered to life, fan belts screeching.

The unit inched forward, and Michael raised his gun to fire again.

Parker sat up behind the steering wheel and took control of the pedals, using the bucar for cover. By the time Michael ran around the grille and into the middle of the street, Parker was scattering the traffic well down the block, speeding toward the east side of town.

Michael kept his pistol at eye level but didn't bring any pressure to bear on the trigger.

Too far. Too risky.

But then the brake lights to the fleeing unit flashed. At first, Michael didn't know what to think, although his stomach knotted up at the possibility of another round of gunplay. Then he believed Parker meant to turn off the main street, and so it seemed until he made a complete U-turn and started back toward them. With a sharp jerk of the front wheels, as if he'd made a sudden and desperate decision.

"What's he doing?" the captain asked from behind. "What the hell is he doing?"

Calmly, Michael walked back to his vehicle and lay across the hood. It was hot on his belly, but he focused to draw a bead on the side window to the unit. Striking the windshield with anything but a high-velocity round was futile. The curvature of the safety glass would deflect the slug. So Michael figured his one chance was to hit the side window as Parker rocketed by.

That wasn't long in coming.

But, from the corner of his eye, he caught pedestrians on the opposite sidewalk, window shopping, oblivious to all that was happening just yards away. Michael started to yell for them to drop, but by then all sound was covered by the howl of the approaching engine.

The bystanders froze and gaped stupidly at Parker in the unmarked sedan.

Helpless now, Michael rolled off the hood of his own car and crouched. Something metallic glinted in the air as it flew over the top of the bucar and came to rest where the captain knelt. Between the man's boots.

Michael stood, hoping to get off at least one round. But again, Parker was too far down the street for a pistol shot.

He looked back at the captain, who was examining what appeared to be his own handgun. Parker had just returned it to him. "Why in the name of Sam Hill would he do something like this?" the man asked in amazement.

"You just had coup counted on your sorry ass."

"Coup?"

But Michael was already running to get behind the wheel of his car. He didn't wait for the captain. He wanted to be alone when he met Parker for what he hoped would be the last time.

* * *

Emmett headed east again as soon as he could, taking Chandler Road all the way out to the Muskogee Turnpike. He had only doubled back on Mangas because he'd seen a city patrol car farther down Okmulgee Street, coming right at him. Tossing the police captain's pistol back to him had been a sudden impulse. Part of it had come out of sheer contempt for the captain's and Mangas's botched arrest attempt—if that's what it'd been—and part had come from realizing the fix they were in. Bearing down on them, Emmett saw the bystanders who were keeping the cop and Mangas from using their weapons. For that reason, he hadn't opened up with the 9mm, although he wondered if he'd regret that in the coming minutes.

Barreling up the southbound on-ramp, he switched from yelp to high-low to clear the traffic ahead of him on the turnpike. It was handy to have a siren again. And the mutual aid frequency on the Motorola was abuzz with confused reports about what had just gone down in front of Fredericksen's Computer World—although he had yet to hear suspect information about him being broadcast.

Still, he could have all the sirens and radios in the world, and they wouldn't add ten minutes to his time at large before a well-coordinated dragnet got him.

He had to get off the roads.

And quickly, too—it looked like the Fourth of July in his rearview mirror. All the emergency lights. At least three cruisers in pursuit of him, about two miles back and gaining.

A sign caught his attention. The next get-off was to the public airport at Davis Field. The tower jutted above the trees to the west. The idea of locking himself inside a Piper Cub or a Cessna for several hours with an anxious pilot-hostage, being dogged all the while by a swarm of U.S. Customs aircraft, didn't appeal to him. But his options were growing fewer by the minute.

Had to get off the turnpike. Soon.

He started to take the Davis Field exit. Then he saw the Oklahoma Highway Patrol unit blocking the bottom of the off-ramp. *Shit.* The trooper was busily laying down puncture strips, which would blow all of Emmett's tires and guarantee a gunfight.

Emmett swerved back into the right lane and continued south on the turnpike. Forty-seven miles to Sallisaw. The sign might as well have said forty-seven million miles. He wasn't going to make it out of the area in this sedan, even if it was unmarked. The Arkansas River ran slow and muddy just to the east. This stretch was part of the McClennan-Kerr Navigation System, and a barge tow was navigating down the channel. The hopper barges were piled high with tawny-colored grain.

Can I swim out to them?

They could take him all the way to New Orleans, where he could lay low while his trail cooled down and then venture back to Eufaula in search of Eli Cusseta. But this stretch of river was straight and well-dredged, and the barge tow was moving at a fast clip. He would have to get miles ahead, ditch the P.D. car so it wouldn't be found anytime soon, and swim out to mid-channel in the hope one of the barges or boats would be trailing a tire for a bumper or something, anything, he could latch on to and pull himself aboard. Otherwise, his day might end in the chop of the knife-sharp propellers.

Can I even hide this unit?

He wondered if the sedan was fitted with a Global Positioning System transmitter, telling dispatch where it was located at all times.

He shut off the siren. The traffic south of town was moderate enough for him to weave from lane to lane without having to force anybody off the turnpike.

Over the radio came mention of the captain's sedan. It was teal in color, according to the sheriff's dispatcher. Emmett hadn't paid attention before. All at once, he was terribly tired. It was oppressively hot, and there was a dusty, wilted quality to the foliage along the way. He was thirsty, and he'd strained one of his half-healed pectoral muscles while waltzing with the captain on the sidewalk. And, as if this all wasn't enough, the engine temperature warning light had come on.

"Emmett . . . ?"

The voice came to him as if out of a dream. He hesitated with his right hand on the microphone.

"Emmett, this is Michael Mangas. Do you read me?"

To the southeast, a train was curving out of the woods and fields toward the river, the locomotive's headlight oscillating through the gray onset of dusk. No matter where the tracks crossed the turnpike, they would run either under or over it—so he couldn't use the freight cars to block off his pursuers.

"Emmett, I'll guarantee your personal safety."

That angered him enough to sweep the mike up to his mouth. "Is that the same guarantee you gave Jerome?"

Mangas came right back at him: "You know more about what happened on Mt. Scott than I do. Care to discuss it?"

"I did not kill Crowe, you son of a bitch, and as soon as I confirm that either you or Ramsey did—you're both thirty seconds from hell!"

"Is that the last thing you told the guy we fished out of Buffalo Lake?"

Continuing to clutch the mike, Emmett glanced left. He'd passed the grain barges. Dirt lanes crisscrossed the thick growth between the turnpike and the river. He checked the rearview mirror: The nearest chase car was much closer now, a sheriff's unit. Maybe only a mile behind. "I had nothing to do with your second floater, Mangas, but I'm sure you'll try to pin it on me, too." He gambled that combined law enforcement could block most but not all the off-ramps between here and Sallisaw. He took the next one. No one awaited him at the quiet, wooded intersection at the bottom, and he passed under the twin tunnels of the turnpike. When he emerged again, the dusk had turned mysteriously windy. The trees and shrubs were being rocked back and forth. He leaned over the steering wheel for an upward glance. *Son of a bitch!* An O.H.P. helicopter was descending on him, the rotors buffeting the wildwood around him, raising a torrent of dust and dead leaves.

He headed south along one of the unpaved lanes he'd spied from the turnpike, trusting that the taller cottonwoods would back off the chopper.

Mangas's voice came at him from the radio speaker: "Emmett, you still there?"

Like you don't know.

"Talk to me, Emmett."

Later. He'd seen something else from the turnpike. A railroad bridge over the Arkansas. The bridge the freight train would soon cross, somewhere downriver of him. But he couldn't see the span through the trees. Bridges had maintenance roads leading to them, but he was afraid of betting on the wrong track through the woods and winding up with his back to the river and nowhere to go. Search helicopters had infrared, letting the crew look right through greenery and catch a human figure by its own body heat, particularly an overheated man.

"Emmett," Mangas continued, "what were you trying to do in Muskogee?"

Emmett was tempted to answer. What if he turned the FBI onto Eli Cusseta? Was that his way out of this? But then all he had to do was recall Jerome dying with a knife in his gut. Ramsey and Mangas had been the only others on the mountain that night. He would say nothing about Cusseta and hoped Fred, the computer store owner, wouldn't either.

He decided it was time to bet on a side road.

"Tell me, Emmett," Michael asked with a catch in his voice, "why'd you come to Muskogee?"

Silence.

Michael selected *scan* again on the radio. Just in time to hear the O.H.P. pilot report that Parker had left the turnpike and was speeding eastbound along a dirt road near Devil's Peak, a promontory forming a big bend in the Arkansas before the river straightened out again. His detour made no sense. Except for the Webbers Falls lock and dam, there were no highway bridges over the river until U.S. 64, miles to the south.

Michael switched back to the local police band on which he'd been communicating with Parker. "Talk to me, Emmett . . . please."

More silence.

"If you need me to check something out for you, I'm listening." Michael followed a trooper down the off-ramp and into dense woods that could swallow Parker in the blink of the eye, but for the fortunate presence of the helicopter.

Suddenly, Parker's voice made him sit straight: "Why, Mangas? You seem to have all the answers."

"No, I don't," Michael quickly said. "Isn't that way at all. I'm looking for the truth. You know that."

"Then instead of chasing me all over two states, you should be figuring out what Calvin Ushuk had to do with that Russian who's lying dead in an oil field between Wheatland and Will Rogers Airport. There's a connection there. I know it. But something's come up and I haven't been able to break away to Alaska. You been up there lately, Mangas? You got any ties up there?"

A honk startled Michael. He'd stopped in the middle of the road, knowing that he'd lose contact with Parker until he got to the other side of the underpasses. Now, a Muskogee P.D. unit overtook him.

Emmett couldn't see the helicopter but knew it was still overhead because the rotor wash was fanning the foliage all around. There was something strangely serene about the woods beyond this restless tussling. They looked dark and quiet and inviting. He wanted to melt into them and lie down.

But a Muskogee County sheriff's cruiser was only a few hundred yards off his rear bumper.

He also wanted to talk to Wendell one last time. The old man could prepare you for anything. Even death. What had the last instruction in his letter for the Palo Duro been? *Now sleep.* Maybe he had foreseen all this. He'd certainly tried to prepare Emmett for life. He still recalled what the elder had said to Malcolm and him after the two of them had run away from school once again: *Be happy with what you've got. It's probably better than what you want.* And he had wanted too much. Women. Excitement in his job. Glory, for he had to admit that glory was an insatiable thirst in the soul of his people. He'd wanted everything, and now he had nothing. Except himself. The diamond hard essence of himself. And enemies worth fighting to the death.

The rail bed loomed around the next dogleg. He felt no relief in finding it. Just resignation. As he'd hoped, the lane climbed the side of the rail bed up to the tracks. And the west anchorage of the bridge. Emmett bounded over the first rail—and blew the left front tire. Didn't matter. It just added slightly to his bumpy ride over the ties. He began passing over water. There were no guard rails on the span, and his view to both sides was good. The chopper hovered upstream of him, agitating the surface of the river. The observer lifted the visor on his helmet and stared at Emmett. As if he couldn't believe his eyes. Meanwhile, the pilot suddenly climbed a hundred feet: The barge tow was bearing down on the chopper, the lead boat less than a half mile away.

With his free right hand, Emmett fumbled under the dashboard for something he trusted was there. It was. A button that sprung the clasp to the shotgun lock. He yanked the scatter gun free and jacked a round into the chamber before resting the weapon across the passenger seat.

Blue and red lights behind caught his attention.

A deputy was pursuing him onto the bridge. Emmett smiled to himself. Nothing crazier in this world than an Oklahoma deputy sheriff. Except perhaps a *Nuhmuhnuh* warrior. *And that's what I am today. Finally, today. I'm home.*

At that moment, the headlight of the locomotive broke from the east bank of the Arkansas. Emmett powered down his window to listen for a sound. Not the *blat-blat* of the horn, which he anticipated, but the squeal of the brakes locking the iron wheels on the tracks.

It came with an ear-splitting shriek. The engineer was doing everything humanly possible to stop the train, but it wasn't easy with the weight of hundreds of loaded freight cars behind him.

The gyrating headlight got bigger and the horn louder.

Emmett thrust the barrel of the shotgun out his open window. He didn't aim directly at the chopper, although close enough to make believers of the pilot and observer. He knew the double-aught balls would fall short of the craft.

Boom!

The pilot swooped under the bridge and was swiftly gone across the river. Out of sight.

Emmett checked the rearview mirror. The deputy was backing up. He didn't think it was a good day to die.

The headlight now filled the sedan's windshield.

Thank you, Creator. Thank you for this day.

Something big had happened, and it took Michael a minute to decipher what all the incredulous chatter was about. As insane as it sounded, Parker had driven onto the railroad bridge and into an onrushing train. The locomotive had demolished the police captain's sedan and swept it along, a fiery ball of crushed metal, nearly all the way to the west bank. Before tossing it over the side into the river.

Finally, Michael could take no more. He transmitted, "People—don't let up. Continue the search. I want every square inch of these woods searched. I want divers in the river to locate that car. *Now.*"

23

IT WAS LATE when Fe Cornplanter left the tavern just outside the entrance to the RV park. She had to walk home through the breathlessly hot night along a winding campground road. But her way was lit by the curtained windows of the travel trailers and motor homes and the quicksilver sheen of Lake Eufaula beyond. Months ago, she'd asked Morris if they could buy a small car to toodle around in once they set up the Winnebago in a park, but he'd said he didn't like towing *a g.d. trailer* and sure as hell didn't want to tow *a g.d. car.*

Thinking of Morris got Fe weeping, and she was racked by big sobs by the time she got to her coach. She unlocked the door and swung it back—but didn't enter. Not without taking in hand the nickel-plated .38 special she now kept under the entry mat whenever she went out for the evening. She would've carried the revolver in her handbag all the time, if not for that close call in the Shawnee bank. Morris had impressed upon her the penalty for carrying a concealed weapon without a permit. She'd been in jail once, briefly, some confusion on a blind date that resulted in an absurd solicitation charge, and didn't want to repeat the experience in that crowded holding tank among such vile and trashy women.

She peered around the darkened interior of the Winnebago, snuffling softly. She tried to listen over her own crying and the hum of the roof air conditioners for somebody waiting for her inside.

Murder changed your home like nothing else, transformed it from a sanctuary to a place of horrors. She still refused to bathe in the fiberglass stall where poor Morris had hung. Thank God there was a ladies' shower room in the park, otherwise she didn't know what she'd do.

Revolver clenched before her, she climbed the two steps up to the kitchenette and flipped on a wall switch, bringing on lights both front and back. She spun this way and that like of those female detectives on the television, making herself dizzy but covering every conceivable place she imagined Hola might lurk. She staggered on her way to the rear, scratching the pantry door with the barrel of the gun.

No matter.

She hated this Winnebago now. She'd go to some big city and sell it. You always got a better price in a big city. Everything was better in the city. She was sick to death of small Midwestern towns, their bland yellow brick buildings and clapboard houses surrounded by rolling monotonies of wheat and corn. You felt as if you were adrift at sea in the Midwest, especially if you'd ever lived somewhere like New York or Los Angeles.

It came to her that she may have had a little too much to drink down at the tavern, for she wasn't as scared as she should be. Vaguely, she realized that terrible things could happen to her at any moment, but she was also sick to death of being on guard all the time.

Buck up, lady, and watch out.

Taking a deep breath, she threw open the door to the bathroom. Morris was there. For a split second. Hanging limp and bloody in death. Then he was gone. As gone as he truly was, and she turned away from the empty bathroom.

She set down the .38, took the vodka from the cupboard and filled a glass without even bothering to see if it was already dirty. She knew she was sliding downhill, but how to stop was beyond her anymore. She wanted an end to this pointless existence on the road, even though she feared the unknowns beyond.

What a crazy world. Cheers.

The Popov's began to numb her despair. That's what was wrong: Walking through the steamy night had sobered her up, and all she needed was to top off her buzz a little to feel on top of things again. Then she might take a dip in the lake, or even inflate the kayak and go for a paddle in the moonlight.

She sat at the table to drink. After a while, her eyes roved over the cabin. Something was wrong, but she couldn't quite put her finger on it.

Then she found it: the lock.

She'd forgotten to lock the door.

Flying up from the seat, she twisted her ankle. Yowling, she nevertheless hopped over to the door and secured it. That ruled out walking down to the lakeshore for a dip, and it now seemed like too much trouble to inflate the kayak. Sitting again, she took a big swallow of vodka on account of her ankle, which she believed was already swelling up. She wanted out of this life, with all its frights and annoyances. She drifted off to Hollywood in her mind. Rode down Sunset Boulevard in a convertible awash in neon and that California night air, which was as light and smooth as good champagne.

Something was still wrong.

She examined the interior of the motor home with wet-lipped suspicion. *Yes.* Things were not as she had left them earlier this evening. That was it. Objects had been moved around. She was now sure of it, even though she couldn't recall where the items had been placed, precisely. There was no permanence to life in a motor home. Your possessions rocked and slid around whenever you hit the road. Yet she was convinced somebody had been inside the coach during her brief absence.

Brief.

She narrowed her eyes to bring the wall clock into focus. It was now eleven o'clock. *Impossible.* She'd just gone down to the tavern for an hour or so after an early supper of Vienna sausages on Ritz crackers.

How had five hours fizzled away in the smoky darkness of the little bar?

Her heart sank under the weight of her growing weaknesses. It was all becoming so pathetic. She wasn't sure where she was. How she'd gotten here. Where she was headed.

Her gaze fell on the combination TV-VCR built into the cabinet over the windshield. A cassette projected slightly from the slot. A twinge of wifely remorse came over her: Damned if she hadn't rented a tape and neg-lected to return it to whichever store she'd gotten it. Morris would give her the devil. There was no way the store could ever trace them, not under the assumed identities they donned and cast off at will, but he was funny about this. He didn't like to steal videocassettes.

Then, for the thousandth time in the past weeks, she remembered that Morris was dead and began crying again.

She longed for the film—whatever it was—to sweep her away from this tomb on wheels. Rising on her sore ankle, she nudged the tape all the way into the slot and turned off the lights. Watching a movie, she liked to imag-ine that she was in a theater. A nice one, like the Egyptian or the Chinese in Los Angeles. Palaces.

There were no titles to open the film.

Abruptly, a human figure appeared, lashed with ropes to a cross. No landscape or real set, just a background of static gray. Shot all jerky in black and white. It wasn't a religious picture, at least any kind of period religious picture she'd ever seen, for, despite the crucifix, the man was in modern costume, Levi's and a white turtleneck, disheveled and torn. To her, he looked Asian or American Indian, or something like that. His head drooped so his chin rested on his breastbone, and there was blood on his teeth and in the corners of his mouth. Like he'd been smacked around. He had a wispy goatee, but other than that she saw no resemblance to Jesus. *What is this piece of garbage?* How could she have ever been so out of it as to pick something like this off the shelf? She knew her cinema and de-tested art-house stuff. This was clearly one of those low-budget artsy-fartsy films.

The figure tied to the cross muttered something through his puffy and bloodied lips. "No, no."

"Brilliant," she said sarcastically.

Then she realized that someone off-screen was putting questions to him. The voice was garbled, diabolically deep. She thought it had been dis-guised on purpose.

"Calvin," the poor man said deliriously, "my name is Calvin Ushuk." He had a funny accent. She couldn't place it.

The voice asked something, but it was impossible make out the words. The tone was unmistakable. Accusatory.

"No idea," the character named Calvin Ushuk said. "I kayaked over to Big Diomede like usual. And when I got back to the weather station, guys from Customs were waiting for me."

The voice barked, and Calvin cringed like somebody afraid of getting hit. *Kayaked.* Fe thought of her own kayak and wondered again if she felt up to inflating it and taking a paddle on the lake.

"That's the truth. I swear it. I never told 'em anything. Nothing about the money. Nothing. I guess they thought I was trading in walrus tusk or something. Nothing was ever said about the money."

Another guttural question.

"Same guy," Calvin replied. "Goldilocks. Same big Russian. He's got gold hair, so I call him Goldilocks. He took the shipment from me and got inside their helicopter. I guess they flew back to Siberia. That's all I know. The Russians flew away. Like usual."

The next question hit him like a hammer blow.

"I didn't!" he wailed. "I did nothing to bring attention to myself!"

Then he was gone, replaced by a flash of full-screen black followed by another image. Although still recognizably human, this one was fuzzy. Awful gurgling noises came from the TV. Fe leaned forward, trying to make out the blurred face. Gradually, it became Morris's. The video camera was jumping all over the place, almost as if it were being held under somebody's arm, but the shot was a definite close-up of her husband in the shower stall being garroted with a coiled towel. "We didn't talk to anybody," he gasped. "Anybody!" Then the videocam must have been dropped, for the screen became a tilted view of his bare feet and the floor of the stall. Morris screamed like she'd never heard him make a sound before, and big gouts of dark liquid splashed around his feet and whorled down the drain.

Fe lunged for the TV, spilling her drink across the table. She ripped the cassette out of the VCR and hurled it into the back of the coach. Then she stumbled down the steps and out the door. She couldn't stay a minute longer inside the place where Morris had died. She didn't scream. You need air to scream. She stood outside under the uncaring stars, trying to force a breath down into her lungs. At last, one made it down her windpipe with a sharp wheeze, and she collapsed to the grass.

Then she must have passed out.

For when she came to, warm grass clung to the side of her face as if she'd been lying there for some time.

We're in the money . . . we're in the money . . .

It was Morris's cell phone. Despite her confusion, she knew she had no choice but to answer its jingle of a ring. But her body felt impossibly heavy, and it was all she could do to sit up.

We're in the money . . .

If she failed to answer, he might come in person. Hola. And she knew she couldn't deal with him in person. She didn't have the strength for that.

Whimpering, she used the exterior step to pull herself to her feet. She wobbled on her stiffening ankle up into the kitchenette. The cell phone had been last left on the dashboard, directly beneath the TV, which was hissing, its screen snowy. She pressed a touch-tone key, any key, and brought the phone up to the side of her pounding head. But she couldn't bring herself to say hello.

"Once again," he said, "I trust that my point has been well taken."

"Oh, yes."

"Very well," Hola went on in that creepy, high voice of his, the same voice—she now realized from its cadence—that had been electronically altered on the tape, "you may be a stupid cunt, but you have your uses. As long as you do just what I say and don't draw attention to yourself, I'll let you live. Is that agreeable to you?"

"Oh, yes," she repeated.

"Good. Listen, shut the door. It's late, your lights will draw attention. That's the big no-no from now on. Attention. It's what got us all in this screwed-up mess."

She shuddered involuntarily. He was watching her. Again, he was watching her every move, just as he had on her nightmare drive out of Amarillo, with poor Morris thudding from side to side in the shower stall on her way to Buffalo Lake and her last view of him lying motionless on the shore. She fought a wave of hysteria by biting her lower lip.

She closed the door.

"Thank you," he said.

She used the remote to switch off the power to the TV, afraid that he was somehow watching her through her own television. Was that even possible? He was a wizard with electronic things. His genius for evil was boundless.

"You'll be fine as long as you don't talk to anybody. As long as you don't draw attention to yourself. The first fellow on the tape did both things, and he wound up in Lake Lawtonka."

"But my Morris . . ." She didn't know how to finish.

"He talked back to me. That won't do either, Fe. You can add that to the list. Morris talked back me, and he wound up in Buffalo Lake. Have you noticed how our lives revolve around lakes? Our deaths, too?" He paused. "Fe means *faith* in Spanish, doesn't it?"

"Yes."

"Well, you must have faith that nothing bad will happen to you as long as you obey me and keep to the program."

"Please, Hola—"

"We're finally close enough for you to address me correctly. I'm called *Yahola*."

"Is that an Indian name for a boy?"

"For a guardian, a god—not a mere mortal. I can be your guardian, Fe, watching over you night and day, making sure no harm comes to you. Making sure you prosper. Would you like that?"

She started to cry again.

"Calm down," he said soothingly. "Everything's going to be fine in the end. I know things have been a mess for some weeks now. But this was inevitable. Change is messy, and you have to be patient while things get sorted out. It had to end. Me sucking hind teat. Me getting the lesser share. You and Morris got a piece of my action. That's how it always worked. The more I made, the more you two made. But that wasn't fair. Not for everything you and I do. That's what this is all about, making things fair. And out of the ashes, a new program will rise. A new, leaner, meaner program."

"I don't understand," she said, seeing that she'd left the revolver on the sink-board.

"Sure you do. Remember last time when we talked about duplication?"

"I think so."

"When two people can do the same job, you eliminate one of them in the interest of efficiency. Except there was a lot more deadwood than just Morris involved in this. A lot."

"Don't kill me," she begged.

"Wouldn't dream of it, girl. You're my best little check casher. You're absolutely tops. When things get squared away, it's going to be just you and me for a while. What do you say to that?"

"Oh, thank you," she said more gratefully than she wanted, for it felt like betraying Morris. Yet, her husband had no more worries and she had many. "Thank you so much, Yahola."

"Now, go find the tape and toss it out the door. Do you understand?"

"Yes."

"Then please do it. Stay on the phone, Fe."

The tape had landed in the back among the developing equipment. On the way to it, she glanced aside at the revolver, visualizing herself throwing the tape outside onto the grass, as he wanted—but waiting behind the barely cracked door with the gun in hand, waiting for him to creep out of the night to retrieve his cassette. She would liberate herself with a flurry of bullets, drive off, and leave this all miles and miles behind. Start a new life in a neat little house in a suburb next to a big, bright city, a real house on dirt she'd own and could plant with flowers and a few vegetables.

She got the tape from the back but couldn't make herself pick up the .38 special on her way past it. She felt so very inept. So hopelessly inept.

She lobbed the cassette out, locked the door, then slumped at the table, the cell phone still scrunched against her ear.

Never once did she hear him approach the Winnebago, but after several minutes of silence he said, "Good night, Fe," and disconnected.

She sat at the table again. Thinking of Morris. Thinking of their lives all these years, not really lives but existences played out at the ends of Yahola's strings.

Grinding her teeth together, she got up from the table and seized the snub-nosed handgun. She took it out into the night, halting in the darkness of the grassy slope that fell away to the lake. An engine fired up. Not a car engine. It sounded more like a snowmobile. Then she saw an object about the size of a snowmobile race away from the shore. A Jet Ski, she realized, ridden by Yahola. She just knew it was her tormentor. The water craft left a luminous wake across Eufaula, then vanished around the backside of an island she could barely make out in daylight.

She lowered the revolver to her side. And wept.

"Michael, I've been shot."

Two days after returning to Lawton from Muskogee, Michael Mangas sat at the computer in his office, finishing a report on Eli Cusseta, the alleged computer expert Emmett Parker had been seeking, according to the owner of Fredericksen's Computer World. Michael inserted *alleged* in his narrative because nearly forty-eight hours of investigation, including ground-pounding by Muskogee FBI agents in the area and a tedious name-by-name search of BIA records and Creek Tribe enrollments, had failed to produce any proof that Eli Cusseta had ever existed, other than as a temporary alias long since shed like an old snakeskin. Fredericksen claimed to have heard nothing about Cusseta in more than a decade.

As Michael typed in frustration, his direct phone line rang. Dagen Kirsch, without greeting him or identifying herself, declared, "Michael, I've been shot."

"Dagen?"

"Yes."

"What're you talking about?"

"I was shot a couple of hours ago."

"*What?*"

"I was shot. Twice."

"Are you all right?"

"I'll survive," she said without much conviction.

"Where are you now?"

"In your parking lot."

Michael swiveled around in his chair and parted the Venetian blinds on a white sedan below. She was seated behind the wheel. The lot lights fell across her torso, but her face was in shadow. "I'll be right down," he said.

Less than a minute later, he opened the driver's side door on her. The dome light revealed her wan face and unhappy smile—plus two bandages, a large one around her upper left arm and a smaller one pasted to her right cheek. "Jesus Christ," he burst out.

"I could've used Him about three hours ago."

"What happened, for God's sake?"

"Let's drive." She scooted over into the passenger seat, nursing her left arm. Still, she winced. "I'll tell you everything, but I just can't sit still. I feel like a sitting duck unless I'm moving."

He started the engine. "Where to?"

"I don't care. Into the sunset. Nice, isn't it?"

He hadn't noticed the last light, thin and pink on the cloudless horizon. In fact, he'd lost track of time. It was nine-thirty. As soon as he drove out of the lot, she closed her eyes and rested them until they were passing through the open country west of town. "What a day," she said, looking over at him.

"Tell me about it."

"Well, it started in the West Wing . . ." She paused, and he realized that she was wearing business attire. "I got fired, Michael," she said with false cheer, as if trying not to cry. "The chief of staff called me back to Washington to fire me. Damned decent of him, don't you think? Doing it face-to-face? These days they seem to prefer doing it doggie style—over the phone or even a discreet leak to the media."

"I'm sorry, Dagen." He wanted to be sympathetic, but found this turn of events understandable. You didn't embarrass the President. Less understandable was how a day that'd begun at the White House ended in gunplay.

As far as he knew, the Secret Service discouraged that sort of thing. "Who shot you . . . and where'd this go down?"

"I caught the first flight back to Will Rogers—"

"Dagen, how are your wounds?" he interrupted. "Should you even be out of the hospital?"

"I'm okay," she said. "The graze to the cheek may or may not scar. The bullet that went through my arm missed anything important."

"Are you on pain medication?"

"No. I don't want to be drugged."

"And the hospital released you?"

"Pretty much." When he looked skeptical, she added, "They do that these days. Before long, brain surgery will be a drive-through thing."

He didn't want to get too far from Lawton, knowing that he'd have to assemble help to deal with this. Best to stop and talk somewhere private. The exit for the town of Cache gave him an idea. "Go on—you flew home from D.C."

"And I set off for Anadarko. I was feeling pretty blue. I'd just turned off Forty-four when it really hit home—the sons of bitches *fired* me. After everything I've done for the President and the party, the sons of bitches let me go!" There were tears in her eyes. Natural. But the bright fury in them surprised him. "I could barely drive. So I parked on the side of the road and cried. This is so fucking unfair."

"I know. You've worked yourself to death." He took an unpaved lane just past a trading post.

"I don't how long I cried. . . ." Sniffling, she popped the glove compartment for a packet of Kleenexes. "Where are you taking me?"

"Star House," he said. "We can sit on the porch and talk."

She was moved. "Thank you, Michael. I know what a special place it is to you."

"So you stopped on the way home to Anadarko to cry . . ."

"That's right, and after a while there was a tap on the window." She startled slightly, as if reliving the moment. "I hadn't noticed the car. It'd pulled in behind me."

"What kind of car?"

"I . . . I'm not sure. New, expensive, pearl-colored. An Infiniti, maybe."

"Are you sure of the make?"

"No," she admitted, "I'm not good with cars."

"Oklahoma plates?"

"I don't remember anything like that, Michael. I was shook, okay? Two men were standing there, staring down at me. One I'd never seen before. Tall and skinny with braids."

"Indian?"

"Definitely. He held the gun while the other one opened the door. It happened so fast from there. The skinny one shot me—"

"Shot you while you sat inside *this* car?"

"Yes, Michael. He had a silencer. At least that's what I think it was. There wasn't much noise. Nothing was said. But he looked so cruel as he pulled the trigger . . ." She wiped her eyes with a wad of Kleenexes, streaking her mascara. "Like he enjoyed doing it."

Parking in front of a shuttered mansion, Michael shut off the engine and switched on the dome light. "Lean forward." As she did, a hole was revealed in the trim panel on the passenger-side door. It was the size of a small caliber bullet. And there was a tear in the upholstery along the back of the bucket seat she now occupied. That would account for both rounds that had struck her.

"Describe the other man. The one who opened the door for the shooter."

"I don't have to, Michael," she said in a hushed voice.

"What do you mean?"

"It was Emmett Parker."

Michael sat still, saying nothing.

After a while, he got out of the sedan and stood before the Star House. The name came from the thirteen large stars painted on the roof, inspired by the stars on a placard the general at Ft. Sill had before his residence. This twelve-room mansion had been built for Quanah Parker by a Texas battle baron in thanks for giving him tribal grazing leases. Here, with his seven wives and many children, Quanah lived in comfort and entertained notables such as Theodore Roosevelt until his death in 1911.

And now Emmett Parker was dead, too.

That was the consensus.

The crushed unmarked police car had been recovered from the muddy bottom of the Arkansas River with no body in it. Yet, everyone Michael had interviewed was certain Parker had died inside. The O.H.P. chopper pilot had been busy evading shotgun fire from the fugitive, but both he and his observer believed that Parker had been inside the car at the moment of impact. Even more convincingly, the locomotive engineer, although rattled by the experience, said that he had been looking right into Parker's *crazed eyes* at the split second of the crash.

But Michael wasn't convinced.

And he'd insisted that search teams comb the banks of the river and the Marine Division of the O.H.P. stop and board the barge tow that, everyone else seemed to forget, had been passing under the railroad bridge at the time of the impact. The sheriff's tactical commander insisted it was improbable Parker had survived the leap into one of the grain-filled hoppers. Grain became cement at the end of a fall like that.

But Michael pressed.

Ultimately, the teams found no sign of the fugitive along the river banks. And the troopers probed the mounds of grain with long rods and interviewed the barge crew with equal thoroughness.

Nada.

Now, Michael had his first solid indication that he'd been right. Parker had survived. And somehow linked up with the suddenly real Eli Cusseta, for Dagen had just described the same person the computer store owner had as the proprietor of now defunct YaholaWare.

However, a voice of caution told Michael not to feel vindicated. Not yet.

While all of this ran through his mind, Dagen stepped out of her car and eased down onto the edge of the front veranda, her platinum hair looking metallic in the star-shine.

Michael joined her. "How'd you get away from them?"

"I'd never turned off my motor. Thank God. I stomped on the gas and headed back for the interstate."

"Did they follow you in their car?"

"I don't know. I was bleeding, Michael. And so damned scared." She leaned against him, as if pleading for an end to his questions. She wanted understanding, not questions.

He took her under his arm, careful not to brush her bandage with his fingers. But he still had much to ask. "Where off Forty-four did this happen?"

"I don't know. Someplace along the Amber cutoff. A wide spot in the road. That's all I remember. Nothing around. Nobody to help me."

"Which hospital did you go to?"

"Come again?"

"You made a U-turn, so I assume you didn't head for Muni in Anadarko."

"I knew that'd be the first place they'd come looking for me. Any hospital, Michael."

"Who treated you, then?"

"My personal physician. He was in family practice for years. Before he went into his specialty. He wants me to drop by a hospital later this evening. Just for some follow-up."

"What's his specialty?"

"Does any of this matter?" she asked with rising anger.

"Did he report the gunshot wounds?"

"I explained my life was in danger and I was on my way to find you. I told him my best friend is an FBI special agent. Okay? I don't give a damn what the legal protocol is."

"Sorry," he muttered. But his mind had shifted to something else. *Small caliber bullets.*

Dropping his arm from her shoulders, he couldn't help but recall Parker's mention over the airwaves during the pursuit of the homicide victim found in the oil field west of the airport. Presumably the Russian energy attaché, although he'd served the Houston consul in that capacity for all of two weeks prior to his death—their foreign ministry had been less than forthcoming to the field office with details about the victim's personal history. Regardless, the four mashed slugs extracted from his corpse had been .22 shorts. The same caliber the hole in Dagen's door trim panel appeared to be.

"Michael, what's coming over you? You're so cold."

"I don't mean to be, Dagen." But he was distracted. He was weighing his options on how to proceed. The shooting evidence left in this car was not particularly perishable, so that much could wait. How would she react if he ordered that her hands be swabbed by an evidence technician for traces of gunpowder residue? How could he make use of her reaction to determine the truth about this afternoon's attack?

If there had been a real attack.

He seriously wondered if her wounds had been self-inflicted. All the pressures of the past month, especially her firing this morning, might have unhinged her, making her grab for any sympathy she could get. For the first time, ever, he realized how desperately she craved sympathy.

He could feel her eyes on him, but he quietly rose and looked over the darkened house. Dark for generations now. This wasn't even its original location. In Quanah's time, the mansion had stood closer to the Wichita Mountains. The Army had condemned it to make room for more artillery ranges, and a white salvager had moved it here. Anything Indian seemed to get moved. Again and again.

She broke their long silence first. "You can't get him, can you?"

"Parker?"

"Yes. You and the entire Federal Bureau of Ineptitude can't seem to catch him."

Her sudden fit of temper struck him as childish. There was something laughably juvenile about it, except that she seemed so disturbed. He knew better than to touch her now. "We may have gotten him, Dagen," he explained. "This week near Muskogee."

"No, you didn't. You bungled that, too. He murdered poor Jerome right in front of one of your agents, and the nincompoop couldn't keep him from driving off!"

Already thinking ahead, he wondered if she'd ever met or seen Ramsey. "I understand why you're so upset."

"The hell you do!" she shouted. "Parker and his sidekick tried to kill me this afternoon, and all you can do is quibble about who treated me!" Then she hurried back to her car.

Michael had left the keys in the ignition, so he followed her before she drove off, stranding him. He had much to do in the coming hours. First, get her to the hospital in Lawton. For her own good. He wasn't sure if he was prepared to put a psychiatric hold on her, even though he wanted a look under those bandages for powder tattooing on her skin—evidence that the weapon had been fired from very close range. And to further substantiate the possibility she'd shot herself, he needed her hands swabbed.

Yet, in the course of the coming night, everything had to do be done at just the right moment, or not at all.

"Let's get you some help, Dagen," he said as he restarted the engine.

24

NOTHING WAS QUITE as frustrating as scanning the radio dial at three in the morning for yesterday's baseball scores. Unless it was searching a country road for the scene of a crime that may or may not have occurred. Four hours ago, Ramsey had been kicking back in his easy chair, electronically transported out of the Midwest by an ESPN-televised game between the Yankees and the Athletics in Oakland—*now there was a sports town*—and seriously thinking about finishing the last two beers in a six pack he'd bought this evening on the way home from the office. Then his bureau-issued cellular rang, the replacement he'd gotten for the phone Parker had taken from him. As was the case after hours these days, Ramsey knew without answering who was calling: "Hello, *compadre.*"

He was right. It was Michael, who—*surprise, surprise*—needed a favor, which meant he wanted something handled discreetly: "Keep off the radio about this, but look along the Amber cutoff for any evidence of a shooting that may have gone down there this afternoon. I don't care how flimsy it seems."

"*May* have gone down?"

"I'll explain later." Mangas's motto.

"Where's the Amber cutoff . . . ?"

Now Ramsey knew. Technically, it was County Road E1280, which Anadarko-bound locals used to reach the Chisholm Trail Highway, letting them avoid the stoplights in Chickasha.

He gave up trying to find out in whose favor a three-three tie in the ninth inning had been resolved and flicked off the radio. Once again, he drove east along the county road, so he could begin the process all over again from I-44.

For the third time.

According to Mangas, the victim—or nonvictim, as the case might be—had been westbound when she stopped alongside the road in a wide spot to compose herself. Why she'd needed to compose herself would be explained later. Where that wide spot was might never be explained.

As he worked his way east, Ramsey ran his spotlight over the shoulder, watching for where the victim might have parked. It seemed unlikely to him that she, driving westbound, would've crossed the center line to park on the opposite edge of the road, but he didn't limit his search to his lane. There was a single pull-out along the north side of E1280 that showed recent tire tracks.

Once more, Ramsey parked shy of it to preserve any possible physical evidence, trained his spotlight on the dusty crescent of dirt and approached it on foot. He knelt, swept his flashlight flush to the surface. He was looking for the glint of a brass casing. The victim, or nonvictim, had been shot twice, not critically, but shot nonetheless, and unless the shooter had used a re-volver there might be ejected casings on the ground. Bits of broken glass and smashed aluminum cans glittered everywhere, but no brass.

While standing up, he caught of glimpse of something white. It was far off, across a barren field of dirt clods in a small stand of trees.

Ramsey returned to his bucar and swung the spotlight around on the object.

It was a car. He wondered if it'd been there, partially hidden by the trees, the other two times he'd stopped at this turn-out. He hoped not, otherwise his powers of observation stank. On the other hand, its sudden appearance might mean that somebody had just driven up, running lights blacked out, to lie in wait for him. Mangas had been clear about one thing: Ramsey was not to summon a backup from the local cops or deputies unless he had a reason he could later justify to God Almighty.

Getting back in his sedan, Ramsey drove down the county road to the next farm track, along which he believed the white car was parked. Before he got to it, he crossed a bridge. A sign bore the name of the sluggish ribbon of water it spanned: West Bitter Creek. He mentally noted it, in case he needed to tell responding help where he was.

Ramsey turned up the unpaved track, the dust curling over his view to the rear. His hand was poised on the microphone. He wanted to start some help this way. He'd feel better if a backup moseyed this way.

Moseyed. Jesus, I'm beginning to think like an Okie.

But he wouldn't feel better when Mangas got in his face about needlessly involving another law enforcement agency. Reluctantly, he let go of the mike.

Besides, he had arrived in the middle of the trees. He centered his spot on the off-white Lincoln. Its driver's door was wide open, and the engine was still running. Nobody was visible in or around the car. Ramsey didn't like that. He wrote down the Missouri license plate on his clipboard. It wouldn't help now, but at least he'd leave behind a solid lead if something happened to him.

Small comfort.

He stepped out of his car, angled his door to deflect bullets away from him and hailed the Lincoln: "FBI, anybody there . . . ?"

There was a green sticker on the trunk lid. Enterprise Rentals. For some reason, that touched a feather to his memory, but he kept his focus on the Lincoln. The open door and the air of hasty abandonment around the vehicle made Ramsey draw his 9mm, but he kept it down at his side as he crept up on the car with his flashlight clamped under his left armpit.

Then it hit him.

The Russian attaché had rented from Enterprise at Will Rogers Airport upon his arrival from Houston. The vehicle had never been recovered. What make and color? Ramsey thought it had been a foreign job, but maybe not. Could it have had Missouri plates?

Suddenly, none of that mattered.

There was blood on the driver's seat. As if it'd collected between the spread of a man's legs. Also, the floor mat was flecked with the same reddish brown.

Ramsey tested the biggest pool of the stuff with his forefinger. It was faintly sticky.

He turned off the Lincoln's engine. The sound was unnerving him. But then the silence that followed seemed even more haunted. Haunted by driver's unexplained absence.

Ramsey ransacked the storage compartment in the center console and then the glove box. No rental agreement to tell him who might have bled here, but the Missouri registration was to an Enterprise outlet in Kansas City.

He gazed all around. Then down at the ground between his shoes.

The dust had transformed droplets of blood into hard little balls. No shoe sole impressions, other than his own, were to be seen, but there were scrapes and other signs of disturbance, as if the driver had sprung the door and tumbled outside in a heap.

Ramsey stepped back.

A long scuff tended off into the darkness, beyond the reach of his spotlight.

He followed it out of the trees and down to the creek.

There, he cried out, "Holy shit!"

A large man lay spread eagle with his back to the bank and his legs submerged in the slow-moving creek. He had lain there long enough for a raft of algae to have collected around his hips. He wasn't moving, and he didn't appear to be breathing. Adding to the impression of death was the fact that he had plucked at his white shirt, even going so far as to undo the lower buttons so he could have a final look at the bullet hole in his fat stomach.

He had a round but brutish face, not unlike that of the Russian corpse found in the oilfield, and a very bad toupee that had shifted forward over his brow. Ramsey had been called in to assist the Oklahoma City agents with that crime scene investigation in the oil field near Wheatland. Why had this man crawled down to the creek? For a drink? Ramsey recalled reading somewhere that a belly wound left a man with a ravenous thirst. He dressed nothing like most Oklahomans. A shiny suit coat and dress shirt, although no tie. The attaché from the Houston consulate had carried his credentials in the inner pocket of his coat. A suit coat like this victim was wearing.

Ramsey holstered his semiautomatic and slowly crouched over the body. He had just reached past the lapel when the man's eyes clicked open and he seized Ramsey by the wrist.

Yahola parked his pearl-colored Infiniti sedan in his private space at Brush Hill Landing and strolled out to the private dock where his boat awaited him. The predawn darkness was deep, but Lake Eufaula suggested itself beyond the breakwater as a sheet of tar. He made certain that his Chris Craft hadn't been tampered with during his absence tonight, even going so far as to sweep for electronic bugs. Yahola paid the marina owner an extra hundred a month to keep an eye on his boat, plus report on anyone who asked about him in any of his various aliases—and deny knowing him.

At last, he warmed up the throaty-sounding inboard engines.

He had ten more miles, ten nautical miles, in front of him before he could sleep. But he always enjoyed the cruise home. He cast off the mooring lines and bounded back up the ladder into the pilothouse.

Soon, he was building speed across the glass-smooth lake. The water was fathomlessly black, but it held the reflections of the stars. The wind made his braids whip his shoulders. He went to full throttle and enjoyed the speed. He felt good this morning. Not all the reports were in, but things were going well. Everything he had patiently programmed over the years was beginning to bear fruit.

The lights to the town of Eufaula showed off to starboard. Just north of them was the RV park where Fe Cornplanter's Winnebago was parked, a GPS transmitter concealed in one of the air conditioners on the roof, informing Yahola's receiver at home of the motor home's whereabouts. Amazing, devices that had once been only the toys of the national security agencies could now be made from components purchased at Radio Shack. High tech was now available to the masses, and the federal government had yet to fully understand the implications of that. Most people, like Fe, had no clearer idea how their world operated than how their vehicles ran.

Sweet dreams, Fe. May you float away the night on your lake of vodka.

She would do fine again, as soon as her nerves settled down. In all the time he'd observed her, she'd never been much of a boozer, and he didn't believe drying her out now would be a challenge. All she needed was time. And she'd be given that respite as Yahola continued to gear the operation down for the investigative siege that was already underway. The problem was simple. Things had gotten too big. Too many moving parts in the whole. Those parts were human beings of varying degrees of trustworthiness. Some hadn't been as steady and predictable as Fe, and so they were dead now. Like her hubby Morris. As far as the investigation, eventually it would peter out as had all the other inquiries over the years into the missing trust funds, the bigwigs at Justice satisfied with a partial solution. As soon as that happened, Yahola would gear up the operation for another run. A more modest and stealthy operation.

But he would be sole proprietor now.

He sped past his island. As was his habit, he continued south for a mile before swinging around and approaching it from the direction of the wildlife refuge, a tule-choked marshland that was uninhabited, except for Brother Kingfisher and Brother Loon and all his other informants who flew far and wide to tell him what was unfolding in his world.

Slowing for the pine-sheltered cove in which his dock lay, Yahola was reassured to see the silhouettes of his geodesic dome, his arrays of antennas and satellite dishes. *Home, sweet home.* His island, referred to as Choctaw Islet on the topo maps, consisted of six wooded acres up one of the remote arms of the lake. He moored his boat, grabbed his flashlight and strode up an overgrown path to the bunker in which his big diesel generator was concealed. He fired it up, and the heart of his idyll began to beat.

Yahola was back in residence.

Michael took one more long and careful look through the viewing window into the operating room at Anadarko Municipal Hospital. Then he gave his verdict to Ramsey, who was nursing a cup of coffee beside him. "No Russian."

"What do you mean?"

"His name is Anthony Brosnahan. He's tied to the Kansas City Family, does hits for them as well as some freelance work."

Gesturing at the corpulent figure on the operating table, Ramsey whined, "You telling me this guy is a made-man from here in the Midwest?"

"Midwest, yes. *Made*, no. Tony's mother was Sicilian, but his dad was Irish, so he'll never be a full member of the congregation. We suspected him in a body dump we had off I-Forty-four years ago."

Ramsey looked crestfallen.

And, to tell the truth, Michael wasn't wildly happy about this development, either. The discovery of a badly wounded Tony Brosnahan a few hundred yards off the same highway along which Dagen claimed to have been attacked complicated this exponentially.

Had she shot the hit-man in self-defense?

Or was this entirely the wrong tack? Had Eli Cusseta, whatever his true identity, and Parker attacked her, as she'd claimed? Then might Brosnahan have run afoul of that unlikely pair? Or could he have been with them, unseen by her in the Lincoln? The Lincoln wasn't foreign, as she'd described, but its off-white color was close to pearl.

One thing was certain. Brosnahan would never tell what'd he'd been doing on County Road E1280 yesterday evening. Michael had asked the Evidence Response Team to roll to the site on West Bitter Creek where Brosnahan had lain for several hours like a beached catfish, suffering and out of his element, but very much alive. Perhaps waiting for help that never arrived—folks who hired hit men were notoriously unreliable. The techies were to search the entire length of the dirt lane in from the county road, as well as wade the creek, for a cell phone, wallet and weapon—none of which Brosnahan had had on his person when found by Ramsey.

"Surgeon get to the bullet yet?" Michael now asked him.

"Nope. It'll be a while in that tub of guts."

Michael checked his phone's signal strength. "Got to step out a minute to make a call."

On his way outside, he passed the ICU unit in which Royce Eschiti had lain. He'd tried to help Emmett and paid the price: He was now back in

McAlester, albeit the prison hospital. And this is where Michael had last seen Wendell under a cloud of mutual suspicion. When this was over, he had to repair the damage. But that would have to wait.

Standing in the warmth of the newly risen sun, he punched up a number on his speed dialer. It connected him to the head evidence technician's cell phone. "Mangas, here. You still out on the scene along the Amber shortcut?"

"Yeah." Cranky. Probably no caffeine this morning, no chance for a bowel movement.

"Can you free up one of the guys?"

"Why?"

"I want a pair of hands swabbed for powder blowback."

"Where?"

"Lawton Community Hospital."

"How soon?"

Michael checked his wristwatch. Almost six. "Have him meet Ramsey and Weeks there in forty-five minutes."

"Okay," the technician said, sounding no less disgruntled.

Late last night, Michael had stood by at Lawton Community as the ER physician examined Dagen's wounds. No powder tattooing around either of them, meaning that it was now less likely that they were self-inflicted. The doctor had ordered her into a bed for observation, and Michael had ordered one of his resident agents, Weeks, a steady Kansan, to stand guard on her car and make sure she didn't check herself out and drive away.

It was no longer a mystery who had initially treated Dagen. At five this morning, Michael got a message on his beeper to call Dr. Hawzeepa. In a voice ragged from apparent sleeplessness, the medical examiner explained that Dagen, a long-time friend, had come to him with two superficial gunshot wounds. *"She said Parker and somebody else had attempted to kill her, and she was afraid to go to an area hospital. She promised to go straight to you, Michael, as soon as I was done with her."* Hawzeepa paused. It was refreshing—his meek tone. Plus, for the first time, he'd called Michael by his given name instead of Agent Mangas. *"Did Dagen report to you?"*

"No," Michael replied, just to have the pleasure then of hearing the man squirm.

"*Well, that won't do at all, will it? I only treated her because the wounds were superficial and because of the peculiar circumstances of this whole episode. If there's anyone who knows what Parker is capable—*" He cut himself off. "*Are you positively sure, Michael, she didn't report this incident?*"

"*Don't sweat it, Silas. I'll handle the formalities.*"

Michael paused. "*How is it you and Ms. Kirsch are long-time friends?*"

"*Oh, years ago, when I had a family practice in Anadarko, she was one of my patients.*"

"*Interesting,*" Michael said.

"*What's interesting?*"

"*I was just wondering out loud if doctor-patient confidentiality still applies.*"

"*Michael, she told me nothing I'm sure she wouldn't tell you or the rest of the FBI. This is truly confounding. . . .*" He was in an absolute dither now. "*Truly.*"

Despite the pre-dawn hour, Michael had been reluctant to terminate the call, it'd been so amusing.

Now, he went back inside Anadarko Muni to Ramsey. "Brosnahan isn't going anywhere soon. I want you to go down to Lawton Community right away. Evidence should be arriving there same time you do. Weeks is already down there. Tell him to go inside with the techie and observe as Ms. Kirsch's hands are tested for residue."

Ramsey interjected, "Shouldn't that have been done right away last night?"

Michael ignored the question. The book no longer applied. "Listen—tell Weeks not to say a word to her. Just stare."

"Why . . . ?" Then the young agent shook his head. "You'll explain later."

"Right."

"And what do I do?"

"Nothing," Michael said. "Unless she bolts from the hospital. If she does, hang back so she doesn't spot you and contact me."

"Solo?"

"Solo."

"Michael, what's this all about?"

"Get going, please."

Shaking his head again, Ramsey started down the corridor. "Later."

His question had been a fair one. At its core, it asked how a five-foot-six-inch female and Washington paper-pusher had managed to best the professional hit man now laid out on the operating table before Michael. Not likely, yet this line of speculation inferred a side to Dagen that Brosnahan had never anticipated, to his detriment, and Michael had never imagined.

To his detriment as well, perhaps, he realized.

25

LIVING IN ISOLATION on Choctaw Islet held its challenges for Yahola. The biggest had been Internet connectivity. Dial up was out of the question—the nearest telephone line was three miles away on the east shore of Lake Eufaula. But the advent of satellite broadband nicely solved that for him. His connections weren't fast, but they were fast enough to carry on the cautiously invasive kind of business he was in. His satellite dish enabled him to play the cowbird on the Internet.

The modern world, he believed, even the technological world, was still best described in animalistic terms.

This North American blackbird stealthily lays its eggs in the nest of a bird of another species. The host bird then raises the cowbird's young as if they were its own. In Yahola's case, the "eggs" were Internet traffic he'd created to resemble someone else's. Like transactional orders from the BIA to the U.S. Treasury. Emails between various law enforcement agencies—that masquerade was especially fun. Finally, to protect himself from other cowbirds, or hackers, and to cloak himself in a reasonable amount of secrecy, he'd hooked up a corporate firewall and other state-of-the art equipment he'd taken from the entity for whom he'd performed his last outsource contract—the U.S. Department of the Interior.

Fresh and flushed from a long shower, Yahola sat at his console, braiding his hair for the start of what promised to be a busy day. It was one in the afternoon, his morning, for he liked to do his most demanding work in the dead of night. Through the components he'd stacked on his long desk, he had a view of the lake of which he never tired. It spangled under a cloudless sky. Farther up, the lake waters were stained red by the silt-heavy Canadian River. But down here, around his island, they were clear enough to see schools of fish darting under the surface. He didn't refer to his home as Choctaw Islet. He called it *Nunne Chaha,* in commemoration of the first hill-shaped land to emerge from the waters of creation.

A Porky Pig voice stuttered out from one of his speakers, "You have m-mmm-mail."

Indeed he did. The response he'd been waiting for.

It came from a free web mail account at an Internet café in Tulsa, but still he knew who had sent it—the I.T. manager at the biggest oil service company in the country, the kingpin of a conglomerate grown fat on lucrative contracts from all over the globe.

They wanted a face-to-face meeting to discuss his proposal.

"No shit!" Laughing, Yahola slapped the table top. "No shit you want a meeting, buckaroo!"

But then, sobering, he began crafting his reply. The Big Boy in Tulsa was doing some outsourcing of his own, the kind that employed the likes of Tony Brosnahan. According to a Secret Service briefing memo Yahola had tapped into late last evening, the Kansas City hit man had been left bleeding along a creek in Grady County with a bullet hole in his stomach but very much alive, something that no doubt had the Big Boy on pins and needles. Yahola monitored the Secret Service more actively than any other law enforcement agency. It was their responsibility to investigate the theft of government checks.

Yahola typed out his conditions.

Their representative—unarmed and alone, of course—was to leave Tulsa within the next twenty minutes and drive south along U.S. Route 75 at precisely 57 miles an hour. Yahola was to be given a complete description of the vehicle and a cell phone number at which the driver could be reached to arrange a yet unspecified meeting place. No aircraft or other cars were to be involved. No enforcer types were to shadow the designated vehicle. A violation of these conditions, in either letter or spirit, would instantly result in a rather unpleasant report being downloaded to the U.S. Attorney's Office in Oklahoma City.

Yahola hit the SEND button, then made himself breakfast.

He was wolfing down scrambled eggs with fry bread when the answer came back. The Big Boy agreed to all his conditions. The vehicle, which was just leaving Tulsa, was a lime-green 1963 Volkswagen beetle. Yahola smiled as he chewed. Some mail room boy at corporate headquarters had been made to cough up his car for the day.

Fifteen minutes later, he was pounding over some light chop in his Chris Craft. He spotted a bald eagle roosting in a tall pine along the shore. "Awesome!" he cried, pinching together his forefinger and thumb in imitation of the noble bird's head and splaying his last three fingers like its wing feathers.

A good omen for the rest of the day.

Yet, if the truth were known, he'd always had exceptional luck. In being adopted by an elderly and childless Choctaw couple—not Creek, as he'd led many to believe—who owned one hundred and sixty acres along the Canadian River. Yahola had not known the two weren't his biological parents until one day, when he was thirteen, he stuck their sow with a pitchfork and laughed while the pig shrieked and bled around its pen. That moment, incomprehensible to his Choctaw father, was the one in which the old man chose to tell Yahola that he was adopted. *You were an orphan, son.* More specifically, as Yahola later learned for himself, he'd been a foundling, an infant abandoned by his mother. That had occurred in an alley behind a rescue mission on Reno Avenue in Oklahoma City, which made it highly probable that she'd been a prostitute. Yahola was undeniably Indian, but which tribe or mix of tribes could never be determined, short of exhaustive DNA analysis, and he really didn't give a shit. He was generically Indian, which in his mind gave him a range of choices not possessed by the members of an individual tribe or band.

Tribes were so parochial.

Luck was with him again when the dammed waters of the Eufaula Project slowly rose and inundated all but the crown of a hill on his parent's allotment, kind of like the *Nunne Chaha* creation story in reverse. Stung by criticism of its uprooting of other native peoples to build reservoirs throughout Oklahoma, the federal government let Yahola's family retain possession of what remained of their holding, now a six-acre island.

For most of his life, Yahola had felt a strong connection to reservoirs. They were his sanctuaries. Repositories for those who had crossed him.

His adopted parents, diabetic and in their seventies, died within six months of each other when he was seventeen. By that time, Yahola was already in college. Not just any college. The Massachusetts Institute of Technology. Yahola, the foundling, the cast-off issue of a Reno Avenue hooker, had a gift for math, particularly calculus and linear algebra, and his high school counselor had seen to it that he got a full scholarship. Today, according to the alumni magazine, one percent of MIT's student body, about ninety kids, were native. But, back in the eighties Yahola had been among only a handful of Indians in attendance, and the ribbing had been insufferable. Finally, tired of being nicknamed *chief*, exasperated with having to explain for the thousandth time that most modern tribes didn't have *freaking chiefs*, he lost his temper and stuck another student with a penknife. The wound was so superficial the attack wasn't even reported, but the impact on Yahola was profound.

To his amazement, he enjoyed sticking human flesh even more than he had pig flesh. Enjoyed it infinitely more than the spiritless masturbation he resorted to on occasion. This urge grew and grew and eventually drove him across the Charles River into Boston's skid row in search of flesh to stick. He thrust an ice pick into a black vagrant sheltering in a cardboard box. Stuck him again and again. Then as soon as the bum twitched his last, Yahola arranged his corpse with arms outstretched and ankles joined. Like one of the crucifixes his Choctaw father had been forced to worship at St. Benedict's Indian Mission. His father had been a mild and sober man, but that hadn't kept him from ranting against Catholicism now and again. And so, Yahola began the practice of honoring his adoptive father in this way.

Back on campus in the weeks that followed, he was sick with dread, believing that homicide detectives were lurking around every corner, waiting to pounce on him. They never did, and from that his confidence had swelled that he could satisfy his urge without being caught.

No one can catch Yahola. No one can catch a god who lives alone in the sky.

Now, reaching the breakwater outside the marina, he idled his engines. A switch on his instrument panel automatically dropped the bow anchor. This done, he grabbed his binoculars and went down a short flight of stairs into the main cabin. Through one of its tinted windows, he glassed the front porch of the store and the parking lot for anything unusual.

Last night, his namesake, the Great Yahola, had appeared to him in a dream. Dressed in a tweed jacket with leather patches at the elbows, his guardian had been standing at a chalkboard, a being of light and vapor. A Massachusetts morning pressed grayly against the windows of this imaginary classroom. The god was scribbling out an equation on the board: Yahola now couldn't remember which, but the nth term or the sum of the n terms approached a finite limit.

What did that mean? What did it portend for today?

His parents' allotment had been farther north than most Choctaw holdings and he'd lived among Creeks all his life. He spoke better Creek than Choctaw. A boy of nine, he'd contracted rheumatic fever and was close to death when their deity appeared to him in a broiling dream. The Great Yahola would make sure the boy survived, but only if he offered up his allegiance. His parents would not have found it seemly for him to honor a Creek god, but the choice had been simple—life or death.

The man Yahola had kept his bargain to the god Yahola.

Setting down his binoculars, he frowned. A faint uneasiness had come over him as he suddenly realized that he was being warned about something. As often the case with messages from the gods, the threat would remain cloudy until it presented itself. The gods were grudging in their gifts and offered human beings only a slight head start on danger.

May it prove to be enough.

Going up to the pilothouse again, he raised anchor and continued on to his slip. He moored and went ashore, keeping a sharp eye out.

The Great Yahola didn't make his nocturnal visits without cause.

He examined his Infiniti, especially the undercarriage, then drove away from the marina. But not far. He took a side road through the oaks and pines. It wound up to a bluff from which he had a view of both the landing to the south and the exit off I-40 to the north.

He parked his Infiniti and got out.

The leafy woods had looked cool from the air-conditioned comfort of his car's interior, but in reality they were hot and dank. And cicadas were skirling so loudly, Yahola could barely hear himself think. He got back in the Infiniti, although his phone's signal strength wouldn't be as good, and restarted the motor to run the air conditioner.

He checked the dash clock. It was 2:12 P.M.

He dialed the number he'd received via email.

"Hello." A familiar voice answered before the second ring, a voice Yahola hadn't expected, at least not coming from a common little car like a Volkswagen. Unless they were already playing tricks with him. Tricks of the electronic variety.

"Where are you right now?" Yahola snapped.

"Just passing the get-off to Schulter."

"If you're sitting on your fat ass in Tulsa, there will be hell to pay."

"Honest. I'm passing by Schulter."

That put him well down U.S. Route 75 from Tulsa. The main man. The Big Boy. A mover and shaker. One of the elect who got invited for barbecues at the President's ranch. Yahola knew that this was a milestone in his life: He was being taken seriously.

"All right," he ordered, "head east on I-Forty. You'll get another call along the way."

"Understood. I . . ."

"What?"

"I thought it was important we finally talk face-to-face."

"Just head east on Forty," Yahola said coldly, then disconnected. But he was smiling. What a rush—*the main fucking dude.* And, on this happy realization, something else hit him: What the Great Yahola had been scribbling on the blackboard in the dream.

Convergence.

He had mathematically described the properties of convergence. Everything was coming together at a unified point. Naturally, there was peril in that. But there was also tremendous opportunity to settle all scores with a single blow.

The cosmos was shifting in the man Yahola's favor. Soon, he, too, would be a god.

Michael got off I-40 seventy miles east of Oklahoma City. The main road, U.S. Route 62, led north a few miles into the town of Okemah, but within a block of the freeway was a budget motel. Mid-afternoon, the parking lot was empty, except for Dagen's white Ford sedan.

Michael didn't approach the motel.

Instead, he took a frontage road that soon ended in a cul de sac with a view of the place. Well, the back and south side of the motel. He was reasonably sure that Dagen couldn't have left without being observed by Ramsey, who was sitting inside his bucar parked there.

Michael pulled in behind the sedan and joined him.

"Find it okay?" the young agent asked.

With Michael sitting beside him, the question would have been patently superfluous but for the faint clues over the radio by which Ramsey had directed him here. Per Mangas's instructions, there had been no mention of Dagen. No mention or description of her car put out over the airwaves. "What time did she get here?" he asked.

"Around noon. Checked in. Re-parked in front of room thirty-seven and went inside. She hasn't stirred since."

"You sure?"

"Nope," Ramsey said. "I couldn't cover the front of the building without burning myself. You told me to do this solo, and I can't be everywhere at once."

"Could the motel manager be the reason she came here?"

"Doubt it," Ramsey replied, yawning.

"But did you see them interact?"

"She was in and out of the office in no time. Last thing I saw was her going inside her room and opening the drapes. That's what made me move to this location. Okay . . . ?" The agent fell silent.

After a minute, Michael asked, "Are you up to doing some research for me?"

"Like what?"

"Modern trends in money laundering."

"I'm a trained accountant. What makes you think I wouldn't be up to doing something like that, *compadre?*"

"Nothing. Great, I'd appreciate it." Michael smiled to himself. Self-esteem was beginning to rear its head.

And then, after a bit, Ramsey revealed that self-esteem was very much on his mind. "Was Parker really the cop they say he was?"

"Yes," Michael replied impatiently, not wanting to wallow in that right now. He neither wanted nor needed to think well of Emmett. "Nobody else came to the motel?"

"Just the linen service guy."

"Did *he* have any contact with the subject?"

"Not that I saw."

"What about any maids?"

"Oh, yeah. One walked from the motel to the bus stop up the street around one o'clock. Caught a bus that headed toward Okemah."

Michael was leaving nothing to chance. So far, in investigative terms at least, things had gone well. His decision to send in the evidence techie to swab her hands had paid off. Not only had the test come up positive, meaning that she'd recently fired a weapon, she'd been spooked enough to check herself out of the Lawton hospital and drive east, doubtlessly with the expectation of contacting someone or finding something. Who or what Michael had no idea.

"She drove like a fool all the way from the city," Ramsey reported, yawning again.

"Fast?"

"Sometimes. Other times so slow, truckers were honking at her."

Distracted. Someone had hired Brosnahan to kill her. That had to be eating away at her, and maybe she knew little more than Michael did at this point. However, she'd been ready for the hit man. Michael couldn't get past that. Had all that sexual pleasure blinded him to her true capabilities? She'd been emotionally prepared for a trained killer—and had beaten off his attack, no worse for wear than a couple superficial wounds.

What makes you think she isn't prepared for you?

"Dammit!" he spat, startling Ramsey. But before the agent could utter a word, Mangas hushed him and dialed information for the motel's number.

The manager answered.

Michael requested, "Ms. Kirsch, please."

The silence that followed lasted long enough for Michael to wonder if he'd blundered in assuming the manager wasn't involved. But then he said with budget-motel curtness, "Hang on a min."

The phone in room thirty-seven rang. And rang. And rang.

"Hit it," Michael ordered, disconnecting.

"What?"

"The goddamn motel!"

As Ramsey rounded the south side of the building, Dagen's Ford came into sight, parked where he had last seen it—in front of her room. But Michael wasn't reassured. Even before Ramsey could shift into park, Mangas was out and running for the door. He glanced over the interior of her sedan. It was empty, even of luggage. He restrained the impulse to bash open the door to thirty-seven with his shoulder and instead tested the knob.

Thankfully.

Because it was unlocked.

He ducked inside with his right hand on his 9mm. He kept his pistol holstered, but he was ready for her. He wasn't going to wind up like Tony Brosnahan.

Yet, as half-expected, Dagen wasn't in the room.

Ramsey rushed past Michael and checked the bathroom. Obviously, she wasn't there, either, for the agent wailed, "You have got to be shitting me!"

"See what the manager has to say." As Ramsey went out, Michael studied the entire room. A shabby place, not to her taste for cleanliness. But her purposes today made taste irrelevant. She had sat upon, not lain upon the bed, judging from the impressions in the coverlet. The phone book was on the nightstand. Closed. But he riffled through it in search of anything remarkable. Perhaps a wrinkled or dog-eared page.

He found more than that.

A yellow page was missing, ripped out, leaving a ragged margin along the spine.

The preceding page left with *Boat Dealers* and the following page listed *Boat Repair* outfits. That left what?

Boat Rentals?

Behind him, Ramsey burst back into the room. "Manager didn't see her leave, and he was at the counter with a view of the lot the whole time. She made no phone calls."

"What about the linen—"

"Deep Fork Linen Service," the agent interrupted, "based in Henryetta."

A town along I-40 about fifteen miles to the east.

"You want me to call them?" Ramsey asked.

Dagen had known she had to shake the FBI before reaching wherever she was headed. One possibility—she had arranged for the truck to swing by the motel. The other—she'd simply seized on the convenience of the driver making his rounds.

Michael wasn't sure which was true.

But if Deep Fork Linen had knowingly helped Dagen, a call would only forewarn her that the FBI was back on her trail.

Michael checked the time: 3:16. "No, don't call," he told Ramsey. "It must be close to the time the truck gets back to the laundry plant. Grab a phone book from another room."

Ramsey pointed toward the nightstand. "What's wrong with that one?"

"It's missing the page I need to find her anytime soon."

"Go into Checotah," Yahola said over his cell phone to the Big Boy.

"Checotah?" he repeated, sounding confused.

"Yeah, it's a town of three thousand that should be about seven miles east of you right now. What are you, a nitwit?"

"No," the man said icily.

"*Ciao.*" Grinning to himself, Yahola disconnected. He wanted to set the tone for the coming confrontation.

It was time to move.

He'd already made two calls from this wooded bluff above the lake, and he had every expectation that they were using all the electronic gadgetry at their disposal to get a fix on him. He raced down to U.S. Route 69, then headed north on it.

His timing was almost perfect.

But only almost, for as he curved east onto I-40, the lime-green Volkswagen appeared in his rearview mirror. He'd wanted to catch it from behind. Now, the only way to do that was to exit the interstate, which he did at the next opportunity. By the time he got back on, the VW was a green speck at least two miles ahead. The driver was doing fifty-seven miles an hour, as told, for at seventy miles per hour, Yahola was steadily gaining on the bug. Weaving through traffic, he examined all the cars along the way. None appeared to be from corporate security, but then again their CEO was disguising himself in a VW bug today.

He dialed the district office of the O.H.P. He didn't use 911, a system guaranteed to have caller identification. "Highway Patrol," a woman's voice answered.

"I'd like to report an accident," Yahola said.

"Are there any injuries?"

"I don't think so. The other guy's holding his neck—does that count?"

"What's your location, sir?"

"Uh, let's see—close to the get-off for Checotah on I-40."

"Your name?"

"Gates. William Gates. From Okmulgee. Can you get a trooper here right away? This joker's getting kind of irate. I don't know what's wrong with—!" Yahola purposely cut himself off mid-sentence and tossed the phone on the passenger seat.

Then he made sure his seatbelt was securely latched.

A hundred or so yards ahead of him, the driver of the green Volkswagen put on his right blinker and started down the turn-off to Checotah. Yahola followed, drawing closer and closer. The driver stopped for the sign at the bottom, but Yahola continued on at ten miles an hour and plowed into the back of the VW. The airbag inflated in his face, and he could see nothing for a few seconds.

Quickly, he took stock of himself. Nothing hurt, although he sneezed from the bag hitting his nose. Jamming his shift into reverse, he backed up a few yards, then drove forward again, jerking the steering wheel back and forth to make sure the fenders hadn't folded in on the tires. His Infiniti still seemed drivable.

Then the Big Boy was screaming at him through his side window, which was still shut. "What's wrong with you, you fucking moron . . . !" He had silver hair that swept back from his brow, and the tendons in his ruddy neck were standing out like ropes. He was badly rattled, probably because he believed he would miss his rendezvous with the mystery caller. So far, he gave no sign that he realized that he'd just met him.

Smirking, Yahola motioned for him to step back so he could get out. The man retreated, but only slightly before he was in Yahola's face, shouting again. "You on drugs?"

Pretending to be dazed, Yahola looked at the crumpled rear to the Volkswagen. Fluids were dribbling from the engine. "What happened?" he asked, altering his voice and playing the dumb Indian. "Where'd you come from?"

"Hell, that's it!" the man cried in self-congratulation. "You're stoned!"

Yahola caught blue and red lights from the corner of his eye. An O.H.P. cruiser was barreling down the ramp toward them.

"You better have insurance," the CEO warned.

"You better believe it," Yahola said.

The trooper had both of them present their licenses and registration cards, then said, "Y'all please step over onto the grass."

A second trooper arrived and started directing traffic around the wreck. The CEO had fallen silent. Yahola quickly saw why: A brown sedan had pulled off on the interstate shoulder on the overpass above. A man with a crew-cut in a business suit got out from behind the wheel and raised the hood as if to troubleshoot the engine. Another man, also neatly shorn and suited up, remained in the shotgun seat, although he'd cracked the door and set one shoe on the pavement—like cops do to be ready to return fire.

But Yahola knew that these two men weren't cops. At least, not recently.

"Sir . . ." The first trooper approached the CEO, holding up a .45 auto, beautifully silvered and engraved with curlicues. "Is this your weapon?"

"Yes, it is," the CEO admitted as he dug a slip of paper out of his billfold. "And I have a permit to carry it concealed."

The trooper examined the permit. "Nice forty-five. I'm going to hang on to it for a couple of minutes. You looked pretty riled when I drove up."

"Well," he said, indicating Yahola, "I'd just been rammed by this moron, who I think should be tested for drugs."

Troopers didn't take advice well from civilians, and this one was no exception. "Sir, I strongly advise against storing your weapon loaded and cocked under the front seat. It wound up jammed under the brake pedal."

"Yes, officer, I'll be more careful."

As the trooper went on about his business, Yahola looked the Big Boy straight in the eye and smiled. "There's a huge difference between a *permit* and *permission*," he said in his normal voice.

The CEO stared back at Yahola, a light sheen of sweat covering his face. "*You*," he growled under his breath.

"*Me*," Yahola growled back at him, mocking him in precisely the same way. "Me pissed off. Me said, '*Come unarmed and alone. . . .*'" He flicked a glance up at the men around the brown sedan. Now, both were out of the car and pretending to deal with some mechanical problem. "You've done neither."

"Listen, you pigtailed yahoo—I grew up in the oilfields of west Texas. Had me only two years of high school, but I was rough-necking by the time I was fifteen and running my own drilling crew at seventeen. My own fucking oil service company at twenty-two. Do you think you can—?"

"Sir," the trooper called from the vicinity his cruiser. He was referring to the CEO. Something things didn't change in Oklahoma, and when a trooper, while handling a dispute between a white and an Indian, addressed one of them as *sir,* it wasn't the Indian. "Would you please step over here a minute so I can take your statement?"

Five minutes later, after he was done with the CEO, the cop took Yahola aside. He gave him a field sobriety test, which he passed. "What happened?"

"I was distracted," Yahola confessed.

"How?"

"By an eagle."

"Pardon?"

"I saw an eagle up there . . ." He indicted the tallest tree beside the off-ramp. "I was saluting him when I ran into the back of this guy."

"Saluting an eagle?" the trooper asked caustically.

"Yeah, it's my religion."

"Well, insurance doesn't take religion into account. Your premiums will go through the roof after this." The trooper handed him back his license and registration. "You need a tow?"

Yahola shook his head.

"Well, the other fella does. I think the impact was hard enough to crack his block."

"That's what he gets for having his motor where the trunk ought to be."

The trooper smiled a little. "In the meantime, you fellas can exchange insurance information."

"Glad to," Yahola said. He strolled over to the CEO, who was looking up to his security men as if waiting for them to do something. "Not likely," he told the silver-haired executive. "The beauty of artificial intelligence is that it can be programmed to go on functioning even after you yourself have ceased to exist. So if they shoot my red ass, that A.I. will spring into action. The truth is—there isn't much you can do in this situation, which I'm sure you find galling, being the dynamic type you undoubtedly are." He reached out and patted the man's shirtfront with his palm. "You're wearing a wire."

The Big Boy recoiled from Yahola's touch. "You son of a bitch," he muttered.

"The best you can do with a wire is take me down with you. But you'd do nearly anything not to go down, being the dynamic type you are, so

I doubt you're transmitting anything that feeds directly to law enforcement."

"You don't know a goddamned thing," the CEO snarled, the hatred in his eyes making them glisten.

"Oh . . . ?" Yahola rolled his tongue around the inside of his cheek. "It so happens that I know everything. But, because of the wire you're so discourteously wearing, I'll limit to my remarks to your direct involvement."

The CEO peered up again at his goons again, one of whom shrugged at him after gesturing at the troopers.

"Yesterday afternoon," Yahola went on, "you sent Tony Brosnahan to kill our lady associate—without the desired result, I might add."

That got the man's attention again. But he recovered from his surprise and mopped his sweaty face with his handkerchief. "You're no associate of mine."

"Don't you wish. I'm the Alpha in this and you're the Omega. I won't bore you with all the technical and needlessly self-incriminating details of how the money gets from the United States Treasury to our friends in Siberia. But I do know how it gets back into this country."

The man had stopped wiping his face.

"False invoices."

"I don't know what you're talking about." But, as the Big Boy said this, he pulled his shirt out of his pants, reached under and ripped off the wire, only to crush the tiny microphone under his heel.

Yahola laughed. "My mama always told me *actions speak louder than words.* Don't worry—who do you think came up with the idea? The problem with capital flight is that the laundered money must at some point come back into this country. Cash is too hot, and that's how amateurs get caught. So why not make a deal with a foreign syndicate, such as the biggest oil exploration firm in Russia, to return those funds—less their cut—disguised as payments on inflated invoices for drilling equipment and pipe from American suppliers? Really just one American supplier—you, and I congratulate your lawyers on your skillful dodging of the antitrust laws, which enables the final phase of this program to work."

The tow truck had pulled up in front of the damaged Volkswagen, but the CEO seemed scarcely aware.

"You and your cronies—excuse me, your *foundation*—are the biggest conduit of soft money to the President's party. In case you still don't know what I'm talking about, these are the contributions that fall outside the hard limits for donating political money. So, in a nutshell, you and your fellow donors take your cut as unwarranted profits, return the rest to the government. Not to the U.S. Treasury, where the money came from in the first place. But to the party that presently holds the White House. That's where our lady associate came in—until two days ago. She didn't care all that much for the cash, but she learned early on how money is translated into power. She wanted power. Except she has neither now, so you decided she was fair game and hired Tony to silence her, right . . . ?"

Two engines fired up, turning the CEO's head: The troopers were departing, and the Volkswagen had been hooked up. The tow driver approached, "Where you want it, sir?"

"The VW dealership in Tulsa."

"That'll cost you. It's closer to Muskogee."

"Tulsa, dammit." The CEO angrily flipped his American Express card to the driver, but then waited until he was out of earshot again. "You said *desired result* in relation to that certain lady."

"Did I?"

"Don't get cute with me. I need to know right this second if that's what you want, too."

"I wouldn't stand in your way," Yahola said airily. "But may I suggest a more discreet means than employing Brosnahan?"

"Such as?"

"Oh, I wouldn't presume to tell a man who was a roughneck at age eleven, or whatever it was." Yahola caught movement on the interstate above. The brown sedan was backing up—to go back to the get-off and start down it. The greatest risk in all this would come in the next sixty seconds, but he smiled at CEO, who looked grim, almost glum, now.

"What are you offering me?" the man asked.

"Silence."

After a moment, the man harrumphed. "Is that all?"

"Yes. Silence is golden."

"What about the usual arrangement—except I keep what comes my way, instead of passing it up?"

"Out of the question."

"Why?"

Yahola could tell by the engine noise that the sedan had parked a few yards behind him, but he didn't turn to face the threat. He kept his focus on the CEO, hoping that his goons would do nothing without a sign from him first. "It's not going to be the same kind of operation in the future," he calmly explained. "It got too big, and that's where all the trouble at present came from."

The Big Boy scowled. "You got balls—not offering me a goddamned thing."

"But I am."

"Like what, you son a bitch?"

"Silence," Yahola repeated. "And for you, silence is life itself."

"Quit talking like a two-bit medicine man. What prevents you from blackmailing me?"

"I don't want to aggravate you. Just retire you."

"Christ, you got balls."

"Look, testosterone notwithstanding, the point's simple—you came perilously close this afternoon to triggering my doomsday mechanism. One, you came armed. And two, you brought them . . ." He jerked his thumb at the figures he'd just heard step out of the car. "I'll overlook that just this once. As a sign I'm negotiating with you in good faith—"

"Negotiating what? I don't see what of value you're offering!"

"Picture this—FBI and Treasury agents massed in the lobby of your corporate towers in Tulsa. You on the ledge outside your fifteenth-story office. Mustering the nerve to jump. The wind on your face. The concrete below, waiting for you. It takes a lot of nerve to simply fall forward into empty space. . . ." Yahola slowly grinned. "My silence gives you a way to crawl back inside your window."

Never before had he seen such raw hatred in a white face.

But finally, the picture Yahola had created dimmed that hatred. The Big Boy tried to say something more, but couldn't. He strode past him as if in a trance and motioned with a limp hand for his goons to get back inside. Then he himself slumped in the back seat, and they left.

The tow driver had reparked the Infiniti on the grass strip. Yahola sat behind the wheel, shut his eyes and bowed his head. After a while, with his eyelids still clenched, he raised his right hand to the side and formed the eagle salute with his fingers.

26

MICHAEL STOOD IN the darkness, mentally replaying the phone conversation he'd had three hours ago with the special-agent-in-charge of the Oklahoma City field office.

As soon as it'd become reasonably clear that Deep Fork Linen Service's staff, especially the driver for the Okemah route, had no idea who Dagen Kirsch was, Michael turned to his next priority—canvassing a full yellow page of boat rental outfits. In this, the wet eastern third of the state, there were nearly sixty marinas. Dagen was headed to one of them, although Michael believed the shaken linen service driver when he claimed that he'd been unaware of the stowaway passenger in the back of his van. Few people were shaken by the appearance of the FBI anymore, and it'd been refreshing to find one. The last stops of the day before his return to Henryetta had been the communities around Lake Eufaula.

Immediately, Michael had realized that he needed more manpower than just Ramsey to cover all the marinas before Dagen wrapped up whatever she had in mind and vanished. And, unavoidably, asking for more manpower meant selling the request to his boss, the head man in Oklahoma City. He'd been a solid investigator in his own right before climbing the ladder and could smell bullshit a mile away. So, Michael had begun the call with a frank admission: *"Kirsch gave me the slip in Okemah."*

"How'd she accomplish that?"

"She's accomplished in a lot of surprising things," Michael replied, instantly recognizing the double entendre and wondering what Freudian impulse had made him say it. Already, it felt as if the conversation was sliding out of control, and he had the dry mouth of a confessor. *"She ditched her Ford and hopped a linen service van. Okfuskee County S.O. will stand by her car until our evidence people arrive. I already rolled them from your office."*

"Any idea where she's headed?"

Michael paused over a small victory—his judgment call not to impound Dagen's car last night wasn't being questioned. Yet. *"Most likely, she's headed for one of fifty-seven boat rental places listed on the page she tore out of the yellow pages at the motel."*

"And you need the manpower to cover them right away."

"Yes, sir."

"Help me put this in perspective, Michael. What's Kirsch up to? What's at the bottom of all this?"

"I'm not sure."

"Any hunches?"

"Yeah, but I don't want to run them up the flagpole yet."

"Well, I need to see at least something flapping in the breeze before I ask a dozen brick agents to drop what they're doing and help you."

Michael rolled his eyes in defeat. *"I've got an idea this has something to do with whoever and whatever Eli Cusseta is."*

"Same guy Parker was looking for in Muskogee before . . . ?" The SAC didn't have to finish for Michael to realize that he believed the former BIA investigator was at the bottom of the Arkansas River, somewhere. No glee was suggested: With Jerome Crowe and now Parker gone, large chunks of the case might go unanswered, forever.

But Michael also realized that, of late, his reports were being read with greater care by the brass. *"Yes, sir, there's a common link among all three subjects here, maybe something to do with Cusseta's computer background. I just don't know and probably won't until I get my hands on him."*

"Is it possible Kirsch means this guy harm?"

At that moment, Michael had looked off at the sun. It was setting into a soft lavender horizon. *"Well, the White House fired her."*

"Meaning?"

"That job was everything to her, and I'm not sure what she'll do now. She's on the ragged edge, but something is keeping her from confiding in me."

"You were friends, right, worked together on Special Olympics . . . ?"

Here it was. And it'd be so easy to postpone this, to let it slide on an explanation of friendship. But as Dagen became a prime focus of the investigation, the truth would be uncovered. The Washington field office would go over her apartment back there; fellow tenants or the manager would reveal that Michael had spent the night numerous times. The truth was unavoidable. *"We were involved."*

"Pardon?"

"We were romantically involved, sir. For about a year, ending eight years ago. My wife doesn't know about this."

Silence. Major silence.

Finally, the SAC said, *"Well, I'm glad you told me, Michael."* There was a hint in his voice that the admission had defused the potential for any disciplinary action arising from Mangas's being less than candid to his superiors. *"Does this past relationship have anything to do with why you let her skate this morning?"* Obviously, the evidence techie who'd swabbed Dagen's hands had briefed him.

"I've asked myself the same thing, sir. But no. I let her leave Lawton this morning hoping she'd eventually lead us to some answers."

"Like why somebody hired Tony Brosnahan to kill her?"

"That's a big part of it now. But, overall, I felt if I stepped back a little, she'd put us on the right track."

"What's your search area?"

"Lake Eufaula, I believe."

"Are you there now?"

"No, Ramsey and I are in Henryetta."

"Why do you ask to use him so much? That have anything to do with Kirsch, too?"

Michael understood the intimation at once. The SAC now suspected he used the Elk City agent, and not one of his own, because Dagen figured so prominently in this mess. *"Maybe,"* he admitted, *"but I like to think I'm mentoring him. Dustin's the kind of kid who will turn out okay as long as he has some firm guidance."*

"Let's hope. Okay, set up a CP someplace convenient on the lake," the SAC said, signaling the end of the conversation. *"I'll send some bodies from here and get the rest you need from the Muskogee office. I want you to stay at the CP and advise me of all major developments, no matter what the hour."*

"Yes, sir." Then Michael couldn't help but add, *"Thank you."*

Now, he waited.

He'd set up shop behind the marina store at Brush Hill Landing. It was here, earlier this evening, that an *unforgettable* blonde with bandages on her right cheek and left arm had strolled in from the highway and rented a fourteen-foot bass boat. She motored out onto the lake, vanishing around the first wooded point to the south. She hadn't been dressed for fishing, and the only item she carried was an overnight bag.

The FBI command post, Michael supposed, consisted of his bucar and a pay telephone on the side of the store. The SAC had told him to stay at the CP, not necessarily run it, and the distinction became clear when the supervising agent of the Muskogee resident agency showed up and took over the operation. He and his agents, plus some SWAT ninjas, had rented the swiftest boats to be had and, assisted by the Highway Patrol Marine Division, fanned out across the lake looking for Dagen.

Michael left his car door ajar so he could monitor radio traffic and listen for the pay phone at the same time. The most secure communications would come over the land line.

Fireflies blinked on and off out in the darkened parking lot and in the mossy oaks beyond. Michael had prevailed upon the owner of the marina to turn off all outdoor lighting except the spot over the main gate and some dock fixtures. The man had claimed not to know anyone by the name of Eli Cusseta, and as far as an Indian with braids, there were many in the area—traditional hair was back in fashion.

The stars were dimmed by the humid air, but Michael tossed a quick and silent prayer in their direction—that Dagen would come to her senses and contact him, let him know what this was all about while there was still time. She'd lied to him, but he wanted to give her a chance to explain herself.

His gaze dropped to some eerie greenish glows speckling the surface of the lake. Fishermen were after catfish by dangling lights over the surface or floating them beside their boats.

A vehicle approached slowly from the direction of highway.

Michael thought it might be one of the many bucars combing the area, an agent returning to give him an update. But then he saw that the sedan had import style. Also, one headlight was out and the other was cocked upward at a crazy angle, making it wash the tops of the trees. The car passed through the gate and under the spotlight. Tinted windows prevented a look inside. However, it was an Infiniti of a white color that was opalescent. How had Dagen described the vehicle that pulled up behind her on the Amber cutoff? *New, expensive, pearl-colored. An Infiniti, maybe.* But Brosnahan's Lincoln from Enterprise Rentals had also been off-white.

Still, the appearance of a pearl-colored Infiniti defied coincidence.

It had front-end collision damage.

Michael closed his car door. He stepped away from the sedan and over into the shadow cast by the store.

The Infiniti proceeded to the parking shed at the back. The lot itself was crowded with pickups and vans, mostly, left by the night fishermen. Michael began threading through them. A bucar looked like a bureau car, and he only hoped that his would be lost among the other vehicles.

He heard a car door shut. This was followed by the *chirp-chirp* of the locks being set.

Michael knelt beside a van.

As footfalls crunched over the lot's pea gravel toward him, he held his breath. If it was Cusseta and the Indian stumbled onto him, Michael decided that he would take him down then and there. Any fancy probable cause could wait for the report. He couldn't afford to let Cusseta find him like this.

The footfalls kept coming on.

Michael was ready to crawl under the van when he saw boots tread down its far side and turn along the grille. The figure—a tall and slender male with braids—crossed the gap formed by the van and the pickup between which Michael crouched. The figure was randomly checking the spaces between the parked vehicles, but by chance he glanced the other way as he walked directly in front of Michael.

Dagen had described this very person in the very sedan he'd shown up in. What did that mean?

Stop thinking. No time for that. It'll only distract you.

Treading softly over the gravel, Michael drew his 9mm and followed the figure. Toward the docks. He was headed for the water and showed no interest in the marina store, which probably meant that his boat awaited him in one of the slips.

Michael halted and looked back the fifty or sixty yards to his car. Did he have time to get his radio handset? Even more time to advise the dispatcher in Muskogee what he was up to? *No,* he quickly decided, not without the risk of losing two subjects within six hours. First Dagen. Now Cusseta. His pride wouldn't stand up to that.

The figure strode down to the entryway to the private anchorage, which was set off from the parking lot by a chainlink fence. He unlocked the gate and secured it again behind him before continuing down a long, covered dock and out of sight among the moored boats.

Big boats. Cabin cruisers and motor-yachts.

Michael followed. He'd borrowed a master key from the owner. He holstered his 9mm and unlocked the gate, leaving it that way in case he had to beat a hasty retreat.

There were disadvantages to working alone.

A whine of electronic ignition announced the firing of boat engines. Michael moistened his fingertips and reached up to unscrew the tin-shaded bulb over his head as the hefty twin inboards burbled the water.

He waited in his little pool of darkness for the figure to show himself again.

When, after a brief but heart-pounding wait, nothing happened, Michael started down the dock. He homed in on the sound, hand on his pistol. Gasoline fumes filled his nostrils, telling him he was close. Then he caught movement. A braided silhouette was busy in the pilothouse of a boat three slips down. Michael leaped aboard the closest cruiser, crossed it amidships and eased down onto the floating dock separating it from the next boat. Climbing onto the second craft, he went prone on the deck over the main cabin. From there, he had a better view of the pilothouse in which the figure had shown.

But no longer.

He was somewhere below. The decks were clear.

Michael took stock of his cruiser—at least a forty-foot Chris Craft. Not bad for a computer nerd. Perhaps it and the Infiniti were the sole remaining fruits of a dot-com boom that had gone bust and turned him toward other pursuits. Like helping bilk individual Indians out of millions of dollars.

The figure emerged from a forward-facing hatch and cast off the bow line. Then he went aft through the hatch again, leaving Michael to ponder his next move.

There was really only one thing to do.

Keeping down, he slid off the neighboring boat onto the gently bobbing dock and stooped alongside the hull of the Chris Craft. He waited for Cusseta, if that's who he was, to cast off the stern line and man the helm again.

A bureaucratic voice of caution nagged him to return to the radio in his car and contact the agents already plying the lake. That was the safe bet. And probably the losing one. There was a good chance those agents might not find the Chris Craft once Mangas broke contact with it. Eufaula had six hundred miles of shoreline.

Still, Michael had no radio. No flashlight.

The big boat began to inch backward. The figure was standing at the controls in the pilothouse, but he had turned aft to back out of the slip.

Standing, Michael grabbed a passing handrail and pulled himself up. As he climbed onto the foredeck, his left shoe thudded against the fiberglass hull. He froze, checking the silhouette.

The figure seemed to glance in Michael's direction, but then he turned his face again, this time to swing the boat around and throttle past the breakwater for the open lake.

Michael scrambled across the deck to the hatch. He opened it as narrowly as he could and still pass through. There was a drop-off, sudden and unexpected, and he tumbled into some sort of darkened space. A cabin or salon. Once more, he didn't move a muscle, believing that he'd given himself away.

He waited for the man in the pilothouse to ease off on the throttles.

Yet, the hull beneath him gained speed over the lake, its noisy vibrations gradually smoothing out.

Michael rose.

Through the rear windows, the lights of the marina grew smaller, and the darkness around him increased. He groped forward, feeling his way. A couch slipped by under his touch, covered with clutter. Computer components, he believed. The sofa ended in the vertical plane of a cabinet or closet sidewall. Michael was running his fingers along its face—when the door swung open.

Something large burst out at him.

Instinctively, he pulled his head down into his shoulders to protect his throat. He whipped out his pistol to use it as a club and started to bring the butt down on his assailant's nose, but the man's weight drove him to the hardwood deck. The back of Michael's head hit hard, and what little he could see vanished in a burst of white sparks behind his eyes. He felt two powerful hands tighten around his gun hand. They began to pry the weapon from his grasp. He bashed the man in the face with his elbow, and the hands fell away from his pistol—only to form fists in the darkness and fly back at Michael's face.

Right-handed. The son of a bitch is right-handed.

Michael knew this because the blows from that fist were more painful. And his attacker was using both hands. Did that mean he had no gun of his own? The thought wasn't much solace, for within seconds he was trying to seize Michael's. Before he could, Mangas drove him back with a thrust from both legs.

The cabin went silent.

Michael held his 9mm before him and swung the muzzle from side to side, searching for movement.

But there was no sign of the man, not even a flicker.

Had he slipped out and gone topside to summon Cusseta to help deal with the armed intruder? Michael hadn't considered the possibility of security being aboard the boat—and now wanted to kick himself for the oversight.

But what kind of security hides in a closet?

The hardwood floor creaked. Farther forward from where Michael believed the man had last been.

Slowly, Michael stood. He kept his semiauto at an arm's length so that, even if he held fire, contact against his hands would alert him to a second attack.

Another creak. Even farther away.

Faint light defined the windows, but it wasn't enough to illuminate the cabin itself. Michael fumbled along the bulkhead in search of a switch or fixture. He'd gone three paces when he found a small wall lamp. But did he really want to give up the darkness that concealed him?

Something made no sense to him. Why hadn't his attacker yelled for Cusseta to help him? Maybe the sounds of the fight hadn't carried up to the pilothouse over the engine and wake noise, but a shout would have.

Michael crept forward.

He had the sense that this cabin narrowed into another, smaller space.

Clattering stopped him in his tracks.

The man was somewhere in this second space, unseen but rummaging through metal objects. Silverware. Kitchenware. The next space was a galley, and he was rooting around for a weapon. Michael could catch nothing of him in the dark, but he kept advancing, dragging his free hand along the passageway—until he found what he needed. A refrigerator. Was it running on battery power, now that the boat had left the dock? Gambling that it was, Michael flung its door open. Jars and bottles cascaded out, shattering against the deck, but also a weak light from within widened over him—just as Michael felt something sharp poke against the underside of his chin.

A tall man in black clothing stood before him. The sharp object was the tip to a butcher's knife he clasped in his right hand. Eyes wild, he was poised to thrust it up into the soft, fleshy vee formed by Michael's lower jaw. The only thing preventing him from doing it right away was the 9mm, which Mangas was pressing tightly against his forehead.

Still, Michael knew that, with even a bullet smashing through his brain, the man would come up with the resolve to drive the blade in a final, killing blow.

Especially this man.

Emmett Parker had been gasping for breath. But, as Michael watched, the fugitive's chest stopped heaving. His respiration grew steady and regular. Through his own shock, Michael could tell that Parker was just as surprised to see him. What it all meant could wait until Michael didn't have the tip of a knife tickling his chin.

"Stand back, Emmett," he ordered.

"My ass." Parker's voice was a rasp, and Michael began to appreciate how beat-up the man was. He stank of weeks on the road. His cheeks were sallow and sagged off the bones, the skin pocked with insect bites, his eyes raw and red. But he didn't blink as he said, "Staying close to you is the only thing I've got going for me right now."

For some reason, Michael found the remark humorous, although he could tell that Parker didn't care for his smile. "What happened to Ramsey's pistol?"

"Lost it in the Arkansas River," Emmett replied.

"Lose anything else on the leap?"

"Just a little mobility in my left ankle. Not enough to lay me up."

As much as the knife allowed, Michael glanced down. The ankle was swaddled in a filthy Ace bandage. "Grain must feel like concrete from that height."

"Don't know," Parker said, lowering his voice slightly. "I missed the barges and hit the water."

Michael knew he had to keep talking. It was the only way out of this. And maybe, just maybe, Parker was looking for his own way out. "Then how'd you make it off the river?"

"Grabbed a car tire used as a bumper on one of those barges. Rode the tow nearly all the way down to Webbers Falls before I let the current swing me ashore."

"Well, I'm glad you made it, *Pabi*."

"Don't you dare call me that," Parker said with a grimace.

Michael stared back at the exhausted-looking fugitive for a long moment, then said evenly, "As you wish." He rolled his eyes upward, indicating the man in the pilothouse, who continued to drive his Chris Craft at the same speed, as if unmindful of the struggle below. "I take it you didn't get permission to come aboard?"

Parker didn't reply. He went on holding the knife to Michael's chin. Mangas's 9mm was growing heavier by the minute, and his joined hands began to be rocked by tiny tremors. This couldn't go on forever, but damned if Michael could think of a quick way out. "Just what do you think I've been doing—other than my job?"

"God help you and Ramsey if you two had *anything* to do with Jerome's murder!"

Parker's tone alarmed Michael, but he also knew he had to resolve this here and now. He had to take risks with the man's explosive temper. "You're the one holding a butcher's knife, and the only latent prints found on Crowe's murder weapon were yours." Michael waited for the reaction. Parker narrowed his eyes as he digested this. That proved he was willing to listen, even to things he didn't want to hear. "You threw me a curve in Elk City. It would've been simple enough for you to take out Ramsey then and there in that elevator. If you'd truly believed he killed Jerome. But you didn't, Emmett. Does that mean you had some serious doubts he gutted Jerome in that parking lot? What you did really threw me for a loop. You counted coup on the poor kid. He didn't have a clue that's what you did, but I'm sure the message was meant for me. You told me you still wanted honor to figure in all this. Ever since, I've respected that as best I could, *Nuhmuhnuh* to *Nuhmuhnuh*, and I resent the fuck out of you insinuating that I haven't!" Michael paused to calm down again. He knew he needed to humanize this before it spun out of control. "If I don't lower my arms pretty quick, they're going to fall off."

"Don't move a muscle," Parker warned.

"How about if I drop one hand and shake the cramp out of it? I'd hate for a cramp to tighten my finger on the trigger when I didn't mean to." After only silence from Parker, Michael dropped his left hand to his side and shook it. That brought movement from Emmett, who dealt with his own apparent stiffness by stepping to the side. With a slight limp. Crunching over the broken glass. Both men shifted around like fighting cocks, facing each other. Both came to a halt closer to the door at the end of the galley. Farther from the refrigerator, there was less light, Michael realized, and a greater chance to mistake each other's physical signals.

"That kid still failed to properly ID himself to me," Parker said. Ramsey, he meant, of course, that night atop Mt. Scott.

"You're probably right about that," Michael said.

He could tell Parker wasn't sure what to make of the admission.

"It was Ramsey's first taste of homicide," Mangas went on, "and he was rattled. Can you perfectly recall everything you said during your first shooting? It was a friendly-fire screw-up with tragic consequences, and that's how I see it now."

"Did you pass that on, so any number of cops who've been chasing me this past month might've been able to decide for themselves if I really ought to be gunned down on sight like a mad dog?"

"No," Michael admitted.

"Why not, you son of a bitch?"

"Partly to cover Ramsey, who's already on thin ice with the bureau for a chicken-shit gambling rap he got pinned on him back at the Boston office." Michael felt his own anger flare again. "And you knew my mother. She was the descendent of warriors, both Comanche and Apache. Don't speak of her in that way ever again."

Parker continued unapologetically, "What's it matter to me if Ramsey's on thin ice?"

"Nothing. Just as it meant nothing to me back at OKC P.D. that Jimmy was on thin ice. Still, you stood by him. Why? Probably because you thought he was basically a good cop and had value to the department. You didn't drop the hammer on him, even after he was dead. I disagreed. I didn't drop the hammer on Ramsey. Now you disagree. I'd say we're even on that score. Secondly, I wasn't at all convinced in June you weren't a murderous nutcase. Mind if I put a question to you on that count . . . ?"

The boat was speeding up, bouncing over some light swells, and Parker glanced upward for a second.

"Who cut up and shot Royce?" Michael asked, talking faster now.

Parker leveled his gaze on Michael, a gaunt and distrustful look.

"Don't worry," Mangas went on, "Eschiti didn't say a word, other than to deny you had anything to do with it."

"Where's he now?"

"Back in McAlester."

The news about his friend clearly pained him. Good. He was capable of feeling emotional pain, something Michael had doubted over these past weeks. "Royce," he said, fighting to hold down his feelings, "did nothing more than try to help a friend in a jam."

"With Dagen's car and seven thousand, five hundred bucks in the trunk for you?" Michael had said it before he'd thought it through. He hadn't wanted to bring her up. But now it was done, and he was surprised by the relief he felt. Admission by admission, he was freeing himself of her, although he understood that an agonizing scene with Jeralyn awaited him down the line. He would rather die in the coming minutes than break her heart. "Dagen hasn't been helping anybody but Dagen."

"You know her."

"Of course I know her."

Parker shook his head. "I mean, you know her better than most folks realize."

Michael thought that the Chris Craft was slowing. "She and I had an affair a while back. How'd you guess?"

"The way you talked to each other in passing at my honor dance."

"Was it that obvious?"

"Yes."

That clinched it. Michael no longer regretted leveling with the SAC.

Maybe everyone had already surmised about Dagen and him, and the notion of secrecy was a sad joke. "You didn't answer me, Emmett. Who cut and shot Royce?"

"Our skipper."

"You sure?"

"Yes. I also watched him execute that Russian in the oil field near Wheatland."

It escaped Michael, again before he could think: "And you didn't step in?"

"I seem to have lost my credentials," Parker said bitterly. "And I couldn't exactly phone the local office of the FBI to help take him down, now could I?"

The hull began to porpoise slightly as it slowed in the water, making Michael clench his teeth each time against the slight jab of the knife tip into his skin. "What about Morris Cornplanter? You also witness his execution while you were passing through the Texas panhandle?"

"You mean the floater in Buffalo Lake?" Parker asked.

"Yes."

"I only learned about him from Royce. After the fact."

"Then Cornplanter might have run afoul of our skipper, too." But Michael was still full of doubts. After learning from the computer store owner in Muskogee that Parker had been seeking Cusseta, Michael had seen to it that agents combed the entire region. They had come up empty-handed. Yet, Parker had zeroed in on Lake Eufaula and the man's boat. "How'd you find this place?"

"Intuition."

"How long have you been waiting here for him?"

"Four days."

"What . . . ?" Michael asked, looking over Parker's tattered clothes, strewn with dirt and bits of dead leaves. "Mostly lying in the woods?"

"And raiding vegetable gardens at night."

"He's the answer to all this, isn't he? That's probably the biggest reason you didn't step in to save that Russian near Wheatland, right?"

Parker refused to answer.

"Dagen's here someplace, searching for him, too."

Clearly, that caught Parker off guard.

"Today," Michael said, "I had Ramsey tail her from Lawton to Okemah, where she gave us the slip."

"Okemah's a piece from here. How do you—?"

"This evening, she rented a boat out of this marina."

Parker's eyes darted back and forth in confusion, as if he'd missed something vital in all his reckoning.

"You didn't see her motor out onto the lake tonight?"

For the first time, Parker looked chagrined. "I was already aboard this boat. I haven't slept in days. Weeks, really. Curled up in the bottom of that closet for a little rest . . ." Then he tottered slightly on the balls of his feet, and his glazed eyes squinted at Michael's 9mm, which was beginning to rub a red spot on his forehead. "I did not . . ." His words were now slurred. "I did not kill Ushuk . . . Jerome . . . anybody. And you know it."

"Yes, Emmett, I know it."

Instantly, Parker snapped out of his fatigue. "What'd you just say?"

"I know. You didn't kill any of them. Also, you have nothing to do with the missing trust funds. I've been sure of this for a day or two now."

Emmett leered at him, obviously trying to make up his mind, trying to determine if this was a trick.

Michael could see only one way to convince him.

Slowly, he lowered his pistol from Parker's head, set the 9mm on the sink-board and dropped his hands to his sides.

But Parker didn't remove the tip of the blade from beneath his chin. It went on poking against the soft flesh there with each bounce of the hull. Michael realized he was out of ways to convince Parker of his sincerity. It was this or death. Had he misjudged? The man's eyes remained fixed on his, unblinking and unreadable. Each trickle of sweat down Parker's drawn face was like an indictment of Mangas for all he'd suffered these past weeks.

"You have no idea," Parker muttered angrily, "you have no idea."

Then, just when it seemed that Emmett was relenting, Michael felt a blade sliding into him like cold fire.

27

UNDERFOOT, THE BOAT raced on. Despite the intrusion. Emmett shoved Mangas to the deck with his left hand and grabbed the 9mm with his right. In the dim light from the refrigerator, he'd just seen the forward door open and close with lightning speed. He fired through it without hesitation, but aimed high. Three quick rounds through the wood. He wanted to spray the stairway beyond, but Mangas had collapsed against the door, pinning it shut. The agent stared up at Emmett, dazed, holding his hand to a bloody spot on his lower back. Parker believed that he'd seen the glint of a blade darting through the crack in the door and catching Mangas in the small of the back.

Now he knew. "How bad?" he asked.

"I'll live."

Emmett began to push him aside, but Mangas grunted obstinately and rose on his short, powerful legs. He tried to fling the door open, but it was jammed by something on the far side. Emmett limped to the rear hatch and found it jammed, too. He returned to Mangas and threw his shoulder into the door. Twice. Before it gave at the hinges and pitched over. "*Ubahani!*" Mangas gasped. *Out of the way!* But then he staggered while passing through. He had to clutch the jambs to keep his balance. "Give me my gun."

Emmett ignored the order and elbowed past him.

The boat, he realized, had gained even more speed.

He expected bullets to fly at them from the top of the stairway, so he crouched as he started up. He used the handrail to take some weight off his ankle. Still, he hobbled, wincing with each step but listening over the noise of the engines for movement above. He knew from a search of the boat earlier today that the stairway led to the pilothouse. He'd found no registration papers aboard, but had seen the braided Indian motor in and dock it this morning, before driving off in an Infiniti. Eli Cusseta, he believed.

A thud behind made him glance back: Mangas had collapsed again, this time to a knee. "Wait for me," he said in an ill-tempered whisper.

Again, Emmett ignored him and climbed on.

He could see stars through glass that was spotted with water. It was the windshield in the pilothouse. He halted. Nothing to indicate where Cusseta was lurking. About six more steps to go. Emmett was getting ready to take them in a rush—when he heard a splash off to one side of the speeding boat.

An anchor being thrown? That made no sense, not at this speed.

Then the deck jerked to a complete stop and he was hurtling through the air. He threw his forearms across his face and tried to hang on to Mangas's pistol as he braced for the on-rushing instrument panel. He slammed into it and dropped to the deck in a heap. Pebbles of safety glass cascaded over him. Below, the engines went on thundering at full throttle, but the Chris Craft was no longer moving. At least not forward.

Was it sinking?

No, it felt more like the boat was falling apart around him. He rubbed a sore shoulder and tried to clear his head.

"Help me," Mangas said from the tumble-down mess that no longer resembled a stairwell.

Emmett rose and immediately tottered. The deck was sloping underfoot. There was light. Not the cold light from the refrigerator, which was buried now in the depths of the wreckage. It was a restless orange glow that had no obvious source. Somehow, he'd managed to hang on to the 9mm. He searched the pilothouse for Cusseta. There was no sign of him. And no one had been at the helm during the collision, although it was now evident that he had run his boat up onto the shore to evade capture. The light was flickering against a screen of moss-draped trees visible through the shattered windshield.

Finally, Emmett understood.

The stern of the Chris Craft was on fire.

"Emmett," Mangas said calmly but firmly, "I smell smoke."

And gasoline. Emmett caught gasoline fumes, too, stronger and closer than any that might be escaping from the engine room. "Hang tight," he told the agent.

"I'm trapped." Again, no panic, but Mangas knew he was in trouble.

Welcome to the club, Emmett thought, as he scanned the shoreline for the braided figure. The splash he'd heard just prior to the boat crashing onto the beach had to have been Cusseta. Jumping ship.

Through a gap in the growth, Emmett could see the rounded top of a building. Antennae and satellite dishes.

Suddenly, a tendril of flame whooshed forward, cloaking the trees behind a wall of crackling vermilion. Another thing became clear. Before jumping, Cusseta had doused the weather decks with gasoline.

Emmett picked his way down the stairs—and was soon confronted by a wall of debris. He guessed that the keel, the spine of the Chris Craft, had been broken directly beneath, twisting the structure above into a mass of splintered wood. Kindling. He could now feel the heat of the spreading fire. Through a fog of smoke, Mangas beseeched him with an outstretched hand. "Come on," he said, choking for the first time.

But Emmett couldn't bring himself to take Mangas's hand. It felt like surrendering, somehow. Embracing a force that had tried to destroy him. Images of the past weeks filled his mind. Jerome dying in that portable toilet. Ramsey shooting at him. Mangas himself chasing Emmett into that storm of hot shrapnel. Saying good-bye to his mother, as if forever, along the Pease River. Royce, cut and shot, headed back to prison. And the endless torment of being falsely accused. That more than anything else. Wittingly or not, they had stolen his honor from him.

"Emmett, *please.*"

He tried to reason with his own anger. Lake Eufaula was probably teeming with FBI agents. He'd sensed activity at the marina earlier this evening but had been unable to see the public dock from the Chris Craft. Without Mangas present to explain his change of heart, those agents would kill him at the drop of a hat. Mangas was his only ticket for safe passage. But still.

Licks of flame could now be seen worming up through the debris behind the man. "Share a pipe with me," Mangas said with a new intensity in his voice. The *Nuhmuhnuh* didn't have a phrase the equivalent to *forgive me* in English. Instead, they had a process for reconciliation. This is what the agent was offering.

At last, Emmett pocketed the pistol. He clasped Mangas's right hand in both of his and pulled. Grudgingly, the man's body came out of the wreckage. Once Mangas was free, Emmett began to feel his limbs for broken bones, but at that second the fire flared up all around them. He seized the agent under the arms and dragged him up the final few steps into the middle of pilothouse. Mangas shouted something ridiculous about being able to make it on his own, but Emmett scarcely heard him over the howl of the fire. There was the stench of scorched hair. His own, he believed. Still hanging on to Mangas, he lunged through a sheet of fire and out onto the open flying bridge. He didn't linger; the heat was no less ferocious there. "Jump!" he cried.

He and Mangas fell into shallow water. It was barely deep enough to cushion their impact against the muddy bottom, which did Emmett's ankle no good. But he hoisted Mangas onto his back and carried him to the beach.

"Put me down," Mangas demanded.

Emmett collapsed at the water's edge. But they couldn't remain there long. The whole of the Chris Craft was engulfed, and butane tanks were cooking off into the sky like fat Roman candles. Soon the gasoline tanks would blow.

They scrambled up into the trees before resting again.

Emmett saw that, sometime over the past few seconds, Mangas had slipped the pistol from his back pocket. "Mine," he said adamantly. Emmett was too winded to argue. The agent looked in command of himself again, and less blood seemed to be leaking through the slash in his shirt. He gestured at Emmett with the 9mm. "Don't ever fuck with me like that again, Parker."

But then he lowered the weapon into his lap.

Both men flinched as shots echoed over them. Aimed at Mangas and him? Emmett didn't know, but he was up, without thinking, hitching through the thick undergrowth toward the dying echoes. Mangas was right behind him.

Four rounds.

Confusing, for they hadn't been sound-suppressed. Cusseta had shot both Royce and the blond Russian with a weapon that was almost noiseless. Somebody had just popped four caps, at least thirty-eight caliber, without regard for the loud reports.

The two men broke from the trees into a clearing that was strewn with sawdust. There was now a source of light other than the burning boat behind them—a geodesic dome that stood just above the clearing. As Mangas and he watched, the windows blew out, disgorging sinuous flames that crept out over the shingled exterior. Accelerant. The fire spread so fast, clearly Cusseta had used an accelerant like gasoline again. And the clearing was so brightly lit Emmett slid in behind a stump to make less of a target of himself. Mangas joined him, huffing for breath and clasping a hand to his back as if applying direct pressure to his wound.

"Give me the gun," Emmett suggested. "You stay here and rest."

"Not on your life."

"Then make sure the barrel is drained."

"Already did."

Atop the stump was a chainsaw, and littered in the sawdust were bits and pieces of sawed timber. Taking all this in, Mangas said, "This explains the crucifixes."

"What crucifixes?"

"Later." Mangas staggered up and made directly for the dome house, perhaps hoping that there was still time for him to check the interior. There wasn't. As before on the boat, the heat was simply too much, and both Mangas and Emmett had to back away from the structure.

For the first time, Emmett saw that they were on a small island. A few wooded acres standing off a darkened stretch of shoreline.

Escape.

To escape, Cusseta had to deal with water again. He'd destroyed his boat on a gamble Mangas and Emmett would be left trapped inside the burning wreck. What did that leave him? With two bonfires now whorling high above the lake, he had to realize that reinforcements would be coming soon. He hadn't pulled that Chris Craft into the anchorage on his island. That, most likely, was a sheltered cove Emmett could just make out through the trees. "Come on," he told Mangas, starting down an overgrown path toward it.

As they drew near the cove, Emmett halted Mangas with a hand signal. He could hear a high-pitched whine. It seemed to be coming from the far side of a tin shed that stood near a floating dock. "What do you think that is?" he asked the agent.

Mangas didn't answer.

Emmett looked at him. Even in the indirect firelight, he could see that blood was oozing blackly through the fingers the man was holding to his wound. "Deep?"

"I'll let you know tomorrow."

Emmett held out his hand for the 9mm. "You stay here. Sit still before you bleed to death."

Reluctantly, Mangas handed over his pistol, then sank to the ground.

Emmett sifted into a dark stand of oaks—the blazing geodesic had now turned the night to day. He threaded his way through some brambles toward the tin shed, skipping every other stride to favor his injured ankle. He wasn't sure if it was broken, but a week after his jump into the Arkansas River it was still painfully swollen.

He was almost to the shore when a thunderous boom made him duck. An orange mushroom cloud rose from the other side of the island and dripped a fiery rain—the fuel tanks aboard the Chris Craft had finally blown.

He flattened himself against the back wall of the shed and waited until the roar of the explosion faded. Gradually through its echoes came the whine again, high-pitched but steady.

Emmett burst around the shed, pistol before him.

The whine was from a Jet Ski. The small craft was tipped on its side in the muddy shallows, the propulsion jets out of the water.

He crept out to it and shut off the engine.

A man was slumped over the seat, his right hand still frozen to the throttle, even though he was face-down in the water. For a distance of two yards all around, his head had stained the lake red. Emmett could clearly make out the two entry wounds at the base of his skull. Taking hold of one of the man's braids, he turned the slack-jawed face out of the water. Eli Cusseta's eyes were open, and he had a fierce expression of confusion, as if he'd had no warning that someone had stepped behind him to pump two bullets into him. At least two, for Emmett had heard four gunshots. He hauled the body up onto the beach and inspected the corpse for other trauma.

None.

Quickly, for the shooter was still here somewhere, he tried to make sense of the scene. The mud was scored where Cusseta had dragged the Jet Ski out of the shed and into the water. The door was still open, although the interior was empty of anyone. Emmett examined the mud more closely. In it, just where the dock started into the lake, he found a single shoe impression. Not Cusseta's. This one was much too small. Too small to be a grown man's print. Here, the shooter had stepped off the dock and onto the beach, possibly to sneak closer to Cusseta as he sat astride his last means of escape, warming it up. Two shots at close range to the back of his head. Two more that went wild, perhaps, as he and the craft capsized.

Emmett turned back for Mangas. Cusseta could now be eliminated as a threat. But they had a new one lurking somewhere on this island. An executioner.

He was surprised to see the agent standing. Mangas was backlit by the conflagration that was still raging from the geodesic. His posture was rigid, which might be blamed on the pain his cut was giving him, except that his hands were also clasped before him. As if he were imploring somebody. Emmett was reminded somewhat of how his mother had looked, there that afternoon along the Pease River.

He melted into the shadows.

Mangas separated his hands and used one behind his back to flash a warning at him—*stay back*. But, in the same moment, a hard but tremulous voice drifted down to him: "Come up here, whoever you are, or I'll blow his brains out!"

She had just done precisely that to Cusseta, so Emmett saw no choice but to join them. He wedged the pistol into the back of his waistband as he continued up the slope.

Dagen Kirsch looked surprised to see him, but she quickly included him in a sweep of her snub-nosed revolver. Her face was streaked with tears, and her clothes were a muddy mess. There were bandages to her face and arm. She was rattled, frightened and deadly. Any patrolman could tell that she was in a lethal mood, even if she herself wasn't fully aware of it.

"Find anything?" Mangas asked Emmett. He was a bit wide-eyed, but other than that he seemed impressively calm for a hostage.

"Just Eli Cusseta with a couple bullets in the back of his head."

Dagen reeled on him. "*What* did you say?"

"You know what I said."

"I did not kill him," she ranted. "I heard the shots, but I didn't kill that bastard. I was up here all the while. There was a crash. The boat, I think. And then I came outside to see what had happened."

"You were waiting inside for him?" Mangas asked innocently.

Lying in wait was the legal term. It indicated premeditation. Despite his circumstances, the veteran agent was taking the time to fish for a voluntary confession.

Emmett looked back to Dagen, who obviously was trying to think through her tears. "Yes," she finally admitted, probably seeing no harm in it. "I came here to tell him to back off."

"Is Cusseta his true name?"

"That doesn't matter, Michael. Things like that no longer matter."

"But why'd you feel the need to back him off . . . ?"

Emmett glanced at Dagen's street shoes. Mud-caked but of a size consistent with the impression he'd seen below. Apparently, much had happened concerning her in the weeks he'd been on the run. Much he knew nothing about. Yet, after she had left so much cash for him in the trunk of her car, he'd come to the conclusion that she might also have planted the $33,000 found by the FBI in Jerome Crowe's room at the Marriott in Lawton—a tidbit he'd picked up from the newspapers in the Norman library.

"You know why I had to come, Michael," she said, her voice cracking on his name. But there followed a quick and accusing shift of her eyes at Emmett. "They tried to kill me there along the Amber cutoff. Parker here and the bastard he just found dead."

"No, they didn't," Mangas said with a tone that inferred she was now skipping over logic like a flat stone over water. "You shot somebody named Brosnahan. He's the only person you faced that day on your way home to Anadarko."

She shifted her aim back on Mangas, blinked dully at him. "What does it matter? What does any of this matter? Don't you see? Parker sent Brosnahan to finish me off. It's all one and the same. Parker's wanted me dead from the beginning."

"I think the opposite's true, Dagen."

Emmett debated drawing the pistol. He asked himself if the moment had come. Never had she ordered him to keep his hands in plain sight, but he now wondered if any sudden movement would frighten her into firing. He decided to wait.

"What are you talking about . . . ?" The betrayed and hurt pitch in her voice brought back the awkward and high-strung girl at the mission to Emmett. Now, more than ever, he saw her scars from St. Benedict's, scars from being white among so many native kids, unpopular, although she would probably have been unpopular even at a white-dominated school. It didn't matter that most of those scars were from self-inflicted wounds. That wasn't how she'd see it. At this moment, her feelings counted for everything. "What are you talking about, Michael?"

"You boosted Emmett to national attention by having the President drop by his honor dance. You needed a big target for a big accusation. Then, when you had Emmett just where you wanted him, you cut the legs out from under him. You and your associates. How far and high this goes remains to be seen, but you all wanted to make it appear that Emmett and Jerome were behind what you yourselves have been doing for years—raiding the trust fund accounts."

"That's absurd," she said, a new quality coming into her voice. Indignant unreality. Emmett noticed, with unease, that the hammer to her revolver kept twitching up and down from varying degrees of pressure she was putting on the trigger.

"Not absurd at all. It was pretty well thought out, given the problems you faced. The first was Calvin Ushuk. The Eskimo brought heat on himself, so you had to eliminate him. Somebody, maybe you, had the brilliant idea of making it look like Emmett whacked him. We at the FBI bought it. At least for a while . . ."

As fascinated as Emmett was in learning how his life had been dumped into the toilet, he recognized what Michael was doing. The agent was drawing this out as long as he possibly could so his backup might arrive. Emmett stifled the urge to glance around for the coming of that help. Dagen might key on to it, and so far she seemed oblivious to everything except her own emotions.

"But then the troubles began for your side," Mangas went on in the same unruffled indictment. "First, you really didn't expect to be blamed for embarrassing the President. Not enough to get fired. You overestimated your importance, sweetheart. That's foolish in Lawton, probably fatal in Washington. And then the in-fighting began. I haven't sorted all that out yet, but with time I will. Like where the money trail ended. Unless you care to tell me now . . . ?"

She started to say something, but then checked the impulse and instead raised her revolver squarely into Michael's face. Emmett was too far from them to reach out and bat the barrel downward, and he would never be able to draw the 9mm and get off a shot before she dropped Mangas. "You're coming with me, Michael."

"Take me instead," Emmett offered.

"No. You have too many lives. You're too strong."

"Michael's wounded."

"How?" she asked.

"Stabbed by Cusseta on the boat. Turn and show her."

As Michael pivoted, Emmett lifted the man's shirt so Dagen could see the knife wound. It was bleeding again, and the entire seat of his pants was soaked with blood. As she fixated on the nasty cut, Emmett inched the pistol out of the back of his waistband, so he was ready, when Mangas turned again, to leave it in the agent's belt holster and flip his shirt-tail over it. Emmett knew full well now that Dagen wasn't going to accept him as a hostage.

She trusted Mangas as much as she could probably trust anybody right now, and that created an opening.

The trick now was not to get shot as she and the agent peeled off from him.

The firelight was still strong, and he could count the glints of copper-tipped bullets inside the visible chambers of her revolver. All four were still loaded with live cartridges. That puzzled him. It was a five-shot Smith and Wesson, and previously he'd heard four reports. That would have left her with a single round, unless she'd reloaded after gunning down Cusseta.

"Let's go, Michael," she ordered.

"How?"

"Boat. I have a boat."

"What about Parker?"

She didn't say, and in that Emmett glimpsed her plan. It had been the mainstay of all her other plans. A frame-up. She would leave Emmett alive on the island—and shoot Mangas in the coming minutes, making it appear that the agent had come out on the losing side of a final confrontation with the fugitive he'd chased so long and hard. Her eyes were almost gloating as she used the muzzle to nudge Mangas toward the western shore of the island, presumably where she'd tied up her boat.

Emmett prepared to leap and roll for the shadows. But there was no need. She simply turned and herded Mangas before her at gunpoint.

They waded into the growth.

Emmett hobbled as fast as he could across the face of the hill, trying to keep them in sight.

28

D AGEN AND MICHAEL hadn't gone far from Parker when she asked, "When'd you realize?"

Michael didn't have to rack his brains to understand what she was asking. For all her other powerful and conflicting emotions at the moment, she was curious as to when he'd figured out that she was involved in the embezzlement. "When I finally got hold of Ed Thorsen . . ." The Secret Service agent with the White House detail she claimed to have contacted regarding her phone conversation with Parker the morning Emmett had counted coup on Dustin Ramsey. "At first, I let it slide with an email, like you wanted," he went on, hoping that the bulge of his 9mm under his shirt wasn't noticeable. "But something wasn't right about his response. It was a carbon copy of yours. Too close to be genuine."

"So you phoned Thorsen to verify?"

"Yes."

"And he said we never discussed Emmett Parker."

Michael felt no need to add to that. Nor bring up her polygraph examination that had never been conducted. But it was worth mentioning his suspicion, which he'd immediately shared with the Secret Service, that their computer system had been compromised. He hadn't known then by whom.

Now it was obvious. "Doesn't take much to figure out who was hacking the Secret Service and no doubt the BIA trust fund data bank, too—you shot him a couple minutes ago."

"I did not shoot him! Quit saying that, goddammit!"

He could tell that she'd stopped walking. He halted too and rested his hands on his knees. Her mood was all over the place. Angry, distracted, but beneath everything—calculating. He could tell that she found this unexpected encounter with him unreal, but he also realized that when she seized upon reality again, it'd be with violence. Curiously, his knife wound was no longer burning. But, more alarmingly, his entire lower back was turning prickly, and in addition to some nausea he was beginning to have trouble breathing.

As he stooped there, he caught something from the corner of his eye: A light that flitted over the brow of the island and went out again. A searchlight. None of his fellow agents would have something that bright on their rental boats, so it probably came from the O.H.P. Marine Division boat. Had Dagen noticed?

"I heard the shots just like you!" she went on, hysterically now. "I did not kill Eli!"

Apparently, she hadn't noticed the light. And apparently Cusseta's first name of Eli was genuine. But he didn't understand her denial, unless it was purely reflexive. "Then you've got nothing to be afraid of, Dagen. Give me your gun. I'll see that nothing bad happens to you."

She laughed bitterly. "Right. Like you did Emmett?"

"At least I didn't send Cusseta to murder Royce and him, like you did that night near Anadarko!" Michael had said it in a fit of temper. But no use backpedaling now. "Taking out Emmett makes sense. You had to silence him. But first you had to shift the blame away from yourself after Calvin Ushuk drew heat from Customs. Again, going after Emmett makes sense. But why poor Royce? What'd he ever do to you?"

"Nothing, really," she admitted, settling down again. The change was unsettling in its abruptness. "He knew about the Alaska connection, and Eschiti could never keep his mouth shut."

"Tell me about that connection."

Instead, she commanded, "Move!"

He didn't. Not for a moment. She took a step but turned her ankle on the uneven, root-latticed ground. Infuriated, she kicked off her street shoes, bent over and—one by one—flung them away. They'd probably had too much heel to make cross-country walking easy, and by all accounts she'd walked into the marina. As she padded on in her bare feet, she barked, "Keep moving!"

Michael obeyed. For the moment.

Her admission about Alaska was the signal he'd been dreading. She meant to kill him, otherwise she wouldn't have said a word about the conspiracy. She'd worked around lawyers all her adult life, so doubtlessly she knew enough to keep her mouth shut. Also, these spasms of rage meant she had to work herself up to homicide. He supposed it was a backhanded compliment: She wasn't finding it easy to shoot an old lover.

"Think, Dagen," he begged her. "*Think.*"

She said nothing to that.

Twice now, he'd heard a muffled crack out in the woods to the left of them. Emmett, plodding along on his bad ankle, was shadowing their progress down to the lake as best he could. It was disconcerting to realize that the unarmed fugitive was risking death to help the man who had chased him all these weeks. But Michael had no time for regret. Especially then, for the distinct snap of a branch breaking underfoot—much closer than before—made Dagen wheel around. She fired twice toward the sound.

Michael scanned the shadows between the oaks and pines for a glimpse, however fleeting, that Parker was still on his feet. He waited for her to pull the trigger again, hoping against hope that she was out of ammunition. But he believed he'd seen the live cartridges in her cylinder, and there was no point in delaying.

It's time . . . it's time . . .

But Dagen was about twenty feet uphill of him, and he needed to be closer for what he had in mind. He held off reaching for his pistol and began to creep toward her, so smoothly he felt as if he were floating. Maybe he was floating; he could barely feel the lower half of his body. Soon, he wouldn't be able to stand, let alone walk, and he might even be on the brink of passing out. He knew that, so he kept inching toward her, pushing on, thinking the whole way that he'd never imagined doing anything like this to her, that it still didn't seem possible.

Suddenly, she spun on him. "Hold it right there!"

He froze and stiffened for a bullet.

After a few seconds, when it didn't come, he said into her unblinking stare, "More than a dozen agents are out on the lake. Looking for you. By now, they've zeroed in on the fires. There's no getting away. Now, I don't understand why you did the things you've done—"

"You're all so pigheadedly strong," she interrupted, her mouth twisting around the words.

"Who's so strong?"

"Indians. Pigheaded Indians." She couldn't conceal her satisfaction in finally saying this. "I didn't worry about Parker. He's strong. Like an animal. It's an animal strength, really. And, damn him, somehow I knew he'd come through it all."

"What about me, Dagen?" he asked simply and calmly. "Am I going to come through this?"

"Get walking," she said mechanically. Now, at the point of doing it, she'd managed to switch off her emotions. Her tone was completely flat.

He walked stiffly, legs sluggish beneath him. The trees parted and below he saw a bass boat half-beached on a strip of sand. He cocked his head a quarter-turn to keep an eye on her and waited for his chance. Now, as the time drew nearer, he struggled with his own sense of unreality, the ridiculous but suddenly unshakable conviction that he'd awaken any second, gasping for breath in the warm and perfumed darkness of her Silver Spring apartment, holding her to him in bed.

Unquestionably now, a searchlight was probing the trees along the crest of the islet. Yet, glancing back, he saw that she was oblivious to it. Her gaze seemed to be riveted to a spot on the base of his skull.

"Dagen!" Emmett cried. He was close, so very close, and she reeled to shoot. Michael didn't hear the shot, but he saw a blue flame sprout from the muzzle of her revolver in Parker's direction. Michael whipped out his pistol and fired once. Low. She cried out, horrible because it was like her cry of sexual pleasure. But she went down. He'd hit her where he intended. In the right leg. And he prayed that was it: She would stay down. It was over.

But then, with an enraged shriek, she sat up and shot back at him. He had no idea if he'd been struck. Everything now was coming fast in a haze of shock. His forefinger worked the trigger as if it had a will of its own. Her head jerked, and she flopped back against the beach.

Emmett stood over Michael, who was holding Dagen's body in his arms. He split his attention between the unresponsive agent and an O.H.P. patrol boat. It had appeared in the last minute and swung its spotlight around on them. He wondered if the troopers aboard could make sense of the tableau on the beach, and his answer came in a voice that boomed over the boat's P.A.: "You there with the weapon—!"

"FBI!" Emmett shouted for Mangas, who still gripped his pistol in hand as he embraced the lifeless body. He hadn't said a word in the few minutes since Emmett had limped down to him, and he seemed unaware of the trooper. Of everything except the body in his grasp.

"Show me—but move slow!"

As ordered, Emmett reached down, removed Mangas's credentials and displayed them. "FBI," he repeated into the dazzle.

But a new voice said anxiously, "That man is not an FBI agent . . . !" Emmett had last heard that voice in the elevator in Elk City, and now it made his heart sink. A second, smaller boat had drifted in behind the glare of the O.H.P.'s spotlight, and from its stern Dustin Ramsey cried, "That man is a federal fugitive!"

"Step away from the others!" the trooper cried.

Emmett complied.

"Place you hands behind your head and turn around—slow!"

Again, Emmett complied, although now his eyes were on the closest trees. *Not far, not really that far.* And the fires from the Chris Craft and geodesic dome were dying, casting far less light than they had just minutes ago. But his ankle felt like a beach ball, and even if he safely made the first trees, he could visualize no way off the island. The Arkansas River had nearly drowned him; that had been days ago, when he'd been in much better shape. This lake would succeed where the Arkansas had failed.

Ramsey was hollering for Mangas's attention, asking him if he was all right. "Talk to me, Michael!"

Emmett had the sense more boats were gathering off the beach to his back. The different timbres of different engines, all massing in a single buzz like a cloud of wasps. Then he heard someone splash ashore. It was Ramsey, for all of a sudden his voice was in Emmett's ear, loud and clear and deliberate: "I am Special Agent Ramsey of the Federal Bureau of Investigation."

"*That's* how it's done, son," Emmett said.

"Thanks. Drop to your knees. You know the drill." The young agent shifted around to Emmett's front so the captive could see the pistol that was trained on him. A replacement 9mm for the one he'd lost in the elevator. "Any weapons, Parker?"

With the side of his face pressed into the sand, Emmett was finished talking.

Someone else, unseen, possibly one of the troopers or even another agent, began to pat him down. The indignity of the groping and sifting hands was almost too much to take, but within seconds yet another man burst out: "Mangas's been knifed!"

"Jesus," Ramsey asked incredulously, "you didn't cut him, did you, Parker?"

Emmett kept silent. They didn't deserve the truth. None of these people deserved the truth.

His left forearm was wrenched back at an unnatural and painful angle. He knew what was coming next, so the bite of the handcuff ratchet around his wrist was no surprise. So tired. This is what the end of resistance had felt like to Quanah. So tired. The spirit willing, the flesh weak, but that spirit strangely consoled by truths that were left unsaid. That was their power. They were left unexplained, all the things he had experienced while evading capture for himself and his people.

"No," a faint male voice said.

"What'd you say, Michael?" Ramsey asked.

"Don't cuff him. Don't do anything to him."

"What are you talking about?"

"Listen to me—"

"Lie down, Mangas, you're in shock," somebody else said. "There's a stretcher on board. We'll carry you."

"No," Michael said weakly but insistently, "Parker just saved my ass. He can help me. Release him—*right now.*"

After a moment, Emmett felt the cuffs being taken off. He spread his arms in exploration of his unexpected freedom. Then, cautiously, he rose to full height and turned. In addition to a trooper, the beach was crowded with FBI agents. A convention of agents, stinking of bug repellant and shining their flashlights in his face.

"Get those lights off him," Mangas told the throng. Finally, he had put Dagen down. He struggled to his knees but could get no higher on his own. His rocked back and forth as he tried to marshal the strength.

Emmett made his way through a gauntlet of agents and took hold of Mangas under the arms. He helped him to his feet.

"Think you can load my lard ass on that boat?" Michael asked with his usual thin scrawl of a smile.

"No problem, *Pabi,*" Emmett said.

"Then let's go home."

It was the nature of life for one threat to be replaced by another as soon as the first was extinguished. Even if that second threat was only the twin phantoms of guilt and self-recrimination. And so, Michael lay on a wire-basket stretcher on the after-deck of the O.H.P. boat, pounding over Lake Eufaula at high speed and wondering how he would feel when the shock wore off. A lethal force review lay ahead, a detail by detail interrogation by his fellow agents. It'd feel like an inquisition. He expected that much, but beyond that he put his trust in peyote, that the homely little cactus bud would help him put this all in perspective. Reveal a dimension in the universe where violence and death did not hold sway. He needed to get back to that place. Soon.

The troopers were Emergency Medical Technicians, and one of them had cleansed and bandaged his wound. Plus given him ten milligrams of morphine sulphate on a surgeon's instructions via radio.

Parker and Ramsey sat on opposite sides of the boat, eyeing each other. As they pulled away from the island, the agent had asked Michael if he might talk to Parker. Obviously, reconciliation had been Ramsey's aim, but Michael said no. First, he and Emmett had to settle their own differences. But he didn't explain this, instead he muttered half-coherently from the morphine, "Not in darkness." He could tell that his words had struck the white agent as being odd. It was an Apache thing. Chiricahuas didn't confide in each other or settle disputes in darkness. That was when witches were most likely to be abroad, eavesdropping, gathering information to use against people.

And Michael suspected a witch was in the boat with them.

He could see her lurking in the dimness of the after-deck lights. She was small and middle-aged, probably Indian. Pretty in an impish sort of way with a crafty and self-satisfied look that further suggested she had powers. There was nothing about her dress—in fact, she wore an old fashioned–looking swimsuit, the kind with a short skirt—to suggest that she worked for the Oklahoma Highway Patrol. She wasn't official-looking in the least. She kept rising from the coiled rope on which she was perched to check over the stern.

As best he could, Michael reared up for a look, too. He saw that the troopers had a kayak in tow.

"Dustin," Michael hailed him.

Ramsey came over to him. "Yeah?"

"Who's the woman?"

Ramsey grinned. "Troopers say they picked her up just before they spotted the fires. Drunker than a skunk. She was paddling along in her in-flatable kayak and pissed as hell they stopped her for showing no lights."

"Where was she picked up?"

"Just south of the island. Damned if she didn't have a revolver on her."

Michael could tell that she was straining to listen in on the two of them. Even more evidence she might be a witch. "Who has the gun now?"

"One of the troopers, I guess."

"Find out if it's been fired."

"You bet."

As Ramsey went up to the bridge, Emmett knelt beside Michael. "How you feeling?"

"I'm not. But that won't last forever. I've been through this before, you know. With Todd . . ." Then Michael began to cry, astonishing himself. Silently. Emmett squeezed his arm. Everything that happened on the beach was cloaked in amnesia. He could recall nothing about her appearance, except a streak of blood in her hair. He placed his hand atop Emmett's. "I have her blood on me, don't I?"

"Yes."

"I never really looked. Know what I mean? Was the entry for my second shot—"

"Instantaneous," Emmett cut him off, having surmised perfectly what Michael was trying to ask.

Ramsey returned. "Trooper says—*yes*. She popped four caps out of five. Mean something to you?"

Wiping his eyes, Michael traded a knowing look with Emmett. Then turned to the woman: "Sister, what's your name?"

"Oh what the hell," she stammered out, "you got me. Woop-de-doo, boys. You big, tough gumshoes finally got poor little Fe Cornplanter. I hope you're all proud of yourselves."

A moment passed before it sank in. Then Michael laughed. He was still chuckling through his tears when they reached Brush Hill Landing, where a chopper was waiting to airlift him to the hospital in McAlester.

He didn't let the pilot lift off until Emmett Parker was allowed to board as well.

29

THIS IS THE *last story I ever heard from my father and he from his fa-ther. It happened long ago, but they told me it's true.*

In the autumn of the year the waters of Lawtonka rose late, all the animals made themselves ready for winter. Because they lived in the lake or along its shores, Muskrat, Salamander and Crawfish could not see the first storm coming, so they asked Kingfisher to fly up to the top of Mt. Scott for a look. Kingfisher agreed because he, too, needed to know when the snow was coming so he could head south.

Day after day, he flew up to the mountaintop at sunset. But the western sky remained clear. Then, on an evening when every last oak leaf had turned gold, he went up and saw that the west was gray and restless with clouds. He was preparing to fly back down to the other animals and warn them of win-ter's approach—when he smelled sacred smoke. He saw two Human Beings standing on a blanket, sharing a pipe. One was stout and one was lean. He recognized them to be First People, and he noted that there were no Second People around the summit at this hour. He hadn't heard the speech of the First People in a long time, so it took him a little while to understand their words.

Just as Kingfisher began to catch on, the stout one said, "My brother and I appeal to the Creator for guidance. We want to put our differences aside so we're of one heart to celebrate the Circle of Life. My brother and I honor the sunrise, the beginning of our lives." He prayerfully blew smoke into the East, as did the lean one after him. "We pay tribute to the waters, which represent our youth, when our blood ran hot and our wisdom was small." They both blew smoke into the South. "We honor the mountains, which stand tall like our maturity as Human Beings." Into the West. And then to the North: "We honor the wind, especially the icy wind that carries us away when our wisdom is complete." In conclusion, they smoked to the Below, Mother Earth, and the Above, from which the Creator reigned.

Even Kingfisher knew these to be the six sacred directions of the First People.

At this point, the stout one said to the lean one, "I want to put our differences aside. These differences sprang from the laws of man and not the laws of the Creator, so it's His desire as well that we become brothers once more. I walk away from our old quarrels once and for all."

The lean one responded, "Subectu-ma."

Then the two Human Beings embraced and sat upon the blanket to talk low and earnestly to each other, even though the cold wind was rising around them.

Kingfisher could stay no longer. He swooped down the mountainside to the other animals and told them that winter was coming, fast, and he himself had to be on his way south. But first he had to ask Muskrat something, the meaning of the words subectu-ma spoken by the lean man. As I said, Kingfisher had not heard the speech of the First People in a long time, and Muskrat had the best memory of all the animals. "What does subectu-ma mean, Brother?"

Muskrat answered, "It is done."